"A CHILLING WALK THROUGH HISTORY . . .

If ever there was a place that could fuel a revolution, it was the streets around Whitechapel. And it is this threatening, despairing atmosphere that Perry captures so vividly in her historical thriller."

—*The Orlando Sentinel*

"A juicy mystery . . . *The Whitechapel Conspiracy* recalls the edginess and romantic spark between Charlotte and Thomas that made the series so appealing to begin with. . . . The novel's ending is exciting and satisfying."

—*The Boston Globe*

"Anne Perry has outdone herself with *The Whitechapel Conspiracy*. . . . The characters are unforgettable and the plotting superb in this thrilling read."

—*Romantic Times Magazine* "Top Pick"

"Perry pulls out the stops and delivers one of the finest performances of her career. . . . A mesmerizing and suspenseful tale, rich in period detail, rife with articulate and believable characters."

—*Publishers Weekly* (starred review)

"One of her best works . . . Perry deftly weaves the different threads of her story into a powerful tale of corruption, patriotism, and loyalty. She uses her extensive knowledge of the period and actual historical events to heighten the suspense. Superb writing and characterization."

—*Library Journal*

By Anne Perry
Published by The Ballantine Publishing Group

Featuring William Monk
THE FACE OF A STRANGER
A DANGEROUS MOURNING
DEFEND AND BETRAY
A SUDDEN, FEARFUL DEATH
THE SINS OF THE WOLF
CAIN HIS BROTHER
WEIGHED IN THE BALANCE
THE SILENT CRY
A BREACH OF PROMISE
THE TWISTED ROOT
SLAVES OF OBSESSION
FUNERAL IN BLUE

Featuring Thomas and Charlotte Pitt
THE CATER STREET HANGMAN
CALLANDER SQUARE
PARAGON WALK
RESURRECTION ROW
BLUEGATE FIELDS
RUTLAND PLACE
DEATH IN THE DEVIL'S ACRE
CARDINGTON CRESCENT
SILENCE IN HANOVER CLOSE
BETHLEHEM ROAD
HIGHGATE RISE
BELGRAVE SQUARE
FARRIERS' LANE
THE HYDE PARK HEADSMAN
TRAITORS GATE
PENTECOST ALLEY
ASHWORTH HALL
BRUNSWICK GARDENS
BEDFORD SQUARE
HALF MOON STREET
THE WHITECHAPEL CONSPIRACY

THE WHITECHAPEL CONSPIRACY

Anne Perry

BALLANTINE BOOKS • NEW YORK

This book contains an excerpt from the forthcoming hardcover edition of *Southampton Row* by Anne Perry. This excerpt has been set for this edition only and may not reflect the final contents of the forthcoming edition.

A Ballantine Book
Published by The Ballantine Publishing Group
Copyright © 2001 by Anne Perry
Excerpt from *Southampton Row* by Anne Perry copyright © 2002 by Anne Perry

www.ballantinebooks.com

ISBN 0-449-00656-5

Manufactured in the United States of America

First Hardcover Edition: February 2001
First International Mass Market Edition: August 2001
First Domestic Mass Market Edition: February 2002

OPM   10   9   8   7   6   5   4   3   2   1

To Hugh and Anne Pinnock,
in friendship

THE
WHITECHAPEL
CONSPIRACY

1

THE COURTROOM at the Old Bailey was crowded. Every seat was taken and the ushers were turning people back at the doors. It was April 18, 1892, the Monday after Easter, and the opening of the London Season. It was also the third day in the trial of distinguished soldier John Adinett for the murder of Martin Fetters, traveler and antiquarian.

The witness on the stand was Thomas Pitt, superintendent of the Bow Street police station.

From the floor of the court Ardal Juster for the prosecution stood facing him.

"Let us start at the beginning, Mr. Pitt." Juster was a dark man of perhaps forty, tall and slender with an unusual cast of feature. He was handsome in some lights, in others a trifle feline, and there was an unusual grace in the way he moved.

He looked up at the stand. "Just why were you at Great Coram Street? Who called you?"

Pitt straightened up a little. He was also a good height, but he resembled Juster in no other way. His hair was too long, his pockets bulged, and his tie was crooked. He had testified in court since his days as a constable twenty years before, but it was never an experience he enjoyed. He was conscious that at the very least a man's reputation was at stake, possibly his liberty. In this case it was his life. He was not afraid to meet Adinett's cold, level stare from the dock. He would speak only the truth. The consequences were not within his control.

He had told himself that before he climbed the short flight of steps to the stand, but it had been of no comfort.

The silence had grown heavy. There was no rustling in the seats. No one coughed.

"Dr. Ibbs sent for me," he replied to Juster. "He was not satisfied with all the circumstances surrounding Mr. Fetters's death. He had worked with me before on other matters, and he trusted me to be discreet should he be mistaken."

"I see. Would you tell us what happened after you received Dr. Ibbs's call?"

John Adinett sat motionless in the dock. He was a lean man, but strongly built, and his face was stamped with the confidence of both ability and privilege. The courtroom held men who both liked and admired him. They sat in stunned disbelief that he should be charged with such a crime. It had to be a mistake. Any moment the defense would move for a dismissal and the profoundest apologies would be offered.

Pitt took a deep breath.

"I went immediately to Mr. Fetters's house in Great Coram Street," he began. "It was just after five in the afternoon. Dr. Ibbs was waiting for me in the hall and we went upstairs to the library, where the body of Mr. Fetters had been found." As he spoke the scene came back to his mind so sharply he could have been climbing the sunlit stairs again and walking along the landing with its huge Chinese pot full of decorative bamboo, past the paintings of birds and flowers, the four ornate wooden doors with carved surrounds, and into the library. The late-afternoon light had poured in through the tall windows, splashing the Turkey rug with scarlet, picking out the gold lettering on the backs of the books that lined the shelves, and finding the worn surfaces of the big leather chairs.

Juster was about to prompt him again.

"The body of a man was lying in the far corner," Pitt continued. "From the doorway his head and shoulders were hidden by one of the large leather armchairs, although Dr. Ibbs told me it had been moved a little to enable the butler

2

to reach the body in the hope that some assistance could be given—"

Reginald Gleave for the defense rose to his feet. "My lord, surely Mr. Pitt knows better than to give evidence as to something he cannot know for himself? Did he see the chair moved?"

The judge looked weary. This was going to be a fiercely contested trial, as he was already uncomfortably aware. No point, however trivial, was going to be allowed past.

Pitt felt himself flushing with annoyance. He did know better. He should have been more careful. He had sworn to himself he would make no mistake whatever, and already he had done so. He was nervous. His hands were clammy. Juster had said it all depended upon him. They could not rely absolutely on anyone else.

The judge looked at Pitt.

"In order, Superintendent, even if it seems less clear to the jury."

"Yes, my lord." Pitt heard the tightness in his own voice. He knew it was tension but it sounded like anger. He cast his mind back to that vivid room. "The top shelf of books was well above arm's reach, and there was a small set of steps on wheels for the purpose of making access possible. It lay on its side about a yard away from the body's feet, and there were three books on the floor, one flat and closed, the other two open, facedown and several pages bent." He could see it as he spoke. "There was a corresponding space on the top shelf."

"Did you draw any conclusions from these things which caused you to investigate further?" Juster asked innocently.

"It seemed Mr. Fetters had been reaching for a book and had overbalanced and fallen," Pitt replied. "Dr. Ibbs had told me that there was a bruise on the side of his head, and his neck was broken, which had caused his death."

"Precisely so. That is what he has testified," Juster agreed. "Was it consistent with what you saw?"

"At first I thought so. . . ."

There was a sudden stirring of attention around the room, and something that already felt like hostility.

"Then, on looking more closely, I saw several small discrepancies that caused me to doubt, and investigate further," Pitt finished.

Juster raised his black eyebrows. "What were they? Please detail them for us so we understand your conclusions, Mr. Pitt."

It was a warning. The entire case rested upon these details, all circumstantial. The weeks of investigation had uncovered no motive whatsoever for why Adinett should have wished harm to Martin Fetters. They had been close friends who seemed to have been similar in both background and beliefs. They were both wealthy, widely traveled, and interested in social reform. They had a wide circle of friends in common and were equally respected by all who knew them.

Pitt had rehearsed this in his mind many times, not for the benefit of the court, but for himself. He had examined every detail minutely before he had even considered pursuing the charge.

"The first thing was the books on the floor." He remembered stooping and picking them up, angry that they had been damaged, seeing the bruised leather and the bent pages. "They were all on the same subject, broadly. The first was a translation into English of Homer's *Iliad*, the second was a history of the Ottoman Empire, and the third was on trade routes of the Near East."

Juster affected surprise. "I don't understand why that should cause your doubt. Would you explain that for us."

"Because the rest of the books on the top shelf were fiction," Pitt answered. "The Waverley novels of Sir Walter Scott, a large number of Dickens, and a Thackeray."

"And in your opinion the *Iliad* does not go with them?"

"The other books on the middle shelf were on the subjects of Ancient Greece," Pitt explained. "Particularly Troy, Mr. Schliemann's work and discourses, objects of art and historical interest, all except for three volumes of Jane Austen, which would more properly have belonged on the top shelf."

"I would have kept novels, especially Jane Austen, in a

4

more accessible place," Juster remarked with a shrug and a tiny smile.

"Perhaps not if you had already read them," Pitt argued, too tense to smile back. "And if you were an antiquarian, with particular interest in Homeric Greece, you would not keep most of your books on that subject on the middle shelves but three of them on the top with your novels."

"No," Juster agreed. "It seems eccentric, to say the least, and unnecessarily inconvenient. When you had noticed the books, what did you do then?"

"I looked more closely at the body of Mr. Fetters and I asked the butler, who was the one who found him, to tell me exactly what had happened." Pitt glanced at the judge to see if he would be permitted to repeat it.

The judge nodded.

Reginald Gleave sat tight-lipped, his shoulders hunched, waiting.

"Proceed, if it is relevant," the judge directed.

"He told me that Mr. Adinett had left through the front door and been gone about ten minutes or so when the bell rang from the library and he went to answer it," Pitt recounted. "As he approached the door he heard a cry and a thud, and on opening it in some alarm, he saw Mr. Fetters's ankles and feet protruding from behind the large leather chair in the corner. He went to him immediately to see if he was hurt. I asked him if he had moved the body at all. He said he had not, but in order to reach it he had moved the chair slightly."

People began to shift restlessly. This all seemed very unimportant. None of it suggested passion or violence, still less murder.

Adinett was staring steadily at Pitt, his brows drawn together, his lips slightly pursed.

Juster hesitated. He knew he was losing the jury. It was in his face. This was about facts, but far more than that it was about belief.

"Slightly, Mr. Pitt?" His voice was sharp. "What do you mean by 'slightly'?"

"He was specific," Pitt replied. "He said just as far as the edge of the rug, which was some eleven inches." He continued without waiting for Juster to ask. "Which meant it would have been at an awkward angle for the light either from the window or the gas bracket, and too close to the wall to be comfortable. It blocked off access to a considerable part of the bookshelves, where books on travel and art were kept, books the butler assured me Mr. Fetters referred to often." He was looking directly at Juster. "I concluded it was not where the chair was normally kept, and I looked at the rug to see if there were indentations from the feet. There were." He took a deep breath. "There were also faint scuff marks on the pile and when I looked again at Mr. Fetters's shoes, I found a piece of fluff caught in a crack in the heel. It seemed to have come from the rug."

This time there was a murmur from the court. Reginald Gleave's lips tightened, but it looked more like anger and resolution than fear.

Again Pitt went on without being asked. "Dr. Ibbs had told me he assumed Mr. Fetters leaned too far, overbalanced, and fell off the steps, cracking his head against the shelves on the corner. The force of the blow, with his body weight behind it, not only caused bruising severe enough for him to lose consciousness, but broke his neck, and this was the cause of his death. I considered the possibility that he had been struck a blow which had rendered him insensible, and then the room had been arranged to look as if he had fallen." There was a sharp rustling in the front row, a hiss of indrawn breath. A woman gasped.

One of the jurors frowned and leaned forward.

Pitt continued without change of expression, but he could feel the tension mounting inside him, his palms sweaty.

"Books he would be likely to read had been pulled out and dropped. The empty spaces left by them had been filled from the top shelf, to explain his use of the ladder. The chair had been pushed close to the corner, and his body placed half concealed by it."

A look of comic disbelief filled Gleave's face. He gazed

6

at Pitt, then at Juster, and finally at the jury. As playacting it was superb. Naturally he had long known exactly what Pitt would say.

Juster shrugged. "By whom?" he asked. "Mr. Adinett had already left, and when the butler entered the room there was no one there except Mr. Fetters. Did you disbelieve the butler?"

Pitt chose his words carefully. "I believe he was telling the truth as he knew it."

Gleave rose to his feet. He was a broad man, heavy shouldered. "My lord, Superintendent Pitt's thoughts as to the butler's veracity are irrelevant and out of place. The jury has had the opportunity to hear the butler's testimony for themselves, and to judge whether he was speaking the truth or not and whether he is an honest and competent person."

Juster kept his temper with obvious difficulty. There was a high color in his cheeks. "Mr. Pitt, without telling us why, since it seems to annoy my honorable friend so much, will you please tell us what you did after forming this unusual theory of yours?"

"I looked around the room to see if there was anything else that might be of relevance," Pitt replied, remembering, describing exactly. "I saw a salver on the small table at the far side of the library, and a glass on it half full of port wine. I asked the butler when Mr. Adinett had left the house and he told me. I then asked him to replace the chair where it had been when he came in, and to repeat his actions as exactly as he was able to." He could see in his mind's eye the man's startled expression and his unwillingness. Very obviously he felt it to be disrespectful to the dead. But he had obeyed, self-consciously, his limbs stiff, movement jerking, his face set in determined control of the emotions which raged through him. "I stood behind the door," Pitt resumed. "When the butler was obliged to go behind the chair in order to reach Mr. Fetters's head, I went out of the door and across the hall and in through the doorway opposite." He stopped, allowing Juster time to react.

7

Now all the jurors were listening intently. No one moved. No one's gaze wandered.

"Did the butler call out after you?" Juster also chose his words with exactness.

"Not immediately," Pitt answered. "I heard his voice from the library speaking in quite normal tones, then he seemed to realize I was not there, and came out to the landing and called me again."

"So you deduced that he had not seen you leave?"

"Yes. I tried the experiment again, with our roles reversed. Crouched behind the chair, I could not see him leave."

"I see." Now there was satisfaction in Juster's voice and he nodded very slightly. "And why did you go into the room opposite, Mr. Pitt?"

"Because the distance between the library door and the stairs is some twenty feet," Pitt explained, seeing the stretch of landing again, the bright bars of sunlight from the end window. He could remember the red and yellow of the stained glass. "Had the butler rung the bell for assistance, I would almost certainly have met with someone coming up before I could have made my way out of the house."

"Assuming you did not want to be seen?" Juster finished for him. "Which had you left rather ostentatiously some fifteen minutes earlier, and then returned through the side door, crept upstairs, and contrived to make murder look like an accident, you would . . ."

There were gasps and rustles around the room. One woman gave a muffled shriek.

Gleave was on his feet, his face scarlet. "My lord! This is outrageous! I . . ."

"Yes! Yes!" the judge agreed impatiently. "You know better than that, Mr. Juster. If I allow you such latitude, then I shall be obliged to do the same for Mr. Gleave, and you will not like that!"

Juster tried to look penitent, and did not remotely succeed. Pitt thought he had not tried very hard.

"Did you see anything unusual while you were in the room across the hall?" Juster enquired artlessly, turning gracefully back towards the jury. "What manner of room was it, by the way?" He raised his black eyebrows.

"A billiard room," Pitt replied. "Yes, I saw that there was a very recent scar on the edge of the door, thin and curving upwards, just above the latch."

"A curious place to damage a door," Juster remarked. "Not possible while the door was closed, I should think?"

"No, only if it were open," Pitt agreed. "Which would make playing at the table very awkward."

Juster rested his hands on his hips. It was a curiously angular pose, and yet he looked at ease.

"So it was most likely to be caused by someone going in or coming out?"

Gleave was on his feet again, his face flushed. "As has been observed, it was awkward to play with the door open, surely that question answers itself, my lord? Someone scratched the open door with a billiard cue, precisely because, as Mr. Pitt has so astutely and uselessly pointed out, it was awkward."

He smiled broadly, showing perfect teeth.

There was complete silence in the courtroom.

Pitt glanced up at Adinett, who was sitting forward in the dock now, motionless.

Juster looked almost childlike in his innocence, except that his unusual face was not cast for such an expression. He looked up at Pitt as if he had not thought of such a thing until this instant.

"Did you enquire into that possibility, Superintendent?"

Pitt stared back at him. "I did. The housemaid who dusted and polished the room assured me that there had been no such mark there that morning, and no one had used the room since." He hesitated. "The scar was raw wood. There was no polish in it, no wax or dirt."

"You believed her?" Juster held up his hand, palm towards Gleave. "I apologize. Please do not answer that, Mr. Pitt. We shall ask the housemaid in due course, and the jury will decide for themselves whether she is an honest and competent person . . . and knows her job. Perhaps Mrs. Fetters, poor woman, can also tell us whether she was a good maid or not."

There was a rumble of embarrassment, irritation and laughter from the court. The tension was broken. For Gleave to have spoken now would have been a waste of time, and the knowledge of that was dark in his face, heavy brows drawn down.

The judge drew in his breath, then let it out again without speaking.

"Then what did you do, Superintendent?" Juster said lightly.

"I asked the butler if Mr. Adinett had carried a stick of any description," Pitt replied. Then, before Gleave could object, he added, "He did. The footman confirmed it."

Juster smiled. "I see. Thank you. Now, before my honorable friend asks you, I will ask you myself. Did you find anyone who had overheard any quarrel, any harsh words or differences of opinion, between Mr. Adinett and Mr. Fetters?"

"I did ask, and no one had," Pitt admitted, remembering ruefully how very hard he had tried. Even Mrs. Fetters, who had come to believe her husband had been murdered, could think of no instance when he and Adinett had quarreled, and no other reason at all why Adinett should have wished him harm. It was as utterly bewildering as it was horrible.

"Nevertheless, from these slender strands, you formed the professional opinion that Martin Fetters had been murdered, and by John Adinett?" Juster pressed, his eyes wide, his voice smooth. He held up long slender hands, ticking off the points. "The moving of a library armchair, three books misplaced on the shelves, a scuff mark on a carpet and a piece of fluff caught in the crack of a heel, and a fresh scratch on a billiard room door? On this you would see a man convicted of the most terrible of crimes?"

"I would see him tried for it," Pitt corrected, feeling the color hot in his face. "Because I believe that his murder of Martin Fetters is the only explanation that fits all the facts. I believe he murdered him in a sudden quarrel and then arranged it to look like—"

"My lord!" Gleave said loudly, again on his feet, his arms held up.

"No," the judge said steadily. "Superintendent Pitt is an

expert in the matter of evidence of crime. That has been established over his twenty years in the police force." He smiled very bleakly, a sad, wintry humor. "It is for the jury to decide for themselves whether he is an honest and competent person."

Pitt glanced over at the jury, and saw the foreman nod his head very slightly. His face was smooth, calm, his eyes steady.

A woman in the gallery laughed and then clapped her hands over her mouth.

Gleave's face flushed a dull purple.

Juster bowed, then waved his hand to Pitt to continue.

"To look like an accident," Pitt finished. "I believe he then left the library, locking the door from the outside. He went downstairs, said good-bye to Mrs. Fetters and was shown out by the butler, and observed to leave by the footman also."

The foreman of the jury glanced at the man beside him, their eyes met, and then they both returned their attention to Pitt. Pitt went on with his description of events as he believed them.

"Adinett went outside, down the road a hundred feet or so, then came back through the side entrance to the garden. A man answering his general description was seen at exactly that time. He went in through the side door of the house, upstairs to the library again, opened it, and immediately rang the bell for the butler."

There was utter silence in the courtroom. Every eye was on Pitt. It was almost as if everyone had held their breath.

"When the butler came, Adinett stood where the open door would hide him," he continued. "When the butler went behind the chair to Mr. Fetters, as he had to, Adinett stepped out, going across the hall to the billiard room in case the butler should raise the alarm and the other servants came up the stairs. Then, when the landing was empty, he went out, in his haste catching his stick against the door. He left the house, this time unseen."

There was a sigh around the room and a rustle of fabric as people moved at last.

"Thank you, Superintendent." Juster bowed very slightly. "Circumstantial, but as you said, the only answer which fits all the facts." He looked across at the jury for a moment, then back again. "And while it would be convenient for us to tell the court why this dreadful thing happened, we are not obliged to—only to demonstrate to them that it did. That I think you have done admirably. We are obliged to you." Very slowly he swung around and invited Gleave to step forward.

Pitt turned to Gleave, his body tense, waiting for the attack Juster had warned him would come.

"After luncheon, I think, my lord," Gleave said with a smile, his heavy face tight with anticipation. "I shall take far longer than the mere quarter of an hour which is available to us now."

That did not surprise Pitt. Juster had said over and over again that the essence of the case depended upon his testimony, and he should expect Gleave to do what he could to tear it apart. Still, he was too conscious of what awaited him to enjoy the mutton and vegetables that were offered him at the public house around the corner from the court, and un-characteristically he left them half eaten.

"He will try to ridicule or deny all the evidence," Juster said, staring across the table at Pitt. He too had little relish for his food. His hand lay on the polished wooden surface, moving restlessly as if only courtesy kept him from drum-ming his fingers. "I don't think the maid will stand up to him. She's frightened enough of just being in a courtroom, without a 'gentleman' questioning her intelligence and her honesty. If he suggests she can't tell one day from another, she's very likely to agree with him."

Pitt took a small drink from his cider. "That won't work with the butler."

"I know," Juster agreed, pulling his lips into a grimace. "And Gleave will know it too. He'll try a different approach altogether. If it were me, I would flatter him, take him into my confidence, find a way of suggesting that Fetters's reputation depended on his death having been an accident rather than murder. Gleave will do the same, I'd wager money on it. Reading character, finding weaknesses is his profession."

Pitt would have liked to argue, but he knew it was true. Gleave's subtle face was that of a man who saw everything and scented vulnerability like a bloodhound on a trail. He knew how to flatter, threaten, undermine, probe, whatever was needed.

Gleave's skill made Pitt angry. The hard lump inside which prevented him from eating was outrage as well as fear of failure. He was certain Martin Fetters had been murdered, and if he did not convince this jury of it, then Adinett would walk away not only free but vindicated.

He returned to the witness stand expecting an attack and determined to face it, to keep his temper and not allow Gleave to fluster or manipulate him.

"Well now, Mr. Pitt," Gleave began, poised in front of him, shoulders squared, feet slightly apart. "Let us examine this curious evidence of yours, on which you hang so much weight and from which you draw so villainous a story." He hesitated, but it was for effect, to allow the jury to savor his sarcasm and prepare for more. "You were sent for by Dr. Ibbs, a man who seems to be something of an admirer of yours."

Pitt nearly retaliated, then realized that was exactly what Gleave would like. Too easy a trap.

"A man who apparently wished to make sure he did not miss any significant fact," Gleave went on, nodding very slightly and pursing his lips. "A nervous man, uncertain of his own abilities. Or else a man who had a desire to cause mischief and suggest that a tragedy was in fact a crime." His tone of voice dismissed Ibbs as an incompetent.

Juster stood up. "My lord, Mr. Pitt is not an expert in the morals and emotions of doctors, in general or in particular. He can have no expert knowledge as to why Dr. Ibbs called him. He knows only what Dr. Ibbs said, and we have heard that for ourselves. He believed the explanation of accident did not entirely fit the facts as he saw them, so he quite rightly called the police."

13

"Your objection is sustained," the judge agreed. "Mr. Gleave, stop speculating and ask questions."

"My lord," Gleave murmured, then looked up sharply at Pitt. "Did Ibbs tell you he suspected murder?"

Pitt saw the trap. Again it was obvious. "No. He said he was concerned and asked my opinion."

"You are a policeman, not a doctor, correct?"

"Of course."

"Has any other doctor ever asked you for your medical opinion? As to cause of death, for example?" The sarcasm was there under his superficial innocence.

"No. My opinion as to interpretation of evidence, that's all," Pitt answered cautiously. He knew another trap lay ahead somewhere.

"Just so." Gleave nodded. "Therefore, if Dr. Ibbs called you because he was dissatisfied, then you surely have sufficient intelligence to deduce that he suspected that the death was not merely an accident but might be a criminal matter . . . one that would involve the police?"

"Yes."

"Then when you said he did not tell you he suspected a crime, you were being a trifle disingenuous, were you not? I hesitate to say you were less than honest, but it inevitably springs to mind, Mr. Pitt."

Pitt could feel the blood heat up his face. He had seen one trap, and sidestepped it directly into another, making him seem evasive, prejudiced—exactly as Gleave had intended. What could he say now to undo it, or at least to not make it worse?

"Discrepancy of facts does not necessarily mean crime," he said slowly. "People move things for many reasons, not always with evil intent." He was fumbling for words. "Sometimes it is an attempt to help, or to make an accident look less careless, to remove the blame from those still alive or to hide an indiscretion. Even to mask a suicide."

Gleave looked surprised. He had not expected a reply.

It was a small victory. Pitt must not allow it to weaken his guard.

"The scuff marks on the carpet," Gleave said, returning to the attack. "When did they happen?"

"At any time since the carpet was last swept, which the maid told me was the previous morning," Pitt answered.

Gleave assumed an air of innocence. "Could they have been caused by anything other than one man dragging the dead body of another?"

There was a titter of nervous laughter in the court.

"Of course," Pitt agreed.

Gleave smiled. "And the tiny piece of fluff on Mr. Fetters's shoe, is that also capable of alternative explanations? For example, the carpet was rumpled at the corner and he tripped? Or he was sitting in a chair and slipped his shoes off? Did this carpet have a fringe, Mr. Pitt?"

Gleave knew perfectly well that it did.

"Yes."

"Exactly." Gleave gestured with both hands. "A slender thread, if you will excuse the pun, on which to hang an honorable man, a brave soldier, a patriot and a scholar such as John Adinett, don't you think?"

There was a murmur around the room, people shifting in their seats, turning to look up at Adinett. Pitt saw respect in their faces, curiosity, no hatred. He turned to the jury. They were more guarded, sober men taking their responsibilities with awe. They sat stiffly, collars high and white, hair combed, whiskers trimmed, eyes steady. He did not envy them. He had never wanted to be the final judge of another man. Even the smooth-faced foreman looked concerned, his hands in front of him, fingers laced.

Gleave was smiling.

"Would it surprise you to know, Mr. Pitt, that the maid who dusted and polished the billiard room is no longer certain that the scratch you so providentially noticed was a new one? She now says it may well have been there earlier, and she had merely not noticed it before."

Pitt was uncertain how to reply. The question was awkwardly phrased.

"I don't know her well enough to be surprised or not,"

he said carefully. "Witnesses sometimes do alter their testimony . . . for a variety of reasons."

Gleave looked offended. "What are you suggesting, sir?"

Juster interrupted again. "My lord, my learned friend asked the witness if he was surprised. The witness merely answered the question. He made no implication at all."

Gleave did not wait for the judge to intervene. "Let us see what we are left with in this extraordinary case. Mr. Adinett visited his old friend Mr. Fetters. They spent a pleasant hour and a half together in the library. Mr. Adinett left. I presume you are in agreement with this?" He raised his eyebrows enquiringly.

"Yes," Pitt conceded.

"Good. To continue, some twelve or fifteen minutes later the library bell rang, the butler answered it, and as he was approaching the library door he heard a cry and a thud. When he opened the door, to his distress, he saw his master lying on the floor and the steps over on their side. Very naturally, he concluded that there had been an accident—as it turned out, a fatal one. He saw no one else in the room. He turned and left to call for assistance. Do you agree so far?"

Pitt forced himself to smile. "I don't know. Since I had not yet given my evidence, I wasn't here for the butler's testimony."

"Does it fit with the facts you know?" Gleave snapped above another ripple of laughter.

"Yes."

"Thank you. This is a most serious matter, Mr. Pitt, not an opportunity for you to entertain the onlookers and parade what you may perceive to be your sense of humor!"

Pitt blushed scarlet. He leaned forward over the rail, his temper boiling.

"You asked me an impossible question!" he accused Gleave. "I was pointing that out to you. If your folly entertained the gallery, that is your own fault—not mine!"

Gleave's face darkened. He had not expected retaliation, but he covered his anger quickly. He was nothing if not a fine actor.

"Then we have Dr. Ibbs being overzealous, for what reason

16

we cannot know," he resumed as if the interruption had never occurred. "You answered his call and found all these enigmatic little signs. The armchair was not where you would have placed it had this beautiful room been yours." His tone of voice was derisive. "The butler thinks it sat somewhere else. There was an indentation on the carpet." He glanced at the jury with a smile. "The books were not in the order that you would have placed them had they been yours." He did not bother to keep the smile from his face. "The glass of port was not finished, and yet he sent for the butler. We shall never know why . . . but is it our concern?" He looked at the jury.

"Do we accuse John Adinett of murder for that?" His face was filled with amazement. "Do we? I don't! Gentlemen, these are a handful of miscellaneous irrelevancies dredged up by an idle doctor and a policeman who wants to make a name for himself, even if it is on the death of one man, and the monstrously wrong accusation against another, who was his friend. Throw it out as the farrago of rubbish it is!"

"Is that your defense?" Juster said loudly. "You appear to be summing up."

"No, it is not!" Gleave retorted. "Although I hardly need more. But have your witness back, by all means."

"Not a great deal to say," Juster observed, taking his place. "Mr. Pitt, when you first questioned the housemaid, was she certain about the scratch on the billiard room door?"

"Absolutely."

"So something has caused her to change her mind since then?"

Pitt licked his lips. "Yes."

"I wonder what that could be?" Juster shrugged, then moved on quickly. "And the butler was certain that the library chair had been moved?"

"Yes."

"Has he since changed his mind?" Juster spread his hands in the air. "Oh, of course you don't know. Well, he hasn't. The bootboy is also quite certain he cleaned his master's boots sufficiently thoroughly that there were no tufts or threads caught in them from the center of the carpet or the fringes."

He looked as if he had suddenly had an idea. "By the way, was the piece you found a thread from the fringe or a piece of soft fluff, as from the pile?"

"Soft fluff, of the color from the center?" Pitt replied.

"Just so. We have seen the shoes, but not the carpet." He smiled. "Impractical, I suppose. Nor can we see the library shelves with their mismatched books." He looked puzzled. "Why would a traveler and an antiquarian, interested most especially in Troy, its legends, its magic, its ruins that lie at the very core of our heritage, place three of its most vivid books on a shelf where he is obliged to climb steps to reach them? And obviously he did want them, or why would he have incurred his own death climbing up for them?" He lifted his shoulders dramatically. "Except, of course, that he didn't!"

That evening Pitt found it impossible to settle. He walked around his garden, pulling the odd weed, noticing the flowers in bloom and those in bud, the new leaves on the trees. Nothing held his attention.

Charlotte came out beside him, her face worried, the late sunlight making a halo around her hair, catching the auburn in it. The children were in bed and the house was quiet. The air was already growing chilly.

He turned and smiled at her. There was no need to explain. She had followed the case from the first days and knew why he was anxious, even if she had no idea of the foreboding he felt now. He had not told her how serious it could be if Adinett were found not guilty because the jury believed Pitt was incompetent and driven by personal emotions, creating a case out of nothing in order to satisfy some ambition or prejudice of his own.

They spoke of other things, trivia, and walked slowly the length of the lawn and back again. What they said did not matter, it was the warmth of her beside him he valued, the fact that she was there and did not press with questions or allow her own fears to show.

The following day Gleave began his defense. He had already done all he could to dismiss the evidence of Dr. Ibbs, of the various servants who had seen the tiny changes Pitt had spoken of, and of the man in the street who had observed someone roughly answering Adinett's description going into the side gate of Fetters's house. Now he called witnesses to the character of John Adinett. He had no shortage from which to choose, and he allowed the whole courtroom to know it. He paraded them one after another. They were drawn from many walks of life: social, military, political, even one from the church.

The last of them, the Honorable Lyall Birkett, was typical. He was slender, fair-haired, with an intelligent, aristocratic face and a quiet manner. Even before he spoke he impressed a certain authority upon his opinions. He had no doubt whatever that Adinett was innocent, a good man caught in a web of intrigue and misfortune.

Since he had given his evidence, Pitt was now permitted to remain in the court, and since he was in command of the Bow Street station he was not answerable to anyone else to return to it. He chose to hear the rest of the trial from a place on the benches.

"Twelve years," Birkett said in answer to Gleave's question as to how long he had been acquainted with Adinett. "We met at the Services Club. You can usually be pretty sure of who you meet there." He smiled very slightly. It was not a nervous smile, not ingratiating, certainly not humorous, merely a gesture of good nature. "Small world, you see? Field of battle tests men. You get to know pretty quickly who's got the mettle, who you can rely on when there's anything to lose. Ask around a bit and you'll run into someone who knows your man."

"I think we can all understand that," Gleave said expansively. He too smiled, at the jury. "Nothing better tests a man's true worth, his courage, his loyalty and his honor in battle than the threat to his own life, or perhaps something worse, the fear of maiming without death, of being left crippled and in permanent pain." An expression of great grief filled his

19

face. He turned slowly so the gallery as well as the jurors might see it. "And did you hear anything ill of John Adinett among all your fellows at the Services Club, Mr. Birkett? Anything at all?"

"Not a word." Birkett still treated the matter lightly. There was no amazement or emphasis in his voice. To him this seemed all a rather silly mistake which was going to be cleared up within a day or two, possibly less.

"But they did know Mr. Adinett?" Gleave pressed.

"Oh, yes, of course. He had served with particular distinction in Canada. Something to do with the Hudson Bay Company and a rebellion of some sort inland. Actually, Fraser told me about it. Said Adinett was more or less co-opted in because of his courage and his knowledge of the area. Vast wilderness, you know?" He raised fair eyebrows. "Yes, of course you know. Up in the Thunder Bay direction. No use for a man unless he has imagination, endurance, utter loyalty, intelligence and courage beyond limit."

Gleave nodded. "How about honesty?"

Birkett looked surprised at last. His eyes widened. "One takes that for granted, sir. There is no place whatever for a man who is not honest. Anyone may be mistaken in one way or another, but a lie is inexcusable."

"And loyalty to one's friends, one's fellows?" Gleave tried to look as if the question were casual and he did not know the answer. But he was in no danger of overplaying his hand. No one else in the room, except Juster, Pitt, and the judge, was sophisticated enough in courtroom histrionics to be aware of his tactics.

"Loyalty is more precious than life," Birkett said simply. "I would trust John Adinett with all I possess—my home, my land, my wife, my honor—and have not a moment's concern that I stood in danger of losing any of it."

Gleave was pleased with himself, as well he might be. The jury were regarding Birkett with admiration, and several of them had looked up at Adinett squarely for the first time. He was winning, and he tasted it already.

Pitt glanced at the jury foreman and saw him frown.

"Did you know Mr. Fetters, by any chance?" Gleave enquired conversationally, turning back to the witness.

"Slightly." Birkett's face darkened and a look of sadness came into it that was so sharp no one could question its reality. "A fine man. It is a bitter irony that he should travel the world in search of the ancient and beautiful in order to uncover the glories of the past, and slip to his death in his own library." He let out his breath silently. "I've read his papers on Troy. Opened up a new world for me, I admit. Never thought it so . . . immediate, before. I daresay travel and a passionate interest in the richness of other cultures were what drew Fetters and Adinett together."

"Could they have had a conflict of any sort over it?" Gleave asked, and the certainty of the answer shone in his eyes.

Birkett was startled. "Good heavens, no! Fetters was a skilled man; Adinett is merely an enthusiast, a supporter and admirer of those who actually made the discoveries. He spoke very highly of Fetters, but he had no ambition to emulate him, only to take joy in his achievements."

"Thank you, Mr. Birkett," Gleave said with a slight bow. "You have reinforced all that we have already heard from other men of distinction such as yourself. No one has spoken ill of Mr. Adinett, from the highest to the most humble. I don't know if my learned friend has anything to put to you, but I have nothing further."

Juster did not hesitate. The jury was slipping away from him, and Pitt could see that he knew it. But the shadow of indecision was in his face for only a moment before it was masked.

"Thank you," he said graciously, then turned to Birkett.

Pitt felt a tightening of anxiety in his chest; Birkett was unassailable, as all the character witnesses had been. In the last two days, by association with the men who admired him and were willing to swear friendship to him, even to appear in a court where he was accused of murder, Adinett had been placed almost beyond criticism. To attack Birkett would alienate the jury, not convince them of the few slender facts.

21

Juster smiled. "Mr. Birkett, you say that John Adinett was absolutely loyal to his friends?"

"Absolutely," Birkett affirmed, nodding his agreement.

"A quality you admire?" Juster asked.

"Of course."

"Ahead of loyalty to your principles?"

"No," Birkett looked slightly puzzled. "I did not suggest that, sir. Or if I did, it was unintentional. A man must place his principles before everything, or he is of no value. A friend would expect as much. At least any man would that I should choose to call friend."

"I too," Juster agreed. "A man must do what he believes to be right, even if it should prove to be at the terrible cost of the loss of a friend, or of the esteem of those he cares for."

"My lord!" Gleave said, standing up impatiently. "This is all very moral sounding, but it is not a question! If my learned friend has a point in all this, may he be asked to reach it?"

The judge looked at Juster enquiringly.

Juster was not perturbed. "The point is very important, my lord. Mr. Adinett was a man who would place his principles, his convictions, above even friendship. Or to put it another way, even friendship, however long or deep, would have to be sacrificed to his beliefs if the two were in opposition. We have established that the victim, Martin Fetters, was his friend. I am obliged to Mr. Gleave for establishing that friendship was not Adinett's paramount concern, and he would sacrifice it to principle, were such a choice forced upon him."

There was a murmur around the room. One of the jurors looked startled, but there was a sudden comprehension in his face. The foreman let out his breath in a sigh, and something within him relaxed.

"We have not established that there was any such conflict!" Gleave protested, taking a pace forward across the floor.

"Or that there was not!" Juster rejoined, swinging around to him.

The judge silenced them both with a look.

Juster thanked Birkett and returned to his seat, this time walking easily, with a slight swagger.

* * *

The following day Gleave began his final assault upon Pitt. He faced the jury.

"This whole case, flimsy and circumstantial as it is, depends entirely upon the evidence of one man, Superintendent Thomas Pitt." His voice was heavy with contempt. "Discount what he says and what have we left? I don't need to tell you—we have nothing at all!" He ticked off on his fingers. "A man who saw another man in the street, turning in towards one of the gardens. This man might have been John Adinett, or he might not." He put up another finger. "A scratch on a door which could have been there for days, and was probably caused by a clumsily wielded billiard cue." A third finger. "A library chair moved, for any number of reasons." A fourth finger. "Books out of place." He shrugged, waving his hands. "Perhaps they were left out, and the housemaid is not a reader of classical Greek mythology, so she put them back wherever she thought they fitted. Her mind was on tidiness of appearance, not order of subject. Very possibly she cannot read at all! A thread of carpet in a shoe." He opened his eyes very wide. "How did it get there? Who knows? And most absurd of all, half a glass of port wine. Mr. Pitt would have us believe this means that Mr. Fetters had no occasion to ring for the butler. All it really means is that Mr. Pitt himself is not accustomed to having servants—which we might reasonably have guessed, since he is a policeman." He pronounced the last word with total scorn.

There was silence in the courtroom.

Gleave nodded.

"I propose to call several witnesses who are well acquainted with Mr. Pitt and will tell you what manner of man he is, so you may judge for yourselves what his evidence is worth."

Pitt's heart sank as he heard Albert Donaldson's name and saw the familiar figure cross the open well of the court and mount the witness stand. Donaldson looked heavier and grayer than he had when he was Pitt's superior fifteen years before, but the expression in his face was just as Pitt recalled, and he knew Donaldson's contempt was still simmering just below the exterior.

The testimony went exactly as he expected.

"You are retired from the Metropolitan Police Force, Mr. Donaldson?" Gleave asked.

"I am."

Gleave nodded slightly.

"When you were an inspector at the Bow Street station was there a Constable Thomas Pitt working there?"

"There was," Donaldson's expression already betrayed his feelings.

Gleave smiled. His shoulders relaxed.

"What sort of a man was he, Mr. Donaldson? I presume you had occasion to work with him often—in fact, he was answerable to you?"

"He wasn't answerable to anybody, that one!" Donaldson retorted, darting a glance towards Pitt where he sat in the crowd. It had taken Donaldson only a moment to pick him out in the front rows. "Law to himself. Always thought he knew best, and wouldn't be told by no one."

He had waited years for his chance to get revenge for the frustration he had felt, for Pitt's insubordination, for the flouting of rules Pitt had viewed as petty restrictions, for the cases Pitt had worked on without keeping his seniors informed. Pitt had been at fault. Even Pitt knew it now, when he had command of the station himself.

"Would arrogant be a fair word to describe him?" Gleave enquired.

"A very fair one," Donaldson answered quickly.

"Opinionated?" Gleave went on.

Juster half rose, then changed his mind.

The foreman of the jury leaned forward, frowning.

Up in the dock, Adinett sat motionless.

"Another good one." Donaldson nodded. "Always wanted to do things his own way, never mind the official way. Wanted all the glory for himself, and that was plain to see from the start."

Gleave invited the witness to give examples of Pitt's arrogance, ambition and flouting of the rules, and Donaldson obeyed with relish, until even Gleave decided he had had enough. He seemed a trifle reluctant to offer Donaldson to Juster, but he had no choice.

Juster took on his task with some satisfaction.

"You did not like Constable Pitt, did you, Mr. Donaldson?" he said ingenuously.

It would have been absurd for Donaldson to deny his feelings. Even he was sensible of that. He had shown them far too vividly.

"Can't like a man who makes your job impossible," he replied, the defensiveness sharp in his voice.

"Because he solved his cases in an unorthodox manner, at least at times?" Juster asked.

"Broke the rules," Donaldson corrected.

"Made mistakes?" Juster stared very directly at him. Donaldson flushed slightly. He knew Juster could trace the records easily enough, and probably had.

"Well, no more than most men."

"Actually, less than most men," Juster argued. "Do you know of any man, or woman, convicted on Mr. Pitt's evidence, who was subsequently found to be innocent?"

The foreman of the jury relaxed.

"I don't follow all his cases?" Donaldson objected. "I've got more to do with my time than trace cases of every ambitious constable on the force."

Juster smiled. "Then I'll tell you, since it is part of my job to know the men I trust," he replied. "The answer is no, no one has been wrongly convicted on Superintendent Pitt's evidence in all his career in the force."

"Because we have good defense lawyers?" Donaldson glanced sideways at Gleave. "Thank God!"

Juster acknowledged the point with a grin. He knew better than to display temper before a jury.

"Pitt was ambitious." He allowed it to be a statement more than a question.

"I said so. Very!" Donaldson snapped.

Juster put his hands in his pockets casually. "I presume he

must be. He has reached the rank of superintendent, in charge of a most important station, Bow Street. Rather higher than you ever reached, isn't it?"

Donaldson flushed darkly. "I didn't marry a well-born wife with connections."

Juster looked surprised, his black eyebrows shooting up. "So he excelled you socially as well? And I hear she is not only well-born but intelligent, charming and handsome. I think we understand your feelings very well, Mr. Donaldson." He turned away. "Thank you. I have nothing further to ask you."

Gleave stood up. He decided he could not retrieve the situation, and sat down again.

Donaldson left the stand, his face dark, his shoulders hunched, and he did not look towards Pitt as he passed on his way to the door.

Gleave called his next witness. This man's opinion of Pitt was no better, if rooted in different causes. Juster could not shake him so easily. His dislike of Pitt was born of Pitt's handling of a case long ago in which a friend of the witness had suffered from public suspicion until being proved not guilty rather late in the affair. It had not been one of Pitt's more skilled or well-conducted investigations.

A third witness recited instances that were capable of unflattering interpretation, making Pitt seem both arrogant and prejudiced. His early years were described unkindly.

"He was the son of a gamekeeper, you say?" Gleave asked, his voice carefully neutral.

Pitt felt cold. He remembered Gerald Slaley, and he knew what was coming next, but he was powerless to prevent it. There was nothing he could do but sit still and endure it.

"That's right. His father was deported for stealing," Slaley agreed. "Always held a grudge against the gentry, if you ask me. Gone after us on purpose, made something of a crusade of it. Check his cases and you'll see. That's why he was promoted by the men who chose him: to prosecute where the powerful and well-to-do were concerned . . . where they thought it politic. And he never let them down."

"Yes." Gleave nodded sagely. "I too have been examining Mr. Pitt's record." He glanced at Juster, and back to Slaley again. "I've noticed how often he has specialized in cases where people of prominence are concerned. If my learned friend wishes to contest the issue, I can rehearse them easily enough."

Juster shook his head. He knew better than to allow it. Too many of them had been notorious cases and might well be resented by members of the jury. One could not know who had been their friends, or men they admired.

Gleave was satisfied. He had painted Pitt as an ambitious and irresponsible man, motivated not by honor but by a long-held bitterness and hunger for revenge because his father had been convicted of a crime of which he still believed him innocent. That was one issue Juster could not retrieve.

The prosecution summed up.

The defense had the final word, again reminding the jurors that its case hung upon Pitt's evidence.

The jury retired to consider their verdict.

They did not find one that night.

The following morning they finally reappeared four minutes before midday.

"Have you reached a verdict?" the judge asked grimly.

"We have, my lord," the foreman announced. He did not look up at the dock; or at Juster, sitting rigidly, black head a little bowed; or at Gleave, smiling confidently. But there was an ease in his bearing, an erectness in the carriage of his head.

"And is it the verdict of you all?" the judge asked him.

"It is, my lord."

"Do you find the prisoner, John Adinett, guilty or not guilty of the murder of Martin Fetters?"

"Guilty, my lord."

Juster's head jerked up.

Gleave let out a cry of outrage, half rising to his feet.

Adinett was set like stone, uncomprehending.

The gallery erupted in astonishment, and journalists scrambled to get out and report to their newspapers that the unbelievable had happened.

"We'll appeal!" Gleave's voice could be heard above the melee.

The judge commanded order, and as the court finally settled to order again, and a kind of terrible silence, he sent the usher for the black cap he would place on his head before he pronounced sentence of death upon John Adinett.

Pitt sat frozen. It was both a victory and a defeat. His reputation had been torn to shreds for the public, whatever the jury had believed. It was a just verdict. He had no doubt Adinett was guilty, even though he had no idea why he had done such a thing.

And yet in all the crimes he had ever investigated, all the hideous and tragic truths he had uncovered, there had never been one for which he would willingly have hanged a man. He believed in punishment; he knew it was necessary, for the guilty, for the victim and for society. It was the beginning of healing. But he had not ever believed in the extinction of a human being, any human being—not John Adinett.

He left the courtroom and went out and walked up to Newgate Street with no sense of victory.

2

"LADY VESPASIA CUMMING-GOULD," the footman announced without requiring to see her invitation. There was no servant of consequence in London who did not know her. She had been the most beautiful woman of her generation, and the most daring. Perhaps she still was. In some people's eyes she could have no equal.

She entered through the double doors and stood at the top of the stairs that led in a graceful curve down to the ballroom. It was already three-quarters full but the steady buzz of conversation lessened for a moment. She could command attention, even now.

She had never been a slave to fashion, knowing well that what suited her was far better than merely the latest craze. This season's slender waists and almost vanished bustles were wonderful, as long as one did not allow the sleeves to become too extravagant. She wore oyster satin with ivory Brussels lace at the bosom and sleeves, and of course pearls, always pearls at the throat and ears. Her silver hair was a coronet in itself, and her clear gray eyes surveyed the room for an instant before she started down to greet and be greeted.

Of course, she knew most of the people there who were over forty, just as they knew her, even if only by repute. There were friends among them, and enemies also. One could not stand for any beliefs at all, or even simple loyalties, and not earn someone's malice or envy. And she had always fought as she believed, not always wisely but always with a whole heart—and all her very considerable wit and intelligence.

The causes had changed over half a century. All life had changed. How could the arbitrary, adoring and unimaginative young Victoria have foreseen the beautiful, ambitious and amoral Lillie Langtry? Or how could the earnest Prince Albert have found anything to say to the scintillating and eccentric Oscar Wilde, a man whose writing was so compassionate and whose words could be so glitteringly shallow?

And there had been an age of change between then and now, terrible wars that killed countless men, and clashes of ideas that probably killed even more. Continents had been opened up and dreams of reform had been born and died. Mr. Darwin had questioned the fundamentals of existence.

Vespasia bowed her head very slightly to an elderly duchess but did not stop to speak. They had long ago said everything they had to say to each other, and neither could be bothered to repeat it yet again. Actually, Vespasia wondered why on earth the woman was even at this diplomatic reception. It seemed a remarkably eclectic group of people, and it took her a moment's thought to perceive what they could have in common. Then she realized that it was a certain value as entertainment . . . except for the duchess.

The Prince of Wales was easily recognizable. Apart from his personal appearance, with which she was perfectly familiar, having met him more times than she could count, the very slight distance of the people surrounding him made him more noticeable. There was a certain attitude of respect. No matter how funny the joke or how enjoyable the gossip, one did not jostle the heir to the throne or allow oneself to trespass upon his good temper.

Was that Daisy Warwick smiling across at him? A little brazen, surely? Or perhaps she assumed that everyone here tonight already knew their intimate relationship, and no one really cared. Hypocrisy was a vice Daisy had never practiced. Equally, discretion was a virtue she exercised selectively. Unquestionably she was beautiful and had a certain air of elegance about her that was worthy of admiration.

Vespasia had never desired to be a royal mistress. She thought the perils far outweighed any advantages, let alone pleasures. And in this instance she neither liked nor disliked the Prince of Wales, but she did rather like the Princess, poor woman. She was deaf, and imprisoned in a world of her own, but still she had to be aware of her husband's self-indulgences.

A far greater tragedy, which she shared with perhaps fewer other women, but still far too many, was the death of her eldest son earlier this year. The Duke of Clarence, like his mother, had also been severely afflicted with deafness. It had been a peculiar bond between them, drawing them closer in their almost silent world. She grieved alone.

A dozen feet from Vespasia, the Prince of Wales was laughing heartily at something told to him by a tall man with a strong, slightly crooked nose. It was a powerful face, intelligent and impatient, although at the moment its expression was alive with humor. Vespasia had not met this man but she knew who he was: Charles Voisey, an appeals court judge, a man of profound learning, widely respected among his peers, if also a trifle feared.

The Prince of Wales saw her and his face lit with pleasure. She was a generation older than he, but beauty had always charmed him, and he remembered her most ravishing years when he himself had been young and full of hope. Now he was tired of waiting, of responsibility without the respect and the reward of being monarch. He excused himself from Voisey and moved towards her.

"Lady Vespasia," he said with undisguised pleasure. "I am so pleased you were able to come. The evening would have lacked a certain quality without you."

She met his eyes for a moment before dropping a slight curtsy. She could still make it seem a gesture of infinite grace, her back ramrod straight, her balance perfect.

"Thank you, Your Royal Highness. It is a splendid occasion." It flickered through her mind just how splendid it was, like so many others these days, extravagant, so much food, the best wine, servants everywhere, music, chandeliers blazing with light, hundreds of fresh flowers. Nothing that could be imagined to add to the glamour was missing, nothing stinted.

There had been so many occasions in the past when there had been more laughter, more joy, and at a fraction of the cost. She remembered them with nostalgia.

But the Prince of Wales lived well beyond his means, and had done so for years. No one was surprised anymore at his huge house parties, shooting weekends, days at the races where fortunes were gambled, made and lost, at his gargantuan dinners or overgenerous gifts to favorites of one sort or another. Many no longer even commented on it.

"Do you know Charles Voisey?" he enquired. Voisey was at his elbow, courtesy demanded it. "Voisey, Lady Vespasia Cumming-Gould. We have known each other longer than either of us cares to remember. We should telescope it all together." He gestured with his hands. "Take out all the tedious bits between and keep only the laughter and the music, the good dinners, the conversations, and perhaps a little dancing. Then we should be about the right age, shouldn't we?"

She smiled. "That is the best suggestion I have heard in years, sir," she said with enthusiasm. "I don't even mind keeping some of the tragedy, or even the quarrels—let us simply get rid of all the tedious hours, the exchanging of phrases that neither of us means, the standing around, the polite lies. That would take years away."

"You are right! You are right!" he agreed, conviction in his face. "I did not realize until this moment how much I had missed you. I refuse to allow it to happen again. I spend years of my life in duty. I swear I am not convinced that those I spend it with are any better pleased with it than I am! We make utterly predictable remarks, wait for the other to reply, and then move on to the next equally predictable response."

"I fear it is part of royal duty, sir," Voisey put in, "as long as we have a throne and a monarch upon it. I can think of no way in which it could be changed."

"Voisey is a judge of appeal," the Prince told Vespasia. "Which I suppose makes him a great man for precedent. If it has not been done before, then we had better not do it now."

32

"On the contrary," Voisey retorted. "I am all for new ideas, if they are good ones. To fail to progress is to die."

Vespasia looked at him with interest. It was an unusual point of view from one whose profession was so steeped in the past.

He did not smile back at her, as a less confident man might have done.

The Prince was already thinking of something else. His admiration for other people's ideas seemed highly limited.

"Of course," he dismissed airily. "The number of new inventions around is incredible. Ten years ago we would not have conceived what they could do with electricity."

Voisey smiled very slightly, his eyes on Vespasia's for an instant longer before he replied. "Indeed, sir. One wonders what may yet be to come." He was polite, but Vespasia heard the faintest thread of contempt in his voice. He was a man of ideas, broad concepts, revolutions of the mind. Details did not hold his regard; they were for smaller men, men whose view was conceived from a lower level.

They were joined by a noted architect and his wife, and the conversation became general. The Prince glanced at Vespasia with regret, a shred of humor, and then played his part in the trivialities.

Vespasia was able to excuse herself and moved on to speak to a politician she had known for years. He looked weary and amused, his face deeply lined, full of character. They had shared personal crusades in the past, triumph and tragedy, and a fair share of farce.

"Good evening, Somerset," she said with genuine pleasure. She had forgotten how fond of him she had been. His failures had been magnificent, as had his successes, and he had carried them both with grace.

"Lady Vespasia!" His eyes were alight. "Suddenly a breath of sanity!" He took the hand she offered, barely brushing it with his lips in a gesture rather than an act. "I wish we had a new crusade, but this is beyond even us, I think." He glanced around at the opulent room and the ever-increasing number

33

of men and women in it, laughing together, diamonds blazing, light on silks and pale skin, swathes of lace, shimmering brocades. His eyes hardened. "It will destroy itself . . . if it doesn't see sense in the next year or two." There was regret in his voice, and confusion. "Why can't they see that?"

"Do you really think so?" She assumed for a moment that perhaps he was speaking for effect, a little dramatic overstatement. Then she saw the tightness of his lips and the shadow over his eyes. "You do. . . ."

He turned to her. "If Bertie doesn't curtail his spending a great deal"—he inclined his head momentarily towards the Prince of Wales ten yards away, laughing uproariously at someone's joke—"and the Queen doesn't come back into public life and start courting her people again." There was another guffaw of laughter a few yards away.

Somerset Carlisle lowered his voice. "Lots of us suffer grief, Vespasia. Most of us lose something we love in our lives. We can't afford to give up—stop working because of it. The country is made up of a few aristocrats, hundreds of thousands of doctors, lawyers, and priests, a million or two shopkeepers and traders of one sort or another, and farmers. And dozens of millions of ordinary men and women who work from dawn to dusk because they have to, to feed those who depend on them, the old and the young. Men die, and women break their hearts. We go on."

Somewhere at the far end of the room the music started. There was a tinkle of glass.

"You can't lead people from more than a certain distance away," he went on. "She isn't one of us anymore. She has allowed herself to become irrelevant. And Bertie is too much one of us, with his appetites—only he isn't indulging them on his own money, as the rest of us have to!"

Vespasia knew that what he said was true, but she had not heard anyone else put it quite so boldly. Somerset Carlisle had an irresponsible wit and a high sense of the bizarre, which she knew only too well. She still felt a note of hysteria rise inside her when she thought of their past battles and the grotesque things he had done in his attempts to force through reform. But she knew him too well to think he was joking or exaggerating now.

"Victoria will be the last monarch," he said almost under his breath, a harsh edge of regret in his voice. "If some people have their way . . . believe me. There is unrest in the country more profound than anything we've had in two centuries or more. The poverty in some places is almost unbelievable, not to mention the anti-Catholic feeling, the fear of the liberal Jews who've come into London after the '48 revolutions in Europe, and of course there are always the Irish."

"Exactly," she agreed. "We've always had most of these elements. Why now, Somerset?"

He remained silent for several moments. People passed them. One or two spoke, and the others nodded in acknowledgment but did not intrude.

"I'm not sure," he said finally. "A mixture of things. Time. It's nearly thirty years since Prince Albert died. That's a long time to live without an effective monarch. We have a whole generation who are beginning to realize we can manage fairly well without one." He lifted one shoulder slightly. "I don't personally agree with them. I think the mere existence of a monarch, whether that monarch does anything or not, is a safeguard against many of the abuses of power, which perhaps we don't realize, simply because we have had that shield so long. A constitutional monarchy, of course. The prime minister should be the head of the nation, and the monarch the heart. I think it is very wise not to have both in the one figure." He gave a twisted, little smile. "It means we can change our minds when we find we are mistaken, without committing suicide."

"It is also who we are," she said, equally softly. "We have had a throne for a thousand years, and the notion of it far longer. I don't think I care to change."

"Nor I." He grinned at her suddenly, lighting his face with a wild humor. "I am too old for it!" He was at least thirty-five years younger than she.

She gave him a look that should have frozen him at twenty paces, and she knew it would not.

They were joined by a slender man, little more than Vespasia's height, with a shock of dark hair threaded through with gray at the temples. He had very dark eyes, a long nose and a sensitive mouth, deeply lined at each side. He looked intelligent, wry, and weary, as if he had seen too much of life and his compassion for it was growing thin.

"Evening, Narraway." Carlisle regarded him with interest. "Lady Vespasia, may I present Victor Narraway. He is head of Special Branch. I'm not sure if that is supposed to be a secret or not, but you know a score of people you could ask, if it interested you. Lady Vespasia Cumming-Gould."

Narraway bowed and made the appropriate acknowledgment.

"Thought you'd be far too busy ferreting out anarchists to waste your time in chatter and dancing," Carlisle said dryly. "England safe for the night, is it?"

Narraway smiled. "Not all the danger is lurking in dark alleys in Limehouse," he replied. "To be any real threat it would have to have tentacles a great deal longer than that."

Vespasia watched him closely, trying to make some estimate in her mind as to whether he believed as Carlisle did, but she could not separate the amusement from the sadness in his eyes. A moment later he was making some remark about the foreign secretary, and the conversation swept past the subject and became trivial.

An hour later, with the strains of a waltz sweet and lilting in the background, Vespasia was enjoying an excellent champagne and a while seated alone, when she was aware of the Prince of Wales a dozen feet away from her. He was in conversation with a solidly built man of middle age with a pleasant, earnest face and a quiff of hair that was thinning markedly on the top. They seemed to be speaking of sugar.

". . . do you, Sissons?" the Prince enquired. The expression on his face was polite but less than interested.

"Mostly through the Port of London," Sissons replied. "Of course, it is a very labor-intensive industry."

"Is it? I admit, I had no idea. I suppose we take it for granted. A spoonful of sugar for one's tea, and so on."

"Oh, there is sugar in scores of things," Sissons said with

feeling. "Cakes, sweet pastries, pies, even some things we might have supposed to be savory. A sprinkle of sugar improves the taste of tomatoes more than you would believe."

"Does it really?" The Prince raised his eyebrows slightly in an attempt to look as if the information were of value to him. "I had always thought of salt for that."

"Sugar is better," Sissons assured him. "It is mostly labor that adds to the cost, you see?"

"I beg your pardon?"

"Labor, sir," Sissons repeated. "That is why the Spitalfields area is good. Thousands of men needing work . . . an almost endless pool to call upon. Volatile, of course."

"Volatile?" The Prince was still apparently lost.

Vespasia was aware of others within earshot of this rather pointless exchange, and also listening. Lord Randolph Churchill was one of them. She had known him in a slight way most of her life, as she had known his father before him. She was conscious of his intelligence and his dedication to his political beliefs.

"A great mixture of people," Sissons was explaining. "Backgrounds, religions and so on. Catholics, Jews, and of course Irish. Lot of Irish. The need to work is about all they have in common."

"I see." The Prince was beginning to feel he had said enough to satisfy courtesy and might be excused for leaving this exceedingly dull conversation.

"It must be profitable," Sissons continued, urgency rising in his voice, his face pink.

"Well, I imagine with a couple of factories, you are in a position to know." The Prince smiled pleasantly, as if to conclude the matter.

"No!" Sissons said sharply, taking a step forward as the Prince took one away. "Actually three factories. But what I meant was not that it was profitable but that there is a great obligation upon me to make it so, otherwise over a thousand men will be thrown out of work, and the chaos and injury that would result from that would be appalling." His words were tumbling out at increasing speed. "I could not even venture a

37

guess as to where that would end. Not in that part of the city. You see, there is nowhere else for them to go."

"Go?" The Prince frowned. "Why should they wish to go?"

Vespasia felt herself cringing. She had a very vivid idea of the soul-destroying poverty of parts of London, most especially the East End, of which Spitalfields and Whitechapel were the heart.

"I mean for work." Sissons was becoming agitated. It was plain in the beads of sweat on his brow and lip, which were glistening in the lights. "Without work they will starve. God knows, they are close enough to it now."

The Prince said nothing. He was clearly embarrassed. It was a most unseemly subject in this gorgeous, lavish display of pleasure. It was poor taste to remind men with glasses of champagne in their hands, and women decked with diamonds, that within a few miles of them thousands had not food and shelter for the night. It made them uncomfortable.

"It is necessary I stay in business!" Sissons's voice rose a trifle, carrying above the hum of other conversations and the beat of the distant music. "I have to make sure I collect all my debts . . . so I can keep on paying them."

The Prince looked bewildered. "Of course. Yes . . . it must be. Very conscientious, I am sure."

Sissons swallowed. "All of them . . . sir."

"Yes . . . quite so." The Prince was looking decidedly unhappy now. His desire to escape this absurd situation was palpable.

Randolph Churchill took the liberty of interrupting. Vespasia was not surprised. She knew his relationship with the Prince of Wales was long and had varied. It had been one of extreme hatred over the Aylesford affair in 1876, when the Prince had actually challenged him to a duel with guns—to be fought in Paris, such a thing being illegal in England. Sixteen years ago the Prince had publicly refused to enter the house of anyone who received the Churchills. Consequently they had been almost entirely ostracized.

Eventually it had all died down, and Jennie Churchill, Randolph's wife, had so charmed the Prince—apparently enough

38

to become one of his many mistresses—that he willingly dined at their home in Connaught Place and gave her expensive gifts. Randolph was back in favor. As well as being appointed leader of the House of Commons and Chancellor of the Exchequer, two of the highest offices in the land, he was the closest personal confidante of the Prince, sharing sporting and social events, giving advice and receiving praise and trust.

Now he stepped in to relieve a tedious situation.

"Of course you have to . . . er . . . Sissons," he said cheerfully. "Only way to conduct a business, what? But this is a time for enjoyment. Have some more champagne; it's excellent." He turned to the Prince. "I must congratulate you, sir, an exquisite choice. I don't know how you do it."

The Prince brightened considerably. He was with one of his own, a man he could trust not only politically but socially.

"It is rather, isn't it? Did well there."

"Superbly," Churchill agreed, smiling. He was a beautifully dressed man of average height with regular features and a very wide, turned-up mustache which gave him a distinguished air. His manner was one of unquenchable pride. "I fancy it calls for something succulent to eat, to complement it. May I have something sent for you, sir?"

"No . . . no, I'll come with you." The Prince grasped the chance to escape. "I really ought to speak to the French ambassador. Good fellow. Do excuse us, Sissons." And he turned and went with Churchill too rapidly for Sissons to do anything but mutter something unheard and take his leave.

"Mad," Somerset Carlisle said softly at Vespasia's elbow.

"Who?" she enquired. "The sugar man?"

"Not so far as I know." He smiled. "Tedious in the extreme, but if that were insanity, then I should lock up half the country. I meant Churchill."

"Oh, of course," she said casually. "But you are far from the first to say that. At least he knows which side his advantage lies, which is an improvement on the Aylesford situation. Who is that very intense-looking man with the gray hair?" She half looked into the distance to indicate who she meant, then back again at Carlisle. "I don't recall having seen him before, and yet he exudes a kind of passion which is almost evangelical."

"Newspaper proprietor," Carlisle replied. "Thorold Dismore. I doubt he would approve your description of him. He is a republican, and a convinced atheist. But you are quite right, there is something of the proselyte about him."

"I have never heard of him," she replied. "And I thought I knew the newspaper proprietors in London."

"I doubt you'd read his paper. It's good quality, but he is not averse to allowing his opinions to shine through rather clearly."

"Indeed?" She raised her eyebrows questioningly. "And why should that prevent me from reading them? I have never imagined people reported the news unfiltered through their own prejudices. Are his any more powerful than usual?"

"I think so. And he is not averse to advocating action in their cause."

"Oh." She felt it as a breath of chill, no more. She should not have been surprised. She looked across at the man more closely. It was a strong face, sharp, intelligent, moved by powerful emotion. She would have judged him a man who yielded no ground to anyone, and whose overt good nature might very easily mask a temper that could be ugly if roused. But first impressions could be mistaken.

"Do you wish to meet him?" Carlisle asked curiously.

"Perhaps," she replied. "But I am quite sure I do not wish him to know that I do."

Carlisle grinned. "I shall make sure he does not," he promised. "It would be grossly presumptuous. I shall certainly not allow him to affect airs above his station. If it is contrived at all, he will believe it was his idea and he is profoundly grateful that I have accomplished it for him."

"Somerset, you verge on the impertinent," she answered, aware that she was very fond of him. He was brave, absurd, passionate about his beliefs, and beneath the flippant exterior, pleasingly unique. She had always loved eccentrics.

It was after midnight and Vespasia was beginning to wonder if she wished to stay much longer, when she heard a voice which dissolved time, hurling her back about half a century to an unforgettable summer in Rome: 1848, the year of revolutions throughout Europe. For a wild, euphoric time—all too brief—dreams of freedom had spread like fire across France, Germany, Austria-Hungary and Italy. Then one by one they had been destroyed. The barricades had been stormed, the people broken, and the popes and kings had taken back their power. The reform had been overturned and trampled under the feet of soldiers. In Rome it had been the French soldiers of Napoleon III.

She almost did not turn to look. Whoever it was, it could only be an echo. It was memory playing a trick, an intonation that sounded the same, some Italian diplomat, perhaps from the same region, even the same town. She thought she had forgotten him, forgotten the whole tumultuous year with its passion, its hope and all the courage and pain, and in the end the loss.

She had been back to Italy since then, but never to Rome. She had always found a way to avoid that, without explaining why. It was a separate part of her life, an existence quite different from the realities of her marriage, her children, of London, even of her recent adventures with the extraordinary policeman Thomas Pitt. Who could have imagined that Vespasia Cumming-Gould, the ultimate aristocrat who could trace her blood to half the royal houses of Europe, could join forces with a gamekeeper's son who had become a policeman? But then worrying what others thought crippled half the people she knew, and denied them all manner of passion and joy, and pain. Then she did turn. It was not really a thought so much as a reaction she could not help.

A dozen feet away stood a man almost her own age. He had been in his twenties when she met him, slender, dark, lithe as a dancer, and with that voice that filled her dreams.

Now his hair was gray, he was a little heavier, but the bones were still the same, the sweep of his brows, the smile.

41

As if he had felt her stare, he turned towards her, for a moment ignoring the man he was speaking with.

His recognition of her was instant, with no moment of doubt, no hesitation.

Then she was afraid. Could reality ever be equal to memory? Had she allowed herself to believe more than had really happened? Was the woman of her youth even remotely like the woman she was today? Or would she find time and experience had made her too wise to be able to see the dream anymore? Did she need to see him in the passion of youth, with the Roman sun on his face, a gun in his hand as he stood at the barricades, prepared to die for the republic?

He was coming towards her.

Panic drenched her like a wave, but habit, the self-discipline of a lifetime, and absurd hope prevented her from leaving.

He stopped in front of her.

Her heart was beating in her throat. She had loved many times in her life, sometimes with fire, sometimes with laughter, usually with tenderness, but never anyone else as she had loved Mario Corena.

"Lady Vespasia." He said the words quite formally, as if they were merely acquaintances, but his voice was soft, caressing the syllables. It was, after all, a Roman name, as he had told her, teasingly, so long ago. The Emperor Vespasian was no hero.

It was her correct title. Should she reply equally correctly? After all they had shared, the hope, the passion, and the tragedy, it seemed like a denial. There was no one else listening.

"Mario . . ." It was strange to say his name again. Last time she had whispered it in the darkness, tears choking her throat, her cheeks wet. The French troops were marching into Rome. Mazzini had surrendered to save the people. Garibaldi had gone north towards Venice, his pregnant wife fighting beside him, dressed as a man, carrying a gun like everyone else. The Pope had returned and undone all the reforms, wiped out the debt, the liberty, and the soul in one act.

But that was all in the past. Italy was united now; that much at least had come true.

He was searching her eyes, her face. She hoped he would not say she was still beautiful. He was the one man to whom it had never mattered.

Should she say something to forestall him? A trite word now would be unbearable. But if she spoke, then she would never know. There was no time left for games.

"I have often imagined meeting you again," he said at last. "I never thought it would happen . . . until today." He gave the tiniest shrug. "I arrived in London a week ago. I could not be here without thinking of you. I quarreled with myself whether I should even enquire for you, or if dreams are best left undisturbed. Then someone mentioned your name, and all the past returned to me as if it were yesterday, and I had no power to deny myself. I thought you would be here." He glanced around the magnificent room with its smooth pillars, its dazzling chandeliers, the swirl of music and laughter and wine.

She knew exactly what he meant. This was her world of money, privilege, all of it passed down by blood. Perhaps in some distant past it had been earned, but not by these men and women here now.

She could so easily pick up the old battles again, but it was not what she wanted. She had believed as desperately as he had in the revolution in Rome. She had labored and argued for it too, worked all day and all night in the hospitals during the siege, carried water and food to the soldiers, in the end even fired the guns beside the last defenders. And she had understood why, in the end, when Mario had had to choose between her and his love of the republic, he had chosen his ideals. The pain of it had never completely left her, even after all these years, but had he chosen otherwise it would have been worse. She could not have loved him the same way, because she knew what he believed.

She smiled back at him, a little bubble of laughter inside her.

"You have an advantage. I would never, in even my silliest dreams, have thought to find you here, all but shoulder to shoulder with the Prince of Wales."

His eyes were soft, old jokes remembered, absurdities

43

within the tears. "Touché," he acknowledged. "But the battle-field is everywhere now."

"It always was, my dear," she answered. "It is more complicated here. Few issues are as simple as they seemed to us then."

His gaze did not waver. "They were simple."

She thought how little he had changed. It was only the superficial things: the color of his hair, the faint lines on his skin. Inside he might be wiser, have a few scars and bruises, but the same hope burned just as strongly, and all the old dreams.

She had forgotten love could be so overwhelming.

"We wanted a republic," he went on. "A voice for the people. Land for the poor, houses for those who slept in the streets, hospitals for the sick, light for the prisoners and the insane. It was simple to imagine, simple to do when we had the power . . . for a brief spell before tyranny returned."

"You hadn't the means," she reminded him. He did not deserve to be patronized by less than the truth. In the end, whether the French armies had come or not, the republic would have fallen because those with the money would not give enough to keep its fragile economy going.

Pain flashed into his face.

"I know." He glanced around the marvelous room in which they stood, still full of music and the chatter of voices. "The diamonds in here alone would have secured us for months. How much do you think these people are served in these banquets in a week? How much is overeaten, how much thrown away because it wasn't needed?"

"Enough to feed the poor of Rome," she answered.

"And the poor of London?" he asked wryly.

There was a bitterness of truth in her reply. "Not enough for that."

He stood staring silently at the throng, his face weary with the long battle against blindness of heart. She watched him, knowing what he thought all those years ago in Rome, and saw beyond doubt that he was thinking the same now. Then it had been the Pope and his cardinals, now it was the Prince and his courtiers, admirers, hangers-on. This was the Crown of Britain and its Empire, not the three-tiered crown of the Pope, but everything else was the same, the splendor and the indifference, the unconscious use of power, the human frailty.

Why was he in London? Did she want to know? Perhaps not. This moment was sweet. Here in this noisy, superficial glamour of the ballroom she could feel the heat of the Roman sun on her face, see the dust, sense the glare in her eyes—and imagine under her feet the stones that had rung to the steps of legions who had conquered every corner of the earth and shouted "Hail Caesar!" as they marched, eagles high, red crests bright. She was back where Christian martyrs had been thrown to the lions, gladiators had fought, St. Peter had been crucified upside down, Michelangelo had painted the Sistine Chapel.

She did not want the past overwhelmed by the present. It was too precious, too deeply woven into the fabric of her dreams.

No, she would not ask.

Then the moment slipped past, and they were no longer alone. A man named Richmond greeted them pleasantly, introducing his wife, and the moment after, Charles Voisey and Thorold Dismore joined them and conversation became general. It was trivial and mildly amusing until Mrs. Richmond made some comment about ancient Troy and the excitement of Heinrich Schliemann's discoveries. Vespasia forced her attention to the present and its trivia.

"Remarkable," Dismore agreed. "Extraordinary persistence of the man."

"And the things they discovered," Mrs. Richmond enthused. "The mask of Agamemnon, the necklace probably worn by Helen. It makes them all real in a way I had never imagined . . . actual flesh and blood, just like ordinary people. It is the oddest sensation to take them out of the realms of legend and make mortals of them, with lives that leave physical remains, artefacts behind."

"Probably." Voisey sounded cautious.

"Oh, I think there's little doubt!" she protested. "Have you read any of those marvelous papers by Martin Fetters? He's brilliant, you know. He makes it all so immediate."

There was a moment's silence.

"Yes," Dismore said abruptly. "He is a great loss."

"Oh!" Mrs. Richmond colored deeply. "I had forgotten. How terrible. I am sorry. He . . . fell . . ." She stopped, clearly uncertain how to continue.

"Of course he fell!" Dismore said tartly. "God knows how any jury came to the conclusion they did. It's patently absurd. But it will go to appeal, and it will be reversed." He looked at Voisey.

Richmond turned to look at him as well.

Voisey stared back.

Mario Corena was puzzled.

"Sorry, Corena, can't give an opinion," Voisey said tersely. His face was pale, his lips pinched. "I shall almost certainly be one of the judges to sit when it comes to appeal. But this much I do know, that damned policeman Pitt is an ambitious and irresponsible man with a grudge against those of better birth and fortune than himself. He's determined to exercise the power his position gives him, just to show he can. His father was deported for theft, and he's never got over it. This is some kind of revenge against society. The arrogance of the ignorant when they are given a little responsibility is terrifying."

Vespasia felt as if she had been slapped. For a moment she had been at a loss for words. She heard the anger in Voisey's voice, saw the heat in his eyes. Her own anger was equal.

"I was not aware you were acquainted with him," she said icily. "But then I am certain a member of the judiciary such as you are would not judge any man, regardless of his birth or status, other than on the most carefully tested evidence. You would not allow other men's words or deeds to weigh with you, least of all your own feelings. Justice must be equal to all, or it is no justice at all." Her voice dripped sarcasm. "Therefore I must presume you know him far better than I do."

Voisey's skin was so pale the freckles on it stood out. He drew in his breath but did not speak.

"He is a relative of mine, by marriage," Vespasia finished. A very distant relative, but she had no need to add that. Her great-nephew, now dead, had been Pitt's brother-in-law.

Mrs. Richmond was astounded. For a moment she found it almost amusing, then she realized how seriously everyone else was taking it; the emotion was charged in the air like a coming storm.

"Unfortunate," Dismore said in the silence. "Probably the fellow was doing his duty as he saw it. Still, no doubt at all the appeal will reverse the verdict."

"Ah . . . yes," Richmond added. "No doubt at all."

Voisey kept his discretion.

3

A LITTLE OVER three weeks later Pitt was home early from Bow Street and pottering happily in the garden. May was one of the most beautiful months, full of pale blossom, new leaves and the brilliant flare of tulips, the heavy scent of wallflowers rich as velvet. The lupines were beginning, tall columns of pinks, blues and purples, and he now had at least half a dozen Oriental poppies opening, fragile and gaudy as colored silk.

He was doing more admiring than actual work, even though there were sufficient weeds to have kept him fully occupied. He was hoping Charlotte would finish whatever domestic duties she had and would join him, and when he heard the French doors open he turned with pleasure. But it was Ardal Juster who walked down the lawn, his dark face grim.

Pitt's first thought was that the appeal judges had found some flaw in the procedure and the verdict had been overturned. He did not believe there was new evidence. He had searched everywhere at the time and questioned everyone.

Juster stopped in front of him. He glanced to right and left at the flower beds, then up at the sunlight pouring through the chestnut leaves at the far end of the lawn. He drew in a deep breath of the fragrance of damp earth and blossoms.

Pitt was about to break the tension himself when Juster spoke.

"Adinett's appeal failed," he said quietly. "It will be in the newspapers tomorrow. A majority verdict—four to one. Voisey delivered it. He was one of the four. Abercrombie was the only dissenting voice."

Pitt did not understand. Juster looked as if he had brought news of a defeat, not a victory. He seized on the only explanation he could think of, the one he felt himself, that to hang a man was a solution that degraded yourself and allowed the man no answer to his sin, no time to change. Certainly he believed Adinett had committed a profound evil, but it had always troubled him that he had no idea of the reason. It was just conceivable that had they known the whole truth everything might have looked different.

But even if it did not, and whatever Adinett was, to demand the final payment from him diminished those who exacted it more than it did him.

Juster's face in the evening sun was bleak with anxiety. There was only reflected light in his eyes.

"They'll hang him." Pitt put it into words.

"Of course," Juster answered. He pushed his hands into his pockets, still frowning. "That's not why I came. You'll read about it in the newspapers tomorrow, and anyway, you know as much about that as I do. I came to warn you."

Pitt was startled. A chill grew inside him, in spite of the balmy evening.

Juster bit his lip. "There was nothing wrong with the conviction, but there are many people who can't believe a man like John Adinett really murdered Fetters. If we could have provided them with a motive then they might have accepted it." He saw Pitt's expression. "I don't mean the ordinary man in the street. He's perfectly happy that justice has been done . . . possibly even agreeable that a man in Adinett's position can meet with the same justice as he would. Such people don't need to understand." He squinted a little in the light. "I mean men of Adinett's own class, men of power."

Pitt was still uncertain. "If they didn't overturn the verdict, then the law accepts both his guilt and that the trial was fairly conducted. They may grieve for him, but what else can they do?"

"Punish you for your temerity," Juster answered, then

smiled lopsidedly. "And perhaps me too, depending on how far they consider it my choice to prosecute."

The warm wind stirred the leaves of the chestnut tree, and a dozen starlings swirled up into the air.

"I thought they had already hurled every insult that they could think of at me when I was on the witness stand," Pitt replied, remembering with a flash of anger and pain the charges against his father. He had been taken by surprise that it still hurt so much. He thought he had pushed it into the background and allowed it to heal over. It startled him that the scab was so easily ripped off and that the wound should bleed again.

Juster looked unhappy, a faint flush on his cheeks. "I'm sorry, Pitt. I thought I had warned you enough, but I'm not sure that I did. It's far from over."

Pitt felt a catch in his throat, as if for an instant it was hard to breathe. "What could they do?"

"I don't know, but Adinett has powerful friends . . . not powerful enough to save him, but they'll take losing hard. I wish I could warn you what to expect, but I don't know." His distress was plain in his eyes and the slight droop to his shoulders.

"It wouldn't have changed anything," Pitt said honestly. "If you don't prosecute a case because the accused has friends the whole law is worth nothing, and neither are we."

Juster smiled, the corners of his mouth turning down. He knew it was true, but the price was far from as simple, and he knew Pitt was speaking with bravado, and irony as well. He held out his hand. "If I can help, call me. I can defend as well as I can prosecute. I mean it, Pitt."

"Thank you," Pitt said sincerely. It was a lifeline he might need.

Juster nodded. "I like your flowers. That's the way to do it, lots of color all over the place. I can't bear straight rows. Too easy to see the faults, apart from anything else."

Pitt made himself smile. "That's my belief as well."

Together they stood drinking in the color in the evening air, the lazy droning of bees, the sound of children laughing in the distance, and the chattering birds. The perfume of the wallflowers was almost like a taste in the mouth.

Then finally Juster took his leave, and Pitt walked slowly back into the house.

The morning newspapers were all that Pitt had feared. In bold letters they announced the failure of Adinett's appeal and that he would be executed in three weeks' time. Pitt had already known, but seeing it in print made it more immediate. It tore away the last shred of evasion.

Almost underneath that news, where no one could miss it, was a long article by Reginald Gleave, who had defended Adinett and very openly still believed in his innocence. He spoke of the verdict as one of the great miscarriages of British justice in the current century, and predicted that the people would one day be bitterly ashamed of the establishment which had, in their name, carried out such a terrible wrong.

He did not castigate the judges of appeal, although he had some unkind words for the original trial judge. He was lenient with the jury, considering them unlearned men as far as the law was concerned, who were unwittingly led astray by those who were truly at fault. One of those was Ardal Juster. The main culprit was Pitt:

... a dangerously bigoted man who has abused the power of his office in order to carry out his private vendetta against the propertied classes because of the prosecution of his father for theft, when he was at an age not to understand the necessity and the justice of such a thing.

Since then he has defied authority in every way his imagination could conceive, short of actually losing his job and thus forfeiting the power he so profoundly desires. And make no mistake, he is an ambitious man, with an expensive wife to keep, and aspirations to act the gentleman himself.

But the officers who guard the law must be impartial,

fair to all, fearing no one and favoring no one. That is the essence of justice, and it is in the end, the only freedom.

And there was more of the same, but he skipped over it, picking up a phrase here and there.

Charlotte was staring at him across the breakfast table, marmalade spoon in her hand. What should he tell her? If she saw the article it would make her angry first, then possibly frightened for him. And if he hid it, she would know he was being evasive, and that would be worse.

"Thomas?" Her voice cut across his thoughts.

"Reggie Gleave has written a rather vicious piece about the case," he replied. "Adinett lost his appeal, and Gleave has taken it hard. He defended him, you remember. Perhaps he really thinks he's innocent."

She was looking at him narrowly, her eyes worried, reading his expression rather than listening to his words.

He made himself smile. "Is there any more tea?" He folded up the newspaper and hesitated for a moment. If he took it, she was perfectly capable of going out and buying another. And the fact that he had hidden it from her would make her worry more. He put it down again on the table.

She put down the marmalade spoon and poured the tea. She said nothing further, but he knew that the moment he was out of the house, she would read the newspaper.

In the middle of the afternoon Assistant Commissioner Cornwallis sent for Pitt. Pitt knew the moment he stepped into Cornwallis's office that something was seriously wrong. He imagined a highly complex and embarrassing case, possibly even another like Fetters's murder, implicating someone of importance. That was the sort of matter he dealt with lately.

Cornwallis stood behind his desk as if he had been pacing the floor and was reluctant to sit. He was a lithe man of average height. Most of his life had been spent in the navy, and he still looked as if being in command of men at sea would suit his nature better, facing the elements rather than the deviousness of politics and public opinion.

"Yes sir?" Pitt enquired.

Cornwallis seemed deeply unhappy, as if he had spent time searching for words for what he had to say but he had not yet found them.

"Is it a new case?" Pitt asked.

"Yes . . . and no." Cornwallis gazed at him steadily. "Pitt, I hate this! I fought against it all morning, and I lost. No battle has ever sat worse with me. If I knew of anything else to do I would do it." He shook his head very slightly. "But I believe that if I pursue it any more I may only make it worse."

Pitt was confused, and Cornwallis's obvious distress touched him with a chill of apprehension.

"Is it a case? Who's involved?"

"In the East End," Cornwallis replied. "And I have no idea who's involved. Half of the anarchists in London, for all I know."

Pitt took a deep breath, steadying himself. Like all other police officers, and much of the general public, Pitt was aware of the anarchist activities in much of Europe, including the violent explosion at a restaurant in Paris and several explosions in London and various other European capitals. The French authorities had circulated a dossier containing pictures of five hundred wanted anarchists. Several were awaiting trial.

"Who's dead?" he asked. "Why are we called in? The East End is not our patch."

"No one is dead," Cornwallis replied. "It's a Special Branch matter."

"The Irish?" Pitt was startled. Like everyone else, he was perfectly aware of the Irish troubles, of the Fenians, of the history of myth and violence, tragedy and strife which had bedeviled Ireland over the last three hundred years. And he knew what unrest there was in parts of London, for which a special section of police had been set apart so that they might concentrate on dealing with the threat of bombings, assassination or even minor insurrection. It had originally been known as the Special Irish Branch.

"Not Irish in particular," Cornwallis corrected. "General

53

political troubles; they just prefer not to be called political. The public wouldn't accept it."

"Why us?" Pitt asked. "I don't understand."

"You'd better sit down." Cornwallis waved at the chair opposite his desk, and Pitt obeyed.

"It's not us," Cornwallis said honestly. "It's you." He did not look away as he spoke but met Pitt's eyes unflinchingly. "You are relieved of command of Bow Street and seconded to Special Branch, from today."

Pitt was stunned. It was impossible. How could he be removed from Bow Street? He had done nothing even incompetent, far less wrong! He wanted to protest, but no words seemed adequate.

Cornwallis's mouth was stretched into a thin line, as if he felt some physical pain gnawing at him. "The command comes from the top," he said very quietly. "Far above me. I questioned it, then I fought it, but it is beyond my power to reverse. The men concerned all know each other. I am an outsider. I'm not one of them." He searched Pitt's eyes, trying to judge how much of his meaning Pitt had understood.

"Not one of them . . ." Pitt echoed. Old memories came flooding like a tide of darkness. He had seen the subtlest of corruption in the past, men who had secret loyalties which superseded every other honor or pledge, who would cover each other's crimes, who offered preference to their own and excluded all others. It was known as the Inner Circle. Its long tentacles had gripped him before, but he had thought little of it for a couple of years. Now Cornwallis was telling him that this was the enemy.

Perhaps he should not have been surprised. He had dealt them some hard blows in the past. They must have been biding their time to retaliate, and his testimony in court had given them the perfect opportunity.

"Friends of Adinett?" he said aloud.

Cornwallis nodded fractionally. "I have no way of knowing, but I would lay any odds you like on it." He too avoided mentioning the name, but neither of them doubted the meaning. Cornwallis drew in his breath. "You are to report to Mr.

Victor Narraway, at the address I shall give you. He is the commander of Special Branch in the East End, and he will tell you your exact duties." He stopped abruptly.

Was he going to say that Narraway too was a member of the Inner Circle? If he were then Pitt was more profoundly alone than he had imagined.

"I wish I could tell you more about Narraway," Cornwallis said miserably. "But the whole of Special Branch is something of a closed book to the rest of us." Dislike puckered his face. He may have been obliged to accept that a clandestine force was necessary, but it offended his nature, as it did those of most Englishmen.

"I thought the Fenian trouble had died down," Pitt said candidly. "What could I do in Spitalfields that their own men couldn't do better?"

Cornwallis leaned forward over his desk. "Pitt, it has nothing to do with the Fenians, or the anarchists, and Spitalfields is immaterial." His voice was low and urgent. "They want you out of Bow Street. They are determined to break you, if they can. This is at least another job, for which you will be paid. Money will be deposited for your wife to withdraw. And if you are careful, and clever, they may be unable to find you, and believe me, that would be very desirable for some time to come. I . . . I wish it were not so."

Pitt intended to stand up, but found his legs weak. He started to ask how long he was to be banished to chasing shadows in the East End, robbed of dignity, of command, of the whole way of life he was used to . . . and had earned! He was not sure if he could bear the answer. Then, looking at Cornwallis's face, he realized the man had no answer to give.

"I have to live . . . in the East End?" he asked. He heard his own voice, dry and a little cracked, as if he had not spoken for days. He realized it was the sound of shock. He had heard the same tone in others when he had had to tell them unbearable news.

He shook himself. This was not unbearable. No one he loved was injured or dead. He had lost his home for himself, but it was there for Charlotte, and Daniel and Jemima. Only he would be missing.

But it was so unjust! He had done nothing wrong, nothing even mistaken. Adinett was guilty. Pitt had presented the evidence to a jury fairly, and they had weighed it and delivered a verdict.

Why had John Adinett killed Fetters? Even Juster had been unable to think of any reason. In everyone's belief they had been the best of friends, two men who not only shared a passion for travel and for objects treasured for their links with history and legend, but also shared many ideals and dreams for changing the future. They wanted a gentler, more tolerant society that offered a chance of improvement to all.

Juster had wondered if the motive could concern money or a woman. Both had been investigated, and no suggestion could be found of either's being the case. No one knew of even the slightest difference between the two men until that day. No raised voices had been heard. When the butler had brought the port half an hour earlier, the two men had seemed the best of friends.

But Pitt was certain he was not mistaken in the facts.

"Pitt . . ." Cornwallis was still leaning across the desk, staring at him, his eyes earnest.

Pitt refocused his attention. "Yes?"

"I'll do all I can." Cornwallis seemed embarrassed, as if he knew that was not enough. "Just . . . just wait it out. Be careful. And . . . and for God's sake, trust no one." His hands clenched on the polished oak surface. "I wish to God I had the power to do something. But I don't even know who I'm fighting. . ."

Pitt rose to his feet. "There's nothing to do," he said flatly.

"Where do I find this Victor Narraway?"

Cornwallis handed him a slip of paper with an address written on it—14 Lake Street, Mile End New Town. It was on the edge of the Spitalfields area. "But go home first, collect what clothes you'll need, and personal things. Be careful what you tell Charlotte. . . . Don't . . ." He stopped, changing his mind about what he meant to say. "There are anarchists," he said instead. "Real ones, with dynamite."

"Maybe they're planning something here."

"I suppose that's possible. After Bloody Sunday in Trafalgar Square, not much would surprise me. Although that was four years ago."

Pitt walked to the door. "I know you did what you could." It was difficult to speak. "The Inner Circle is a secret disease. I knew that . . . I'd just forgotten." And without waiting for Cornwallis to answer, he went out and down the stairs, oblivious of the men he passed, not even hearing those who spoke to him.

He dreaded telling Charlotte, therefore the only way to do it was immediately. "What is it?" she said as he came into the kitchen. She was standing at the big, black cooking stove. The room was full of sunlight and the smell of fresh bread, and clean linen on the airing rails hauled up to the ceiling. There was blue-and-white china on the Welsh dresser and a bowl full of fruit in the center of the scrubbed wooden table. Archie, the marmalade-and-white cat, was lying in the empty laundry basket washing himself, and his brother Angus was creeping hopefully along the window ledge towards the milk jug by Charlotte's elbow.

The children were at school, and Gracie must be upstairs or out on some errand. This was the home he loved, everything that made life good. After the horror and tragedy of crime, it was coming back here with its laughter and sanity, the knowledge that he was loved, that took the poison out of the wounds of the day.

How would he manage without it? How would he manage without Charlotte?

For a moment he was filled with a blinding rage against the secret men who had done this to him. It was monstrous that from the safety of anonymity they could rob him of the things he held dearest, that they could invade his life and scatter it like dry grass, without being accountable to anyone. He wanted to do the same to them, but face-to-face, so they would know why, and he could see it in their eyes as they understood.

"Thomas, what is it?" Her voice was sharp with fear. She had swung around from the stove, the oven cloth in her hand, and was staring at him. He was dimly aware that Angus had reached the milk and was beginning to lap it.

"They've put me into Special Branch," he replied.

"I don't understand," she said slowly. "What does that mean? Who are Special Branch?"

"They work against bombers and anarchists," he replied. "Mostly Fenians to begin with, until last year. Now it's anyone who wants to cause riot or political assassination."

"Why is that so terrible?" She was looking at his face, reaching his emotions rather than the words he had said. She was not doubting the pain of it, only the reason.

"I shan't be in Bow Street anymore. Not with Cornwallis. I'll work for a man called Narraway . . . in Spitalfields."

She frowned. "Spitalfields? The East End? You mean you'll have to travel to the Spitalfields police station every day?"

"No . . . I'll have to live in Spitalfields, as an ordinary person."

Slowly understanding dawned in her eyes, then loneliness and anger.

"But that's . . . monstrous!" she said incredulously. "They can't do that! It's totally unjust! What are they afraid of? Do they think a few anarchists are really going to put all London in danger?"

"It's got nothing to do with catching anarchists," he explained. "It's about punishing me because John Adinett is part of the Inner Circle, and I gave the evidence that will get him hanged."

Her face tightened, her lips pale. "Yes, I know. Are they listening to people like Gleave, in the newspaper? That's ridiculous! Adinett was guilty—that's not your fault!"

He said nothing.

"All right." She turned away, her voice thick with tears. "I know that has nothing to do with it. Can't anyone help? It's so unjust." She swung back. "Perhaps Aunt Vespasia . . ."

"No." The ache inside him was almost intolerable. He

stared at her face, flushed with anger and despair, her hair escaping its pins, her eyes full of tears. How was he going to bear living in Spitalfields, alone, not seeing her at the end of every day, not sharing a joke or an idea, or even arguing an opinion, above all not touching her, feeling the warmth of her in his arms?

"It won't be forever." He said it as much to himself as to her. He had to look to a time beyond this, whenever it might be. He would not endure this a day longer than he had to. There would be some way of fighting it . . . in time.

She sniffed hard. Her eyes brimmed over and she hunted through her apron pockets for a handkerchief. She found one and blew her nose fiercely.

He was suddenly undecided. He had thought since before he came into the kitchen that he would pack his things and leave straightaway, not dragging out good-byes. Now he wanted to stay as long as he could, hold her in his arms, and since the house was empty, even go upstairs and make love for what would be the last time for as long as he could foresee.

Would that make it better . . . or worse, harder when the time came, as it would—soon?

In the end he did not think about it at all, he simply clung to her, kissed her, held her so tightly she cried out against it and he let her go, but only an inch or two, only enough not to hurt. Then he took her upstairs.

After he was gone, Charlotte sat in front of the bedroom mirror brushing her hair. She had to take out the few pins that remained and redo it anyway. She looked dreadful. Her eyes were red and still burning with tears, although now they were also of anger, as well as shock and loneliness.

She heard the front door close, and Gracie's footsteps along the hall.

Quickly she wound up her hair and repinned it rather wildly, then went down and into the kitchen.

Gracie was standing in the middle of the room.

"Wotever's 'appened?" she said in dismay. "Yer new bread's

ruined. Look at it." Then she realized it was something far more serious. "S'it Mr. Pitt? S'e 'urt?" All the color drained from her face.

"No!" Charlotte answered quickly. "He's all right. I mean, he isn't hurt."

"Wot then?" Gracie demanded. Her whole body was rigid, her shoulders hunched tight, her small hands clenched.

Charlotte deliberately sat down on one of the chairs. This was not something to tell in a few words. "They've dismissed him from Bow Street and sent him into Special Branch, in the East End." She never thought of not confiding in Gracie. Gracie had been with them for eight years, since she had been a thirteen-year-old waif, undernourished and illiterate, but with a sharp tongue and a will to improve herself. To her, Pitt was the finest man in the world, and the very best at his job. She considered herself better than any other maid in Blooms-bury because she worked for him. She pitied those who worked for mere useless lords. They had no excitement, no purpose in life.

"Wot's Special Branch?" she asked suspiciously. "W'y 'im?"

"It used to be about the Irish bombers," Charlotte said, explaining the little she knew. "Now it's more about anarchists in general, and nihilists, I believe."

"Wot's them?"

"Anarchists are people who want to get rid of all governments and create chaos—"

"Yer don't 'ave ter get rid o' governments ter do that," Gracie said with scorn. "Wot's them other 'ists?"

"Nihilists? People who want to destroy everything."

"That's daft! What's the point o' that? Then yer got nuffink yerself!"

"Yes, it is daft," Charlotte agreed. "I don't think they have much sense, just anger."

"So is Mr. Pitt goin' ter stop 'em, then?" Gracie looked a little more hopeful.

"He's going to try, but he has to find them first. That's why he's going to have to live in Spitalfields."

60

Gracie was aghast. "Live! They in't never gonna make 'im live in Spitalfields? Don' they know wot kind of a place that is? Blimey, it's the dregs o' the East End there. Filthy, it is, and stinkin' o' Gawd knows wot! Nobody's safe from nuffink, not robbers nor murderers nor sickness nor bein' set on in the dark." Her voice rose higher and higher. "They got the fevers an' the pox an' everything else besides. Dynamite some o' them places there an' yer'd be doin' the world a favor. Yer'll 'ave ter tell 'em it in't right. 'Oo der they think 'e is? Some kind o' useless rozzer?"

"They know what it's like there," Charlotte said, misery overwhelming her again. "That's why they're doing it. It's a kind of punishment for finding the evidence against John Adinett and swearing to it in court. He's not head of Bow Street anymore."

Gracie hunched into herself as if she had been beaten. She looked very small and thin. She had seen too much injustice to question its reality.

"That's wicked," she said quietly. "It's real wrong. But I s'pose if them toffs is after 'im, 'an 'e got one of 'em wot 'e 'ad comin' ter 'im, then 'e's safest out o' their way, w'ere they can't see 'im, like. I s'pose they'll pay 'im, won't they, in this Branch wotever?"

"Oh, yes. I don't know how much." That was something Charlotte had not even thought of. Trust Gracie to be practical. She had been poor too often to forget it. She had known the kind of cold that makes you feel sick, the hunger where you eat scraps that other people throw away, when one slice of bread is wealth and nobody even imagines tomorrow, let alone next week.

"It will be enough!" she said more forcefully. "No luxuries, maybe, but food. And the summer's coming, so we won't need anything like as much coal. Just no new dresses for a while, and no new toys or books."

"An' no mutton," Gracie added. " 'Errings is good. An' oysters is cheap. An' I know w'ere yer can get good bones fer soup an' the like. We'll be o'right." She drew in a deep breath. "But it still in't fair!"

61

* * *

It was difficult to explain to the children too. Jemima at ten and a half was already growing tall and slim and had lost a little of her roundness of face. It was possible to see in her a shadow of the woman she would become.

Daniel, at eight, was sturdier of build and very definitely a child. His features were developing strength, but his skin was soft and the hair curled at the back of his head exactly the way Pitt's did.

Charlotte had tried to tell them that their father would not be home again for a long time in such a way that they understood it was not of his choosing, that he would miss them terribly.

"Why?" Jemima said immediately. "If he doesn't want to go, why does he do it?" She was fighting against accepting, her whole face full of resentment.

"We all have to do things we don't wish to sometimes," Charlotte answered. She tried to keep her voice level, knowing that both children would pick up her emotions as much as her words. She must do all she could to disguise from them her own distress. "It is a matter of what is right, what has to be done."

"But why does *he* have to do it?" Jemima persisted. "Why couldn't someone else? I don't want him to go away."

Charlotte touched her gently. "Neither do I. But if we make a fuss it will only be harder for him. I told him we would look after each other, and would miss him, but we'd be all right until he comes back."

Jemima thought a few moments about that, uncertain if she was going to accept it or not.

"Is he after bad men?" Daniel spoke for the first time.

"Yes," Charlotte said quickly. "They must be stopped, and he is the best person to do it."

"Why?"

"Because he's very clever. Other people have been trying for a while, and they haven't managed to do it, so they've sent for Papa."

"I see. Then I suppose we'll be all right." He thought for a few minutes more. "Is it dangerous?"

"He's not going to fight them," she said with more assurance than she felt. "He's just going to find out who they are."

"Isn't he going to stop them?" Daniel asked reasonably, his brow puckered up.

"Not by himself," she explained. "He'll tell other policemen, and they'll all do it together."

"Are you sure?" He knew she was worried, even though he was uncertain why.

She made herself smile. "Of course. Wouldn't you?"

He nodded, satisfied. "But I'll miss him."

She forced the smile to remain. "So will I."

Pitt went by train straight to the address to the north of Spitalfields that Cornwallis had given him. It proved to be a small house behind a shop. Victor Narraway was waiting for him. Pitt saw that he was a lean man with a shock of dark hair, threaded with gray, and a face in which the intelligence was dangerously obvious. He could not be inconspicuous once one met his eyes.

He surveyed Pitt with interest.

"Sit down," he ordered, indicating the plain wooden chair opposite him. The room was very sparsely furnished, with no more than a chest with drawers, all of which were locked, a small table, and two chairs. Probably it had originally been a scullery.

Pitt obeyed. He was dressed in his oldest clothes, the ones he used when he wished to go into the poorer areas unnoticed. It was a long time since he had last found it necessary. These days he employed other people for such tasks. He felt uncomfortable, dirty, and at a complete disadvantage. It was as if his years of success had been swept away, nothing but a dream, or a wish.

"Can't see that you'll be a great deal of use to me," Narraway said grimly. "But I shouldn't look a gift horse in the mouth, I suppose. You've been foisted on me, so I'd better make the best of it. I thought you were noted for your handling of scandal among the gentry. Spitalfields doesn't seem like your patch."

"It isn't," Pitt said grudgingly. "Mine was Bow Street."

"And where the hell did you learn to speak like that?" Narraway's eyebrows rose. His own voice was good—he had the diction of birth and education—but it was not better than Pitt's.

"I was taught in the schoolroom along with the son of the house," Pitt replied, remembering it sharply even now, the sunlight through the windows, the tutor with his cane and his eyeglasses, the endless repetitions until he was satisfied. Pitt had resented it at first, then become fascinated. Now he was grateful.

"Fortunate for you," Narraway said with a tight smile. "Well, if you're going to be any use here, you'll have to unlearn it, and rapidly. You look like a peddler or a vagrant, and you sound like a refugee from the Athenaeum!"

"I can sound like a peddler if I want to," Pitt retorted. "Not a local one, but I'd be a fool to try that. They'll know their own."

Narraway's expression eased for the first time, and a glint of acceptance shone for an instant in his eyes. It was a first step, no more. He nodded.

"Most of the rest of London has no idea how serious it is," he said grimly. "They all know there is unrest. It's more than that." He was watching Pitt closely. "We are not talking of the odd lunatic with a stick of dynamite, although we've certainly got them too." A brief flicker of irony crossed his face. "Only a month or two ago we had a man who tried to flush dynamite down the lavatory and blocked the drains up until his landlady complained. The workmen who took up the drains and found it had no idea what it was. Some poor fool thought it would be useful to mend cracks in something or other, and put it on the floor of his loft to dry out, and blew the whole place to smithereens. Took half the house away."

It was farce, but bitter and deadly. One laughed at the absurdity of it, but the tragedy was left.

64

"If it's not the odd nihilist achieving his ambition," Pitt asked, "then what is it we are really looking for?"

Narraway smiled, relaxing a little. He settled in his chair, crossing his legs. "We've always had the Irish problem, and I don't imagine it'll go away, but for the moment it is not our main concern. There are still Fenians around, but we arrested quite a few last year, and they're fairly quiet. There is strong anti-Catholic feeling in general."

"Dangerous?"

He looked at Pitt's expression of doubt. "Not in itself," he said tartly. "You have a lot to learn. Start by being quiet and listening! Get something to do to explain your existence. Walk 'round the streets here. Keep your eyes open and your mouth closed. Listen to the idle talk, hear what is said and what isn't. There's an anger in the air that wasn't here ten years ago, or perhaps fifteen. Remember Bloody Sunday in '88, and the murders in Whitechapel that autumn? It's four years later now, and four years worse."

Of course Pitt remembered the summer and autumn of '88. Everyone did. But he had not realized the situation was still so close to violence. He had imagined it one of those sporadic eruptions which happens from time to time and then dies down again. Part of him wondered if Narraway were overdramatizing it, perhaps to make his own role more important. There was much rivalry within the different branches of those who enforced the law, each guarding his own realm and trying to increase it at the cost of others.

Narraway read his face as if he had spoken.

"Don't rush to judgment, Pitt. Be skeptical, by all means, but do as you are told. I don't know whether Donaldson was right about you or not on the witness stand, but you'll obey me while you're in Special Branch or I'll have you out on your ear so fast you'll fetch up living in Spitalfields or its like permanently, and your family with you! Am I clear enough for you?"

"Yes, sir," Pitt answered, still hideously aware of what a dangerous path he trod. He had no friends, and far too many enemies. He could not afford to give Narraway any excuse to throw him out.

"Good." Narraway recrossed his legs. "Then listen to me, and remember what I say. Whatever you think, I am right, and you will need to act on what I say if you are to survive, let alone be any actual use to me."

"Yes, sir."

"And don't parrot back at me! If I wanted a talking bird I'd go and buy one!" His face was tight. "The East End is full of poverty—desperate, grinding poverty such as the rest of the city can't even imagine. People die of hunger and the diseases of hunger . . . men, women, and children." A suppressed anger made his voice raw. "More children die than live. That makes life cheap. Values are different. Put a man in a situation where he has little to lose and you have trouble. Put a hundred thousand men in it and you have a powder keg for revolution." He was watching Pitt steadily. "That's where your Catholics, your dynamiting anarchists, nihilists and Jews are a danger. One of them could be the single spark which could unintentionally set off all the rest. It only needs a beginning."

"Jews?" Pitt said curiously. "What's the problem with the Jews?"

"Not what we expected," Narraway confessed. "We have a lot of fairly liberal Jews from Europe. They came after the '48 revolutions, all of which were crushed, one way or another. We expected their anger to spill over here, but so far it hasn't." He shrugged very slightly. "Which isn't to say it won't. And there's plenty of anti-Semitic feeling around, mostly out of fear and ignorance. But when things are hard, people look for someone to blame, and those who are recognizably different are the first targets, because they are the easiest."

"I see."

"Probably not," Narraway said. "But you will, if you pay attention. I have found you lodgings in Heneagle Street, with one Isaac Karansky, a Polish Jew, well-respected in the area. You should be reasonably safe, and in a position to watch and listen, and learn something."

It was still very general, and Pitt had little idea of what was expected of him. He was used to having a specific event to investigate, something that had already happened and was his task to unravel so he could learn who was responsible, how it had been done, and—if possible—why. Trying to learn about some unspecified act which might or might not happen in the future was completely different, and something too indefinite to grasp. Where did he begin? There was nothing to examine, no one to question, and worst of all, he had no authority.

Once again he was overwhelmed by a sense of failure, both past and to come. He would be no use at this job. It required both skills and knowledge he did not possess. He was a stranger here, almost a foreigner in the ways that would matter. He had been sent not because he would be of use but as a punishment for accusing Adinett, and succeeding. Perhaps as far as Cornwallis was concerned it was also for his safety, and so that he still had a job of some sort, and an income for Charlotte and the children. He was grateful for at least that much, even if at the moment it was well buried beneath fear and anger.

He must try! He needed more from Narraway, even if it meant stifling his pride and making himself ask. When he left this tiny, drab room it would be too late. He would be more completely alone than he had ever been professionally in his life, until now.

"Do you believe there is someone deliberately trying to foment violence, or is it just going to happen by a series of unguarded accidents?" he asked.

"The latter is possible," Narraway answered him. "Always has been, but I believe this time it will be the former. But it will probably look spontaneous, and God knows, there is enough poverty and injustice to fuel it once it is lit. And enough racial and religious hatred for there to be open war in the streets. That's what it is our job to prevent, Pitt. Makes one murder more or less look pretty simple, doesn't it, even close to irrelevant—except to those concerned." His voice was sharp again. "And don't tell me all tragedy or injustice is made up of individual people . . . I know that. But even the best societies in the world don't eradicate the private sins of jealousy, greed and rage, and I don't believe any ever will. What we are talking about is the sort of insanity where no one is safe and everything of use and value is destroyed."

Pitt said nothing. His thoughts were dark, and they frightened him.

"Ever read about the French Revolution?" Narraway asked him. "I mean the big one, the 1789 one, not this recent fiasco."

"Yes." Pitt shivered, thinking back to the classroom on the estate again, and the word pictures of the streets of Paris running with human blood as the guillotine did its work day after day. "The High Terror," he said aloud.

"Exactly." Narraway's lips thinned. "Paris is very close, Pitt. Don't imagine it couldn't happen here. We have enough inequality, believe me."

Against his will, Pitt was considering the possibility that there was at least some truth in what Narraway was saying. He was overstating the case, of course, but even a ghost of this was terrible.

"What do you need of me, exactly?" he asked, keeping his voice carefully controlled. "Give me something to look for."

"I don't need you at all!" Narraway said in sudden disgust. "You've been wished on me from above. I'm not entirely sure why. But since you're here, I may as well do what I can with you. Apart from being able to provide you with as reasonable a place to live as there is in Spitalfields, Isaac Karansky is a man of some influence in his own community. Watch him, listen, learn what you can. If you find anything useful, tell me. I am here every week at some time or another. Speak to the cobbler in the front. He can get a message to me. Don't call unless it's important, and don't fail to call if it could be! If you make a mistake, I'd rather it were on the side of caution."

"Yes, sir."

"Right. Then go."

Pitt stood up and walked towards the door.

"Pitt!"

He turned. "Yes, sir?"

Narraway was watching him. "Be careful. You have no

68

friends out there. Never forget that, even for an instant. Trust no one."

"No, sir. Thank you." Pitt went out of the door feeling cold, in spite of the close air and the semisweet smell of rotting wood, and somewhere close by an open midden.

A couple of enquiries led him through the narrow, gray byways to Heneagle Street. He found the house of Isaac Karansky on the corner of Brick Lane, a busy thoroughfare leading past the towering mass of the sugar factory down to the Whitechapel Road. He knocked on the door. Nothing happened, and he knocked again.

It was opened by a man who appeared to be in his late fifties. His countenance was dark, very obviously Semitic, and his black hair was liberally flecked with gray. There were both gentleness and intelligence in his eyes as he regarded Pitt, but circumstances had taught him to be cautious.

"Yes?"

"Mr. Karansky?" Pitt asked.

"Yes . . ." His voice was deep, slightly accented, and very wary of intrusion.

"My name is Thomas Pitt. I am new to the area, and looking for lodging. A friend of mine suggested you might have a room to let."

"What was your friend's name, Mr. Pitt?"

"Narraway."

"Good, good. We have one room. Please come in and see if it will suit you. It's small, but clean. My wife is very particular." He stood back to allow Pitt to pass him. The hall was narrow and the stairs were no more than a couple of yards from the door. It was all dark, and he imagined that in the winter it would be damp and bitterly cold, but it smelled clean, of some kind of polish, and ahead of him there was an aroma of herbs he was unused to. It was pleasant, a house where people led a family life, where a woman cooked, swept and did laundry, and was generally busy.

"Up the stairs." Karansky pointed ahead of them.

Pitt obeyed, climbing slowly and hearing the creak with every step. At the top Karansky indicated a door and Pitt opened it. The room beyond was small with one window so grimed it was difficult to see what lay outside, but perhaps it was a sight better left to the imagination. One could create one's own dream.

There was an iron bedstead, already made up with linen that looked clean and crisp. There seemed to be several blankets. A wooden dresser had half a dozen drawers with odd handles, and a ewer and basin on top. A small piece of mirror was attached to the wall. There was no cupboard, but there were two hooks on the door. A knotted rag rug lay on the floor beside the bed.

"It will do very well," Pitt accepted. Years fled away and it was as if he were a boy again on the estate, his father newly taken away by the police, he and his mother moved out of the gamekeeper's cottage and into the servants' quarters in the hall. They had counted themselves lucky then. Sir Matthew Desmond had taken them in. Most people would have turned them onto the street.

Looking around this room, remembering poverty again, cold, fear, it was as if the intervening years had been only a dream and it was time to wake up and get on with the day, and reality. The smell was oddly familiar; there was no dust, just the bareness and the knowledge of how cold it would be, bare feet on the floor, frost on the window glass, cold water in the jug.

Keppel Street seemed like something of the imagination. He would miss the physical comfort he had become used to. Immeasurably more than that, unbearably more, he would miss the warmth, the laughter and the love, the safety.

"It will be two shillings a week," Karansky said quietly from behind him. "One and sixpence more with food. You are welcome to join us at the dinner table if you wish."

Remembering what Narraway had said about Karansky's position in the community, Pitt had no hesitation in accepting. "Thank you, that would be excellent." He fished in his pocket and counted out the first week's rent. As Narraway had said, he must find work of some sort, or he would arouse

70

suspicion. "I am new in the area. Where is the best place to look for a job?"

Karansky shrugged expressively, regret in his face. "There's no best place. It's a fight to survive. You look like you have a strong back. What are you prepared to do?"

Pitt had not thought seriously about it until this moment. Only as he counted out the money for his rent did he realize that he would have to have a visible means of earning it or he would invite undue suspicion. It was many years since he had put in great physical effort. His work was hard on the feet sometimes, but mostly it was his mind he used, more especially since he had been in charge in Bow Street.

"I'm not particular," he answered. At least he was not close enough to the docks to have to heave coal or lift crates. "What about the sugar factory? I noticed it just along Brick Lane. Can smell it from here."

Karansky raised one black eyebrow. "Interested in that, are you?"

"Interested? No. Just thought it might have a job offering. Sugar uses a lot of men, doesn't it?"

"Oh yes, hundreds," Karansky agreed. "Every second family around here owes at least some of its living to one of them. Belongs to a man called Sissons. He has three of them, all around here. Two this side of the Whitechapel Road, one the other."

There was something in his expression that caught Pitt's attention, a hesitation, a watchfulness.

"Is it a good place to work?" Pitt asked, trying to sound completely casual.

"Any work is good," Karansky answered. "He pays fair enough. Hours are long and the work can be hard, but it's enough to live on, if you are careful. It's a lot better than starving, and there's already enough around here that do that. But don't set your heart on it, unless you know someone who can get you in."

"I don't. Where else should I look?"

Karansky blinked. "You're not going to try for it?"

"I'll try. But you said not to count on it."

71

There was a movement on the landing beyond the door, and Karansky turned. Pitt saw past him where a handsome woman stood just behind. She must have been almost Karansky's age, but her hair was still thick and dark although her face was lined with weariness and anxiety and her eyes held a haunted look, as if fear were a constant companion. Nevertheless her features were beautifully proportioned, and there was a dignity in her that experience had refined rather than destroyed.

"Is the room right for you?" she asked tentatively.

"It is good, Leah," Karansky assured her. "Mr. Pitt will stay with us. He will look for a job tomorrow."

"Saul needs help," she said, looking past her husband to Pitt. "Can you lift and carry? It is not hard."

"He was asking about the sugar factory," Karansky told her. "Perhaps he would rather be there."

She looked surprised, worried, as if Karansky had done something which disappointed her. She frowned. "Wouldn't Saul's be better?" Her expression indicated that she meant far more than the simple words, and she expected him to understand.

Karansky shrugged. "You can try both, if you want."

"You said I wouldn't get anything at the sugar factory unless I knew someone," Pitt reminded him.

Karansky gazed back in silence for several seconds, as if trying to decide how much of what he had said was honest, and the truth of it eluded him.

It was Mrs. Karansky who broke the silence.

"The sugar factory is not a good place, Mr. Pitt. Saul won't pay as much, but it's a better place to work, believe me."

Pitt tried to balance in his mind the advantages of safety and the appearance of ordinary common sense against the loss of opportunity to discover what was so dangerous about the sugar factories which supported half the community, either directly or indirectly.

"What does Saul do?" he asked.

"Weave silk," Karansky answered.

Pitt had a strong feeling that Karansky expected him to be

interested in the sugar factory, to go for that job in spite of any warning. He remembered Narraway's words about trust.

"Then I think I'll go to see him tomorrow, and if I'm lucky, he may give me some work," he replied. "Anything will be better than nothing, even a few days."

Mrs. Karansky smiled. "I'll tell him. He's a good friend. He'll find a place for you. May not be much, but it's as certain as anything is in this life. Now you must be hungry. We eat in an hour. Come, join us."

"Thank you," Pitt accepted, remembering the smell from the kitchen and recoiling from the thought of going out again into the sour, gray streets with their smell of dirt and misery.

"I will."

4

I T WAS NOT the first night on which Pitt had been away from home, but Charlotte felt a kind of loneliness that she had not experienced at other times, perhaps because now she had no idea when he would be back, or even if. When he was, it would be only temporary.

She lay awake a long time, too angry to sleep. She tossed and turned, pulling the bedclothes with her until she had made a complete mess of them. Finally at about two o'clock she got up, stripped the bed and remade it with clean sheets. Half an hour later she finally slept.

She woke in broad daylight with a headache—and a determination to do something about the situation. It was not tolerable simply to endure it. It was completely unjust, firstly and mostly of course to Pitt, but also to the whole family.

She dressed and went downstairs to the kitchen, where she found Gracie sitting at the table. The scullery door was open and a shaft of sunlight fell across the scrubbed floor. The children had already gone to school. She was angry with herself for missing them, especially today.

"Mornin', ma'am." Gracie stood up and went over to the kettle, which was singing on the hob. "I got fresh tea ready." She poured it into the pot as she spoke and carried it back to the table, where there were two cups waiting. "Daniel and Jemima's fine this mornin', off wi' no trouble, but I bin thinkin'. We gotta do summink about this. It in't right."

74

"I agree," Charlotte said instantly, sitting down opposite her and wishing the tea would brew more quickly.

"Toast?" Gracie offered.

"Not yet." Charlotte shook her head very slightly. It still throbbed. "I was also thinking about it half the night, but I still don't know what there is we can do. Mr. Pitt told me that Commander Cornwallis said it was for his own safety, as well as to keep him in a job of some sort. The people he's upset would be happy to see him with nothing, and where they can reach him." She did not want to put it into words, but she needed to explain. "They might have meant him to have an accident in the street, or something like that . . ."

Gracie was not shocked; perhaps she had seen too much death when she was growing up in the East End. There was nothing about poverty she had not known, even if some of it was receding into memory now. But she was angry, her thin, little face hardened and her lips drawn into a tight line.

"All because 'e done 'is job right an' got that Adinett 'anged? Wot der they want 'im ter do? Pretend like it in't wrong 'e murdered Mr. Fetters? Or just act daft like 'e never realized wot 'appened?"

"Yes. I think that's exactly what they wanted," Charlotte answered. "And I think not every doctor would have seen anything wrong. It was just their bad luck that Ibbs was quick enough to realize there was something odd, and it was Thomas he called."

" 'Oo is this Adinett, anyway?" Gracie screwed up her brows. "An' why does anyone want 'im ter get away wi' murderin' Mr. Fetters?"

"He's a member of the Inner Circle," Charlotte said with a shiver. "Isn't the tea ready yet?"

Gracie looked at her shrewdly, probably guessing how she felt, and poured it anyway. It was a little weak but the fragrance of it was easing, even while it was still too hot to drink.

"Does that mean they can get away wi' murder, an' nuffink is supposed ter 'appen to 'em?" Gracie was clenched up with anger.

"Yes, unless perhaps someone either brave or reckless gets in the way. Then they get rid of him too." Charlotte tried to sip the tea, but knew she would burn herself, and more milk would spoil it.

"So wot are we goin' ter do?" Gracie stared at her with wide, unflinching eyes. "We gotter prove 'e were right. We dunno 'oo's in this circle, but we know there's more o' us than there is o' them." It was not a possibility to her that Pitt could have been mistaken. It was not even worth denying it.

Charlotte smiled in spite of the way she felt. Gracie's loyalty was more of a restorative than the tea. She could not let her down by being less brave or less positive. She said the first thing that came into her mind, so as not to leave silence.

"The thing that made this trial so different was that no one knew of any reason why Adinett should do it. The two men had been friends for years, and no one knew anything of a quarrel, that day or any other time. Some people couldn't believe he had any reason, and all the evidence was about things, not feelings. They were a lot, when added together, but each one by itself didn't seem much." She sipped the tea. "And some of the witnesses retreated a bit when it came to swearing in court and sticking to their stories in spite of the defense lawyer's cross-questioning them and trying to make them look foolish."

"So we gotta find out w'y 'e done it," Gracie said simply. " 'E must 'ave 'ad a reason. 'E wouldn't 'a done it fer nuffink."

Charlotte was already beginning to think. Very little had come out in the newspapers about either man, except their general worthiness, their social standing and the incomprehensibility of the whole affair. If the evidence was right, and she did not question it, then there must be a great deal more to know, including something so monstrous and so ugly it had led to the murder of one of them and the sentence to death of the other. And yet it had remained totally hidden.

"Why would a man who is going to be hanged not tell anyone, in his own defense, the reason he killed a friend?" she said aloud.

" 'Cos it don't excuse 'im none," Gracie answered. "If it did, 'e'd a' said."

Charlotte followed her train of thought, sipping at the tea again. "Why do people kill friends, people they know but aren't related to, can't inherit money from, or aren't in love with?"

"Yer lash out 'cos yer 'ate someone or yer scared of 'em," Gracie said reasonably. "Or they got suffink yer want an' they won't give it yer. Or yer crazy jealous."

"They didn't hate each other," Charlotte answered, reaching for the bread and the knife. "They had been friends for years, and no one knows of a quarrel."

"A woman?" Gracie suggested. "Mebbe Fetters caught 'im doin' suffink wi' Mrs. Fetters?"

"I suppose that's possible," Charlotte said thoughtfully, taking butter and marmalade. "He wouldn't put that up as a defense because it isn't. People would only think worse of him for it. Except he could say it wasn't true, Fetters just imagined it, and accused him, wouldn't listen to reason and attacked him." She took a deep breath, and a bite of the bread, realizing she was hungry. "Except he'd hardly do it from on top of the library ladder, would he? I wouldn't believe that if I were a juror."

"Yer wouldn't be a juror," Gracie pointed out. "Yer a woman. An' yer've gotta 'ave yer own 'ouse an' yer own money."

Charlotte did not bother to answer. "What about money?"

Gracie shook her head. "I can't fink o' nuffink as I'd 'ave a quarrel about from the top o' a set o' steps, 'specially ones wot's got w'eels on!"

"Actually, neither can I," Charlotte agreed. "Which means that whatever it was about, Adinett took a lot of trouble to conceal it and pretend he wasn't involved. So it was something he was ashamed of." They were back to the beginning.

"We gotta find out more," Gracie said. "An' yer should 'ave a proper breakfast. D'yer want summink 'ot? I can make an egg on toast, if yer like?"

"No, this is enough, thank you," Charlotte declined. Maybe

77

from now on they should not be so extravagant as to eat eggs except for the main meal. They were not working men, only women and children.

Gracie was used to the practicalities of poverty and she accepted the answer without argument.

"I think I'll go and see Mrs. Fetters," Charlotte said at last, when she had finished a third slice. "Thomas said she was very agreeable and believed absolutely that Adinett was guilty. She must want to know why her husband died almost as much as we do. I would!"

"That's a good idea." Gracie started to clear away the dishes and put the butter and marmalade back in the pantry. "She's gotta know suffink about Adinett, and lots about 'er 'usband, poor soul. I reckon as mournin' must be awful. If I'd jus' lost someone as I loved, I'd 'ate ter sit around by meself in an 'ouse all muffled up, winders dark, mirrers covered an' clocks stopped, like I was dead meself! Wearin' black'd be bad enough. I wore black fer me granddad's burial, an' 'ad ter slap meself silly ter get a bit o' color in me face, or I'd a bin scared they'd a put me in the 'ole, not 'im."

Charlotte smiled in spite of herself. She stood up and poured a little milk into a saucer for Archie and Angus, then scraped the remainder of last night's shepherd's pie into their dish, and they descended on it, purring in anticipation and winding around her ankles.

After she had made sure that Gracie had everything she needed for the day, she went upstairs again. Actually, Gracie had seemed unusually settled about her chores, almost as if she had already sorted them in her mind and was uninterested in them. But they were the last thing on Charlotte's mind either, so it hardly mattered.

She changed her clothes, having selected very carefully from her wardrobe a well-fitting dress of a soft, deep aqua shade. It was very flattering—the reason she had chosen it—but also discreet. She had selected it so it would last several seasons, but that meant it was also not unsuitable for visiting someone in mourning. Prints or yellow would have been insensitive.

She dressed her hair with considerable flair. It had taken her a long time to learn to do this well for herself, but if one's hair looked good, then the rest of one had an excellent chance. Good posture and a smile could achieve most of the rest.

She took the omnibus and then walked. Money should be guarded, and it was a perfectly pleasant day. Of course she knew from Pitt where Martin Fetters had lived, and the newspapers had made the address famous anyway. It was on Great Coram Street, between Woburn Place and Brunswick Square, a handsome house no different from its neighbors except for the drawn curtains. If there had been straw in the street to muffle the passing carriages at the time of Fetters's death, it was not there now.

She went up the steps without hesitation and knocked on the door. She had no real idea whether Mrs. Fetters would welcome her, or be so deep in grief she would consider her call both impertinent and intrusive. But Charlotte did not care. It was a case of necessity.

The door was opened by a somber butler who surveyed her with polite disinterest.

"Yes, madam?"

She had planned what she intended to say. "Good morning." She held out her card. "Would you be kind enough to give this to Mrs. Fetters and ask her if she would spare me a few moments of her time. It concerns a matter of the utmost importance to me, and I believe it may be to her also. It is in regard to my husband, Superintendent Thomas Pitt, who investigated Mr. Fetters's death. He is unable to come himself."

The butler looked startled. "Oh dear." He fumbled for words that were suitable. It was very apparent he had never met with such a circumstance and was still suffering from the distress and the grief of the past two months. "Yes madam, I remember Mr. Pitt. He was very civil to us. If you care to wait in the morning room I shall ask Mrs. Fetters if she will see you." He did not indulge in the polite fiction of pretending he did not know if she were at home.

Charlotte was conducted to a small, bright room facing the early sun and decorated with fashionable Chinese prints, porcelain, and gold chrysanthemums on a silk screen. Within five minutes the butler returned and conducted her to another, very feminine room in rose-pink and green which opened onto the garden. Juno Fetters was a handsome woman, full figured, carrying herself with great dignity. Her skin was very fair even though her hair was an unremarkable brown. Naturally at the moment she was dressed entirely in black, and it became her more than it did most women.

"Mrs. Pitt?" she said curiously. "Please come in and make yourself comfortable. I have left the door open because I like the air." She indicated the door to the garden. "But if you find it cold, I shall be happy to close it."

"No, thank you," Charlotte declined, sitting in the chair opposite Juno. "It is delightful. The smell of the grass is as sweet as flowers. There are times when I prefer it."

Juno regarded her with concern. "Buckland said that Mr. Pitt is unable to come himself. I hope he is not unwell?"

"Not at all," Charlotte assured her. She looked at Juno's intelligent, highly individual face with its direct gaze and lines that at any other time would have suggested humor. She decided to tell her the truth, except where Pitt was, and she knew very little of that anyway. "He has been removed from Bow Street and sent somewhere on a secret mission. It is a sort of punishment for having testified against Adinett."

Juno's face filled with astonishment, and then anger.

"That is monstrous!" Unconsciously she had chosen the very word in Charlotte's mind. "To whom can we speak to have it changed?"

"No one." Charlotte shook her head. "By pursuing the case he has made powerful enemies. It is probably better if he is out of their sight for a while. I came to you because Thomas spoke very highly of you, and he was certain you believed that your husband was the victim of murder, not an accident." She tried to read Juno's expression and was startled to see a moment of unguarded grief in it. Instead of being perceptive, she felt she had intruded.

"I do believe it," Juno said quietly. "I didn't at first. I was simply numb. I couldn't grasp that it had happened. Martin is

80

not . . . was not clumsy. And I know perfectly well that he would never have put his books on Troy and Greece on the top shelf. It made no sense at all. And it was other things as well when Mr. Pitt pointed them out: the chair that wasn't where it usually was, and the pieces of fluff on his shoe." She blinked several times, struggling to keep her emotion in control.

Charlotte spoke, to give her a moment and perhaps take her mind from the acutely personal subject of the shoes. Surely mention of them must make her picture Fetters being dragged backwards across the floor. It would be all but unbearable.

"If you had known why Adinett did it, you would surely have said so at the trial, or before." She leaned forward a little. "But have you had time to reconsider since then?"

"I have little else to do," Juno said with an attempt at a smile. "But I can't think of anything."

"I need to know." Charlotte heard the raw edge of urgency in her own voice. She had intended not to betray herself so completely, but seeing Juno's grief had unlocked her own. "It is the only way I can prove to them that it was a just verdict, and Thomas wasn't being arrogant or irresponsible, and there was no prejudice in his actions. He was following the evidence in a case and he was right. I don't want anyone who matters being allowed an inch of room to doubt that."

"How are you going to do it?"

"Find out all I can about John Adinett and—if you will help me—about your husband, so that I know not only what happened but I can prove why it did."

Juno took a deep breath and steadied herself, looking at Charlotte gravely. "I want to know what happened myself. Nothing will stop me missing Martin or make me feel any better about it, but if I understood it I should be less angry." She shook her head a little. "I wouldn't be so confused, and maybe I would feel as if there was some sense to it. It is all so . . . unfinished. Is that an absurd thing to say? My sister keeps telling me I should go away for a while, try to forget about it . . . I mean, about the way it happened. But I don't want to. I need to know why!"

81

Outside in the garden the birds were singing and the breeze brought in the scent of grass.

"Did you know Mr. Adinett well? Did he call here often?"

"Quite often. At least once or twice a month, sometimes more."

"Did you like him?" She wanted to know because she needed to understand the emotions involved. Did Juno feel betrayed by a friend, or robbed by a man who was relatively a stranger? Would she be angered if Charlotte probed critically into their lives?

Juno thought for a few moments before replying, weighing her words. The question seemed to cause her some difficulty.

"I am not entirely certain. At first I did. He was very interesting. Apart from Martin, I had never heard anyone speak so vividly about travel." Her face lit with memory. "He had a passion about it, and he could describe the great wildernesses of Canada in such a way that their terror and beauty came alive, even here in the middle of London. One had to admire that. I found I wanted to listen to him, even if I didn't always want to meet his eye."

It was a curious choice of words, and Charlotte found it highly expressive. She had not been to the trial so she had only newspaper pictures to re-create a picture of Adinett in her mind, but even in photographs there was a stern quality to his face, an ability to exercise self-control, and perhaps to mask emotion, which she could well imagine might be uncomfortable.

What sort of a man had he been? She could not recall having to find the truth of a murder when both the people most closely involved were unknown to her. Always in the past it had been a question of deducing which of several people were guilty. This time she knew who, but she would never meet him or be able to sense any part of his reality except through the observations of others.

She had read that he was fifty-two, but from a newspaper photograph she had no idea whether he was tall or short, dark or medium of coloring.

"If I were to look for him in a crowd, how would you describe him?" she asked.

Juno thought for a moment. "Military," she answered, certainty in her voice. "There was a kind of power in him, as if he had tested himself against the greatest danger he knew and found he was equal to it. I don't believe he was afraid of anyone. He . . . he never showed off, if you know what I mean. That was one of the things Martin most admired about him." Again her eyes filled with tears, and she blinked them away with annoyance. "I respected it too," she added quickly. "It was a kind of strength of character that is unusual, and both frightening and attractive at the same moment."

"I think I understand," Charlotte said thoughtfully. "It makes people seem invulnerable, a little different from ourselves. Well, from me, anyway. I catch myself talking too much now and again, and I know it is the need to impress."

Juno smiled, her face suddenly warm and alive. "It is, isn't it! Because we know our own weaknesses, we think other people can see them also."

"Was he tall?" Charlotte realized suddenly that she was speaking in the past tense, as if he were already dead, and he was not. Somewhere he was alive, sitting in a cell, probably at Newgate, waiting the legal three Sundays before he could be hanged. The thought made her feel sick. What if they were all wrong, and he was innocent?

Juno was unaware of what was in Charlotte's mind, even of the change inside her.

"Yes, far taller than Martin," she replied. "But then Martin wasn't very tall, only an inch or two more than I."

There was no reason why she should be, but Charlotte was startled. She realized she had formed a picture of him quite differently. If there had been a photograph in the newspapers, she had not seen it.

Perhaps Juno noticed her surprise. "Would you like to see him?" she asked tentatively.

"Yes . . . please."

Juno stood up and opened a small, rolltop desk. She took

out a photograph in a silver frame. Her hand was shaking as she held it out.

Charlotte took the picture. Had Juno kept it in the desk to avoid draping it in black, as if to her he were still alive? She would have done the same thing. And the unbearableness of Pitt's being dead washed over her in a wave so immense for a moment she was dizzy with it.

Then she looked at the face in the frame. It was broad-boned, with a wide nose and wide, dark eyes. It was full of intelligence and humor, almost certainly a quick temper. It was vulnerable, the face of a man with profound emotions. He and Adinett might have had many interests in common, but their natures, as far as one could read, were utterly different. The only link was a bold, direct stare at the camera, the sense of dedication to a purpose. Martin Fetters might also have made people uncomfortable, but it would be by his honesty, and she imagined he was a man who inspired deep friendship.

She gave it back with a smile. He was unique. She could think of nothing to say that would help the pain of his loss.

Juno replaced the picture where she had found it. "Do you want to see the library?" It was a question with many layers of meaning. It was where he had worked, where his books were, the key to his mind. It was also where he had been killed.

"Yes, please." She rose and followed Juno into the hall and up the stairs. Juno stiffened as she approached the door, her shoulders square and rigid, but she grasped the handle and pushed it open.

It was a masculine room, full of leather, strong colors, walls lined with books on three sides. The fireplace had a brass fender padded in green leather. A tantalus stood on the table by the window, and there were three clean glasses.

Charlotte's eyes went to the large chair nearest the corner opposite and to the left, then to the smoothly turned polished ladder pushed hard up against the shelves. It was only three steps high, with a long central pole to hold on to. It would be necessary to use it in order to reach the top shelves, even for a tall man. If Martin Fetters had been little more than Juno's height, he would have had to stand on the top step to see the titles on the uppermost shelf. This made it seem all the more unlikely that he would have kept his most frequently used books there.

She turned to the big chair, which was now placed some six feet from the corner and facing the center of the room. Given the position of the window, and the gas brackets on the wall, it was the obvious situation in which to have it in order to read.

Juno followed her thoughts. "It was over here," she said, pushing her weight against it and heaving it until it was only three feet from the shelves and the wall. "He was lying with his head behind it. The steps were there." She pointed to the far side.

Charlotte went to where his head must have been, squeezing behind the chair on her hands and knees. She turned to look towards the door, and could see nothing of that entire wall. She stood up again.

Juno was regarding her gravely. There was no need for either of them to say that they believed it had happened as Pitt had said and the jury had accepted. Any other way would have been awkward and unnatural.

Charlotte looked around the room more closely, reading the titles of the books. All those on the most easily accessible shelves were on subjects she realized after several minutes held one train of characteristics in common.

Farthest away from the most worn chair were books on engineering; steel manufacture; shipping; the language, customs and topography of Turkey in particular, and of the Middle East in general. Then there were books on some of the great ancient cities: Ephesus, Pergamon, Izmir, and Byzantium under all its names from the Emperor Constantine to the present day.

There were other books on the history and culture of Turkish Islam: its beliefs, its literature, its architecture, and its art from Saladin, in the Crusades, through the great sultans to its current precarious political state.

Juno was watching her.

"Martin began traveling when he was building railways in Turkey," she said quietly. "That was where he met John Turtle Wood, who introduced him to archaeology, and he found he had a gift for it." There was pride in her voice and a softness in her eyes. "He discovered some wonderful things. He would show them to me when he brought them home. He would stand in this room holding them in his hands . . . he had beautiful hands, strong, delicate. And he'd turn them 'round slowly, touching the surfaces, telling me where they were from, how long ago, what kind of people used them."

She took a deep, shaky breath and continued.

"He would describe all he knew of their daily life. I remember one piece of pottery. It wasn't a dish, as I thought at first; it was a jar for ointment. It was fanciful, perhaps, but as I looked at him, his face so full of excitement, I could see a real Helen of Troy, a woman who fired men's imaginations with such passion two nations went to war for her, and one of them was ruined."

Charlotte was angry for Pitt, and for the injustice that men she could not even name had the power to take so much from him. Now she was also touched with the reality of the loss of a man who had been loved, who was full of life, dreams and purpose.

"Where did he meet Adinett?" she asked. Archaeology was interesting, but there was no time to waste on such luxuries.

Juno recalled herself to the task.

"That came long after. Martin learned a lot from Wood, but he moved on. He met Heinrich Schliemann, and worked with him. He learned all sorts of new methods from the Germans, you know." There was enthusiasm in her face. "They were the best at archaeology. They used to map a whole site and draw it all, not just bits and pieces. So afterwards anyone else could form a picture of a way of life, not just one household, or perhaps one aspect, such as from a temple or a palace." Her voice dropped. "Martin loved it."

"When was this?" Charlotte asked, sitting down in one of the chairs.

Juno sat opposite her. "Oh . . . I don't think I know when Martin met Mr. Wood, but I know they started work on the site in Ephesus in '63. I think it was '69 when the British Museum bought the site and they started work on the Temple of Diana, and it must have been the following year that Martin met Mr. Schliemann." Her eyes were distant with memory. "That's when he fell in love with Troy and the whole idea of finding it. He could recite pages of Homer, you know. . . ." She smiled. "In the English translation, not the original. At first I thought I would be bored by it . . . but I wasn't. He cared so much I couldn't help caring too."

"And Adinett was a scholar in the same things?" Charlotte asked.

Juno looked startled. "Oh, no! Not at all. I don't think he ever went to the Middle East, and he had no interest in archaeology that I heard of, and Martin would certainly have mentioned it."

Charlotte was confused. "I thought they were good friends who spent much time together . . ."

"They were," Juno assured her. "But it was ideals which they held in common, and admiration for other peoples and cultures. Adinett had been interested in Japan ever since his elder brother was posted there as part of the British Legation at Yedo—that's the capital city. I believe it was attacked by some of the new reactionary authorities who were trying to expel all foreigners."

"He traveled to the Far East?" Charlotte could not see any value in the information, but since she had not even the first thread of an idea as to the motive for murder, she would gather everything there was.

Juno shook her head. "I don't think so. He was just fascinated by their culture. He lived in Canada for quite a long time, and he had a Japanese friend in the Hudson Bay Trading Company. They were very close. I don't know his name. He always referred to him as Shogun. It was what he called him."

"He talked about him?"

"Oh, yes." Juno's expression was bleak. "He was very interesting indeed. I listened to every word myself. I can see

87

him across the dinner table as he told us of traveling over those great wastes of snow, how the light was, the cold, the vast polar sky, the creatures, and above all the beauty.

"There was something in it he loved, and it was there in his voice.

"Apparently there was a brief uprising in Manitoba in 1869 and 1870 led by a French-Canadian called Louis Riel. They resented the British taking over everything, and executed someone or other." She frowned. "The British sent in a military expedition led by Colonel Wolseley. Adinett and Shogun volunteered to act as guides for them into the interior, and met up with them at Thunder Bay, four hundred miles north-west of Toronto. They led them another six hundred and fifty miles. It was that he used to talk about."

Charlotte could see nothing useful in it at all. It sounded like a far more interesting conversation than was held over most dinner tables. What had happened that led to a quarrel so violent it ended in murder?

"Was the rebellion put down?" She supposed it must have been, but she had not heard of it.

"Oh yes, apparently very successfully." Juno saw Charlotte's confused look. "Adinett formed a very strong sympathy with the French Canadians," she explained. "He spoke of them often, and with great warmth. He admired French republicanism and their passion for liberty and equality. He went to France quite often, even up to a few months ago. That was what he and Martin really had in common, the passion for social reform." She smiled in recollection. "They talked about it for hours, and ways in which it could be accomplished. Martin learned about it from ancient Greece, the original democracy, and Adinett from French revolutionary idealism, but their aims were very close." Again her eyes filled with tears. "I just don't understand what could possibly have led them to quarrel!" She blinked several times and her voice wavered. "Could we be wrong?"

Charlotte was not ready to consider that.

"I don't know. Please, think back if Mr. Fetters expressed any difference of opinion or anger over anything." It seemed a slender thread. Did anyone but a lunatic quarrel to the point of blows over the virtues of one foreign country's form of democracy rather than another'?

"Not anger," Juno said with certainty, staring at Charlotte. "But he was preoccupied with something. I would have said concern, not really anything more than that. But he was always a trifle absentminded when he was absorbed in his work. He was brilliant at it, you know?" There was urgency in her voice. "He used to find antiquarian pieces no one else could. He could see the value in things. Lately he did more writing about it, for various journals, and went to meetings and so on. He was a very gifted speaker. People loved to listen to him."

Charlotte could visualize it easily. His face in the photograph was full of intelligence and enthusiasm.

"I'm so sorry . . ." The words were out before she thought of their effect.

Juno gulped, and it was a few moments before she regained complete control of herself again.

"I . . . apologize," she said with a little shake of her head. "He was worried about something, but he wouldn't discuss it with me, and I couldn't press him, he just became annoyed. I have no idea what it was. I imagined it was something to do with one of the antiquarian societies he belonged to. They do fight among themselves rather a lot. There is tremendous rivalry, you know."

Charlotte was confused. It all seemed so very ordinary and good-natured.

"But Adinett wasn't interested in antiquities?" she reaffirmed.

"Not at all. He listened to Martin, but only because he was a friend, and I could see that sometimes he was bored by it." Juno looked at her with shadowed eyes. "It doesn't help, does it." It was not a question.

"I can't see that it does," Charlotte admitted. "And yet there must be some reason. We just don't know yet where to look first." She rose to her feet. She would learn nothing more at the moment, and she had trespassed long enough on Juno Fetter's time.

Juno stood up also, slowly, as if there were a debilitating tiredness in her.

Charlotte caught a glimpse of the engulfing loneliness of mourning, but she had no idea how to help. She had met Juno less than two hours ago. She could hardly offer to keep her company. And perhaps Juno preferred to grieve alone. The necessity of being courteous to strangers might be the last thing on earth she wanted . . . or it might be the first. At least it would force her to keep control of herself, and occupy her mind for a while, not allowing it to be consumed with memory. The conventions that kept a new widow out of society were probably meant to be kind, and to observe the decencies, and yet they could hardly have been better designed to intensify her grief. Perhaps they were for everyone else, to save them the embarrassment of having to think of something to say, and so one was not reminded too forcefully of death and that eventually it would come to all.

"May I call again?" Charlotte said aloud. She knew she was risking rebuff, but at least that gave the decision to Juno.

Juno's face filled with hope. "Please do . . . I . . ." She breathed in deeply. "I want to know what really happened, apart from the physical facts. And . . . and I want to do something more than just sit here!"

Charlotte smiled back at her. "Thank you. As soon as I can think of anything remotely hopeful to follow, I shall call upon you." And she turned towards the door, knowing that so far she had accomplished almost nothing to help Pitt.

Gracie had plans of her own. As soon as Charlotte left the house she abandoned the rest of her own chores, put on her best shawl and hat—she had only two—and taking enough for a fare in the omnibus, she went out also.

It took her a little over twenty minutes to reach the Bow Street police station, where until yesterday Pitt had been superintendent. She marched up the steps and inside as if she were going to war, and she felt much as if she were. During her childhood, police stations—and their inhabitants, whoever they were—had been places to be avoided at any cost.

Now she was going in deliberately. But it was in a cause for which she would have gone into the mouth of hell, had it been the only way. She was sufficiently angry she would have taken on anyone at all.

She went straight up to the desk sergeant, who looked at her with very little interest.

"Yes, miss? Can I 'elp yer?" He did not bother to stop chewing his pencil.

"Yes, please," she said smartly. "I wish to speak to Sergeant Tellman. It is very urgent, and concerns a case he is working on. I have information for him." That was a complete invention, of course, but she needed to see him, and any story that accomplished that would do. She would explain when she saw him.

The sergeant was unimpressed. "Oh yes, miss. And what would that be?"

"That would be 'very important,' " she replied. "And it'll not make Sergeant Tellman best pleased if you don't tell 'im I'm 'ere. My name is Gracie Phipps. Yer go tell 'im that, and leave 'im ter do the choosin' as ter whether 'e comes out or not."

The sergeant looked for a long moment at her face, her unflinching eyes, and decided that in spite of her diminutive size she was determined enough to be a considerable nuisance. Added to which, he knew very little of Tellman's personal life or family. Tellman was a remarkably taciturn man, and the sergeant was not certain who this girl might be. Discretion was the better part of valor. Tellman could be unpleasant if crossed.

"You wait there, miss. I'll tell 'im, an' see what 'e says."

It took Tellman rather less than five minutes to appear. As always he looked lean, dour and so neatly dressed as to be uncomfortable with his tight collar and slicked-back hair. His hollow cheeks were slightly flushed. He ignored the desk sergeant and walked right across to where Gracie was standing.

"What is it?" he said half under his breath. "What are you doing here?"

91

"I come ter find out wot you're doin', more like," she retorted.

"What I'm doing? I'm investigating burglaries."

Her eyebrows shot up. "You're looking after a bit o' thievin', w'en Mr. Pitt's bin throwed out o' 'is job an' sent ter Gawd knows w'ere, an' Mrs. Pitt's near beside 'erself, an' the children got no father at 'ome . . . an' you're chasin' some bleedin' flimp!"

"It's no pocket-picking!" he said angrily, but still keeping his voice low. "It's a proper cracksman we're after."

"An' that's yer reason, is it?" Her disgust was withering. "Some ruddy safe is more important that wot they done to Mr. Pitt?"

"No, it isn't!" His face was white with anger, both at her, for her misjudgment of him, and with the whole injustice of what had happened. "But there's nothing I can do about it," he said indignantly. "They aren't going to listen to me, are they! They've already got someone else here, while his chair is still warm. Fellow called Wetron, and he told me to let it go, don't even think about it. It's done, and that's that."

"An' o' course yer bein' the soul of obedience, like, yer jus' do like 'e says!" she challenged, her eyes blazing. "Then I reckon as I'll 'ave ter try ter fix it on me own, won't I?" She bit her lip to keep it from trembling. "Can't say as I'm not proper disappointed, though. I counted on yer ter 'elp, knowin' that in spite o' yer grizzlin' an' gurnin' 'alf the time, yer still got a kind o' loyalty, somewhere inside yer . . . ter bein' fair, at least. An' this in't fair!"

"Of course it isn't fair!" His body was rigid and his voice was almost strangled in his throat. "It's wicked, but it comes from the power to do these things. You don't know what they're like, or who they are, or you wouldn't talk about it like it was just a matter of me saying 'Let's do right by Mr. Pitt,' and they'd say, 'Oh, yes, of course we will!' and it'd all change. Mr. Wetron's told me to let the whole thing drop, and I know he's got his eye on me to see if I do. For all I know, he's probably one of them!"

Gracie stared at him. There was real fear in his eyes, and

for a moment she was frightened too. She knew that he was more than fond of her, much as he wanted to deny it to himself, and that allowing her to see how he felt would cost him dearly. She decided to be a little gentler.

"Well, we gotta do summink! We can't just let it 'appen. 'E in't even at 'ome anymore." Her voice trembled. "They sent 'im ter Spitalfields, not jus' ter work but ter live."

Tellman's face tightened as if he had been slapped.

"I didn't know that."

"Well, yer do now. Wot are we gonna do about it?" She stared at him beseechingly. It was very difficult to ask a favor of him, with all the differences that lay between them, and the fighting against any admission of friendship. And yet she had not even considered not coming to him. He was the natural ally. Only now did she wonder at the ease with which she had approached him. She certainly did not doubt it was right.

If he noticed the "we," and wondered at her inclusion of herself in the plan, there was no sign of it in his face. He looked profoundly unhappy. He glanced over his shoulder at the curious gaze of the desk sergeant.

"Come outside!" he said sharply, taking Gracie by the arm and almost dragging her through the door and down the steps into the street, where they could speak without being overheard by anyone but uninterested strangers.

"I don't know what we can do," he said again. "It's the Inner Circle! In case you don't know who they are, they are a secret society of powerful men who favor each other in everything, even to protecting each other from the law, if they can. They'd have saved Adinett, only Mr. Pitt got in the way, and they won't forgive him for that. It's not the first time he's crossed them up."

"Well, 'oo are they?" She was reluctant to let him see how much that thought frightened her. Anyone who could outwit Pitt had to be kin to the devil himself.

"That's the point. Don't you listen, girl? No one knows who they are!" he said desperately. "You look at someone in power, and they might be, and they mightn't. No one else knows."

She found herself shivering. "Yer mean it could be the judge 'isself?"

"Of course it could! Only it wasn't this time, or he'd have found some way of getting Adinett off."

She squared her shoulders. "Well, all the same, we gotta do summink. We can't just let 'im be stuck in a filthy 'ole somewhere an' never able ter come back 'ome again. Yer sayin' as Adinett didn't do in that feller, what's-'is-name?"

"Fetters. No. I'm not. He did it. We just don't know why."

"Then we'd better find out, an' sharpish, 'adn't we?" she responded. "Yer a detective. Where do we start?"

A mixture of expressions crossed his face: reluctance, gentleness, anger, pride, fear.

With a stab of shame she realized how much she was asking of him. She had little to lose compared with what failure would cost him. If the new superintendent had deliberately commanded him to not enquire into the matter anymore, and to forget Pitt, and then Tellman disobeyed, he would lose his job. And she knew how long and hard he had worked to earn his place. He had asked no one any favors, and received none. He had no family still alive, and few friends. He was a proud, lonely man who expected little out of life and guarded his own anger at injustice carefully, cherishing his sense of fairness.

He had bitterly resented it when Pitt had been promoted to command. Pitt was not a gentleman. He was ordinary, a gamekeeper's son, no better than Tellman himself and hundreds of others in the police force like them. But as they had worked together an unadmitted loyalty had grown, and to betray that would be outside Tellman's sense of decency. He would not be able to live with himself, and Gracie knew that.

"Where do we begin?" she said again. "If 'e done it, then 'e done it for a reason. Less'n yer daft, yer don't up and kill someone without a reason so good it's like a mountain yer can't get 'round no other way."

"I know." He stood in the middle of the footpath, deep in thought as carriages and wagons streamed past down Bow Street, and people were obliged to step into the gutter to get around them. "We did everything at the time to find out why. Nobody knew of anything that even looked like a quarrel." He shook his head. "There was no money, no women, no rivalry in business or sports or anything else. They even agreed about politics."

"Well, we in't looked 'ard enough!" She stood squarely in front of him. "What would Mr. Pitt do if 'e were 'ere?"

"What he did anyway," he replied. "He looked at everything they had in common to see what they could possibly have quarreled over. We spoke to all their friends, acquaintances, everybody. Searched the house, read all his papers. There was nothing."

She stood in the bright sun, chewing her lip, staring up at him. She looked like a tired and angry child on the brink of tears. She was still far too thin, and had to take up most of her clothes at the hem or she would have fallen over them.

"Yer don' kill anyone fer nuffink," she repeated stubbornly. "An' 'e did it sudden, so it were summink 'as 'appened just 'afore 'e were killed. Yer gotta find out wot 'appened every day fer a week up until then. There's summink there!" She would not bring herself to say please.

He hesitated, not out of unwillingness, but simply because he could think of nothing useful to be done.

She was staring at him. He had to give her an answer, and he could not bear it to be a denial. She did not understand. She had no idea of the difficulties, of everything he and Pitt had done at the time. She saw only loyalty, a matter of fighting for those she loved, who belonged to her life.

He did not really want to belong to anyone else's life. And he was not ready to admit that he cared about Pitt. Injustice mattered, of course, but the world was full of injustice. Some you could fight against, some you couldn't. It was foolish to waste your time and your strength in battles you could not win.

Gracie was still waiting, refusing to believe he would not agree.

He opened his mouth to tell her how pointless it was, that she did not understand, and found himself saying what he knew she wanted to hear.

"I'll find out about Adinett's last few days before he killed Fetters." It was ridiculous! What kind of a policeman allows a slip of a maid to coerce him into making a fool of himself? "I don't know when," he went on defensively. "In my own time. It won't help anyone if Wetron throws me out of the force."

" 'Course it won't," she said, nodding her head reasonably. Then she gave him a sudden, dazzling smile which sent his heart rocketing. He felt the blood surge up his face and hated himself for being so vulnerable.

"I'll come and tell you if I find anything," he snapped. "Now, go away and leave me to work!" And without looking at her again he swung around and marched back up the steps and in through the doorway.

Gracie sniffed fiercely, and with a lift of hope inside her went to find an omnibus back to Keppel Street.

Tellman began that evening, going straight from Bow Street, buying a hot pie from a peddler as he did most evenings, and eating it as he walked up Endell Street. Whatever he did, he must manage to do it without leaving any trace, not only for his own safety but for the very practical reason that if he were caught he would be unable to continue.

Who would know what Adinett had done, whom he had seen, where he had gone in the time immediately before Fetters's death? Adinett himself had sworn that he had done nothing out of the ordinary.

He bit into the pie, being careful not to squash out its contents.

Adinett was of independent means and had no need to earn his living. He could spend his time as he wished. Apparently that was usually visiting various clubs, many of them to do with the armed services, exploration, the National Geographic Society, and others of a similar nature. That was the pattern of those who had inherited money and could afford to be idle. Tellman despised it with all the anger of a man who had watched too many others work all the hours they were awake and still go to bed cold and hungry.

He passed a newspaper boy.

"Paper, sir?" the boy invited. "Read about Mr. Gladstone? Insulted the laborers o' the country, so Lord Salisbury says. Some get an eight-hour day—mebbe!" He grinned. "Or they brought out a new edition o' *Darkness an' Dawn*, all about corruption an' that, in ancient Rome?" he added hopefully.

Tellman handed over his money and took the late edition, not for the election news but for the latest on the anarchists.

He quickened his pace and turned his mind back to the problem. It would give him more than one kind of satisfaction to find out why Adinett had committed murder, and prove it so all London would be obliged to know, whether they wished to or not.

He was well-used to tracing the comings and goings of people, but always with the authority of his police rank. To do it discreetly would be very different. He would have to call on a few favors done in the past, and perhaps a few yet to come.

He decided to begin at the most obvious place, with hansom cab drivers he knew. They usually frequented the same areas, and the chances were that if Adinett had used a cab—and since he did not own a coach, that was quite likely—then he would more than once have come upon the same driver.

If he had used an omnibus, or even the underground railway, then there was almost no chance at all of learning his movements.

The first two cabdrivers he found were of no assistance at all. The third could only point him in the direction of others.

It was half past nine. He was tired, his feet hurt and he was angry with himself for giving in to a foolish impulse, when he spoke to the seventh cabdriver, a small, grizzled man with a hacking cough. He reminded Tellman of his own father, who had worked as a porter at the Billingsgate fish market all day and then driven a hansom half the night, whatever the weather, to feed his family and keep a roof over their heads. Perhaps it was memory which made him speak softly to the man.

"Got a little time?" he asked.

"Yer wanna go somewhere?" the cabbie responded.

"Nowhere special," Tellman answered. "I need some information to help a friend in trouble. And I'm hungry." He was not, but it was a tactful excuse. "Can you spare ten minutes to come and have a hot pie and a glass of ale?"

"Bad day. Can't afford no pies," the cabbie answered.

"I want help, not money," Tellman told him. He had little hope of learning anything useful, but he could still see his father's weary face in his mind's eye, and this was like a debt to the past. He did not want to know anything about the man; he simply wanted to feed him.

The cabbie shrugged. "If you like." But he moved quickly to leave his horse at the stand and walk beside Tellman to the nearest peddler, and accepted a pie without argument. "Wot yer wanna know, then?"

"You pick up along Marchmont Street way quite often?"

"Yeah. Why?"

Tellman had brought a picture of Adinett which he had not thrown away after the investigation. He took it from his pocket and showed it to the driver.

"Do you recall ever picking up this man?"

The cabbie squinted at it. "That's the feller wot killed the one wot digs up ancient pots an' the like, isn't it?"

"Yes."

"You police?"

"Yes—but I'm not on duty. This is to help a friend. I can't make you tell me anything, and no one else is going to ask you. It's not an investigation, and I'll probably get thrown out if I'm caught following it up."

The cabbie looked at him with awakening interest. "So why yer doin' it, then?"

"I told you, a friend of mine is in trouble," Tellman repeated.

The cabbie looked at him sideways, his eyebrows raised. "So if I 'elp yer, yer'll 'elp me . . . when yer are on duty, like?"

"I could do," Tellman conceded. "Depends if you can help me or not."

"I did pick 'im up, three or four times. Smart-lookin' gent,

98

like an old soldier or summit. Always walked stiff, 'ead in the air. But civil enough. Gave a good tip."

"Where did you take him?"

"Lots o' places. Up west mostly, gennelman's clubs an' the like."

"What sort of clubs? Can you remember any of the addresses?" Tellman did not know why he bothered to pursue it. Even if he knew the names of all the clubs, what use would it be? He had no authority to go into them and ask whom Adinett had spoken to. And if he found out, it would still mean nothing. But at least he could tell Gracie he had tried.

"Not exact. One was a place I never bin ter before, summink ter do wi' France. Paris, ter be exact. It were a year, as I 'member."

Tellman did not understand. "A year? What do you mean?"

"Seventeen summat." The cabbie scratched his head, tipping his hat crooked. "1789 . . . that's it."

"Anywhere else?"

"I could eat another pie."

Tellman obliged, more for the man's sake than as a bribe. The information was useless.

"An' ter a newspaper," the cabbie continued after he had eaten half the second pie. "The one wot's always goin' on about reform an' the like. 'E came out wi' Mr. Dismore wot owns it. I know 'cos I seen 'im in the papers meself."

This was unsurprising. Tellman already knew that Adinett was acquainted with Thorold Dismore.

The cabbie was frowning, screwing up his face. "That's w'y I thought it real odd, a gennelman like that, askin' ter go all the way past Spitalfields ter Cleveland Street, wot's off the Mile End Road. Excited, 'e were, like 'e'd found summink wonderful. In't nuffink wonderful in Spitalfields nor Whitechapel nor Mile End, an' I can tell yer that fer nuffink."

Tellman was startled. "You took him to Cleveland Street?"

"Yeah . . . like I said. Twice!"

"When?"

"Just afore 'e went ter see that Mr. Dismore wot owns the

99

paper. All excited, 'e was. Then a day or two arter that 'e went an killed that poor feller. Strange, in't it?"

"Thank you," Tellman said with sudden feeling. "Thank you very much. Let me get you a glass of ale along the way here."

"Don't mind if I do. Ta."

5

P_{ITT} FOUND IT painfully difficult to endure living in Heneagle Street. It was not that either Isaac or Leah Karansky did not make him as comfortable as their means allowed, or were not friendly towards him on the occasions they were together, such as at the meals they provided. Leah was an excellent cook, but the food was different from the simple and abundant fare he was used to. He could eat only at set times. There were no cups of tea whenever he wished, no homemade bread with butter and jam, no cake. It was all unfamiliar, and he slept with exhaustion at the end of the day, but he did not relax.

He missed Charlotte, the children, even Gracie, more than he would have thought possible. It was some comfort to know that money was provided for Charlotte to collect every week from Bow Street. But watching Isaac and Leah together, the glances between them that spoke of years of shared understanding, the occasional laughter, the way she nagged at him about his health, the gentleness in his hands when he touched her, reminded Pitt the more forcefully of his own loneliness.

Towards the end of the first week he realized the other emotion that was consuming him, knotting his stomach and making his head ache.

He had accepted Isaac's offer to help him find work with Saul, the silk weaver. Of course, it was completely unskilled labor, a matter of bending his back to lift crates and bales, to sweep the floor, fetch or carry everything as needed, run

101

errands. It was the most manual task in the establishment, and the pay corresponded, but it was better than nothing at all, and probably physically easier than labor in the sugar factory. It also offered him far more opportunity to be in the streets, to listen and observe without calling any attention to himself. Although he could see little purpose in it; the capture of anarchists Nicoll and Mowbray was evidence that the Special Branch's detectives were well schooled in their craft and needed no help from a stranger in the area like Pitt.

As he was walking back to Heneagle Street—he could not think of it as home—he heard shouting ahead of him. The anger in it was unmistakable. Voices were high and rough, and a moment later there was a crash as if a bottle had been hurled to the pavement and splintered to pieces. There was a yell of pain, and then a torrent of abuse. A woman screamed.

Pitt broke into a run.

There was more shouting and the sound of a load of barrels cascading onto the ground, several bursting open as they landed on each other. A cry of rage rose above the general hubbub.

Pitt turned the corner and saw about twenty people in the street ahead of him, half of them partly obscured by a wagon whose tailboard was open. Barrels rolled into the street, blocking the traffic in both directions. Men were already beginning to fight, hard and viciously.

Other people came out of shops and workplaces, at least half of them joining in. Women stood on the sidelines shouting encouragement. One stooped and picked up a loose stone and hurled it, her arm swinging wide, her torn brown skirts swirling.

"Go home, yer papist pig!" she screamed. "Go back ter Ireland w'ere yer belong!"

"I in't no more Irish than you are, yer soddin' 'eathen!" the other woman shouted back at her, and whirled a broom handle around so hard that when it caught the first woman across her back it broke in half and sent her flying into the gutter, where she lay winded for a few moments before sitting up slowly and beginning to curse viciously and repetitively.

"Papist!" someone else shrieked. "Whore!"

Half a dozen more people, men and women, joined in the melee, everyone hurling abuse with all the power of their lungs. Several scruffy children were hopping up and down, squealing encouragement, backing whomever they fancied in the scrum.

A police whistle blew, thin and shrill. There was a moment's lull through which came the pounding of feet.

Pitt swung around. It was not his job to stop this, even if he could have. He saw a constable running towards them, and he stepped back near the arch of the gate into a stonemason's yard. Narraway would expect him to observe. Although what he could tell him that would be of the slightest use, he had no idea. It was only one of countless numbers of ugly street scenes that must occur regularly and surprise no one.

More police came and started trying to pull the fighting men apart, and were rewarded for their trouble by becoming the victims themselves. Hatred for the police seemed about the only thing that the crowd had in common.

"Useless bloody rozzers!" one man yelled, flailing his fists in the air, willing to hit anyone and everyone within reach. "Couldn't catch a cold, yer stupid bastards! Pigs!"

A policeman lashed out at him with a truncheon, and missed.

Pitt remained in the shadows. He looked around at the shabby, crumbling buildings grimed with the smoke of thousands of chimneys, the patched windows, the broken cobbles of the streets, the overrunning gutters. The smells of rot and effluent were everywhere. The fighting in the street was vicious. It was not a quick flare of temper but the slow, sullen rage of years of anger and hate shown naked for a few moments, before the police frightened or beat it into silence again . . . until next time.

Pitt turned and walked away before he was noticed—and remembered. He kept his head down, hat jammed forward, hands in his pockets. He went around the first corner he came to, even though it was away from Heneagle Street. He had been aware of a simmering resentment since he came here, an edge to people's voices, a quickness to take offense. Now he had seen how close the rage simmered under the surface. It only needed an insult perceived, one ugly remark, and it broke through.

This time the police had come quickly and some form of order was restored, but nothing was solved. Pitt had been startled by how anti-Catholic feeling had erupted within seconds. It must have been only just controlled all the time. Now, as he walked past a row of small shops, narrow-fronted windows piled with boxes and goods, he remembered other remarks he had heard, slang words for *papist* said not in fun but with vindictiveness driving them.

And the feeling had been given back with good measure added.

He remembered also snatches of conversation about business that would not be done on religious grounds, hospitality denied, even the reasonable help to one in trouble withheld, not out of greed but because the one in need was of the other faith.

The anti-Semitic taunts were less surprising to him simply because he had heard them before: the dehumanizing, the resentment, the blame.

He went into the first public house he came to, and sat down at a table near the bar nursing a tankard of cider.

Ten minutes later a thin-shouldered young man came in with a finger tied up in a bloodstained rag.

"Eh, Charlie!" the barman said curiously. "Wotcher done ter yerself, then?"

"Bitten by a bloody rat, that's wot," Charlie replied angrily. "Gimme a pint. If I were paid 'alf o' wot I work fer, I'd 'ave a shot o' whiskey! But wot poor sod in Spitalfields ever got paid wot 'e was worth?"

"Yer got a job, yer better'n some," a pale-faced man said bitterly, looking up from his half pint of ale. "Don' know w'en yer well orff, that's your trouble."

Charlie turned on him angrily, his cheeks flushing. "My trouble is that greedy men work me night an' day and take wot I make and sell it and grow fat themselves, an' keep all us

104

poor sods on a pittance." He drew in his breath with a rasping sound. "An' bloody gutless cowards like you don't stand up beside me to fight fer justice . . . that's my trouble! That's everyone's trouble 'round 'ere! Just roll over an' play dead every time anyone looks sideways at yer!"

"Yer'll get us all out in the gutter, yer stupid sod!" the other man snapped, clinging onto his mug as if it were some kind of protection to him. His eyes were hot with anger struggling to overmaster the fear that haunted him day and night: fear of hunger, fear of cold, fear of being hurt, fear of being despised and excluded.

A fair-haired man looked from one to the other of them, apparently not noticing Pitt at all. "What d'yer want ter do then, Charlie? If we all stand beside yer, wot then, eh?" he demanded defensively.

Charlie glared at him, considering his answer carefully, his face still creased in anger.

"Then, Wally, we'd see a few changes 'round 'ere," he retorted. "We'd see a day w'en a man gets paid wot 'e's worth, not what some fat swine chooses ter give 'im, because 'e's no use if 'e starves!"

Wally coughed into his beer. "Dream on!" he said witheringly. His tone conveyed his boredom with such empty words he had heard too many times.

Charlie slammed his empty mug on the bar so hard the pewter made a scar on the wood. "Yeah?" he said belligerently. "Well if we 'ad more men wi' the guts ter be men, instead of a lot o' sniveling papists an' Jews creepin' around the place, we'd get up an' fight fer wot's ours! Like the bloody Frogs did in Paris! Cut a few throats an' we'll soon see 'ow quick some o' them fancy bastards can change their minds about 'oo 'as wot!"

A dark-haired man shivered a little, biting his lips. "Yer shouldn't say fings like that!" he warned. "Yer dunno 'oo's listenin'. You'll only make it worse."

"Worse!" Charlie exploded. "Worse? Wot's worse 'n this, eh? Yer expectin' bleedin' crushers ter come in 'ere an' cart us all orff ter the Tower o' London, are yer? All of us, like?" His voice rose, frustration raw and throbbing in his words. "There's 'undreds an' thousan's of us trodden down by a few idle, greedy bastards poncin' around up west, eatin' 'emselves sick an' so fat they can't scarcely 'old their trousers up. An' the rozzers are in their bleedin' pockets, an' all," he added, swinging around, daring anyone to challenge him. "That's w'y they never caught the Whitechapel murderer wot killed them poor cows in '88. You mark my words, 'e's one o' them . . . an' that's the Gawd's truth!"

There was a sudden chill in the room. At the table next to Pitt three men stopped talking. Even now, nearly four years afterwards, it was not done to speak of the Whitechapel murderer. No one made jokes about him, and there were no songs, no music hall references.

"Yer shouldn't say that!" A gray-haired man was the first to speak, his voice hoarse, his face pasty-white.

"I'll say wot I want!" Charlie retaliated, the blood high in his cheeks.

Someone else started to laugh, and then stopped just as suddenly.

A stoop-shouldered man stood up and held his glass tankard high. " 'Ere's ter nothin'!" he said with a grin. " 'Ere's ter terday, 'cos termorrer yer could be dead." He drank down the entire glass without taking it from his lips to draw breath.

"Shut yer mouth, yer fool!" the man nearest to him hissed, hard anger in his face, his fist clenched on the tabletop.

The man subsided sullenly, his grin vanished. "I never said nothin'!" he snarled. "Our day's gonna come! An' soon."

"Then we'll see 'ow much sugar they can eat!" his companion said between his teeth.

"Yer say 'sugar' again an' I'll put yer bleedin' lights out meself!" the first man threatened, his eyes hot and black, and hideously sober. "I'll practice on yer, ready fer all them foreigners wot's poisonin' this city an' takin' wot should be ours."

This time there was no reply.

Pitt hated everything about this public house—the smell of

it, the sudden anger in the air, the defeat, the gleam of gaslight on the battered pewter mugs, the stale sawdust—but he knew it was his job to overhear. He hunched lower down into himself and sipped at the cider.

Half an hour later a couple of street women came in, soliciting business. They looked tired, dirty, overeager, and for a few moments Pitt was as angry as Charlie had been, for the poverty and despair that made women walk alone around streets and public houses trying to sell their bodies to strangers. It was a squalid and often dangerous way to earn a little money. It was also quick, usually certain, and easier to come by than sweatshop or factory labor, and in the short term, far better paid.

There was a burst of laughter, coarse, overloud.

A man at the table next to Pitt was drowning his sorrows, afraid to go home and tell his wife he had lost his job. He was probably drinking the little money he had left, next week's rent, tomorrow's food. There was a gray hopelessness in his face.

A youth named Joe was telling his friend Percy how he planned to save enough money to buy his own barrow and start selling brushes farther west, where it was safer and he could make a better profit. One day he would move and find rooms somewhere else, maybe in Kentish Town, or even Pinner.

Pitt stood up to leave. He had learned all he was going to, and none of it was anything Narraway would not already know. The East End was a place of anger and misery where one incident would be enough to set it alight with rebellion. It would be put down by force, and hundreds would die. The rage would be submerged again, until next time. There would be a few articles about it in the newspapers. Politicians would make statements of regret, and then return to the serious business of making sure that everything stayed as much as possible the same.

He trudged back towards Heneagle Street with his shoulders hunched and his head down.

The remarks about sugar had seemed irrelevant to the rest of the conversation, at least on the surface, and yet they had

107

been said with such bitterness of feeling that they stayed in his mind over the next few days. He had realized from snatches of conversation overheard in the various places he called at in the course of his duties just how many people were dependent in one way or another on the three sugar factories in Spitalfields. The money that was earned from them was spent in the shops, in the taverns and on the streets.

Had the remarks made been anything more than a bitterness at such dependence, and the fear that the only source of income might fail them? Or was there something more specific? Was the reference to a day coming when there would be justice only anger and bravado, or based in fact?

Narraway's words came back to him that there was a mounting danger, not just the usual underlying resentment. Circumstances had changed; the mix of people had been added to and was more volatile than in the past.

But what was there to tell him? That he was right? If so, the solution lay in reform, not policing. Society had cultivated its own destruction; the anarchists were merely going to light the fuse.

Perhaps he should at least look more closely at the sugar factory in Brick Lane, gain some slight knowledge of the place and see the men who worked in it, get a feeling of their temper.

The best way seemed to be to pretend he was interested in a job there. He had no skill in the processes of making sugar, but there might be something simpler he could do.

The following morning he went early down Brick Lane towards the seven-story-high building with its squat windows overlooking the entire town. The smell of cane syrup, like rotting potatoes, filled the air.

It was easy enough to enter at the yard gates. Huge hogshead barrels were piled up and carts were being unloaded, having just come up from the docks. Men hauled and lifted; cranes were maneuvered into position.

" 'Oo are yer, then?" a bull-chested man asked abruptly. He was dressed in worn dun-colored trousers and a leather jerkin shiny with constant rubbing. He stood squarely in front of Pitt, blocking his way.

"Thomas Pitt. I'm looking for any extra work that might be going." That was almost true.

"Oh yeah? An' wot are yer good fer, then?" He looked Pitt up and down disparagingly. "Not local, are yer." That was an accusation, not a question. "We got all we need 'ere," he finished.

Pitt stared around him at the high, flat sides of the building, the cobbled yard, the wide doors open to the ground floor, and men coming and going.

"Do you work all night?" he asked curiously.

"Boilers do. Gotter keep 'em alight. Why? Yer wanner work nights?"

Pitt most assuredly did not want to work at night, but his curiosity impelled him to pursue the matter.

"Why? Is there night work available?"

The man squinted at Pitt. "Mebbe. Yer wanner stand in if one o' the night watchmen goes sick?"

"Yes," Pitt said immediately.

"Where'd yer live, then?"

"Heneagle Street, on the corner of Brick Lane."

"Yeah? Well, mebbe we'll send fer yer . . . an' mebbe we won't. Leave yer partic'lars at the office." He pointed towards a small door in the side of the building.

"Right," Pitt accepted. "Thank you."

For several days there was no word from the sugar factory, but work at Saul's silk-weaving shop was more interesting than Pitt had expected. He found himself admiring the bright, delicate fibers, and without having intended to, watching how they were woven into brocades, the subtle blending of colors into patterns.

Saul observed him with amusement, his dark, narrow face relaxed for a change.

"You're not from around here, are you?" he said in the middle of one Monday afternoon early in June. "Why are you doing this? It's not your trade!"

"It's a living," Pitt replied, turning his face away. He liked

109

Saul, who had been more than fair to him, but he remembered Narraway's warning to trust no one. "Isaac said it was hard to get into the sugar factories unless you knew someone."

"So it is," Saul agreed. "Everyone wants work. And selling on the street is hard. You can make enemies easily. Everyone's got their own patch. Get your throat cut for pinching someone else's."

Pitt wondered what pressures Narraway had used to persuade Saul to take him on. He noticed most of the other Jews he visited employed their own people, as did all the other identifiable groups.

"I'm sure." Pitt smiled. "And who in Spitalfields cares about sweeping crossings?"

Saul grunted. "There's worse places."

Pitt gave him a glance of incredulity.

"Believe me!" Saul said with sudden fierceness, his dark eyes brilliant. "Spitalfields may be dirty and poor, and smell like a hole in hell . . . but it's safer than the places I've been . . . at least for the moment. Here you can say what you think, read what you like, walk out in the street without being arrested." He leaned forward, his shoulders hunched, his face tense. "Robbed . . . perhaps? Set on by hooligans and religious bigots . . . some days." He gave a little grunt. "But that's probably so most places. Here at least it's random, not organized by the state." He smiled lopsidedly. "Some of the police are corrupt, and most of them are incompetent—but they're not vicious, bar the odd one or two."

"Corrupt?" Pitt could not help asking. He had not meant to, but the words were out before he guarded them.

Saul shook his head. "You're really not from around here, are you!"

Pitt said nothing.

"There's all sorts of things going on," Saul continued gravely. "You just keep your head down, mind your own business and look after your own. If gentlemen come down here from up west, you don't see them, don't know them. Understand?"

"You mean after women?" Pitt was surprised. There were plenty of better-class prostitutes from the Haymarket to the

110

park and anywhere else. No one had need to come this way where it was dark, dirty and quite possibly dangerous as well.

"And other things." Saul bit his lip, his eyes anxious. "Mostly things you shouldn't ask. Like I said, better you don't know."

Pitt's mind raced. Was Saul talking about private vice or the plans of insurrection that Narraway feared?

"If it's going to affect me, it's my business," Pitt argued.

"It won't, if you look the other way." Saul's face was grave; the urgency of his advice was too vivid to deny.

"Dynamiters affect everyone," Pitt said quietly, afraid the moment he had said it that he had gone too far.

Saul was startled. "Dynamiters! I'm talking about gentlemen from up west who drive around Spitalfields at night in big, black coaches and leave the devil's business behind them." His voice trembled. "You tend to your work, run your errands and look after your own, and you'll be all right. If the police ask you about anything, you don't know. You didn't hear. Better still, you weren't there!"

Pitt did not argue any further, and that evening as he sat over the table with the last of the food, his attention was taken up by a friend of Isaac's coming to the door bruised and bleeding, his clothes torn.

"Samuel, whatever happened to you?" Leah said in dismay, starting up from her chair as Isaac led him in. "You look like you were run over by a carriage." She looked at him with concern puckering her face, judging what she should do to help him.

"Had a bit of trouble with a bunch of local men," Samuel answered, dabbing a bloodstained handkerchief to his lip and wincing as he tried to smile.

"Here! Don't do that," Leah ordered. "Let me look at it. Isaac, fetch me some water and ointment."

"Did they rob you?" Isaac asked without moving to obey.

Samuel shrugged. "I'm alive. It could be worse."

"How much?" Isaac demanded.

"Never mind how much," Leah said sharply. "We'll deal with that afterwards. Fetch me some water and the ointment.

111

The man's in pain! And he's bleeding all over his shirt. Do you know how hard it is to get blood out of good cloth?"

Pitt knew where the pump was, and the ewer. He went out of the back door and came back five minutes later with the ewer full of water. How clean it was he had no idea.

He found Leah and Isaac together, heads bent, talking quietly. Samuel was sitting back in a chair, his eyes closed. The conversation stopped the moment Pitt came in.

"Ah, good, good," Isaac said quickly, taking the ewer. "Thank you very much." He set it down and poured about a pint into a clean pan and put it on the stove. Leah already had the ointment.

"It's too much," Leah demanded, her voice low and fierce, her fingers clenched on the jar. "If you give all that this time, then what about next time? And there will be a next time, never mistake it!"

"We'll deal with next time when it happens," Isaac said firmly. "God will provide."

Leah let out a snort of impatience. "He's already provided you with brains! Use them." She moved fractionally to place her back to Pitt. "It's getting worse, and you can see that as well as anyone," she urged. "With Catholics and Protestants at each other's throats, and dynamiters all over the place, each one crazier than the last, and now talk about blowing up the sugar factory . . ."

Samuel sat patiently and silently between them. Pitt leaned against the dresser.

"No one's going to blow up the sugar factory!" Isaac said tensely, with a warning glance at her.

"Oh? You know that, do you?" she challenged him, her eyebrows arched, eyes wide.

"Why would they do such a thing?" He kept his tone calm.

"They need a reason?" she demanded with amazement. She lifted her shoulders dramatically. "They're anarchists. They hate everybody."

"That's got nothing to do with us," he pointed out. "We look after our own."

"They blow up the sugar factory, it'll have to do with everyone!" she retorted.

"Enough, Leah!" he said, finality in his tone. Now it was an order. "Look after Samuel. I'll find him some money to tide him over. Everyone else'll help. Just do your part."

She stared at him solemnly for several seconds, on the edge of further argument, then something in his face deterred her, and without saying anything further she obeyed.

The water reached the boil, and Pitt carried it over so she could minister to Samuel.

An hour later, in the privacy of the room Isaac used to work on his books, Pitt offered him a contribution of a few shillings towards the fund for Samuel. He was unreasonably delighted when it was accepted. It was a mark of belonging.

Tellman said nothing to anyone about his interest in John Adinett or his conversation with the cabdriver. It was three days before he was able to take the matter any further. Wetron had spoken to him again, questioning him about his present case more closely, wanting a detailed accounting of his time.

Tellman answered with exactness, obedient and unsmiling. The man had taken Pitt's place, and he had no right to it. It might not have been of his choosing, but that excused nothing. He had forbidden Tellman to contact Pitt or take any further interest in the Adinett case. That was his fault all right. Tellman stared at his round, smooth-shaven face with bland, dumb insolence.

By late Tuesday afternoon he again had time to himself, and the first thing he did was to leave Bow Street, buy a ham sandwich from a peddler, and a drink of fresh peppermint, then walk slowly up towards Oxford Street, thinking hard.

He had taken another look at the notes he had made during the investigation and had seen that there were several spaces of time, often as much as four or five hours, in which they did not know where Adinett had been. It had not seemed to matter then, because they were concerned with the details of the physical facts. Where Adinett had spent his time seemed to be irrelevant, only a matter of catching all the details. Now it was all he had.

He walked more slowly. He had no idea where he was going, except that he must pursue something definite, both for Pitt's sake and because he had no intention of going back to Gracie empty-handed.

Why would a man like John Adinett go three times to a place such as Cleveland Street? Who lived there? Was it possible he had odd tastes in personal vice which Fetters had somehow discovered?

Even as he said it to himself, he did not believe it. Why should Fetters care anyway? If it were not criminal, or even if it was, it was no one else's concern.

But perhaps Fetters had discovered something about Adinett which he could not possibly afford to have known. That would have to be something criminal. What?

He increased his pace slightly. Perhaps the answer was in Cleveland Street. It was the only thing so far that was unexplained.

At Oxford Street he caught an omnibus going east, changed at Holborn, and went on towards Spitalfields and Whitechapel, still turning the question over and over in his mind.

Cleveland Street was very ordinary: merely houses and shops, tired, grubby, but reasonably respectable. Who lived here that Adinett had come to see three times?

He went into the first shop, which sold general hardware.

"Yes sir?" A tired man with thinning hair looked up from a kettle he was mending. "What can I get yer?"

Tellman bought a spoon, more for goodwill than because he wanted it. "My sister's thinking of getting a house around here," he lied easily. "I said I'd look at the area for her first. What's it like? Quiet, is it?"

The ironmonger thought about it for a moment, the metal patch in one hand, the kettle in the other.

Tellman waited.

The ironmonger sighed. "Used ter be," he said sadly. "Got a bit odd five or six years ago. Got kids, 'as she, yer sister?"

"Yes," Tellman said quickly.

"Better a couple o' streets over." He indicated where he meant with a nod of his head. "Try north a bit, or east. Keep away from the brewery an' the Mile End Road. Too busy, that is."

Tellman frowned. "She thought of Cleveland Street. The houses look about right for her. Right sort of price, I should think, and well enough kept. But it's busy, is it?"

"Please yerself." The ironmonger shrugged. "I wouldn't live 'ere if I didn't already."

Tellman leaned forward and lowered his voice. "There are not houses of ill repute, are there?"

The ironmonger laughed. "Used ter be. Gorn now. Why?"

"Just wondered." Tellman backed away. "What's all the traffic, then? You said it was busy lately."

"Dunno." The ironmonger had obviously changed his mind about being so candid. "Just people visiting, I expect."

"Carriages and the like?" Tellman tried to assume an air of innocence.

He must have failed, because the ironmonger was imparting nothing more. "Not more than most places." He returned his attention to the kettle, avoiding Tellman's eyes. "Quieter now. Just a bit busy a while back. Forget what I said. I in't 'eard there was nothin' for sale, but if the price is right, you go fer it."

"Thank you," Tellman said civilly. There was no point in making an enemy. Never knew when you might want to speak to him again. He left the shop and walked slowly down the street, looking from side to side, wondering what had taken Adinett's attention, and why.

There were several houses, a few more shops, an artist's studio, a small yard that sold barrels, a maker of clay pipes, and a cobbler. It could have been any of a thousand streets in the poorer parts of London. The smell of the brewery not far away was sweet and stale in the air.

He stopped and bought a sandwich from a peddler at the end of the road where it turned into Devonshire Street.

"Glad to find you," he said conversationally. "Do much business here? I've hardly seen a soul."

115

"Usually stop down the Mile End Road," the peddler replied. "On me way 'ome now. Yer got the last one." He smiled, showing chipped teeth.

"My luck's changed," Tellman said sourly. "Been here all evening on an errand for a friend of my boss's who came here a few weeks back and dropped a watch fob. 'Go and look for it,' he tells me. 'I must have left it behind.' Wrote it down for me, and I lost the paper."

"Name?" the peddler asked, staring at Tellman with wide blue eyes.

"Don't know. Lost it before I read it."

"Watch fob?"

"That's right. Why? You know where it might be?"

The peddler shrugged, grinning again. "No idea. What's your boss like, then?"

Tellman instantly described Adinett. "Tall, military-looking gentleman, very well dressed, small mustache. Walks with his head high, shoulders back."

"I seen 'im." The peddler looked pleased with himself. "Not in a few weeks, like," he added.

"But he was here?" Tellman tried not to let his eagerness betray him, but he could not keep it out of his voice. "You saw him?"

"I jus' said I did. Din't yer say as 'e were yer guvner an' 'e sent yer ter fetch 'is fob?"

"Yes. Yes, I know. But if you saw him, maybe you knew which house he went into." Tellman lied to cover his mistake. "He's a hard man. If I go back without a good explanation, he'll say I took it!"

The peddler shook his head, sympathy in his face. "Times I'm glad I don't work fer no one. Get good days an' bad days, but nob'dy's on me back, like." He pointed down the road. "Were that one down there, on that side. Number six. Tobacconist and confectioner. Lots o' folk comin' an' going there. That's w'ere all the trouble were, four or five year back."

"What trouble?" Tellman said casually, as if it were of no real interest.

"Carriages comin' and goin' at all hours, and that bit o' a

116

fight wot there were," the peddler replied. "Not that much, I s'pose. Bin a lot worse since then, in Spitalfields and 'round there. But it seemed kind o' nasty at the time. Lot o' yellin' an' cursin' an' so on." He screwed up his face. "Odd thing, though, they was all strangers! Not a one o' them local, like." He looked at Tellman narrowly. "Now w'y would a lot o' strangers wanner come 'ere just ter fight each other? Then quick as yer like, they was all gorn again."

Tellman could feel his heart beating in his chest.

"At the tobacconist's?" His voice caught. It was ridiculous. It probably meant nothing.

"Reckon so." The peddler nodded, still watching him. "That's w'ere yer guv'ner went, any'ow. Asked me the same thing, 'e did, an' then went orff like a dog wi' two tails w'en I told 'im."

"I see. Thank you very much. Here." Tellman fished in his pocket and brought out a sixpence. His fingers were shaking. It was a bit extravagant, but he felt suddenly optimistic and grateful. "Have a pint on me. You've probably saved me a packet."

"Ta." The peddler took the sixpence and it disappeared instantly. " 'Ere's ter yer 'ealth."

Tellman nodded and then walked quickly down to where the peddler had indicated. It looked much like any other shop on the outside, a small area for selling sweets and tobacco, with living quarters above. What on earth could be here that John Adinett had found exciting? He would have to come back when the shop was open. He would find a way of doing that tomorrow, when Wetron would not find out.

He walked back towards the Mile End Road with a spring in his step.

But when he managed to return to Cleveland Street in the middle of the next afternoon, after some considerable difficulty, and having stretched the truth to his inspector so far it bore little resemblance to the facts, the shop seemed exactly like a thousand others.

He bought threepence worth of mint humbugs and tried to start a conversation with the owner, but there was little to talk about except the weather. He was becoming desperate when he made a remark about heat and fevers, and poor Prince Albert's having died of typhoid.

"I suppose no one's safe," he said, feeling foolish.

"Why should they be?" the tobacconist said ruefully, chewing his lip. "Royals ain't no better off than you nor me when it comes to some things. Eat better, I s'pose, an' certainly wear better." He fingered the thin cloth of his own jacket. "But get sick like we do, an' die, poor sods." There was a sharp note of pity in his voice which struck Tellman as extraordinary from a man in such an area, who obviously owned little and worked hard. This was the last place he would have expected compassion for those who seemed to have everything.

"You reckon they've got troubles like ours?" Tellman said, trying to keep all expression out of his voice.

"Yer free to come an' go as yer please, aren't yer?" the tobacconist asked, gazing at Tellman with surprisingly clear gray eyes. "Believe what yer want, Catholic, Protestant, Jew, or nothin'? God wi' six arms, if that's what takes yer fancy? An' marry a woman wot believes anything, if she's willing?"

Gracie's sharp little face came instantly to Tellman's mind with its bright eyes and determined chin. Then he was furious with himself for his weakness. It was ridiculous. They disagreed about everything. She would have felt with this tobacconist and his sympathies. She saw nothing wrong in being in service, whereas Tellman was outraged that anyone, man or woman, should be fetching and carrying and calling other people "sir" and "ma'am" and cleaning up after them.

"Of course I can!" he said far more tartly than he meant. "But I wouldn't want to marry a woman who couldn't believe the same things I do. More important than religion, about rights and wrongs on how people behave, what's just and what isn't."

The tobacconist smiled and shook his head patiently.

"If yer fall in love, yer won't think about w'ere she came from or what she believes, yer'll just wanna be with 'er." His voice was soft. "If yer sittin' arguin' over rights an' wrongs o'

118

things, yer in't in love. 'Ave 'er fer a friend, but don't marry 'er." He shook his head, his voice making plain his opinion of such a choice. " 'Less she's got money or summink, an' that's wot yer want, like?"

Tellman was offended. "I wouldn't marry anyone for money!" he said angrily. "I just think that a person's sense of fairness matters. If you're going to spend your whole life with someone, have children, you should agree on what's decent and what isn't."

The tobacconist sighed heavily, his smile vanishing. "Could be yer right. Gawd knows, fallin' in love can bring yer enough grief, if yer beliefs an' yer station in life is different."

Tellman put one of the humbugs in his mouth as the shop door opened behind him. He turned instinctively to see who it was, and he recognized the man who came in but could not place him.

"Afternoon, sir." The tobacconist dismissed Tellman from his mind and looked to the new customer. "What can I get yer, sir?"

The man hesitated, glanced at Tellman, then back at the tobacconist. "That gentleman was before me," he said politely.

" 'E's bin served," the tobacconist answered. "Wot will it be fer you?"

The man looked at Tellman again before replying. "Well, if you're sure. Half a pound of tobacco . . ."

The tobacconist's eyebrows shot up. "Half a pound? Right you are, sir. What kind'll it be? I got all sorts . . . Virginia, Turkish—"

"Virginia," the man cut him off, fishing in his pocket for his money.

It was the voice that Tellman recognized. It took him a moment or two, then he knew where he had heard it before. The man was a journalist named Lyndon Remus. He had followed Pitt around asking questions, probing, during the Bedford Square murder. It was he who had written the piece which had done so much damage, implying scandal.

What was he doing here in Mile End? Certainly not buying tobacco, half a pound at a time! He didn't know Virginia from

119

Turkish, or care. He had come in for something else, then changed his mind when he saw Tellman.

"Thank you," Tellman said to the tobacconist. "Good day." And he went out into the street and along about forty yards to a wide doorway where he could stand almost unseen and watch for Remus to come out.

After about ten minutes he began to wonder if there were a way out of the shop and into a back street. What could Remus be doing in there so long? There was only one answer which made any kind of sense—Remus was there for the same reason he had come himself, scenting a story, a scandal, perhaps an explanation for murder. It must be to do with John Adinett. There could hardly be two murderers tied to that small tobacconist's shop.

The minutes went by. Traffic passed along the street, some towards the Mile End Road, some the other way. After another ten minutes Remus came out at last. He looked to left and right, crossed the road and walked south, passing within a yard of Tellman, then realizing who he was, stopped abruptly.

Tellman smiled. "Onto a good story, Mr. Remus?" he asked.

Remus's sharp, freckled face was a total blank for a matter of seconds, then he recovered his composure. "Not sure," he said easily. "Lot of ideas, all disconnected at the moment. Since you're here, maybe it does mean something."

"Humbug," Tellman said with a smile.

"Oh no . . . I don't . . ." Remus began.

"Mint humbugs," Tellman clarified. "That's what I bought there."

Remus's expression smoothed out.

"Oh! Yes, of course."

"Better than tobacco," Tellman went on. "I don't know one tobacco from another. Neither do you."

"Not your beat, is it?" Remus said, shifting the subject back to Tellman. "Still on the Adinett case, are you? Interesting man." His eyes narrowed. "But why bother? You got your conviction. What more do you want?"

120

"Me?" Tellman said, affecting surprise. "Not a thing. Why? What more do you think there is?"

"Motive," Remus said reasonably. "Did Fetters ever come here?"

"What makes you think that? Did the tobacconist say he had?"

Remus raised his eyebrows. "I never asked him."

"So it's not Fetters you're after," Tellman deduced.

Remus was momentarily taken aback. He had let slip more than he'd intended. He recovered, looking at Tellman with a sly smile. "Fetters and Adinett . . . it's all the same thing, isn't it?"

"You didn't say you were after Adinett," Tellman pointed out.

Remus pushed his hands into his pockets and started to walk slowly in the direction of the Mile End Road, allowing Tellman to keep pace with him.

"Not exactly news now, is he?" he said thoughtfully. "For me or for you. He'd have to have had a really interesting reason for killing Fetters for me to bother to write it up. And I reckon it would have to be connected with another crime, a pretty big one, before you'd still be following it too . . . don't you think?"

Tellman had no intention whatsoever of allowing him to know anything about Pitt. "Sounds sensible," he agreed. "Presuming I wasn't just after a mint humbug."

"Humbug, maybe," Remus said with a twisted smile, and increased his pace slightly. They walked in silence for a few moments, crossing an alleyway leading towards the brewery. "But be careful! There's a lot of very important people'll try to stop you. I suppose Mr. Pitt sent you here?"

"And Mr. Dismore sent you?" Tellman countered, remembering what the cabbie had said about Adinett's going to Dismore's newspaper after leaving Cleveland Street the last time.

Remus was momentarily nonplussed, then again he disguised his emotions and replied blandly. "I'm independent. Don't answer to anyone. I thought you would know that . . . a sharp detective like you!"

Tellman grunted. He was not sure what he believed, except

that Remus thought he was onto a story which he had no intention of sharing.

They reached the Mile End Road, and Remus said goodbye and plunged into the stream of people going west.

Tellman decided on the spur of the moment to follow him. It proved more difficult than he had expected, partly because of the amount of traffic which was trade carts and wagons rather than hansoms, but mostly because Remus very apparently did not wish to be followed and was aware of Tellman behind him.

It took him a succession of very rapid sprints, a good deal of bribery, and a little luck not to lose him, but half an hour later Tellman was in a hansom crossing London Bridge. Just beyond the railway terminus, Remus stopped ahead of him and got out. He paid his fare, then ran up the steps of Guy's Hospital and disappeared through the doors.

Tellman alighted also, paid off his driver and went up into the hospital as well.

But Remus was nowhere to be seen.

Tellman walked over to the porter and described Remus to him, asking which way he had gone.

"Asked after the offices," the porter replied. "That's that way, sir." He pointed helpfully.

Tellman thanked him and went the same way, but search as he might, he found no further trace of Remus, and finally after nearly half an hour of wandering corridors, he left the hospital and took the train north over the river again. He found himself at Keppel Street just before six o' clock in the evening.

He stood at the back door for several minutes before he summoned enough courage to knock. He wished there were some way he could see Gracie without having to encounter Charlotte. He was embarrassed by the fact that he had done nothing to help Pitt. He was sure she was going to be distressed, and he had no idea what to say or do.

It was only the very vivid imagination of Gracie's total scorn for him that stopped him from turning around and hurrying away. He would have to face her sometime. Putting it off would only make it even more difficult. He took a deep breath, then let it out again, still without knocking. Perhaps he should find out more before he spoke to her. After all, he didn't have very much. He had no idea why Remus had gone to Guy's Hospital, not even a guess.

The door opened and Gracie let out a shriek as she almost ran into him. The saucepan she was holding slipped out of her hands and fell onto the step with a crash.

"Yer stupid great article!" she said furiously. "Wot d'yer think yer doin' standin' there, wi' a face like a pot lion? Wot's the matter with yer?"

He bent down and picked up the saucepan and handed it back to her. "I came to tell you what I've found out," he said tartly. "You shouldn't drop the good saucepans like that. You'll chip them and then they'll be no good."

"I wouldn't 'a dropped it if yer 'adn't give me the fright o' me life," she accused. "Why din't yer knock, like any ordinary person?"

"I was about to!" That was not really a lie. Of course he would have knocked any moment.

She looked him up and down. "Well, yer'd better come in. I s'pose yer've got more ter say than can be done on the step?" She whisked around, her skirts swirling, and went back inside, and he followed her through the scullery into the kitchen, closing both doors behind him. If Charlotte were at home, she was nowhere to be seen.

"An' keep yer voice down!" Gracie warned, as if reading his thoughts. "Mrs. Pitt's upstairs reading ter Daniel and Jemima."

"Jemima can read herself," he said, puzzled.

"O' course she can!" she said with an effort at patience. "But 'er papa's not 'ome anymore, an' we 'aven't 'eard a thing from 'im. Nobody knows wot's goin' ter 'appen, if 'e's bein' looked after, or what! It does yer good ter be read to." She sniffed and turned away from him, determined he should not see the tears spill down her face. "So wot 'ave yer found out, then? I s'pose yer want a cup o' tea? An' cake?"

"Yes, please." He sat down at the kitchen table while she

123

busied herself with the kettle, the teapot, two cups, and several wedges of fresh currant cake, all the time keeping her back to him.

He watched her quick movements, her thin shoulders under the cotton dress, a waist he could have put his hands around. He ached to be of some comfort to her, but she was far too prickly proud to let him. Anyway, what could he say? She would never believe lies that everything would be all right. More than twenty-one years of life had taught her that tragedy was real. Justice sometimes prevailed, but not always.

He must say something. The kitchen clock was ticking the minutes by. The kettle was beginning to sing. It was the same warm, sweet-smelling room as always. He had been ridiculously happy here, so comfortable, more than anywhere else he could remember.

She banged the teapot down, risking chipping it.

"Well, are yer goin' ter tell me or not?" she demanded.

"Yes . . . I am!" he snapped back, furious with himself for wanting to touch her, to be gentle, to put his arms around her and hold her close. He cleared his throat and nearly choked. "Adinett went to Cleveland Street in Mile End at least three times. And the last time he was really excited about something. He went straight from there to visit Thorold Dismore, who owns the newspaper that's always going on against the Queen and saying that the Prince of Wales spends too much money."

She stood still, her brows furrowed, confusion in her eyes.

"Wot does a gentleman like Mr. Adinett go ter Mile End fer? If 'e's lookin' for an 'ore, there's plenty closer, an' cleaner! 'E could get 'isself done in, down Mile End way."

"I know that. And that isn't all. The place he went to isn't a brothel, it's a tobacconist's shop."

" 'E went ter Mile End ter buy tobacco?" she said in disbelief.

"No," he corrected her. "He went to the tobacconist's shop for some other reason, but I don't know what it was yet. But when I went back there today, and went into the shop myself, who should come in but Lyndon Remus, the journalist who

124

was trying to dig up all that dirt back when Mr. Pitt was working on the murder in Bedford Square." He leaned forward urgently, putting his elbows on the scrubbed wood of the table. "He wouldn't say anything while I was there, but he stayed another twenty minutes after I'd gone. I know because I waited for him. And when he left I spoke to him."

She was transfixed, her eyes wide, the teapot forgotten. Only the screaming of the kettle brought her back to the moment. She pulled it off the hob and then ignored it.

"So?" she demanded. "Wot'd 'e want? Wot's so special about Cleveland Street?"

"I don't know yet," he admitted. "But he's after scandal, and he thinks he's really onto something. He tried to ask me what I was doing there. He was sort of excited to see me. He thought it proved he was right. It's to do with Adinett, he as good as admitted that."

She sat down in the chair opposite him. "Go on!" she urged.

"When he left I followed him. He tried to make sure I didn't, but I stuck with him."

"W'ere'd 'e go?" Her eyes never left his face.

"South of the river, to Guy's Hospital . . . the offices. But I lost him there."

"Guy's 'Ospital," she repeated slowly. Finally she stood up and made the tea and set it on the table to brew. "Now whyever did 'e not want yer ter know 'e went there?"

"Because it has something to do with Adinett," he answered. "And Cleveland Street. But I'm damned if I know what."

"Well, yer'll just 'ave ter find out," she said without hesitation. " 'Cause we gotta prove Mr. Pitt is right an' Adinett were as guilty as 'e said, an' fer a wicked reason. D'yer want a piece o' cake?"

"Yes, please." He took the largest piece on the plate she offered. He had long ago stopped pretending to be polite. Gracie made the best cake he had ever eaten.

She was looking at him earnestly. "Yer goin' ter find out wot it is, in't yer . . . I mean, wot really 'appened, an' why?"

Tellman wished she had even a shred of the admiration for him that she had for Pitt. And yet the belief in her face now, even if it was born of desperation, was both wonderful and frightening. Could he live up to it? He had very little idea what to do next. What would Pitt have done were their roles reversed?

He liked Pitt, he had to admit that, in spite of not wanting to, not agreeing with him over dozens of things. He had disapproved violently of Pitt's appointment. He was not a gentleman and had no more right to expect the rest of them to obey him than any other ordinary policeman had. But on the other hand he had been reasonable—most of the time. He was eccentric, took a lot of getting used to.

But for better or worse, Tellman was part of Pitt's life. He had sat at their table too often, shared too many cases, good and bad. And there was Gracie.

"Yes, of course I will," he said with his mouth full of cake.

"Yer goin' ter foller this Remus?" she pressed. " 'E's onter it . . . whatever it is. Mrs. Pitt's tryin' ter find out more about Mr. Fetters, but she don't 'ave nothin' yet. I'll tell yer if she does." She looked tired and frightened. "Yer won't stop, will yer?" she insisted. "No matter wot! There's nob'dy ter do it but us."

"I told you," he said, meeting her eyes steadily. "I'll find out! Now, eat some of your cake. You look like a fourpenny rabbit! And pour the tea!"

"It in't brewed yet." But she poured it anyway.

6

CHARLOTTE OPENED the morning newspaper more out of loneliness than any real interest in the political events which filled it as the various parties prepared for the coming election. They were very hard on Mr. Gladstone, berating him for ignoring all issues except Irish Home Rule and apparently abandoning any effort towards achieving the eight-hour working day. But she did not expect the newspapers to be fair.

There was tragic news of a railway crash at Guisley, in the north. Two people had been killed and several injured. Doctors were on their way.

The New Oriental Bank Corporation had been compelled to withdraw funds and suspend certain payments. The price of silver was seriously down. They had sustained losses in Melbourne and Singapore. The liquidation of the Gatling Gun Company had affected them badly. A hurricane in Mauritius was the crowning blow.

She did not read the rest of it. Her eye moved down the page, and in spite of herself was caught by the dark type announcing that John Adinett was to be executed at eight o'clock that morning.

Instinctively she glanced at the kitchen clock. It was a quarter to eight. She wished she had not opened the paper until later, even half an hour would have been enough. Why had she not thought of that, counted the days and been careful not to look?

Adinett had killed Martin Fetters, and the more Charlotte

learned about Fetters the more she believed she would have liked him. He had been an enthusiast, a man who grasped at life with courage and enjoyment, who loved its color and variety. He had a passion to learn about others, and it seemed from his writings that he was equally eager to share what he knew so that anyone else could see the same enchantment he did. His death was a loss not only to his wife—and to archaeology and to curators of ancient artefacts—but to anyone who knew him and to the world in general.

Still, ending the life of Adinett did not improve anything. She doubted it would even deter anyone else from future crime. It was the certainty of punishment that stopped people from killing, not the severity. Each one presumed he or she would get away with it, so the penalty was irrelevant.

Gracie came in from the back door, where she had been collecting herrings from the fishmonger's boy.

"These'll do dinner for us," she said briskly, swirling through the kitchen and putting the dish into the larder. She continued talking to herself absentmindedly about what would do for which meal, how much flour or potatoes they had left, and if the onions would last. They had used a lot of onions lately to flavor very plain food.

She had been preoccupied recently. Charlotte thought it had to do with Sergeant Tellman. She knew he had been at the house the other evening, even though she had not seen him herself. She had heard his voice and deliberately not intruded. Having Tellman sitting in the kitchen, exactly as if Pitt were still at home, made her sense of loneliness even more overwhelming.

She was happy for Gracie, and she was very well aware, rather more than Gracie was herself, that Tellman was fighting a losing battle against his feelings for her. Just at the moment she found it difficult to make herself seem cheerful about anything. Missing Pitt was hard enough. The evenings seemed endless when she was not listening for his step. There was no one to tell about her day, even if it had been entirely uneventful. The high point might have been something as trivial as a new flower in the garden, or a piece of gossip, perhaps a joke. And if things somehow went wrong, perhaps she would not mention it, but the knowledge that she could made all the irritation seem temporary, something that could be ignored. It was odd how happiness unshared was only half as great, and yet any kind of misfortune alone was doubled.

But far worse than loneliness was her anxiety for Pitt, the ordinary day-to-day worry as to whether he was eating properly, was warm enough, had anyone to wash his clothes. Had he found somewhere even remotely comfortable and kind to live? The real misery in her mind was for his safety, not only from anarchists, dynamiters or whomever he was looking for, but from his secret and far more powerful enemies in the Inner Circle.

The clock chimed and she was dimly aware of it. Gracie riddled the stove and put more coal on the fire.

Charlotte tried not to think, not to imagine, and during the day she was quite good at it. But at night, the moment her mind was blank, the fears came rushing in. She was emotionally exhausted and physically not tired enough. She had never been to Spitalfields, but she pictured it all too easily, narrow dark streets with figures lurking in doorways, everything damp and flickering with movement, as if it were only waiting to catch the unwary.

She woke too many times in the night, aware of every creak in the house, of the empty space beside her in the bed, wondering where he was, if he were awake also, feeling his loneliness.

Sometimes the fact that she had to pretend she was all right for the children's sake seemed an impossible task, at other times it was a discipline for which she was grateful. How many women down the centuries had pretended while their men were away at war, exploring unknown lands, at sea carrying goods over the oceans, or simply had run away because they were feckless and disloyal? At least she knew Pitt was none of these things and he would return when he could—or when she could find some answer to why Adinett had murdered Martin Fetters that was strong enough so even the members of the Inner Circle would have to believe it and the world in general would have no doubt left.

She closed the newspaper and pushed her chair away from the table just as Daniel and Jemima came into the room, eager for breakfast before going to school. There would be plenty to do today, and if not, then she would find it, or create it.

The kitchen clock rang a single chime. It was a quarter past eight. It had rung eight o'clock and she had not heard it. John Adinett would be dead now, his body, broken-necked—like Martin Fetters—being removed, ready for an unhallowed grave, and his soul to answer for his acts before the judge who knows all things.

She smiled at the children and began to prepare breakfast.

It was just after ten o'clock and she was sorting out the linen cupboard for the second time that week when Gracie came upstairs to tell her that Mrs. Radley had called—except that that was unnecessary, because Emily Radley, Charlotte's sister, was only a step behind Gracie. Emily looked devastatingly elegant in a dark green riding habit with a small, dark, hard-brimmed hat with a high crown, and a jacket cut so superbly it flattered every line of her slender figure. She was a trifle flushed from exertion, and her fair hair had come loose and had gone into curls in the damp air.

"Whatever are you doing?" she asked, surveying the piles of sheets and pillowcases strewn around.

"Sorting the linen for mending," Charlotte answered, suddenly aware of how shabby and untidy she looked compared with her sister. "Have you forgotten how to do that?"

"I'm not sure that I ever knew," Emily said airily. As Charlotte had married socially and financially beneath her, so Emily had married correspondingly above. Her first husband had possessed both title and fortune. He had been killed some time ago, and after a period of mourning, and loneliness, Emily had married again, this time to a handsome and charming man who owned almost nothing. It was Emily's ambition which had driven him to stand for a seat in Parliament and eventually to win it.

Gracie disappeared downstairs again.

Charlotte turned her back and resumed folding pillow-cases and piling them neatly where they had originally been.

"Is Thomas still away?" Emily asked, lowering her voice a little.

"Of course he is," Charlotte replied, a trifle sharply. "I told you, it's going to be a long time, I don't know how long."

"Actually you told me very little," Emily pointed out, taking one of the pillowcases herself and folding it neatly. "You were rather mysterious and sounded upset. I came to see if you were all right."

"What are you going to do about it if I'm not?" Charlotte started on one of the sheets.

Emily picked up the other end. "Give you the opportunity to pick a quarrel and be thoroughly beastly to someone. It looks as if that is what you need this moment."

Charlotte stared at her, ignoring the sheet. Emily was being bright, but beneath the glamorous surface there was anxiety in her eyes—and no humor underlying the smart retort.

"I'm all right," Charlotte said more gently. "It's Thomas I'm worried about." She and Emily had shared in many of his past cases, and Emily knew the passion and the loss that could be involved. She was no stranger to fear, and she already knew of the Inner Circle. Charlotte could not tell her where Pitt was, but she could tell her why.

"What is it?" Emily sensed that there was more than she had been led to believe before, and now her voice was sharp with anxiety.

"The Inner Circle," Charlotte said very quietly. "I think Adinett was one of them—in fact, I'm sure he was. They won't forgive Thomas for convicting him." She took a shivering breath. "They hanged him this morning."

Emily was very somber. "I know. There was more in some of the newspapers about whether or not he was really guilty. No one seems to have any idea why he would do such a thing. Doesn't Thomas have any clues?"

"No."

"Well, isn't he trying to find out?"

"He can't," Charlotte said quietly, looking down at the

linen on the floor. "He's been removed from Bow Street and sent . . . into the East End . . . to look for anarchists."

"What?" Emily was aghast. "That's monstrous! Who have you appealed to?"

"No one can do anything about it. Cornwallis already tried everything he could. If Thomas is somewhere in the East End, where nobody knows, anonymous, at least he is as safe from them as he can be."

"Anonymous in the East End?" Emily's face showed only too clearly her horror and all the dangers her imagination foresaw.

Charlotte looked away. "I know. Anything could happen to him, and it would be days before I'd even hear."

"Nothing will happen to him," Emily said quickly. "And I can see that he's safer there than still where they can find him." But there was more courage in her voice than conviction. She hurried on. "What can we do to help?"

"I've been to see Mrs. Fetters," Charlotte replied, mimicking the same positive tone. "But she doesn't know anything. I'm trying to think what to do next. There has to be some connection between the two men that they quarreled over, but the more I learn about Martin Fetters, the more he seems an unusually decent man who harmed no one."

"Then you aren't looking in the right places," Emily said frankly. "I assume you have tried all the obvious things: money, blackmail, a woman, rivalry for some position or other?" She looked puzzled. "Why were they friends anyway?"

"Travel and political reform, so far as his wife knows." Charlotte finished folding the last of the sheets. "Do you want a cup of tea?"

"Not especially. But I'd rather sit in the kitchen than stand here in the linen cupboard," Emily responded. "Does anyone quarrel seriously over travel?"

"I doubt it. And they didn't even travel to the same places. Mr. Fetters went to the Near East, and Adinett went to France, and he had been to Canada in the past."

"Then it's politics." Emily followed her down the stairs and along the corridor to the kitchen. She said hello to Gracie in a matter-of-fact way. In no one else's house would she have spoken to the maid, but she knew of Charlotte's regard for her.

Charlotte put on the kettle. "They both wanted reform," she went on.

Emily sat down, flicking her skirts expertly so they were not crushed. "Doesn't everyone? Jack says it's getting pretty desperate." She looked down at her hands on the table, small and elegant, and surprisingly strong. "There have always been rumblings of unrest, but it's a lot worse now than even ten years ago. There are so many foreigners coming into London and not enough work. I suppose there have been an-archists for years, but there are more of them now, and they are very violent."

Charlotte knew that. It was in the newspapers often enough, including the trial of the French anarchist for the as-sassination of Carnot. And she knew that in London they were largely in the East End, where the poverty was worst and the dissatisfaction the highest. That was the official excuse for sending Pitt there.

"What?" Emily said quickly, seeing her sister's expres-sion. "What is it?"

"Are they really a danger, do you think? I mean, more than the individual lunatic?"

Emily considered for a moment before answering. Char-lotte wondered whether it was to search for the right words, to examine her knowledge, or worst of all, if it were a matter of tact. If it were the last, then the instinctive answer must be very ugly. It was not Emily's nature to be indirect, which was quite different from being devious, at which she was brilliant.

"Actually," she said quietly when Gracie had brewed the tea and brought it, "I think Jack is really worried, not about anarchists, who are only individual madmen, but about the feeling everywhere. The monarchy is very unpopular, you know, and not just with the sort of people you would expect, but with some who are very important and perhaps you would not think."

"Unpopular?" Charlotte was puzzled. "In what way? I know people think the Queen should do far more, but they've

133

said that for thirty years. Does Jack think it's any different now?"

"I don't know that it's different." Emily was very grave. She chose her words carefully, weighing them before she spoke. "But he says it is much more serious. The Prince of Wales spends an enormous amount of money, you know, and most of it is borrowed. He owes all over the place, and to all kinds of people. He doesn't seem to be able to stop himself, and if he realizes what harm it is doing, then he doesn't care."

"Political harm?" Charlotte asked.

"Eventually, yes." Emily lowered her voice. "There are some people who think that when the old Queen dies that will be the end of the monarchy."

Charlotte was startled. "Really?" It was a surprisingly unpleasant thought. She was not quite sure why she minded. It would take some of the color out of life, some of the glamour. Even if you never saw the countesses and the duchesses, if there was no way in the world you would ever be a lady, far less a princess, it would make things a little grayer if they should not exist anymore. People would always have heroes, real or false. There was nothing essentially noble about the aristocracy. But then the heroes who would be put in their places would not necessary be chosen for their virtue or achievement; it might as easily be for wealth or beauty. Then the magic would be gone for no reason, no gain.

All of which was a silly argument, and she knew it. What mattered was the change, and a change born of hatred was frightening because so often it was done without thought or knowledge. So much could not be foreseen.

"That's what Jack says." Emily was watching her closely, her tea forgotten. "And what bothers him the most is that there are powerful interests who are royalist and will do anything to keep things as they are . . . and I mean anything!" She bit her lip. "When he said that, I pressed him what he meant, and he wouldn't answer me. He went quiet and sort of . . . into himself, the way he does if he isn't well. It seems an odd thing to say, but I think he was afraid." She stopped abruptly, looking down at her hands again, as if she had said something of which she was ashamed. Perhaps she had not meant to reveal so much of what was vulnerable, and therefore private.

Charlotte felt chilled. There was too much to be afraid of already. She wished to know more, but there was no point in pressing Emily. If she had been able to tell her then she would have done so. It was an ugly and lonely thought. "You don't realize how much you value what you have, with all its problems, until someone threatens to destroy it and put his own ideas in its place," she said ruefully. "I don't mind a little change, but I don't want a lot. Can you have a little change, do you suppose? Or does it have to be all or nothing? Do they have to smash everything in order to make any of it different?"

"That depends on the people," Emily replied with a tight, sad little smile. "If you'll bend, then no. If you won't, if you do a Marie Antoinette, then perhaps it's either the crown or the guillotine."

"Was she really so stupid?"

"I don't know. It's just an example. No one's going to behead our Queen. At least I don't imagine so."

"I don't suppose the French imagined so either," Charlotte said dryly. "I wish I hadn't thought of that!"

"We aren't French." Emily's voice was firm, even angry.

"Tell Charles I," Charlotte retorted, picturing in her mind Van Dyke's sad, brilliant portrait of that unfortunate man, stubborn to his beliefs right to the scaffold.

"That wasn't a revolution." Emily retreated to the literal.

"It was a civil war. Is that any better?" Charlotte argued.

"It's only talk! Politicians having nightmares. If it wasn't over that, it would be something else—Ireland, taxes, an eight-hour day, or drains." She shrugged elegantly. "If there isn't something awful to solve, why would we need them?"

"We probably don't . . . at least, most of the time."

"That's what they're afraid of." Emily stood up. "Do you want to come with us to the National Gallery and see the exhibition?"

"No, thank you. I'm going to see Mrs. Fetters again. I think you may be right—it's probably politics."

* * *

Charlotte arrived at Great Coram Street a little after eleven o'clock. It was a most unsuitable time for calling on anyone, but this was not a social visit, and it had the one advantage that she would be excessively unlikely to run into anyone else and have to explain her presence.

Juno was delighted to see her and made no pretense to conceal it. Her face was full of relief that she should have company.

"Come in!" she said enthusiastically. "Do you have any news?"

"No, I'm sorry." Charlotte felt guilty that she had achieved nothing more. After all, this woman's loss was far greater than her own. "I have thought a great deal, but to no avail, except more ideas."

"Can I help?"

"Perhaps." Charlotte accepted the offered seat in the same lovely garden room as before. Today it was cooler and the door was closed. "It seems that ambition for political reform was the obvious thing that Mr. Fetters and John Adinett had in common and about which they both cared very deeply."

"Oh, Martin cared intensely," Juno agreed. "He argued for it and wrote many articles. He knew a lot of people would feel the same, and he believed it would come."

"Do you have any of the articles?" Charlotte asked. She was not sure what use it would be to see them, but there was nothing better she could think of.

"They will be among his papers." Juno stood up. "The police went through them, of course, but they are all still in his desk in the study. I . . . I haven't had the heart to read them again myself." She spoke softly, with her back to Charlotte, and she went straight out and across the hall to the study, leading the way in.

It was a smaller room than the library, and without the tall windows and sunlight, but it was still pleasant and very obviously well used. A single bookcase was full, and there were two more volumes on the leather inlaid desk. Shelves behind were stacked with papers and folios.

Juno stopped, the light going from her face. "I don't know

what we could find here," she said helplessly. "The police didn't find anything more than the odd note regarding a meeting, and two or three written when John ... Mr. Adinett ... went to France once. They weren't in the least personal, just very vivid descriptions of certain places in Paris, mostly to do with the Revolution. Martin had written some articles about the same places, and Adinett was saying how much more they meant to him with Martin's vision than they had before." Her voice thickened with emotion as she remembered such a short time ago when so much had been different.

She walked over to the shelves behind the desk and pulled out a number of periodicals, sifting through the pages. "There are all sorts of articles in here. Would you like to read them?"

"Yes, please," Charlotte accepted, again because she knew of no better place to start. She would glance at them, no more.

Juno passed them across. Charlotte noticed on the covers a line saying that they were published by Thorold Dismore. She opened the first and began to read. It was written from Vienna, by Martin Fetters, as he walked about the city and stood in the places where the revolutionaries of the '48 uprising had struggled to force the simpleminded Emperor Ferdinand's government into some kind of reform of the crushing laws, the burden of taxes and the inequalities.

She had intended only to skim through, catch a flavor of his beliefs, but she could not omit a sentence. The words leapt vividly to life with a passion and a grief that held her so completely she forgot the study in Great Coram Street, and Juno sitting a few feet away. She heard Martin Fetters's voice in her mind and saw his face full of enthusiasm for the courage of the men and women who had fought. She felt his outrage at their defeat in the end, and a longing that someday their goals would be achieved.

She turned to the next one. This was written from Berlin. In essence it was the same. The love of the beauty of the city and individuality of the people was there, the story of their attempts to curb the military power of Prussia, and in the end, their failure.

He wrote from Paris, perhaps the article to which John

137

Adinett had referred in the letters Pitt had found. This piece was longer, filled with an intimate love of a glorious city stained with terror, a hope so vivid it hurt, even through the printed words on the page. Fetters had stood where Danton had lived, followed his last ride in the tumbrel to the guillotine, where Danton had been at his greatest, where he had already lost everything and seen the Revolution consume its own children in body—and more dreadfully, in spirit.

Fetters had stood on the Rue St. Honoré outside the carpenter's home where Robespierre had lodged, who sent so many thousands to their bloody deaths and yet never saw the engine of destruction until he rode to it himself, for the last time.

Fetters had walked in the streets where the students manned the barricades for the '48 revolution that gained so little and cost so much. Charlotte found tears thick in her throat when she finished it, and she had to force herself to pick up the next piece. And yet had Juno interrupted her, asked for them back, she would have felt robbed and suddenly alone.

Fetters wrote from Venice, which he found the most beautiful city on earth, even under the Austrian yoke, and from Athens, once the greatest city republic of all, the cradle of the concept of democracy and now a shell of its ancient glory, its spirit defiled.

Finally he wrote from Rome, again of the revolution of '48, the brief glory of another Roman republic, snuffed out by the armies of Napoleon III, and the return of the Pope, the crushing of all the passion for freedom and justice and a voice for the people. He wrote of Mazzini, living in the papal palace, in one room, eating raisins, and of his fresh flowers every day. He wrote of the deeds of Garibaldi and his fierce, passionate wife, who died after the end of the siege, and of Mario Corena, the soldier and republican who was willing to give everything he owned for the common good: his money, his lands, his life if need be. If only there had been more like him, they would not have lost.

She put down the last paper on the desk, but her mind was filled with heroism and tragedy, past and present alive together, and above all the inescapable presence of Martin Fetters's voice in her mind, his beliefs, his personality, his fierce, life-giving love of individual liberty within a civilized whole.

Surely if John Adinett had known him as well as everyone said he did, he must have had an overwhelming reason for killing such a man, something so powerful it could conquer friendship, admiration, the common love of ideals? She could not think what such a thing could be.

Then a thread of thought came, like a shadow passing across the sun. Could they have been wrong about murder after all? Had Adinett told the truth all along?

She kept her eyes down so Juno would not see the doubt in her. It was as if she had betrayed Pitt that the thought had even existed.

"He wrote brilliantly," she said aloud. "I not only feel as if I have been there and learned what happened in those streets, but as if I cared about it almost as much as he did."

Juno smiled very slightly. "He was like that . . . so alive I couldn't have imagined he would ever die, not really." Her voice was gentle, far away. She sounded almost surprised. "It seems ridiculous that for everybody else the world goes on just the same. Part of me wants to put straw down on the streets and tell everyone they must drive slowly. Another part wants to pretend it never happened at all, he's just away somewhere again, and he'll be back in a day or two."

Charlotte looked up at her and saw the struggle in her face. She could understand it so easily. Her own loneliness was only a fraction of this. Pitt was all right; he was just a few miles away in Spitalfields. If he gave up the police force he could come home any day. But that would answer nothing. Charlotte had to know that he had been right about Adinett, and why, and she had to prove it to everyone.

Perhaps Juno had to know just as urgently, and the darkness in her face was fear as to what she might find out about her husband. There had to be something vast . . . and at least to Adinett, unendurable.

And secret! He had gone to the gallows rather than speak of it, even to excuse himself.

"We had better look further," she said at last. "What we want may not be here in this room, but it is the best place to begin." It was also the only place, so far.

Juno bent obediently and opened the desk drawers. For one of them Juno sent to the kitchen for a knife, and then pried it open, splintering the wood.

"A pity," she said, biting her lip. "I don't suppose it can be mended, but I didn't have the key."

They began there since it was the only one specifically protected from intrusion.

Charlotte had read three letters before she started to see a pattern. They were carefully worded; the casual glance would have found nothing remarkable in them—in fact, they were rather dry. The subject matter was theoretical: the political reform of a state which had no name, whose leaders were spoken of personally rather than by office. There was no drama, no passion, only ideals; as if it were an exercise of the mind, something one writes for an examination.

The first letter was from Charles Voisey, the appeals judge.

My dear Fetters,

I read your paper with the greatest interest. You raise many points with which I agree, and some I had not considered, but on weighing what you have to say, I believe you are quite right in your thinking.

There are other areas in which I cannot go as far as you do, but I understand the influences which have affected you, and in your place I might share your view, even if not the extremity of it.

Thank you for the pottery, which arrived safely, and now graces my private study. It is a most exquisite piece, and a constant reminder to me of the glories of the past, and the spirits of great men to whom we owe so much . . . as you have said, a debt for which history will hold us accountable, even if we ourselves do not.

I look forward to conversing with you further,

Your ally in the cause,
Charles Voisey

The next one was in a similar tone; it was from Thorold Dismore, the newspaper proprietor. It too was largely in admiration for Fetters's work, and requested that he write a further series of articles. It was very recently dated, so presumably the articles were yet to be written. There was a rough draft of Fetters's acceptance. There was no way of telling whether the final had been sent or not.

Juno held out a letter from the pile she had taken, her eyes filled with distress. It was from Adinett. Charlotte read:

My dear Martin,

What a marvelous piece you have written. I cannot praise you enough for the passion you display. It would be a man devoid of all that distinguishes the civilized from the barbaric who would not be fired by what you have said, and determined at all costs to spend all his strength and his substance in creating a better world.

I have shown it to various people, whom I will not name, for reasons you will know, and they are as profound in their admiration as I am.

I feel there is real hope. It is no longer a time merely of dreams.

I shall see you on Saturday.

John

Charlotte looked up.

Juno stared at her, her eyes wide and hurt. Then she passed over a sheaf of notes for further articles.

Charlotte read them with growing misgiving, then alarm. The mention of reform became more and more specific. The Roman revolution of '48 was referred to with passionate praise. The ancient Roman Republic was held as an ideal and kings as the pattern of tyranny. The invitation to a modern republic, after the overthrow of the monarchy, was unmistakable.

There were oblique references to a secret society whose members were dedicated to the continuation of the royal house in its power and wealth, by any means at all, and the

141

implication was there that even the shedding of blood was not beyond them if the threat was serious enough.

Charlotte put down the final sheet and looked across at Juno, who sat white-faced, her shoulders slumped.

"Is that possible?" Juno asked hoarsely. "Do you think they really planned a republic here in England?"

"Yes . . ." It seemed a brutal answer, but a denial would have been a lie neither of them could have believed.

Juno sat quite still, leaning a little on the desk, as if she needed its strength to support her. "After . . . after the Queen dies?"

"Perhaps."

Juno shook her head. "That's too soon. It could be any day. She's into her seventies. What about the Prince of Wales? What are they going to do about him?"

"There's nothing said here," Charlotte answered very quietly. "I think they would be too careful to commit that to writing, if there is a plan, not just dreaming. Especially if there is a secret society, as they say."

"I understand reform." Juno searched for words. "I want it too. There's terrible poverty and injustice. Funny how they don't mention women." She tried to smile, but it was too difficult. "They don't say anything about us having more rights or more voice in decisions, even for our own children." She shook her head, her lips quivering. "But I don't want this!" She gestured with one hand as if to push it away. "I know Martin admired republics, their ideals, their equality, but I never had the slightest idea he wanted one for us! I don't . . . I don't want so much change." She gulped. "Not so violently. I like too much of what we have. It is who we are . . . who we have always been." She looked at Charlotte pleadingly, willing her to understand.

"But we are the fortunate ones," Charlotte pointed out. "And we are a very small minority."

"Is that why he was killed?" Juno asked the question that hung between them. "Adinett was actually a member of this other society, the secret one, and he murdered Martin because of this . . . plan for a republic?"

"It would explain why he said nothing, even in his own defense." Charlotte's mind was racing. Was the Inner Circle monarchist? Was that what it was about, and Adinett had discovered what his friend planned, that his idealism was not merely about the glories of the past or the tragedies of '48, but meant something urgent and immediate for the future?

Even if it were true, how could that help Thomas?

Juno was still sitting and staring across the room. Something inside her had crumbled. The man she had loved for so many years had suddenly moved, revealing another dimension which altered everything that was already perceived, making it radically different, dangerous . . . perhaps irredeemably ugly.

Charlotte was sorry, desperately sorry, and she wanted to say so, but that would be condescending, as if she had uncovered this situation alone, relegating Juno to a spectator, a sufferer, not a protagonist.

"Do you have a safe?" she said aloud.

"Do you think there's more in it?" Juno asked miserably.

"I don't know, but I think you should keep these letters and papers there, since this drawer won't lock anymore. You shouldn't destroy them yet, because we are only guessing what they mean. We may be wrong."

There was no light in Juno's eyes. "You don't believe that, and neither do I. Martin cared intensely about reform. Even now I can look back and remember things he said about republics as opposed to monarchies. I've heard him criticize the Prince of Wales and the Queen. He said that if the Queen had been answerable to the people of Britain, like any other holder of office, she would have been dismissed years ago. Who else can afford to abandon their job because they lost a husband or wife?"

"No one," Charlotte agreed. "And there are plenty of other people who say the same. I think I do myself. That doesn't mean I would rather have a republic . . . or even if I would, that I would do anything to make that happen."

Juno gathered the papers together, frowning slightly.

"There's no proof in these," she said quietly, as if the words hurt her and she had to force them out.

Charlotte waited, uncertain, her mind fumbling towards the next conclusion. Before she reached it Juno spoke.

"There are other papers somewhere, ones that are more specific. I have to find them. I have to know what he meant to do . . . as if it were only what he wished for."

Charlotte felt the tightness inside her. "Are you sure?"

"Wouldn't you have to know?" Juno asked.

"Yes . . . I . . . I think so. But I meant are you sure there is anything more to find?"

"Oh, yes." There was no doubt in Juno's voice. "These are only bits of something, notes. I may be entirely wrong about what Martin was working on, but I know the way he worked. He was meticulous. He never trusted solely to memory."

"Where would it be?"

"I don't—"

They were interrupted by the maid, who had come to say that Mr. Reginald Gleave had called, and begged her pardon for the inconvenience of the hour, but he would very much like to see her, and commitments he could not escape made the traditional time impossible for him.

Juno looked startled. She turned to Charlotte.

"I'll wait wherever you wish," Charlotte said quickly.

Juno swallowed. "I will receive him in the withdrawing room," she told the maid. "Give me five minutes, then show him in." As soon as the maid had gone she turned to Charlotte. "What on earth can he want? He defended Adinett!"

"You don't have to see him." Charlotte spoke out of compassion, but she knew it was the refusal of an opportunity to learn more. Juno was exhausted, frightened of what she might discover, and profoundly alone. "I'll go and tell him you are unwell if you wish."

"No . . . no. But I should be grateful if you would remain with me. I think that would be quite seemly, don't you?"

Charlotte smiled. "Of course."

Gleave looked startled when he was shown in and saw two women present. It was immediately apparent that he had not met Juno before and was for a moment uncertain which she was.

"I am Juno Fetters," Juno said coolly. "This is my friend, Mrs. Pitt." There was a challenge in her voice, the lift of her chin. He must remember the name and not fail to associate it. Charlotte saw the recognition in his eyes, and the flare of anger.

"How do you do, Mrs. Fetters. Pitt. I had no idea you were acquainted." He bowed very slightly.

Charlotte regarded him with interest. He was not particularly tall but he gave an impression of great size because of his powerful shoulders and heavy neck. It was not a face she liked, but there was no mistaking the intelligence in it, or the immense strength of will. Was he no more than a passionate advocate who had lost a case, he believed unjustly? Or was he a member of a secret and violent society prepared to commit private murder or public riot and insurrection to achieve its ideals?

She looked at his face, his eyes, and had no idea.

"What may I do for you, Mr. Gleave?" Juno asked with a little shiver in her voice.

Gleave's eyes moved from Charlotte's back to hers.

"First, may I offer my condolences upon your loss, Mrs. Fetters? Your husband was a fine man in every respect. No one else's grief can match yours, of course; nevertheless, we are all the poorer for his passing. He was a man of high morality and great intellectual gifts."

"Thank you," she said politely, her expression almost bordering on impatience. They both knew he had not come to tell her this. It would have been better said in correspondence, more memorable and less intrusive.

Gleave lowered his gaze, as if he felt awkward.

"Mrs. Fetters, I care very much that you should know that I defended John Adinett because I believed him innocent, not because were he guilty I would have imagined any excuse whatever for what he did." He looked up quickly. "I still find it almost impossible to imagine that he could have done such a thing. There could have been . . . no . . . reason!"

Charlotte realized with a shiver that he was watching Juno intently, his eyes fixed upon her face so completely he must see even the faintest flicker of breath, the wavering of her gaze for an instant. He watched as an animal watches its prey. He had come to learn how much she knew, if she had found anything, guessed or suspected.

Charlotte willed Juno to tell him nothing, to be bland, innocent, even stupid if necessary. Should she intervene, take matters into her own hands? Or would that tell him she was afraid, which could only be because she knew something? She drew in her breath and let it out again.

"No," Juno said slowly. "Of course he wouldn't. I admit, I don't understand it either." She allowed herself to relax, deliberately, starting with her hands. She even smiled very slightly. "I always saw them as the best of friends." She added nothing more, leaving him to pick up the thread.

It was not what he had expected. For a moment uncertainty flashed in his face, then it was gone. His expression eased.

"That is what you saw also?" He smiled back at her, avoiding Charlotte's gaze. "I wondered if perhaps you had any perception as to what may have gone so tragically wrong . . . not evidence, of course," he added hastily, "or you would have spoken of it to the appropriate authorities. Just thoughts, intuition even, born of your understanding of your husband."

Juno said nothing.

Gleave's voice was unctuous, but Charlotte saw the flash of doubt again. He had not expected the conversation to go this way. He was not controlling it as he had intended. Juno was obliging him to speak more because she offered less. Now he had to explain his interest.

"I apologize for pursuing it, Mrs. Fetters. The case troubles me still because it seems so . . . unresolved. I . . ." He shook his head a little. "I feel as if I failed."

"I think we all failed to understand, Mr. Gleave," Juno replied. "I wish I could clarify it for you, but I am afraid I cannot."

"It must be very troubling for you also." His voice was full of sympathy. "It is part of grief to wish to understand."

146

"You are very kind," she said simply.

A flare of interest quickened in him, so faint as to be almost indiscernible, but Charlotte knew Juno had made a mistake. She had been careful rather than frank. Should she intervene? Or would that only make it worse? Again she hovered on the edge of speech. What was Gleave? Simply a defense lawyer who had lost a client he felt to be innocent, and perhaps for which his peers held him accountable? Or a member of a powerful and terrible secret society, here to judge how much the widow knew, if there were papers, evidence they needed to destroy?

"I confess," Juno went on suddenly, "I should like to know why . . . what . . ." She shook her head, and her eyes filled with tears. "Why Martin died. And I don't! It doesn't make any sense at all."

Gleave responded the only way possible to him. "I am so sorry, Mrs. Fetters. I did not mean to distress you. It was clumsy of me to have raised the subject at all. Do forgive me." She shook her head. "I understand, Mr. Gleave. You had faith in your client. You must be distressed also. There is nothing to forgive. In truth, I would have liked to ask you if you know the reason, but of course even if you did, you would not be free to say so. Now at least you have made it plain you know no more than I do. I am grateful for that. Perhaps now I shall be able to let it go and think of other things."

"Yes . . . yes, that would be best," he agreed, and for the first time he looked fully at Charlotte. His eyes were dark, clever, searching her mind, perhaps warning her also.

"Delighted to have met you, Mrs. Pitt." He added nothing more, but meanings unsaid hung in the air.

"And you, Mr. Gleave," she responded charmingly.

As soon as he was gone and the door closed behind him, Juno turned to her. Her face was pale and her body was trembling.

"He wanted to know what we have found," she said huskily. "That's why he came . . . isn't it?"

"Yes, I think so," Charlotte agreed. "Which means you are

right in there is something more. And he doesn't know where it is either . . . but it matters!"

Juno shivered. "Then we must find it! Will you help me?"

"Of course."

"Thank you. I shall think where to look. Now, would you like a cup of tea? I would!"

Charlotte had not told Vespasia what had happened to Pitt. At first she was embarrassed to, although it was in no way due to his negligence, rather the opposite. Still, she felt it a blow she would rather not allow anyone else to know of, particularly someone whose opinion Pitt cared about as much as he did Vespasia's.

However, now the whole matter had become one she was unable to carry alone, and there was no one else she could trust both as to loyalty and ability to understand the issues and be able to advise on what next to do.

Therefore she arrived on Vespasia's doorstep the morning after having visited Juno Fetters. She was shown in by the maid. Vespasia was at breakfast, and invited Charlotte to join her in the yellow-and-gold breakfast room, at least for tea.

"You look a little harassed, my dear," she observed gently, spreading her wafer-thin toast with a smear of butter and a large dollop of apricot preserves. "I presume you have come to tell me about it?"

Charlotte was glad not to pretend. "Yes. Actually it happened three weeks ago, but I only realized how serious it was yesterday, I really have no idea what to do."

"Does Thomas not have an opinion?" Vespasia frowned and allowed her toast to go unregarded.

"Thomas has been removed from Bow Street and put into Special Branch to work in Spitalfields." Charlotte let the words pour out with all the distress she felt, the wondering and the fear she had to hide from the children, even in part from Gracie.

"Worst of all, he has to live there. I haven't seen him. I can't even write to him because I don't know where he is! He writes to me—but I can't answer!"

"I'm so sorry, my dear," Vespasia said, sorrow filling her face. If she was angry also, it came second. She had seen too much injustice to be surprised anymore.

"It is partly in revenge for his testimony against John Adinett," Charlotte explained. "And partly to protect him . . . from the Inner Circle."

"I see." Vespasia bit into the toast delicately. The maid brought fresh tea and poured it for Charlotte.

When the maid had gone, Charlotte resumed her story. She told Vespasia how she had determined to find the motive for Martin Fetters's death, and had gone to visit Juno for that purpose. She recounted as exactly as she could recall what she had read in the papers in Fetters's desk, and then spoke of Gleave's visit.

Vespasia remained silent for several minutes.

"This is extremely unpleasant," she said at length. "You are quite right to be afraid. It is also highly dangerous. I am inclined to share your opinion as to the purpose of Reginald Gleave's visit to Mrs. Fetters. We must assume that he has a profound vested interest in the matter and may be prepared to pursue it regardless of what means may be necessary."

"Including violence?" Charlotte made it only half a question.

Vespasia made no pretense. "Assuredly, if there is no other opportunity open to him. You must be extremely discreet."

Charlotte smiled in spite of herself. "Anyone else would have said I must leave it alone."

The light shone in Vespasia's silver eyes. "And would you have?"

"No . . ."

"Good. If you had said yes it would either have been a lie, and I should not care to be lied to, or it would have been the truth, and I should have been very disappointed in you." She leaned forward a little across the polished table. "But I mean the warning very seriously, Charlotte. I am not certain how much there is at stake, but I think it is a very great deal. The Prince of Wales is ill-advised, at best. At worst he is a spendthrift and careless of his reputation for financial honesty. Victoria has

149

long since lost her sense of duty. Between them they have invited republican sentiment to flourish, and it has done so. I had not realized it was so close to violence, or involved men as much admired as Martin Fetters. But what you have discovered would explain his death as nothing else so far has done."

Charlotte realized she had been half hoping Vespasia would say she was mistaken, that there was some other, more personal answer, and society as they were familiar with it was in no danger. Her agreement swept away the last pretense.

"Is it the Inner Circle who support the monarchy at any cost?" Charlotte asked, lowering her voice in spite of the fact there was no one to overhear them.

"I don't know," Vespasia admitted. "I do not know what their aims are, but I have no doubt they are willing to follow them regardless of the rest of us.

"I think it is best you keep silent," Vespasia went on gravely. "Speak to no one. I believe Cornwallis is an honorable man, but I do not know it beyond doubt. If what you have suggested is true, then we have stumbled into something of immense power, and one murder more or less will be of no consequence at all, except to the victim and those who loved him or her. I hope Mrs. Fetters will do the same."

Charlotte felt numb. What had begun as her private sense of outrage at injustice to Pitt had developed into a conspiracy that could threaten everything she knew.

"What are we going to do?" she asked, staring at Vespasia.

"I have no idea," Vespasia confessed. "At least not yet."

After Charlotte had left, looking confused and deeply unhappy, Vespasia sat for a long time in the golden room, staring out of the window and across the lawn. She had lived through the whole of Victoria's reign. Forty years ago England had seemed the most stable place in the world, the one country where all the values were certain, money kept its worth, church bells rang on Sundays, and parsons preached of good and evil and few doubted them. Everyone knew their places and largely accepted them. The future stretched out ahead endlessly.

That world was gone, like summer flowers.

She was startled how angry she was that Pitt should have been robbed of his position and his life at home, and sent to work in Spitalfields, almost certainly uselessly. But if Cornwallis was the man Vespasia judged him to be, then at least Pitt was relatively safe from the vengeance of the Inner Circle; that was one good thing.

She no longer received the vast number of invitations she once had, but there were still several from which to choose. Today she could attend a garden party at Astbury House, if she wished to. She had meant to decline, and had even said as much to Lady Weston yesterday. But she knew various people who would be there—Randolph Churchill and Ardal Juster, among others. She would accept after all. Perhaps she would see Somerset Carlisle. He was one man she would trust.

The afternoon was fine and warm, and the gardens were in full bloom. It could not have been a better day for a party in the open air. Vespasia arrived late, as was her habit now, and found the lawns bright with the silks and muslins of beautiful gowns, the cartwheels of hats decked with blossom, swathed with gauze and tulle, and like everyone else she was in constant danger of being skewered by the point of some carelessly wielded parasol.

She wore a gown of two shades of lavender and gray, and a hat with a brim which swept up like a bird's wing, arching rakishly to one side. Only a woman who did not care in the slightest what others thought would dare to choose such a thing.

"Marvelous, my dear," Lady Weston said coldly. "Quite unique, I'm sure." By which she meant it was out of fashion and no one else would be caught wearing it.

"Thank you," Vespasia said with a dazzling smile. "How generous of you." She glanced up and down Lady Weston's unimaginative blue dress with total dismissal. "Such a wonderful gift."

"I beg your pardon?" Lady Weston was confused.

"The modesty to admire others," Vespasia explained, then,

with another smile, flicked her skirt and left Lady Weston furious, knowing she had been bested and only now realizing how.

Vespasia passed the newspaper proprietor Thorold Dismore, whose keen face was sharp with heightened emotion. He was talking with Sissons, the sugar manufacturer. This time Sissons too seemed to be driven by some vigor and enthusiasm. He was barely recognizable as the same man who had been such a thundering bore with the Prince of Wales.

Vespasia watched for a moment with interest at the change in him, wondering what they could be discussing which could so engage them both. Dismore was passionate, eccentric, a crusader for causes in spite of being born to wealth and position. He was a brilliant speaker, a wit at times, if not on the subject of political reform.

Sissons was self-made and had seemed leaden of intellect, socially inept when faced with royalty. Perhaps he was one of those who simply freeze when in the presence of one in direct line to the throne. With some people it was genius which paralyzed them, with some beauty, with a few it was rank.

Still, she was curious to know what they held in common that so engrossed them.

She was never to know. She found herself face-to-face with Charles Voisey, whose eyes were narrowed against the sun. She could not read the emotion in his face. She had no idea whether he liked or disliked her, admired or despised her, or even dismissed her from his thoughts the moment she was out of sight. It was not a feeling she found comfortable.

"Good afternoon, Lady Vespasia," he said politely. "A beautiful garden." He looked around them at the profusion of color and shape, the dark, trimmed hedges, the herbaceous borders, the smooth lawn and a stand of luminous purple irises in bloom with the light through their curved petals. It was lazy in the warmth, dizzy with perfume. "So very English," he added.

So it was. And even as they stood there she remembered the heat of Rome, the dark cypresses, the sound of falling water from the fountains, like music in stone. During the days her eyes had been narrowed against the lush sun, but in the evening the light was soft, ocher and rose, bathing everything in a beauty that healed over the scars of violence and neglect.

But that was to do with Mario Corena, not this man in front of her. It was a different battle, different ideals. Now she must think of Pitt and the monstrous conspiracy of which he was one of the victims.

"Indeed," she replied with equally distant courtesy. "There is something particularly rich about these few weeks of high summer. Perhaps because they are so brief and so uncertain. Tomorrow it may rain."

His eyes wandered very slightly. "You sound very reflective, Lady Vespasia, and a trifle sad." It was not quite a question.

She looked at his face in the unforgiving sunlight. It found every flaw, every trace left by passion, temper, or pain. How much had it hurt him that Adinett had hanged? She had heard a raw note of rage when he had spoken at the reception, before the appeal. And yet he had been one of the judges who had been of the majority opinion, for conviction. But since it had been four to one, had he voted against, it would have betrayed his loyalty without altering the outcome. That must have galled him to the soul!

Was he driven by personal friendship or political passion? Or simply a belief in John Adinett's innocence? The prosecution had never been able even to suggest a motive for murder, let alone prove one.

"Of course," she replied noncommittally. "Part of the nature of one's joy in summer's fleeting beauty is the knowledge that it will pass too soon, and the certainty that it will come again, even if we will not all see it."

He was watching her intently now, all pretense of casual politeness gone. "We do not all see it now, Lady Vespasia."

She thought of Pitt in Spitalfields, and Adinett in his grave, and the unnamed millions who did not stand amid the flowers in the sun. There was no time to play.

"Very few of us do, Mr. Voisey," she agreed. "But at least it exists, and that is hopeful. Better flowers bloom for a few than not at all."

153

"As long as we are of the few!" he returned instantly, and this time there was no disguising the bitterness in his face.

She smiled very slowly; there was no anger in her for his rudeness. It had been an accusation.

Doubt flickered in his eyes that perhaps he had made an error. She had wished him to show his hand, and he had done so. It cost him an effort; he was not a man who smiled superficially, but his face relaxed now, and he smiled at her widely, showing excellent teeth.

"Of course, or how else would we speak of them, except in dream? But I know you have worked for reforms, as I have, and injustice outrages you also."

Now she was uncertain. He was not an easy man, but perhaps it was a rare integrity which made him so. It was not impossible.

Had Adinett killed Martin Fetters to prevent a republican revolution in England? That was a very different thing from reform by changing the law, by persuasion of the people who had the power to act.

She smiled back at him, and this time she meant it.

A moment later they were joined by Lord Randolph Churchill, and the conversation was no longer personal. With an election so close, naturally politics arose: Gladstone and the whole troubled issue of Irish Home Rule, the rise of anarchy across Europe, and dynamiters here in London.

"The whole East End is like a powder keg," Churchill said softly to Voisey, apparently having forgotten Vespasia was still within earshot. "It will only take the right spark and it will all go up!"

"What are you doing?" Voisey asked, his voice full of concern, his brow puckered.

"I need to know whom I can trust and whom I can't," Churchill replied bitterly.

A cautious expression flickered in Voisey's face. "You need the Queen to come out of seclusion and start pleasing the public again, and the Prince of Wales to pay his debts and stop living as if there were no tomorrow—and no reckoning."

"Given all that I shouldn't have a problem," Churchill rejoined. "I knew Warren, and Abberline to a degree, but I'm not sure of Narraway. Clever, certainly, but I don't know where his loyalties are, if it comes to it!"

Voisey smiled.

A group of young women passed, laughing together, glancing sideways and hastily composing themselves to a more decorous manner. They were pretty, fair-skinned and blemishless, dressed in pastel laces and muslin, skirts swirling.

Vespasia had no hunger to be their age again, for all its hope and innocence. Her life had been rich, her regrets were few; there had been an act of selfishness or stupidity here and there, but never for anything she had failed to grasp, nothing flinched from out of cowardice—although perhaps there should have been.

She did not find Somerset Carlisle and was conscious of a feeling of disappointment, suddenly aware that she had been standing a long time. She was about to excuse herself and leave when she was aware of hearing Churchill's voice again just beyond a rose arbor. He was speaking hurriedly, and she could barely distinguish the words.

". . . refer to it again! It has been dealt with. It won't happen again."

"It had damned well better not!" another voice said in hardly more than a whisper, the emotion in it so intense the voice was unrecognizable. "Another conspiracy like that could mean the end—and I don't say that lightly!"

"They're all dead, God help us," Churchill replied hoarsely. "What did you think we were going to do—pay blackmail? And where do you imagine the end of that would be?"

"In the grave," came the response. "Where it belongs."

At last Vespasia turned away. She had no idea of the meaning of what she had overheard.

Ahead of her, Lady Weston was telling an admirer about Oscar Wilde's latest play, *Lady Windermere's Fan*. They both laughed.

Vespasia moved out into the sunlight and joined them, for once actually intruding into someone else's conversation. It

155

was sane, trivial, funny, and she desperately needed to be part of it. It was brightly glittering and familiar. She would hold on to it as long as she could.

7

TILLMAN WAS STRETCHED to the end of his patience, trying to keep his attention on the string of burglaries that had been assigned to him. All the time he was asking questions, looking at pictures of jewelry, his mind was on Pitt in Spitalfields, and what Adinett had been doing in Cleveland Street that could possibly have been of such intense interest to Lyndon Remus.

His intelligence told him that if he did not apply his mind to the problem of the robberies he would not solve them, and that would do nothing but add to his troubles. Nevertheless his imagination wandered, and completely uncharacteristically, as soon as the hour came when he could excuse himself from duty for the day, he did so. Without waiting for a word from anyone, he left Bow Street and started making serious enquiries as to the habits of Remus: where he lived, where he ate, which public houses he frequented and to whom he sold the majority of his stories. That pattern had changed over the last year or so, there being a steady increase in the number sold to Thorold Dismore, until over the months of May and June it had been almost exclusively so.

It took him until nearly midnight, after the public houses closed, before he had sufficient information to feel he could find Remus when he wanted him. He would lie to his immediate superior in the morning, a thing he had never done before. There was no evasion that would cover the situation, or

157

his driving need to follow this far more urgent mystery. He would have to find an excuse later, if he were caught.

He slept badly, even though his bed was comfortable enough. He woke early, partly because his mind was teeming with ideas about all manner of personal vices or secrets that Adinett might have found in Mile End, and over which Martin Fetters had in some way threatened him. Nothing he thought of seemed to match his impression of the small tobacconist's shop on such an ordinary street.

He had a quick cup of tea in the kitchen and bought a sandwich from the first peddler he passed as he hurried to the corner opposite Remus's lodgings so he could follow him wherever he might go.

He had nearly two hours to wait, and was angry and miserable by the time Remus finally emerged looking freshly shaved, clean white collar high around his neck, and stiff enough to be uncomfortable. His hair was brushed back, still damp, and his face was sharp and eager as he walked rapidly within a few yards of Tellman, who was standing head down in the arch of a doorway. Remus was obviously intent upon where he was going and all but oblivious to anyone else on the footpath.

Tellman turned and followed him some fifteen yards behind, but prepared to move closer if the streets should become more crowded and he was faced with the prospect of losing him.

Half a mile later he had to sprint and only just caught the same omnibus, where he collapsed in a seat next to a fat man in a striped coat who looked at him with amusement. Tellman gasped for breath and cursed his overcaution. Never once had Remus glanced behind him. His mind was apparently absorbed in his purpose, whatever it was.

Tellman was perfectly aware it might have nothing whatsoever to do with Pitt's case. He could have concluded that story already and have found anything, or nothing. But Tellman had scanned the newspapers every morning for articles to do with Adinett, or Martin Fetters, or even a byline for Remus, and found nothing. The front pages were all filled with the horror of the Lambeth poisonings. Seemingly there were seven young prostitutes dead already. Either the Cleveland Street story had been eclipsed by this latest atrocity, or else Remus was still pursuing it . . . apparently towards St. Pancras.

Remus got off the bus and Tellman followed him, taking care not to get too close, but still Remus did not look behind him. It was now mid-morning; the streets were busy and becoming choked with traffic.

Remus crossed the street, tipped the urchin sweeping the dung away, and increased his speed on the far side. A moment later he went up the steps of the St. Pancras Infirmary.

A second hospital! Tellman still had no idea why Remus had gone to Guy's, on the other side of the river.

He ran up behind him, glad he had brought a dark-colored cloth cap which he could pull forward to shade his face. Again, Remus made a brief enquiry of the hall porter, then turned and went towards the administration offices, walking rapidly, shoulders forward, arms swinging. Was he after the same thing as he had been at Guy's? Was it because he had failed to find whatever it was the first time? Or was there something to compare?

Remus's footsteps echoed on the hard floor ahead of him, and Tellman's own seemed like a mockery behind. He wondered that Remus did not turn to see who it was.

Two nurses passed, going in the opposite direction, middle-aged women with tired faces. One carried a pail with a lid on it, and from the angle of her body, it was heavy. The other carried a bundle of soiled sheets and kept stopping to pick up the trailing ends.

Remus turned right, went up a short flight of steps and knocked on a door. It was opened and he went in. A small notice said that it was the records office.

Tellman followed immediately behind. There was nothing to be learned standing outside.

It was a kind of waiting room, and a bald man leaned on a counter. There were shelves of files and paper folders behind him. Three other people were there seeking information of one sort or another. Two were men in dark, ill-fitting suits; from

159

their resemblance to each other they were possibly brothers. The third was an elderly woman with a battered straw hat.

Remus took his place in the queue, shifting from one foot to the other with impatience.

Tellman stood closer to the door, trying to be inconspicuous. He stared at the floor, keeping his head down so his cap fell forward naturally, obscuring his face.

He could still watch Remus's back, see his shoulders high and tight, his hands clenching and unclenching behind him. What was he seeking that was so important to him he was unaware of being followed? Tellman could almost smell the excitement in him, and he had not even the shred of an idea what it was about, except that it had to do with John Adinett.

The two brothers had learned what they wished and went out together. The woman moved up.

It was several more minutes before she was satisfied and at last it was Remus's turn.

"Good morning, sir," he said cheerfully. "I am informed that you are the right person to ask if I have any enquiries about the patients in the infirmary. They say you know more about the place than any other man."

"Do they?" The man was not thawed so easily. "And what was it yer would be wanting to know, then?" He pushed out his lower lip. "I'm guessin' it in't about your own family, or yer'd 'a said so simple enough. Nor about the price of bein' cared for, which you could find out without the least trouble. You look like far too smart a gentleman to need my help for anything easy."

Remus was taken aback but he made the best of it very quickly.

"Of course," he agreed. "I'm trying to trace a man who may be a bigamist, at least that is what a certain lady has told me. I'm not so sure."

The clerk drew in his breath to make some remark, then apparently thought better of it. "And you think he may be 'ere, sir? I got records of the past, not who's 'ere now."

"No, not now," Remus replied. "I think he may have died here, which closes the matter anyway."

"So what's 'is name, then?"

"Crook. William Crook," Remus replied, his voice shaking a little. He seemed to be short of breath, and Tellman could see the back of his neck, where his stiff collar was so tight it pinched the flesh. "Did he die here, back end of last year?" Remus went on.

"And if 'e did?" the clerk questioned.

"Did he?" Remus leaned over the counter, his voice rising, his body rigid. "I . . . I need to know!"

"Yes, 'e did, poor soul," the man answered respectfully. "So do scores o' folk every year. You could find that out by lookin' in public records."

"I know!" Remus was not deterred. "What day did he die?"

The man remained motionless.

Remus put half a crown on the counter. "Look up the record for me, and tell me what religion he was."

"Wot religion?"

"Yes—isn't that plain enough? And what family: who came to see him, who outlived him."

The man looked at the half crown—a considerable amount of money—and decided it was easily enough earned. He swiveled around to the shelves behind him and took down a large blue bound ledger and opened it. Remus's eyes never left him. He was still oblivious of Tellman standing near the door, or of the thin man with sandy hair who came in the moment after.

Tellman racked his brain. Who was William Crook, and why did his death in an infirmary matter? Or his religion? Since he had died last year, what could he possibly have to do with Adinett or Martin Fetters? Was there any way in which he could have been murdered by Adinett, and Fetters had known of it? That would be motive to kill him.

The clerk looked up. "Died fourth o' December. A Roman Catholic, 'e was, accordin' ter 'is widder, Sarah, wot registered 'im."

Remus leaned forward. His voice was carefully controlled,

161

but a pitch higher. "A Roman Catholic. Are you certain? That's what the record says?"

The clerk was irritated. "I jus' told yer, didn't I?"

"And his address before he came here?"

The clerk looked down at the page and hesitated.

Remus understood and produced another shilling, putting it on the counter with a sharp click.

"Nine St. Pancras Street," the clerk replied.

"St. Pancras Street!" Remus was stunned, his voice empty with disbelief. "Are you certain? Not Cleveland Street?"

"St. Pancras Street," the clerk repeated.

"How long had he been there?" Remus demanded.

" 'Ow would I know?" the clerk said reasonably.

"Number nine?"

"That's right."

"Thank you." Remus turned and left, his head bent in thought, and he did not even notice Tellman go after him without having taken his turn at the counter.

Tellman followed at a slight distance as Remus retraced his steps to the street, still apparently consumed in disappointment and confusion, but he did not hesitate to plunge into the crowd and walk briskly towards the end of St. Pancras Street and find number 9. He knocked and stepped back to wait.

Tellman remained on the footpath on the opposite side. Had he crossed to be close enough to overhear, even Remus in his preoccupied state would have noticed him.

The door was opened by a large woman, very tall indeed—Tellman judged her to be over six feet—and with a fierce expression.

Remus was very deferential, as if he held her in the greatest respect, and she seemed to soften a little. They spoke for several minutes, then Remus half bowed, doffed his hat and turned and walked away very quickly, so excited he all but skipped a couple of steps, and Tellman had to run to keep up with him.

Remus went straight to the St. Pancras railway station and in at the main entrance.

Tellman fished in his pockets and felt three half crowns, a

couple of shillings and a few pennies. Probably Remus was only going a stop or two. It would be easy enough to follow him—but was it worth the risk? Presumably the tall woman at the door of number 9 had been William Crook's widow, Sarah. What had she told Remus that had banished his confusion and despondency? It must be that her late husband was the same William Crook who had once lived in Cleveland Street, or had some other close connection with it. They had spoken for several minutes. She must have told him more than he wished to know. Something about Adinett?

Remus went up to the ticket window.

At least Tellman should find out where he was going. There were other people in the hall. He could move closer without attracting attention. He kept half behind a young woman with a cloth bag and a wide, light blue skirt.

"Return to Northampton, please," Remus asked, his voice quick and excited. "When is the next train?"

"Not for another hour yet, sir," the ticket seller replied. "That'll be four shillings and eight pence. Change at Bedford."

Remus handed over the money and took the ticket.

Tellman turned away quickly and walked out of the station hall, down the steps and into the street. Northampton? That was miles away! What possible connection could be there? It would cost him both time and money, neither of which he could afford. He was a careful man, not impulsive. To follow Remus there would be a terrible risk.

Without making a deliberate decision he began walking back towards the infirmary. He had an hour before the train left; he could allow forty minutes at least and still give himself time to return, buy a ticket and catch the train—if he wanted to.

Who was William Crook? Why did his religion matter? What had Remus asked his widow, apart from whether they had any connection with Cleveland Street? Tellman was angry with himself for pursuing this at all, and angry with everyone else because Pitt was in trouble and no one was doing anything about it. There was injustice everywhere, while people went about their own affairs and looked the other way.

163

He thought how he would tell Gracie that it all made very little sense, and possibly had nothing to do with Adinett anyway. Every time he tried for the right words they sounded like excuses. He could see her face in his mind so clearly he was startled. He could picture her exactly, the color of her eyes, the light on her skin, the shadow of her lashes, the way she always pulled a strand or two of her hair a little too tightly at her right brow. The curve of her mouth was as familiar to him as his own in the shaving glass.

She would not accept defeat. She would despise him for it. He could see the expression in her eyes now, and it hurt him too much. He could not allow it to happen.

He changed direction and went westward towards number 9 St. Pancras Street. If he stopped to consider what he was doing his nerve would fail, so he did not think. He walked straight up to the door and knocked, his police identification already in his hand.

It was opened by the same giant of a woman.

"Yes?"

"Good morning, ma'am," he said, his breath catching in his throat. He showed her his identification.

She looked at it closely, her face immobile. "All right, Sergeant Tellman, what is it you want?"

Should he try charm or authority? It was difficult to be authoritative with a woman of her size and her frame of mind. He had never felt less like smiling. He must speak; she was losing patience and it was clear in her expression.

"I am investigating a very serious crime, ma'am," he said with more certainty than he felt. "I followed a man here about half an hour ago, average height, light reddish hair, sharp face. I believe he asked you certain questions about the late Mr. William Crook." He took a deep breath. "I need to know what they were, and what you told him."

"Do you? And why would that be, Sergeant?" She had a marked Scottish accent, soft, from the West Coast, surprisingly pleasing.

"I can't tell you why, ma'am. It would be breaking confidence. I just need to know what you told him."

164

"He asked if we used to live in Cleveland Street. Very urgent about it, he was. I'd a mind not to tell him." She sighed. "But what's the use? My daughter Annie used to work in the tobacconist's shop there." There was a sadness in her face which for a moment twisted at Tellman as if he had seen into a terrible grief. Then it was gone, and he heard himself press on.

"What else did he ask, Mrs. Crook?"

"He asked if I were related to J. K. Stephen," she answered him. There was a weariness in her voice as if she had no more will to fight the inevitable. "I'm not, but my husband was. His mother was J. K. Stephen's cousin."

Tellman was puzzled. He had never heard of J. K. Stephen.

"I see." All he knew was that it had mattered to Remus so intently he had gone straight to the station and booked a ticket to Northampton. "Thank you, Mrs. Crook. Was that all he asked?"

"Yes."

"Did he give you a reason why he wanted to know?"

"He said it was to correct a great injustice. I didn't ask him what. It could be any one of a million."

"Yes, it could. He was right in that . . . if that's why he cared." He inclined his head. "Good day, ma'am."

"Good day." She pushed the door closed.

The journey to Northampton was tedious, and Tellman spent the time turning over in his mind all the possibilities he could think of as to what Remus was chasing, getting more and more fanciful as the minutes passed. Perhaps it was all a wild-goose chase? The injustice might have been no more than his way of engaging Mrs. Crook's sympathy. Perhaps it was only some scandal he was pursuing? That was all he had cared about in the Bedford Square case, because the newspapers would buy it fast enough if it increased their readership.

But surely that was not why Adinett had been to Cleveland Street, and also left in excitement and gone to Dismore? He was no chaser of other people's misfortunes.

No, there was a reason here, if Tellman could only find it.

When they reached Northampton, Remus got off the train.

Tellman followed him out of the station into the sunlight, where he immediately took a hansom cab. Tellman engaged the one behind it and gave the driver orders to follow him. Tellman sat forward, anxious and uncomfortable as he moved at a fast pace through the provincial streets until they finally drew up at a grim asylum for the insane.

Tellman waited outside, standing by the gate where he would not be noticed. When Remus emerged nearly an hour later, his face was flushed with excitement, his eyes were brilliant and he walked with such speed, arms swinging, shoulders set, that he could have bumped into Tellman and barely noticed.

Should he follow the reporter again and see where he went to now or go into the asylum himself and find out what he had learned? The latter, definitely. Apart from anything else, he had only a limited time to get to the station and catch the last train to London. It would be difficult enough as it was to explain his absence to Wetron.

He went into the office and presented his police identification. The lie was ready on his tongue.

"I'm investigating a murder. I followed a man from London, about my height, thirty years old or so, reddish colored hair, hazel eyes, eager sort of face. I need you to tell me what he asked you and what you answered him."

The man blinked in surprise, his faded blue eyes fixed on Tellman's face, his hand stopped in the air halfway to his quill pen.

"He wasn't askin' about no murder!" he protested. "Poor soul died as natural as yer like, if yer can call starvin' yerself natural."

"Starving yourself?" Tellman had not known what he was expecting, but not suicide. "Who?"

"Mr. Stephen, of course. That's who he was askin' about."

"Mr. J. K. Stephen?"

"S'right." He sniffed. "Poor soul. Mad as a hatter. But then 'e wouldn't 'a bin in 'ere if 'e were all right, would 'e!"

"And he starved himself?" Tellman repeated.

"Stopped eatin'," the man agreed, his face bleak. "Wouldn't take a thing, not a bite."

"Was he ill? Perhaps he couldn't eat?" Tellman suggested.

" 'E could eat, 'e just stopped sudden." The man sniffed again. "Fourteenth o' January. I remember that, 'cos it were the same day as we 'eard the poor Duke o' Clarence were dead. Reckon that's wot did it. Used ter know the Duke, real well. Talked about 'im. Taught 'im ter paint, so 'e said."

"He did?" Tellman was totally confused. The more he learned the less sense it made. It seemed unlikely that the man who had starved himself to death here in this place knew the Prince of Wales's eldest son. "Are you certain?"

"O' course I'm certain! Why d'yer wanna know?" His look narrowed considerably, and there was a note of suspicion in his voice. He sniffed again, then searched his pockets for a handkerchief.

Tellman controlled himself with an effort. He must not spoil it now.

"Just have to make sure I've got the right man," he lied, hoping it sounded believable.

The man found his handkerchief and blew his nose fiercely.

"Used ter be tutor to the Prince, didn't 'e!" he explained. "Reckon w'en 'e 'eard the poor feller'd died, 'e jus' took it too bad. 'E weren't right in the 'ead any'ow, poor devil."

"When did 'e die?"

"Third o' February," he said, putting his handkerchief away. "That's an' 'orrible way ter go." There was pity in his face. "Seemed ter mean summink ter the feller yer followin', but I'm blessed if I know wot. Some poor, sad lunatic decides ter die—o' grief, for all I know—an' 'e goes rushin' out of 'ere. Went orff like a dog after a rabbit. Fair shakin' wi' excitement, an' that's the truth. I don't know nuthink more."

"Thank you. You've been very helpful." Tellman was suddenly unpleasantly aware of the train timetable. "Thank you!" he repeated, and took his leave, sprinting down the corridor and outside, in search of a cab back to the railway station.

He just caught the train, and was glad to sit back in his seat.

He spent the first hour writing down all he had learned, and the second trying to concoct in his mind a story for tomorrow that would somehow resemble the truth and still satisfy Wetron that he was on justifiable police business. He did not succeed.

Why had poor Stephen chosen to starve himself to death when he heard the news that the young Duke of Clarence had died? And what interest was that to Remus? It was tragic. But then the man had apparently been judged insane anyway, or he would not have been incarcerated in the Northampton asylum.

And what had it to do with William Crook, who had died last December in the St. Pancras Infirmary of perfectly natural causes? What was the connection with the tobacconist's shop in Cleveland Street? Above all, why should John Adinett have cared?

When they reached London, Tellman jumped out onto the platform and turned one way then the other to see Remus. He had almost given up when he saw him climb slowly out of the carriage two ahead of him. He must have fallen asleep. He stumbled a little, then set off towards the exit.

Again Tellman followed, running the risk of being seen rather than that of losing him. Fortunately it was close to the middle of summer, and the long evenings meant that at nine o' clock it was still sufficiently light to keep someone in sight for up to fifteen or twenty yards or more, even along a reasonably busy street.

Remus stopped at a public house and had a meal. He seemed to be in no hurry, and Tellman was on the point of leaving himself, having come to the conclusion that Remus was finished for the day and would shortly go home. Then Remus glanced at his watch and ordered another pint of ale.

So time mattered to him. He was going somewhere, or he expected somebody.

Tellman waited.

In another quarter of an hour Remus stood up and walked out into the street. He hailed a cab, and Tellman very nearly lost him before he could find one himself, urging the driver to follow him and keep up at all costs.

They seemed to be heading in the general direction of Regent's Park. Certainly this was not anywhere near where Remus lived. He was going to meet someone, to keep an appointment. Tellman held up his watch to catch the light of the next lamppost they passed. It was nearly half past nine, and growing darker.

Then without warning the cab stopped and Tellman leapt out.

"What's happened?" he asked abruptly, staring ahead. There were several cabs along the street next to the park.

"That one!" His driver pointed ahead. "That's the one you want. It'll be one and threepence, sir."

This was becoming a truly expensive exercise. Tellman cursed himself for his stupidity, but he paid quickly and walked towards the figure he could see dimly ahead. He recognized him by his gait, the urgency in him, as if he were on the brink of some tremendous discovery.

They were on Albany Street, just short of the entrance to Regent's Park to the left. Tellman could see the Outer Circle quite clearly, and the smooth grass beyond stretching in the dusk all the way to the trees of the Royal Botanical Gardens, about a quarter of a mile away.

Ahead of him, Remus set out to walk towards the park. Once he turned to look behind him, and Tellman stumbled in his step. It was the first time Remus had taken the slightest notice of his surroundings. There was nothing Tellman could do but continue as if this were the most natural thing in the world for him. He swung his arms and increased his pace a fraction.

Remus resumed his own journey, but now looking around. Was he expecting someone, or afraid of being observed?

Tellman moved closer under the shadows of the trees and dropped back a little.

There were several other people out, some in twos and threes, strolling together, one not far off, a man alone. Remus hesitated in his step, peered forward, then seemed satisfied and moved urgently again.

Tellman went after him as close as he dared.

Remus stopped next to the man.

Tellman ached to know what was said, but they spoke in voices little above a whisper. Even starting forward, hat pulled over his brow and walking within ten feet of them, he caught no distinct words, but he noticed their expressions. Remus was fiercely excited and listened to the other man with total attention, not even glancing around as Tellman passed on the other side of the path.

The other man was extremely well dressed, of more than average height, but his bowler hat was drawn so far forward and his coat collar so high that half his face was hidden. All Tellman could see for certain was that his boots were polished leather, beautifully cut, and his coat was fine and fitted him perfectly. It would have cost more than a police sergeant earned in months.

He continued to walk along the Outer Circle to the turnoff back to Albany Street, then went as far as the next omnibus stop to take him home. His mind was whirling. None of it fitted into a pattern, but now he was certain that there was one. He simply had to find it.

The next morning he slept later than he had meant to and arrived at Bow Street only just in time. There was a message waiting for him to report to Wetron's office. He went up with a sinking heart.

This was Pitt's office, even though his personal books and belongings had been removed and replaced already with Wetron's leather-bound volumes. A cricket bat, presumably of some personal significance, hung on the wall, and there was a silver-framed photograph of a fair-haired woman on the desk. Her face was soft and pretty and she wore a pale lace dress.

"Yes sir?" Tellman said without hope.

Wetron leaned back in his chair, his colorless eyebrows raised.

"Would you care to tell me where you were yesterday,

Sergeant? Apparently you found it outside your ability to inform Inspector Cullen . . ."

Tellman had already decided what to say, but it was still difficult. He swallowed hard. "I didn't have the opportunity to tell Inspector Cullen yet, sir. I was following a suspect. If I'd stopped, I'd have lost him."

"And the name of this suspect, Sergeant?" Wetron was staring at him fixedly. He had very clear blue eyes.

Tellman pulled a name out of memory. "Vaughan, sir. He's a known handler of stolen goods."

"I know who Vaughan is," Wetron said tartly. "Did he have the Bratbys' jewels?" There was deep skepticism in his voice.

"No, sir." Tellman had considered embroidering the account, and decided it offered too much scope for being caught out. It was unfortunate that Wetron knew of Vaughan. He had not expected that. Please heaven no one could prove Vaughan had been in custody in some other station!

Wetron's mouth closed in a thin line. "You surprise me. When did you last see Superintendent Pitt, Sergeant Tellman? And your answer had better be the exact truth."

"The last day he was here at Bow Street, sir," Tellman said swiftly, allowing offense to bristle in his tone. "Nor have I written to him or had any other communication, before you ask."

"I hope that is the truth, Sergeant." Wetron's voice was icy. "Your instructions were very clear."

"Very," Tellman agreed stiffly.

Wetron did not blink. "Perhaps you would like to tell me why you were seen by the beat constable calling at Superintendent Pitt's house late in the afternoon two days ago?"

Tellman felt the cold shudder through him. "Certainly, sir," he replied steadily, hoping his color had not changed. "I'm courting the Pitts' maid, Gracie Phipps. I called on her. No doubt the constable reported that I went to the kitchen door. I had a cup of tea there, and then I left. I did not see Mrs. Pitt. I believe she was upstairs with the children."

"You're not being watched, Tellman!" Wetron said, the

faintest color mounting his cheeks. "It was chance that you were observed."

"Yes sir," Tellman responded expressionlessly.

Wetron glanced at him, then down at the papers spread out on the desk in front of him. "Well, you'd better go and report to Cullen. Burglary is important. People expect us to keep their property safe. It's what we are paid for."

"Of course, sir."

"Are you being sarcastic, Tellman?"

Tellman opened his eyes very wide. "Me, sir? Not at all. I'm sure that is what the gentlemen of Parliament pay us for."

"You are damned insolent!" Wetron snapped. "Be careful, Tellman. You are not indispensable."

Wisely, Tellman did not answer this time, but excused himself to go to find Cullen and try to satisfy him as to where he had been and why he had nothing to report.

It was a long, hot and extremely difficult day, mostly spent trudging from one unproductive interview to another. It was not until nearly seven in the evening that Tellman, his feet burning, was able to extricate himself from duty and finally take an omnibus to Keppel Street. He had been waiting since yesterday night to tell Gracie what he had learned.

Fortunately again Charlotte was upstairs with the children. It seemed she had made a habit of reading to them at about this hour.

Gracie was folding linen and it smelled wonderful. Freshly laundered cotton was one of his favorite things. This was rough dry, ready for the iron, warm from the airing rail.

"Well?" she asked as soon as he was inside, before he had even sat down at the table.

"I followed Remus." He made himself comfortable, easing the laces of his boots and hoping she would put the kettle on soon. And he was hungry too. Cullen had not allowed him time to eat since midday.

"W'ere'd 'e go?" She looked at him with rapt attention, the last few pieces of linen forgotten.

"St. Pancras Infirmary, to check on the death of a man called William Crook," he answered, leaning back in the chair.

She looked blank. " 'Oo was 'e?"

"I'm not sure," he admitted. "But he died there naturally, the end of last year. Remus seemed to care that he was Roman Catholic. The only thing I can see that mattered about him was that he had a daughter who worked at the tobacconist's in Cleveland Street—and his mother was cousin to the Mr. Stephen who starved himself to death in the madhouse in Northampton."

"Wot?" She was aghast. "Wot are yer talkin' about?"

He told her briefly about his train journey and what he had learned at the asylum. She sat in complete silence, her eyes fixed on him.

"An' 'e were the teacher o' poor Prince Eddy 'oo just died?"

"That's what they said," he agreed.

She frowned. "Wot's that got ter do wi' Cleveland Street? Wot were Adinett doin' there?"

"I don't know," he had to admit again. "But Remus is sure it all ties together. If you'd seen his face you'd know that. He was like a bloodhound on the scent. He practically quivered with excitement, his face was alight, like a child at Christmas."

"Summink 'appened at Cleveland Street, wot started all this goin'," she said thoughtfully, screwing up her face. "Or else it 'appened arter that, because o' wot 'appened at Cleveland Street. An' Fetters an' Adinett knew about it."

"It looks that way," he agreed. "And I intend to find out what it was."

"You be careful!" she warned him, her face pale, eyes frightened. Unconsciously she reached across the table towards him.

"Don't worry," he answered her. "Remus has no idea I'm following him." He put his hand over hers. He was amazed how small it was, like a child's. She did not pull away from him, and for a moment that was all he could think of.

"Not Remus, yer daft article," she whispered huskily. "Yer new boss wot took Mr. Pitt's place. 'E'll have yer if 'e catches

173

yer out o' line, an' then w'ere will yer be? Out on the street wi' nuffink!"

"I'll be careful," he promised, but he was cold inside. He could not afford to have Cullen complain of him again, or to be seen by anyone where he should not be. He had worked since he was fourteen to reach the position he was in now, and if he were thrown out of the police force he would lose his income, and perhaps his character when he needed references for another job. Although there was no other job he wanted or was qualified to do. His whole life would be damaged, every value he had lived by overturned.

And with no job, and soon no lodgings, how could he ever be the man he wanted to be, like Pitt, with a home and a wife . . . how could he be the man Gracie wanted him to be?

He went on speaking to drive out the thoughts. He was committed now, whatever it cost him. He had to find out the truth—for Pitt, for Gracie, for the sake of honor.

"After Remus got back from Northampton he didn't go home. He had a meal in a public house, then he went by cab to Regent's Park and met a man there, by appointment, because he kept looking at his watch."

"Wot kind o' man?" she asked very quietly, still not moving her hands from his, but keeping them very still, as if not to remind him they were there.

"Very well dressed," he replied, feeling the small bones under his fingers and longing to hold them tighter. "Bit taller than ordinary, wearing a coat with the collar turned up, even at this time of year, and his hat pulled down. I couldn't really see his face. And even though I was only a few yards away, I couldn't hear a word they said."

She nodded without interrupting.

"Then Remus went off quickly again, excited, eager. He's after something so big he hardly knows how to contain himself—or he thinks he is. If it's to do with Adinett, it might be the proof that Mr. Pitt is right."

"I know that," she agreed quickly. "I'll follow 'im. No rozzer's gon' ter notice me, nor think anythin' of it if they do."

"You can't . . ." he began.

174

She took her hands away. "Yeah, I can. Least I can try. 'E don't know me, an' even if 'e saw me, it won't mean anythin' to 'im. Anyway . . . you can't stop me."

"I could tell Mrs. Pitt not to let you off," he pointed out, leaning back in his chair again.

"Yer wouldn't!" The look of dismay in her face was momentarily comical. "What about Mr. Pitt stuck in Spitalfields, an' all the lies they're sayin' about 'im?"

"Well, be careful," he insisted. "Don't follow too close. Just remember where he goes. And come home as soon as it begins to get dark. Don't go into any public houses." He fished in his pockets one after another and took out all his change. He put it on the table. "You'll need money for cabs, or omnibuses."

It was plain in her face that she had not thought of that. She stared across at him, struggling with herself over accepting it.

"Take it!" he ordered. "You can't follow him on foot. And if he goes outside the city again, leave him be. Do you understand?" He looked at her sharply, his stomach knotting. "You're not to go on any trains. No one would know where you are. Anything could happen to you, and where would we even begin to look?"

She swallowed hard. "O'right," she said meekly. "I'll do that."

He was not entirely sure he believed her. He was startled how deeply the fear bit into him that some harm might come to her. He drew breath to say something to stop her from doing it at all, then realized how absurd it would sound. He had no power to command her in anything, as she would be the first to point out. And also it would betray to her how he felt, and he was in no way ready to do that. He did not even know how to deal with it himself, let alone explain it to her. Friendship he could cope with, just. Even that much made demands he was unused to coping with and opened him up to hurt. It was a loss of the independence which had always been his greatest safety.

But he admired her for being willing to take up following Remus in his place. There was a deep warmth inside him when he thought of it. That was a kind of safety also, a knowledge of trust.

"Be careful!" was all he said aloud.

" 'Course I will!" She attempted to be indignant, but her eyes did not leave his, and she stayed still for several minutes before she finally stood up and went to get them both something to eat.

Next morning she asked Charlotte for the day off, saying it was something rather urgent she had to do. She had prepared an explanation if it was asked for, but Charlotte seemed satisfied to busy herself with various domestic chores. It took her mind off her anxieties, and if she had further plans to pursue the case herself, she did not share them.

Gracie took the first opportunity to leave. The last thing she wished for was a discussion which might too easily betray her own intentions.

She had very little idea where to find Lyndon Remus at this hour of the day. It was already nearly ten o'clock. But she knew how to get to Cleveland Street on the omnibus, and that was a very good place to begin.

It was a long ride, and she was glad now of Tellman's money, even though it made her feel uncomfortable to have accepted it. But it was definitely a case of necessity. Something had to be done to help Mr. Pitt, and personal feelings must be set aside. She and Tellman could sort out their relationship later, and if that proved to be difficult, well, they would just have to manage.

She reached the last stop for the omnibus in Mile End Road, and alighted. It was five past eleven. She walked along until she came to Cleveland Street, and turned left. It looked very unremarkable, a great deal wider and cleaner than the street where she had been born and grown up . . . really quite respectable. Not if you compared it with Keppel Street, of course—but then this was the East End.

Where should she start? The direct approach at the tobacconist's, or indirect, asking someone else about them? Indirect was better. If she went there first, and failed, then she would have spoiled it for trying to be discreet.

She looked around at the worn pavements, the uneven cobbles, the grimy, brick-faced buildings, some whose upper windows were broken or boarded. Smoke curled lazily from a few chimneys. Yard or alley entrances gaped darkly.

What shops were there? A maker of clay pipes and an artist's studio. She knew nothing about art, and not much about pipes, but pipes she could guess about. She walked over to the door and went in, the story ready on her tongue.

"Mornin', miss. Can I 'elp yer?" There was a young man, a year or two older than she was, behind the counter.

"Mornin'," she replied cheerfully. "I 'eard yer 'ave the best pipes any place east o' St. Paul's. Matter o' taste, o' course, but I want summink special fer me pa, so wot 'ave yer got?"

The lad grinned. His hair grew in a cowlick at the front, giving him a casual, cheeky expression. "Did yer? Well, 'oever told yer that were right!"

"Were a while back," she responded. " 'E's dead now, poor soul. William Crook. 'Member 'im?"

"Can't say as I do." He shrugged. "But then we gets 'undreds through 'ere. Wot kind of a pipe did yer fancy, then?"

"Maybe it were 'is daughter as bought it for 'im?" she suggested. "She used ter work up at the tobacconist's." She gestured up towards the farthest end of the street. "Knew 'er, didn't yer?"

His face stiffened. "Annie? 'Course I did. She were a decent girl. 'Ave yer seen 'er lately? This year, like?" He looked at her eagerly.

"In't yer seen 'er yerself?" she countered.

"Nobody 'ere seen 'er in more'n five years," he replied sadly. "There were an 'ell of a row one day. A bunch o' strangers, real ruffians, suddenly started ter fight. Bangin' seven bells outa each other, they was. Two carriages come up, one ter number fifteen, w'ere the artist used to be, an' the other ter number six. I remember, 'cos I were out in the street meself. Two men went inter the artist's place, an' a few minutes later they

177

come out again draggin' a young feller wif 'em, fair strugglin' and yellin'. 'E were terrible upset, but din't do 'im no good. They bundled 'im inter the carriage an' drove off like the devil was be'ind 'em."

"And the others?" she said breathlessly.

He leaned forward over the counter. "They went up ter number six, like I said, and they came out carryin' poor Annie, an' she were took, an' all, an' I never seen 'er since then. Nor 'as anyone else, far as I know."

She frowned. It seemed a long time ago for Remus to be interested in now, or John Adinett.

" 'Oo were the feller they took?" she asked.

He shrugged.

"Dunno. Gent, I know that. Lots o' money, an' real classy. Kind o' quiet most o' the time. Nice-lookin', tall wi' fine eyes."

"Were he Annie's lover?" she guessed.

"Reckon so. 'E came 'ere often enough." His face darkened and his tone became defensive. "Though she were a decent girl, Catholic, so don't go readin' nothin' scandalous inter it, because yer got no right."

"Maybe it were a tragic love?" she suggested, seeing the pity in his face. "If 'e weren't Catholic, maybe their families kept 'em apart?"

"Reckon so?" He nodded, eyes sad and far away. "It's a shame. Wot kind o' pipe d'yer want fer yer pa?"

She really could not afford a pipe. She must return as much of Tellman's money to him as she could, and he certainly would have no use for a clay pipe—and she did not want him smoking one anyway.

"I reckon I'd best ask 'im," she said regretfully. "In't the kind o' thing yer can come back wif' if it in't right. Ta fer yer advice." And before he could attempt to persuade her differently, she turned and went out of the door.

In the street she kept walking back the way she had come, towards the Mile End Road, simply because it was familiar and busy, and she had very little idea what lay in the other direction.

Where should she go now? Remus could be anywhere. How much of this had he known? Probably all of it. It seemed to be common knowledge and easily enough obtained. But apparently Remus knew what it meant. He had been elated, and then gone to find out about William Crook's death. Although that was apparently quite ordinary too.

From Cleveland Street he had gone first to Guy's Hospital to ask something. What? Was he looking for William Crook then too? Only one way to find out: go there herself. She would have to invent a good story to explain her interest in that.

It took her all the bus journey back westwards, and south over London Bridge towards Bermondsey and the hospital, before she had worked it out in her mind. If you were going to lie, you might as well do it thoroughly.

She bought a fruit pie and a drink of lemonade from a peddler and stood looking at the river while she consumed them. It was a bright, windy day and there were lots of people out enjoying themselves. There were pleasure boats on the water, flags flying, people clutching onto their hats. Somewhere not very far away the sound of a hurdy-gurdy was cheerful and a little off-key. Half a dozen boys chased each other, shouting and squealing. A couple walked arm in arm, close to each other, the girl's skirts brushing the young man's trousers.

Gracie finished her pie, straightened her shoulders and turned towards Borough High Street and the hospital.

Once inside she went straight to the offices, composing her face into a serious expression and doing her best to look pathetic. She had tried this many years ago, before going to the Pitts' to work. She had been small and thin then, with a sharp little face, usually dirty, and it had been very effective. Now it was not quite so easy. She was a person of some consequence. She was employed by the best detective in London, which meant the best in the world—even if he was temporarily unappreciated.

"What can I do for you?" the old man behind the desk asked her, peering down over the top of his spectacles.

"Please sir, I'm tryin' ter find out wot 'appened ter me

179

grandpa." She guessed that William Crook's age made that the most believable relationship to use.

"Was 'e brought in sick?" the man asked kindly.

"I reckon as 'e must 'a bin." She sniffed. "I 'eard 'e died, but I in't sure."

"What was his name?"

"William Crook. It'd a bin a while back. I only just bin told." She sniffed again.

"William Crook," he repeated, puzzled, pushing his spectacles back up so he could see through them. "Don't recall 'im, not off 'and, like. Yer sure 'e was brought 'ere?"

She tried to look lost and abandoned. "That's wot they tol' me. Yer got nobody called Crook bin' 'ere? Not ever?"

"I dunno about ever." He frowned. "We 'ad an Annie Crook 'ere fer ages. Sir William hisself brought 'er 'ere. Mad, she were, poor soul. Did everything 'e could fer 'er, but it weren't no good."

"Annie?" Gracie gulped, trying not to let the edge of excitement in her voice betray her. "She come 'ere?"

" 'Course." She did a rapid calculation. "She were me aunt. Not that I ever knew 'er, like. She . . . she kind o' vanished, years back, around '87 or '88. Nobody never said as she were mad, poor soul. I suppose they wouldn't, would they?"

"I'm sorry." He shook his head slowly. "It can 'appen to all kinds o' folk. That's wot I told the other young man as asked. But 'e weren't family to 'er." He smiled at her. "She got the very best care there is, I can promise yer that. Yer still want as I should look for yer granpa?"

"No, ta. I reckon as I must 'a got it wrong."

"I'm sorry," he said again.

"Yeah. I am too." She turned and walked out of the office, closing the door quietly behind her and hurrying away before he sensed the excitement inside her.

Once again in the street and the bright sharp wind and the sun, she ran down towards the place where the omnibuses stopped. Now she must go back home and catch up with some of her work. And with luck, Tellman would come this evening and she could tell him what she had found out. He would be impressed—very impressed. She was singing a little song to herself as she stood in the queue.

"You went where?" Tellman demanded, his thin face pale, his jaw tight.

"Cleveland Street," Gracie replied, pouring the tea. "I'll follow Remus tomorrow."

"You won't! You'll stay here and do the work you're supposed to do, where you're safe!" he retorted harshly, leaning forward across the table. There were shadows under his eyes and a smudge on his cheek. She had never seen him look so tired.

He was certainly not going to tell her what she could or could not do . . . but on the other hand, it gave her a pleasant, warm, almost comfortable feeling that he was concerned that she not be in danger. She could hear the edge of fear in his voice and knew that it was real. It might make him furious, and he might very well deny it the next minute, but he cared very much what happened to her. It was in his eyes, and she recognized it with a little bubble of pleasure.

"Don't yer wanna 'ear wot I found out?" she asked, aching to tell him.

"What?" he said grudgingly, sipping the tea.

"There were a girl called Annie Crook, 'oo were the daughter o' William Crook wot died in St. Pancras." Her words fell over each other. "An' she were kidnapped from the tobacconist's in Cleveland Street about five year ago and took ter Guy's 'Ospital, w'ere the poor creature were called mad, an' no one ever seed 'er again." She had the cake out but in her excitement she had forgotten to cut him a slice. "It were somebody called Sir William wot said as she were mad, an' 'e couldn't 'elp 'er no more. An' someone else just asked about 'er too. I reckon as that were Remus. An' that's not all! There were a young man kidnapped from the artist's place in Cleveland

Street the same time, a real fine-lookin' feller wi' good clothes, a gentleman. 'E were taken out kickin' an' strugglin', poor soul."

"Do you know who he was?" He was too elated with the information to remember his anger—or the cake. "Any idea at all?"

"The lad at the pipe-maker's thought 'e were Annie's lover," she answered. "But 'e don't know fer sure. But 'e said as she were a decent girl, Catholic, an' I shouldn't spread scandal about 'er, 'cos it wouldn't be right or true." She took a deep breath. "Maybe their families did it 'cos she were Catholic an' 'e weren't?"

"What could that have to do with Adinett?" He frowned, pursing his lips.

"I dunno yet. Gimme a chance!" she protested. "But there's a lot o' people wot's off their 'eads, poor devils. There's the feller wot died up in Northampton too. D'yer reckon as there's madness somewhere where it really matters, then? Maybe Mr. Fetters knew about it too?"

He was quiet for several minutes. "Maybe," he said at last, but there was no lift in his voice.

"Yer scared, in't yer?" she said softly. "That mebbe it don't 'ave nothin' ter do wi' Mr. Pitt, an' we aren't 'elpin' 'im?" She wished she could say something to comfort him, but it was the truth, and they were in it together, neither pretending. He was on the point of denying it; she could see it in his face as he drew in his breath. Then he changed his mind.

"Yes," he admitted. "Remus thinks he's on a big story, and I wish I believed it was the reason Adinett killed Fetters. But I can't see any way Fetters fits into it at all."

"We will!" she said determinedly. " 'Cos, 'e must 'a done it fer some reason, an' we'll go on until we find out wot it is."

He smiled. "Gracie, you don't know what you're talk-ing about," he said softly, but the light in his eyes denied his words.

"Yeah, I do," she argued, and she leaned forward and kissed him very lightly, then drew back quickly and picked up the knife to cut the cake for him, looking away. She did not see the color rush up his face or his hand tremble so hard he had to leave his cup on the table in case he spilled it.

8

Pɪᴛᴛ ᴄᴏɴᴛɪɴᴜᴇᴅ to work at the silk weaver's and to run as many errands as possible, watching and listening. At night now and then he took a watch at the sugar factory, standing under the shadow of the huge building and hearing the steady hiss of steam from the boilers, kept going around the clock, and the occasional clatter of footsteps across the cobbles. The smell of the waste washed off the syrup filled the darkness like an oversweet rot.

Occasionally he patrolled inside, carrying a lantern along the low passages, hunting the shadows, listening to the myriad small movements. He exchanged a little gossip, but he was an outsider. He would have to be here years before he would be accepted, trusted without question.

Increasingly he heard the ugliness of anger under the surface of what appeared casual conversation. It was everywhere: in the factory, in the streets, in the shops and public houses. A few years ago it would have been a good-natured complaining; now there was an undertone of violence in it, a rage close under the surface.

But the thing that frightened him the most was the hope that flashed every now and again among men sitting and brooding over a pint of ale, the whispers that things would soon change. They were not victims of fate but protagonists who governed their own lives.

He was also aware how many different kinds of people there were in Spitalfields, refugees from all over Europe fleeing one kind of persecution or another, financial, racial, religious or political. He heard a dozen languages spoken, saw faces of every cast and color.

On the fifteenth of June, the day after a series of poisonings in Lambeth occupied all the headlines, he arrived back late and tired at Heneagle Street to find Isaac waiting for him. His face was strained with anxiety and his eyes were shadowed as if he had slept little in many nights.

Pitt had developed a considerable affection for him, apart from the fact that Narraway had trusted him with Pitt's safety. He was an intelligent man, well-read, and he liked to talk. Perhaps because Pitt did not belong to Spitalfields, he enjoyed their time after dinner when Leah was in the kitchen or had gone to bed. They argued over all manner of philosophy and belief. Pitt learned much from him of the history of his people in Russia and Poland. Sometimes Isaac told the tale with a wry, self-mocking humor. Often it was unimaginably tragic.

Tonight he obviously wished to talk, but not in the general way of conversation.

"Leah is out," he said with a shrug, his dark eyes watching Pitt's face. "Sarah Levin is sick and she has gone to be with her. She has left dinner for us, but it's cold."

Pitt smiled at him, following him into the small room where the table was set ready. The polished wood and the unique aromas were already familiar to him, Leah's embroidery on the linen, the picture of Isaac as a young man, the matchstick model of a Polish synagogue just a trifle crooked with age.

They had barely sat down to it when Isaac began talking.

"I'm glad you went to work for Saul," he remarked, cutting a slice of bread for Pitt and one for himself. "But you shouldn't be at that sugar factory at nights. It's not a good place."

Pitt knew him well enough now to be aware that this was only an opening gambit. There was far more to follow.

"Saul is a good man." Pitt took the bread. "Thank you. And

185

I like going around the neighborhood. But I see a different side of things at the factory."

Isaac ate in silence for a while.

"There is going to be trouble," he said presently, looking not at Pitt but down at his plate. "A lot of trouble."

"At the sugar factory?" Pitt remembered what he had heard said in the taverns.

Isaac nodded, then looked up suddenly, his eyes wide and direct. "It's ugly, Pitt. I don't know what, but I'm frightened. Could be we'll get blamed for it."

Pitt did not need to ask whom he meant by "we." He was speaking of the immigrant Jewish population, easily recognizable, natural scapegoats. Pitt already knew from Narraway of the suspicions held of them by Special Branch, but it was his observation that they were, if anything, a stabilizing influence in the East End. They cared for their own, they set up shops and businesses and gave people something to work for. He had told Narraway that. He had not told him about their collection of money for those in trouble. He kept that a private thing, a matter of honor.

"It's only a whisper," Isaac went on. "It's not gossip. That's what makes me think it's real." He was watching Pitt closely, his face puckered with anxiety. "Something is planned, I don't know what, but it isn't the usual crazy anarchists. We know who they are, and so do the sugar makers."

"Catholics?" Pitt asked doubtfully.

Isaac shook his head. "No. They're angry, but they're ordinary people, like us. They want houses, work, a chance to get on, something better for their children. What good would it do them to blow up the sugar factories?"

"Is that what it is, dynamite?" Pitt said with a sudden chill, imagining the sheet of flame engulfing half Spitalfields. If all three factories were set alight, whole streets would be ablaze.

"I don't know," Isaac admitted. "I don't know what it is, or when, just that something definite is planned, and at the same time there is going to be a big event somewhere else, but concerning Spitalfields. The two are to happen together, one built upon the other."

186

"Any idea who?" Pitt pressed. "Any names at all?"

Isaac shook his head. "Only one, and I'm not sure in what connection . . ."

"What was the name?"

"Remus."

"Remus?" Pitt was startled. The only Remus he knew was a journalist who tended to specialize in scandal and speculation. There were no scandals among the inhabitants of Spitalfields that would interest him. Perhaps he had misjudged Remus, and he was concerned with politics after all. "Thank you," he acknowledged. "Thank you for that."

"It's not much." Isaac dismissed it with a wave of his hand. "England has been good to me. I am at home here now." He smiled. "I even speak good English, yes?"

"Definitely," Pitt agreed warmly.

Isaac leaned back in his chair. "Now you tell me about this place you grew up in, the country with woods and fields and wide-open sky."

Pitt looked at the remnants of their meal on the table.

"What about this?"

"Leave it. Leah will do it. She likes to fuss. She will be angry if she catches me in her kitchen."

"You ever been in it?" Pitt said skeptically.

Isaac laughed. "No . . ." He gave a lopsided grin. "But I'm sure she would!" He pointed to a pile of linen on the side table. "There are your clean shirts. She makes a good job, yes?"

"Yes," Pitt agreed, thinking of the buttons he had found sewn on as well, and her shy, pleased smile when he had thanked her. "Very good indeed. You are a fortunate man."

Isaac nodded. "I know, my friend. I know. Now sit, and tell me about this place in the country. Describe it for me. How does it taste first thing in the morning? How does it smell? The birds, the air, everything! So I can dream it all and think I am there."

It was early the following morning as Pitt was walking to the silk-weaving factory that he heard the steps behind him and swung around to see Tellman less than two yards away. His stomach lurched with fear that something was wrong with Charlotte or the children. Then he saw Tellman's face, tired but unafraid, and he knew that at least the news was not devastating.

"What is it?" he said almost under his breath. "What are you doing here?"

Tellman fell into step beside him, pulling him around to continue the way he had been going.

"I've been following Lyndon Remus," he said very quietly. Pitt started at the name, but Tellman did not notice. "He is into something to do with Adinett," he went on. "I don't know what it is yet, but he's alight with it. Adinett was in this area, bit farther east, actually: Cleveland Street."

"Adinett was?" Pitt stopped abruptly. "What for?"

"Looks like he was following a story five or six years old," Tellman answered, facing him. "About a girl kidnapped from a tobacconist's shop there and taken to Guy's Hospital, then found insane. Seems as if he went straight to Thorold Dismore with it."

"The newspaper man?" Pitt asked, starting forward again and skirting around a pile of refuse and only just jumping back onto the footpath in time to avoid being struck by a cart loaded precariously with barrels.

"Yes," Tellman repeated, catching up with him. "But he's taking orders from someone he meets by appointment in Regent's Park. Someone who dresses very well indeed. A lot of money."

"Any idea who?"

"No."

Pitt walked in silence for another twenty yards, his mind whirling. He had determined not to think any more about the Adinett case, but of course it had plagued his mind, teasing every fact to try to make sense of a crime which seemed contrary to all reason or character. He wanted to understand, but more than that, he wanted to prove that he had been right.

"Have you been to Keppel Street?" he asked aloud.

"Of course," Tellman answered, keeping up with him.

188

"They're all fine. Missing you." He looked away. "Gracie found out something about this girl from Cleveland Street. She was Catholic and she had a lover who looked like a gentleman. He disappeared too."

Pitt caught the mixture of emotions in Tellman's voice, the pride and the self-consciousness. At another time he would have smiled.

"I'll tell you if I find out anything else," Tellman went on, keeping his eyes straight ahead of him. "I've got to get back. We've got a new superintendent . . . Wetron's his name." His voice was laden with disgust. "I don't know what this is all about, but I don't trust anyone, and you'd be best not to either. Do you come this way every morning?"

"Usually."

"I'll tell you everything I find out." He stopped abruptly and swung around to face Pitt, his lantern jaw hollow in the gray light, his eyes dark. "You be careful." Then, as if he had said too much and embarrassed himself by showing his concern, he swiveled on his heel and strode off back the way he had come.

Gracie was still determined to follow Lyndon Remus, but she had no intention of allowing either Charlotte or Tellman to know it. That meant it was necessary that she give Charlotte some other reason for wanting to leave the house so early—and for remaining absent, possibly all day. It required considerable imagination to come up with a series of excuses, and she hated lying. If it were not absolutely necessary in order to rescue Pitt from injustice and get him home again, she would not even have contemplated it.

She got up just after dawn to have the range lit and the water boiling and the kitchen scrubbed and spotless before anyone else came down. Even the cats were startled to see her at half past five, and not at all sure it was a good idea, especially since she disturbed their sleep in the laundry basket without offering them breakfast.

When Charlotte came down at half past seven Gracie was ready with her story.

189

"Mornin', ma'am," she said cheerfully. "Cup o' tea?"

"Good morning," Charlotte replied, looking around the kitchen with surprise. "Were you up half the night?"

"Got up a bit early." Gracie kept her voice quite casual, moving the kettle back onto the hob to bring it to the boil again. " 'Cos I wanted a favor, if that's all right." She knew Charlotte was aware of Tellman's regard for her, because they had conspired in the past to take advantage of it—only as a matter of necessity in the cause of detection, of course. She took a deep breath. This was the lie. She kept her back to Charlotte; she did not think she could do it looking at her.

"Mr. Tellman asked me ter go ter a fair wif 'im, if I could get the day off. An' I got an errand as well, bit o' shoppin', not much. But if I could go w'en the laundry's finished, I'd be ever so grateful. . . ." It did not sound as good as she had hoped. She knew Charlotte was finding it increasingly hard to endure the loneliness and the worry, especially since there was so little she could do to help.

Charlotte had been back to see Martin Fetters's widow at least twice, and they were at a loss where to search for his missing papers. However, by now she probably knew as much of Fetters's career as anyone. She had told Gracie of John Adinett's travels, military skill and exploring adventures in Canada. But neither of them could see in any of it a reason why one man had murdered the other, only terrible, dangerous ideas. They had spoken of them together, often late into the evening, after the children were in bed. But without proof none of it helped.

Now it was up to Gracie to find the next link between John Adinett and the forces of anarchy . . . or oppression, or whatever it was that he had been doing in Cleveland Street and Remus was so excited about. She really had very little idea what it could be, only that Tellman was certain it was ugly and dangerous, and very big.

"Yes, of course," Charlotte replied to Gracie. There was reluctance in her voice, perhaps even envy, but she did not argue.

"Thank you," Gracie accepted, wishing she could tell the

truth as to what she was doing; it was on the edge of her tongue. But if she did, Charlotte would stop her, and she must not allow that. It would be self-indulgent and stupid to say anything. She must pull herself together and get on with it.

She still had quite a bit of Tellman's money, and all she could collect of her own. She was ready to follow Remus wherever he went, and she was outside his rooms waiting for him by eight o'clock.

It was a very pleasant morning, warm already. Flower sellers were out with fresh blossoms come in during the early hours. She was glad she did not have to stand all day on corners, hoping to sell.

Delivery boys with fish, meat, vegetables passed by, knocking on scullery doors. There was a milk cart at the next crossroads. A thin woman was carrying a full can back to her kitchen. She walked leaning a little sideways from the weight of it.

A newspaper boy took up his position on the farther corner, every now and then shouting the latest headlines about the coming election. There had been a tornado in Minnesota in America. Thirty-three people had been killed. Already Adinett was forgotten.

Lyndon Remus came out of his front door and started to walk smartly along towards the main thoroughfare and— Gracie hoped profoundly—the omnibus stop. Hansoms were very expensive, and she guarded Tellman's money carefully.

Remus looked purposeful, his head forward, stride long and swinging. He was dressed very ordinarily, in old jacket and with no collar to his shirt. Whomever he intended calling on, it was not gentry. Perhaps he was going back to Cleveland Street?

She followed after him quickly, running a little to catch up. She must not lose him. She could stay quite close; after all, he did not know her.

She was right; he went to the omnibus stop. Thank heaven for that! There was no one else there, so she was obliged to stand more or less beside him to wait. But she need not have been concerned he would remember her if he saw her again.

191

He seemed oblivious to anyone else, straining his eyes to watch the traffic for the omnibus and shifting from one foot to the other in his impatience.

She went with him as far as Holborn, then, as he changed for another omnibus eastwards, she did the same. She was taken unaware and nearly left behind when he got off at the farther end of Whitechapel High Street opposite the railway station. Surely he was not going somewhere else by train?

But he walked up Court Street towards Buck's Row and then stopped, staring around him, facing right. Gracie followed his gaze. She saw nothing even remotely interesting. The railway line north was ahead of them, the board school to the right, and the Smith & Co. distillery to the left. Beyond that was a burial ground. Please heaven he wasn't come to look at graves.

Perhaps he was! He had already enquired into the deaths of William Crook and J. K. Stephen. Was he after a trail of dead men? They couldn't all have been murdered . . . could they?

There was plenty of traffic in the street, carts and wagons, people going about their business.

She was shivering in spite of the close, airless warmth of the day. What was Remus looking for? How did a detective know, or find out? Perhaps Tellman was cleverer than she had given him credit for. This was not so easy.

Remus was moving forward, looking around him as if now he had something definite in mind, yet he did not seem to be reading numbers, so perhaps it was not an address.

She moved very slowly after him. In case he turned around, she glanced at doors, pretending to be searching also.

Remus stopped a man in a leather apron and spoke to him. The man shook his head and walked on, increasing his pace. He turned up Thomas Street, at the end of which Gracie could just see a notice proclaiming the Spitalfields Work-house. Its huge, gray buildings were just visible, shelter and imprisonment at once. She had grown up dreading this place more than jail. It was the ultimate misery that awaited the destitute. She had known those who would rather die in the street than be caught in its soulless regimentation.

Remus spoke to an old woman carrying a bundle of laundry.

Gracie moved close enough to overhear. He seemed so absorbed in what he was asking she hoped he would not be aware of her. She stood sideways, staring across the street as if waiting for someone.

"Excuse me . . ." Remus began.

"Yeah?" The woman was civil but no more.

"Do you live around here?" he asked.

"White's Row," she answered, pointing a few yards to the east, where apparently the street changed its name. It was only a short distance before it finished in the cross street, facing the Pavilion Theater.

"Then perhaps you can help me," Remus said urgently.

"Were you here four or five years ago?"

"O' course. Why?" She frowned, narrowing her gaze. Her body stiffened very slightly, balancing the laundry awkwardly.

"Do you see many coaches around here, big ones, carriages, not hansoms?" Remus asked.

Her expression was full of scorn. "Does it look ter yer like we keep carriages 'round 'ere?" she demanded. "Yer'll be lucky if yer can find an 'ansom cab. Yer'd be best off ter use yer legs, like the rest of us."

"I don't want one now!" He caught hold of her arm. "I want someone who saw one four years ago, around these streets."

Her eyes widened. "I dunno, an' I don't wanner know. You get the 'ell out of 'ere an' leave us alone! Gorn! Get out!" She yanked her arm away from him and hurried away.

Remus looked disappointed, his sharp face surprisingly young in the morning light. Gracie wondered what he was like at home relaxed—what he read, what he cared about, if he had friends. Why did he pursue this with such fervor? Was it love or hate, greed, the hunger for fame? Or just curiosity?

He crossed the road past the theater and turned left into Hanbury Street. He stopped several people, asking the same questions about carriages, large closed-in ones such as might have been cruising to pick up prostitutes.

Gracie stayed well behind him as he went the length of the street right up to the Free Methodist Church. Once he found someone who gave him an answer he seemed delighted with. His head jerked up, his shoulders straightened and his hands moved with surprising eloquence.

Gracie was too far away to hear what had been said.

But even if there had been such a carriage, what did that tell her? Nothing. Some man with more money than sense had come to this area looking for a cheap woman. So he had coarse tastes. Perhaps he found a kind of thrill in the danger of it. She had heard there were people like that. If it had been Martin Fetters, what of it? If it were made public, would it matter so much, except to his wife?

Was Remus really chasing after the reason for Fetters's murder anyway? Perhaps she was wasting her time here, or to be more honest, Charlotte's time.

She made a decision.

She came out of the doorway, squared her shoulders, and strode towards Remus, trying to look as if she belonged here and knew exactly what she was doing and where she was going. She was nearly past him when at last he spoke.

"Excuse me?"

She stopped. "Yeah?" Her heart was pounding and her breath was so tight in her throat her voice was a squeak.

"I beg your pardon," he apologized. "But have you lived here for some time? I am looking for someone with some particular knowledge, you see."

She decided to modify her reply a bit, so as not to be caught out by recent events—or the geography of the area, of which she knew very little.

"I bin away." She gulped. "I lived 'ere a few years back."

"How about four years ago?" he said quickly, his face eager, a little flushed.

"Yeah," she said carefully, meeting his sharp, hazel eyes.

"I were 'ere then. Wot is it yer after?"

"Do you remember seeing any carriages around? I mean really good quality carriages, not cabs."

194

She screwed up her face in an effort of concentration. "Yer mean like private ones?"

"Yes! Yes, exactly," he said urgently. "Do you?"

She looked steadily at his face, the suppressed excitement, the energy inside him. Whatever he was looking for, he believed it was intensely important.

"Four year ago?" she repeated.

"Yes!" He was on the verge of adding more to prompt her, and only just stopped himself.

She concentrated on the lie. She must tell him what he expected to hear.

"Yeah, I 'member a big, fine-lookin' carriage around 'ere. Couldn't tell about it except, like, as it were dark, but I reckon as it were about then." She sounded innocent. "Someone yer know, was it?"

He was staring at her as if mesmerized. "I'm not sure." His breath caught in his throat. "Perhaps. Did you see anyone?"

She did not know what to answer because this time she was not sure what he was looking for. That was what she was here to find out. She settled for bland; that could mean anything.

"It were a big, black coach, quiet like," she replied. "Driver up on the box, o' course."

"Good-looking man, with a beard?" His voice cracked with excitement.

Her heart lurched too. She was on the brink of the truth. She must be very careful now. "Dunno about good-lookin'!" She tried to sound casual. "I reckon as 'e 'ad a beard."

"Did you see anyone inside?" He was trying to keep his face calm, but his eyes, wide and brilliant, betrayed him. "Did they stop? Did they talk to anyone?"

She invented quickly. It would not matter if the man he was looking for had not stopped. It could have been for any reason, even to ask the way.

"Yeah." She gestured ahead of her. "Pulled up an' spoke ter a friend o' mine, jus' up there. She said as they was askin' after someone."

"Asking after someone?" His voice was high and scratchy. She could almost smell the tension in him.

"A particular person? A woman?"

That was what he wanted to hear. "Yeah," she said softly. "That's right."

"Who? Do you know? Did she say?"

She chose the one name she knew of connected with this story, "Annie summink."

"Annie?" He gasped and all but choked, swallowing hard so he could breathe. "Are you sure? Annie who? Do you remember? Try to think back!"

Should she risk saying "Annie Crook"? No. Better not overplay her hand. "No. Begins with a C, I think, but I in't certain."

There was utter silence. He seemed paralyzed. She heard someone laugh fifty yards away, and out of sight a dog barked.

His voice was a whisper. "Annie Chapman?"

She was disappointed. Suddenly all the sense in it collapsed. She was cold inside.

"Dunno," she said flatly, unable to conceal it. "Why? 'Oo was it? Some feller after a night out on the cheap?"

"Never mind," he said quickly, trying to conceal the importance of it to him. "You've been immensely helpful. Thank you very much, very much indeed." He fished in his pocket and offered her threepence.

She took it. At least she could return it to Tellman, give him something back of what she had spent. Anyway, depending upon where Remus went next, she might need it.

He left without even looking behind him, striding off over the cobbles, dodging a coal cart. Nothing was further from his mind than the possibility that he might be followed.

He went straight back down Commercial Street to the Whitechapel High Street. Gracie had to run every now and then to keep up with him. At the bottom he turned west and went to the first bus stop, but instead of traveling all the way back to the City, as she had expected, he changed again at Holborn and went south to the river and along the Embankment until he came to the offices of the Thames River police. Gracie followed him straight in, as if she had had business there herself. She waited behind him, her head down. She had taken the precaution of letting her hair out of its pins and rubbing a little dirt into her face. She now looked reasonably unlike the young woman Remus had stopped on Hanbury Street. In fact, she appeared rather like the urchins who scrambled for leftovers along the riverbank, and hoped she would be taken for one, if anybody bothered to look at her twice.

Remus was inventive also. When the sergeant who answered his call asked him what he wanted, he answered with a story Gracie was certain was created for the occasion.

"I'm looking for my cousin who's disappeared," he said anxiously, leaning forward over the counter. "I heard someone answering his description was nearly drowned near Westminster Bridge, on the seventh of February this year. Poor soul was involved in a coach accident that nearly killed a little girl, and in his remorse he tried to kill himself. Is that true?"

"True enough," the sergeant answered. "Was in the papers. Feller called Nickley. But I can't say as he really tried to kill 'isself." He smiled twistedly. "Took 'is coat an' 'is boots off afore 'e jumped, an' anyone 'oo does that don't mean it fer real." His voice was laden with contempt. "Swam, 'e did. Fetched up on the bank along a bit, like yer'd expect. Took 'im ter Westminster 'Ospital, but weren't nothin' wrong wif 'im."

Remus became suddenly casual, as if what he was asking now were an afterthought and scarcely mattered.

"And the girl, what was her name? Was she all right too?"

"Yeah." The sergeant's blunt face filled with pity. "Close call, poor little thing, but not 'urt, jus' scared stiff. Said it weren't the first time, neither. Nearly got run down by a coach before." He shook his head, his lips pursed. "Said it were the same one, but don't suppose she can tell one fancy big coach from another."

Gracie saw Remus stiffen and his hands knot by his sides. "The second time? By the same coach?" In spite of himself his voice was sharp as if this new fact had momentous meaning for him.

The sergeant laughed. "No, 'course it weren't! Just a little girl . . . only seven or eight years old. What'd she know about coaches?"

Remus could not contain himself. He leaned farther forward. "What was her name?"

"Alice," the sergeant answered. "I think."

"Alice what?"

The sergeant looked at him a little more closely. "What's this all about, mister? You know sumunink as you should tell us?"

"No!" Remus denied it too quickly. "It's just family business. Bit of a black sheep, you know? Want to keep it quiet, if possible. But it would help a lot if I knew the girl's name."

The sergeant was skeptical. He regarded Remus with the beginning of doubt. "Cousin, you said?"

Remus had left himself no room to escape. "That's right. He's an embarrassment to us. Got a thing about this little girl, Alice Crook. I just hoped it wasn't her."

Gracie felt the name shiver through her. Whatever it was, Remus was still on the track of it.

The sergeant's face softened a little. "Well, I'm afraid it were 'er. Sorry."

Remus put his hands up quickly, covering his face. Gracie, standing behind him, saw his body stiffen, and knew it was not grief he was hiding but elation. It took him a moment or two to recompose himself and look up again at the sergeant.

"Thank you," he said briefly. "Thank you for your time."

Then he turned on his heel and walked out rapidly past Gracie, leaving her to run after him if she wanted to keep up. If the sergeant even noticed her, he might have thought she was with Remus anyway.

Remus walked back away from the river, looking to the right and left of him as if he were searching for something.

Gracie stayed well back, keeping at least half behind other people in the street, laborers, sightseers, clerks on errands, newsboys and peddlers.

Then she saw Remus change direction and walk across the footpath to the post office and go inside.

She went in after him.

She saw him take out a pencil and write a very hasty note in a scribble, his hands shaking. He folded it up, purchased a stamp, and put the letter into the box. Then he set out again at considerable speed. Once more Gracie had to run a few steps every now and then to not lose him.

She was delighted when Remus apparently decided he was hungry and stopped at a public house for a proper meal. Her feet were sore and her legs ached. She was more than ready to sit down for a while, eat something herself, and observe him in comfort.

He chose an eel pie, something she had always disliked. She watched with wonder as he tucked into it, not stopping until he had finished, then wiping his lips with his napkin. She had a pork pie and thought it a lot better.

Half an hour later he set out again, looking full of purpose. She went after him, determined to not lose him. It was early evening by now, and the streets were crowded. She had the advantage that Remus had no idea there was anyone behind him, and he was so set in his purpose that he never once looked over his shoulder or took the slightest steps to be inconspicuous.

After two omnibus rides and a further short walk, Remus was standing by a bench in Hyde Park, apparently waiting for someone.

He stood for five minutes, and Gracie found it taxed her imagination to think of something to explain her own presence. Remus kept looking around, in case whoever he was waiting for came from the opposite direction. He could not help seeing her. In time he had to wonder why she was here.

What would Tellman have done? He was a detective. He must follow people all the time. Try to be invisible? There was nothing to hide behind, no shadows, no trees close enough. Anyway, if she hid behind a tree she would not see whom he met! Think of a reason to explain her being here? Yes, but what? Waiting for someone as well? Would he believe that? Lost something? Good, but why had she not started to look for it as soon as she got here?

Got it. She had only just discovered it was missing.

She started to retrace her steps very slowly, staring at the ground as if searching for something small and precious. When she had gone twenty yards she turned and started back again. She had almost reached her original position when finally a middle-aged man came towards him along the path and Remus stepped out directly in front of him.

The man stopped abruptly, then made as if to walk around Remus and continue on his way.

Remus moved to remain across his path and, from the attitude of the other man, apparently spoke to him, but so softly Gracie, thirty feet away, could not hear more than the faintest sound.

The man was startled. He looked more closely at Remus, as if he expected to recognize him. Perhaps Remus had addressed him by name.

Gracie peered through the soft evening light, but she dared not draw attention to herself by moving. The older man seemed to be in his fifties, handsome enough, of good height and growing a trifle portly. He was very ordinarily dressed, inconspicuous, well tailored but not expensively. It was the sort of clothing Pitt might have worn, had he not a genius for untidiness sufficient to make any garment ill-fitting. This man was neat, like a civil servant or retired bank manager.

Remus was talking to him heatedly, and the man was replying now with some anger himself. Remus seemed to be accusing him of something; his voice was rising higher, sharp, excited, and Gracie could pick out the odd word.

". . . knew about it! You were in on . . ."

The other man dismissed whatever it was with a quick gesture of his hand, but his face was red and flustered. The indignation in his tone rang false.

"You have no proof of that! And if you—" He gulped back his words, and Gracie missed the next sentence or two. "A very dangerous path!" he finished.

"Then you are equally guilty!" Remus was furious, but there was a thin thread of fear clearly audible in his voice now. Gracie knew that with certainty and it sent a chill rippling through her, clenching the muscles in her stomach and tightening her throat. Remus was afraid of something, very afraid indeed.

And there was something in the other man's body, the angle of his head, the lines of his face that she could still see in the shadows and the thin gold of the evening light. She knew that he was afraid also. He was waving his hands now, jerky, angry movements, sharp denial. He shook his head.

"No! Leave it! I'm warning you!"

"I'll find out," Remus retaliated. "I'll uncover every damned piece of it, and the world will know! We'll not be lied to any longer . . . not by you, or anyone!"

The other man yanked his arm up angrily, then turned and strode away, back in the direction from which he had come.

Remus took a step after him, then changed his mind and walked very rapidly past Gracie towards the road. His face was set in tense, furious determination. He almost bumped into a couple who were walking arm in arm, taking a late stroll in the summer dusk. He muttered an apology and kept straight on.

Gracie ran after him. She had to keep running, he was going so rapidly. He crossed Hyde Park Terrace, continuing north over Grand Junction Road and up to Praed Street and straight into the station for the underground railway.

Gracie's heart lurched. Where was he going? How far? What was this all about? Who was the man he had met in the park and accused . . . of what?

She followed him down the steep steps to the ticket window and bought a fourpenny ticket as he did, and went after him. She had been on an underground train before, and seen them coming roaring and screaming out of the tunnels and stop alongside the platform. She had been rigid with terror, and it had taken all the courage she possessed to climb inside that closed tube and be hurtled, in deafening noise, through the subterranean passages.

But she was not going to lose Remus. Wherever he was going, she was going too . . . to find whatever it was he was pursuing.

The train shot out of the black hole and ground to a stop. Remus got in. Gracie got in behind him.

The train lurched and roared forward. Gracie clenched her fists and kept her lips tightly closed so she would not cry out. Around her everyone else sat stolidly, as if perfectly accustomed to charging through holes under the ground, closed inside part of a train.

They came to the Edgware Road station. People got out, others got in. Remus did not even glance up to see where he was.

The train moved off again.

They passed Baker Street, Portland Road and Gower Street the same way. There was a long stretch to King's Cross, then they seemed to lurch to the right and roar on, gathering speed.

Where was Remus going to now? What was it that connected Adinett's trips to Cleveland Street; the girl Annie Crook, who lived there and had been taken away by force, and her lover as well? She had ended up in Guy's Hospital attended by the Queen's surgeon himself, who had said she was mad. What had happened to the young man? It seemed no one had heard of him again.

What were the coaches about in Spitalfields? Were they driven by the same man who had run down the little girl Alice Crook and then jumped into the river—after taking off his coat and boots?

The train stopped at Farringdon Street, then very quickly after that at Aldergate Street.

Remus shot to his feet.

Gracie almost fell in her surprise and haste to go after him.

Remus got to the door, then changed his mind and sat down again.

Gracie collapsed onto the nearest bench, her heart pounding.

The train went on to Moorgate, and then Bishopsgate. It stopped at Aldgate, and Remus made for the door.

Gracie went also, and climbed up the steps, hurrying into the darkness where Aldgate Street changed into the Whitechapel High Street.

Which way was Remus going? She would have to keep

close to him now. The lamps were lit, but they were dim, just pools of yellow here and there.

Was he going back to Whitechapel again, where he'd been before? He was nearly a mile from Buck's Row, which was the other end of the Whitechapel Road, beyond the High Street. And Hanbury Street was a good half mile to the north, more if you took into account all the narrow, winding streets and alleys and dogleg corners.

But instead he turned right into Aldgate Street, back towards the City. Where was he going now? Did he expect to meet with someone further? She remembered the look on his face as he had walked away from the man in Hyde Park. He was angry, furiously angry, yet he was also excited and afraid. This was something of monstrous proportion . . . or he thought it was.

She was unprepared for it when he turned up Duke Street. It was narrower, darker. The eaves dripped in the gloom. The smells of rot and effluent hung in the air. She found herself shivering. The huge shadow of St. Botolph's Church was just ahead. She was on the edge of Whitechapel.

Remus had been walking as if he knew exactly where he was going. Now he hesitated, looking to his left. The dim light gleamed for a moment on his pale skin. What did he expect to see? Beggars, destitutes huddled in doorways, trying to find a place to sleep, street women looking for chance custom?

She thought of the big black carriages he had asked about, the rumble of wheels on the cobbles growing louder and louder, black horses looming out of the night, the huge shape of the carriage, high, square, a door opening and a man asking . . . what? For a woman, a specific woman. Why? What gentleman in a carriage would come here at night when he could stay up west and find somebody cleaner, more fun, and with a room and a bed to go to rather than some doorway?

Remus was crossing the street into an alley beside the church.

It was pitch-dark. She stumbled as she followed him. Where in the devil's name was he going? She knew he was still ahead of her because she could hear his feet on the cobbles. Then she saw him outlined against a shaft of light ahead. There was an opening. There must be a street lamp there, around the corner.

She reached it and emerged. It was a small square. He stood motionless, staring around; for a moment his face was turned towards the yellow glare of the one lamp. His eyes were wide, his lips parted and drawn back in a dreadful smile that was a mixture of terror and exultation. His whole body shook. He raised his hands a little, white-knuckled in the gaslight, clenched tight.

She looked up at the grimy sign on the brick wall above the light. Mitre Square.

Suddenly she was ice-cold, as if the breath of hell had touched her. Her heart heart almost stopped. At last she knew why he had come here—to Whitechapel, to Buck's Row, to Hanbury Street, and now to Mitre Square. She knew who he was after in the big black coach that didn't belong here. She remembered the names: Annie Chapman, known as Dark Annie; and Long Liz; and Kate; and Polly; and Black Mary. Remus was after Jack the Ripper! He was still alive, and Remus believed he knew who he was. That was the story he was going to break in the newspapers to make his name.

She turned and ran, stumbling and gasping back through the alley. Her knees were weak, her lungs hurt as if the air were knives, but she was not staying in that hellish place a second longer. It drenched her imagination with horror, the blinding, paralyzing fear, the blood, the pain, the moment when the women met his eyes and knew who he was—that was the worst of all, seeing into the heart and the soul of someone who had done that . . . and would do it again!

She collided with someone and let out a scream, thrashing with her fists till she felt soft flesh, heard a grunt and a curse. She tore herself free and pounded into Duke Street and raced down towards Aldgate Road. She did not know or care whom she had struck, or whether Remus was behind her or not, whether he knew she had followed him . . . just as long as she could get a bus or a train and get away, out of Whitechapel and its ghosts and demons.

An omnibus was going west. She shouted and ran out into the street, startling the horses and making the driver curse her. She did not care in the slightest. Ignoring his protests, she scrambled on board and collapsed in a heap on the first vacant seat.

"Devil after yer?" a man said kindly, a smile of amusement in his broad face.

It was too close to the truth to be a joke. "Yeah . . ." she said hoarsely. "Yeah . . . 'e is!"

She finally arrived home at Keppel Street after eleven o'clock, to find Charlotte pacing the kitchen floor, pale-faced and hollow-eyed.

"Where have you been?" she demanded furiously. "I've been worried sick for you! You look terrible! What happened?"

Gracie was so relieved to be home safe, in the warmth and light of the familiar kitchen with its smells of clean wood and linen, bread, herbs, and to know that Charlotte cared about her, that now at last she burst into tears and sobbed incoherently while Charlotte held her lightly in her arms.

Tomorrow she would give her a very carefully edited version of the truth, with an apology for lying.

9

TELLMAN TRIED to put Gracie out of his mind. It was difficult. Her eager face kept intruding every moment he relaxed and allowed his attention to wander from what he was doing. However the knowledge that Wetron was watching him and waiting for him to make the slightest error forced him to keep working as hard as he could on the wretched burglaries. He could not afford to be caught in even the smallest mistake.

His diligence was rewarded with a stroke of good luck, bringing the end of the case into sight.

He also thought more often than he wished, and with both discomfort and guilt, about Pitt, living and working in Spitalfields. It was quite obvious why they had put him there. It was ridiculous to think he was going to make any difference one way or the other regarding the anarchists. That was a specialized job and they had men doing it very well already. From Cornwallis's point of view it was an attempt to save him from any further danger; and for those who had commanded it, it was punishment for having convinced the jury that Adinett was guilty.

And he was left vulnerable because he could not prove why Adinett had done it; he could not even suggest a reason. That was why Tellman felt guilty. He was still a policeman, still free to pursue the truth and find it, and he had achieved nothing except to learn that Adinett had been excited about something in Cleveland Street which seemed to have un-ending ramifications, very little of which he understood.

He was standing near the flower market a couple of blocks down from the Bow Street police station when he realized someone had stopped near him and was watching him.

Gracie!

His first reaction was pure pleasure. Then he saw she was scrubbed and pale, and she stood very quietly, unlike her usual self. His heart sank. He walked over to her.

"What is it?" he said urgently. "What are you doing here?"

"I came ter see yer," she retorted. "Wot did yer think— I come for a bunch of flowers?" Her voice was sharp. It alarmed him. Now he was certain there was something badly wrong.

"Is Mrs. Pitt all right? Has she heard from him?" That was his first thought. He had barely seen Charlotte since Pitt had left, and that was over a month ago now. Perhaps he should have spoken with her? But it would have been intrusive, even impertinent, and what would he say? She was a lady, the real thing, and she had family.

What she relied on him to do was find out the truth and show that Pitt had been right, so he could be reinstated in Bow Street, where he belonged. And he had signally failed to do that!

A flower cart trundled past them and stopped a dozen yards away.

"What is it?" he said again, more sharply. "Gracie!"

She swallowed hard. He could see her throat jerk. Now he was really afraid. Too much of his life was tied up in Keppel Street. He could not shrug it off and walk away. He would be left incomplete, hurting.

"I followed Remus, like yer said." She looked at him defiantly.

"I didn't tell you to follow him! I told you to stay at home and do your job!"

"Yer told me first ter follow 'im," she pointed out stubbornly.

A couple walked past them, the woman holding newly bought roses up to smell the perfume.

Gracie was frightened. Tellman could see it in her face and in the way she stood, the stiffness inside her. Her whole body was rigid. It made him angry, made him want to protect her, and he felt the fear as if it had brushed him too with a breath of ice. He did not want this! He was vulnerable, wide open to being hurt, twisted, even broken.

"Well, you shouldn't have! You should stay at home where you're supposed to be, looking after Mrs. Pitt and the house!"

Her eyes were wide and dark, her lips trembling. He was making it worse. He was hurting her and leaving her alone with whatever it was that she had seen, or thought.

"Well, where did he go?" he asked more gently. It sounded grudging, but it was himself he was angry with—for being clumsy, feeling too much and thinking too little. He did not know how to behave with her. She was so young, fourteen years younger than he was, and so brave and proud. Trying to touch her was like trying to pick up a thistle. And there was nothing of her! He'd seen bigger twelve-year-olds. But he had never known anyone of any size with more courage or strength of will. "Well, then?" he prompted.

Her eyes did not waver from his. She ignored the passersby. "I spent all yer money," she said. "An' a bit wot I was give as well."

"You didn't go out of London! I told you . . ."

"No, I didn't," she said quickly, gulping. "But I don' 'ave ter do wot yer tells me. 'E went ter Whitechapel, Remus did . . . ter the back streets, Spitalfields way, Lime'ouse side. 'E asked if anyone seen a big carriage about four years ago, drivin' around, one as don't belong. Which were kind o' daft. Nobody around there's goin' ter 'ave a carriage. Shanks's pony, more like. Omnibus if yer sticks ter the main 'Igh Street."

He was puzzled. But at least this was not sinister. "Looking for a carriage? Do you know if he found anything?"

For a moment he thought she was going to smile, but it died before it began. There was an underlying terror inside her which snuffed out every shred of lightness. It gripped at him with a kind of pain he could hardly bear.

"Yeah, 'cos 'e never recognized me, so I let 'im ask me,

like 'e asked anyone else," she answered. "An' I told 'im I'd seen a big black carriage four years ago. 'E asked me if anyone in it 'ad acted like they was lookin' fer anyone special. So I told 'im they 'ad."

"Who?" His voice came roughly, hoarse with tension.

"I said the first name as came ter me 'ead. I were thinking o' that girl wot wos took from Cleveland Street, so I said 'Annie.' " She shivered violently.

"Annie?" He took a step closer to her. He wanted to touch her, hold her by the shoulders, but she might have pushed him away, so he stood still. "Annie Crook?"

Her face was bleached white. She shook her head very slightly. "No . . . I didn't know it till later, hours later, w'en I followed 'im back to Whitechapel again, arter 'e'd bin ter the river police, wrote a letter ter somebody, an' met up wi' a gent in 'Yde Park an' accused 'im o' summink terrible, an' 'ad a real quarrel wif 'im, an' then gorn all the way back ter Whitechapel—" She stopped, breathless, her chest heaving.

"Who?" he demanded urgently. "If it wasn't Annie Crook, what does it matter?" Unreasonably, he was disappointed. Only the horror in her face held him from looking away.

She gulped again. "It were Dark Annie," she said in a strangled whisper.

"Dark . . . Annie . . . ?" Slowly the horror began to dawn on him, cold as the grave.

She nodded. "Annie Chapman . . . wot Jack cut up!"

"The . . . Ripper?" He could barely say the word.

"Yeah!" she breathed. "The other places 'e were askin' about coaches were Buck's Row, w'ere Polly Mitchell were found, 'Anbury Street w'ere Dark Annie were, an' 'e finished up in Mitre Square, w'ere they got Kate Eddowes, wot wos the worst o' them all."

Horror washed over him as if something nameless, primeval, had come out of the darkness and stood close to them both, death in its heart and its hands.

He could not bring himself to say the name. "If you knew it then, you shouldn't have followed him the rest of the way back to the river police and . . ." he started, hysteria rising in his voice.

"I didn't!" she protested. " 'E went ter the police first, askin' about a coach driver called Nickley tryin' ter run down a little girl about seven or eight, wot 'e did twice, but never got 'er." She caught her breath. "An' after the second time 'e went an' jumped inter the river, but 'e took 'is boots off first, so 'e din't really mean ter kill 'isself, 'e jus' wanted folks ter think 'e did."

"What's that got to do with it?" he asked quickly. He caught hold of her arm and pulled her to the side of the pavement, out of the way of two men passing by. He did not let go of her.

"I dunno!" she said.

He was struggling to find sense in the story, to see the connections to Annie Crook and what it could have to do with Adinett and Pitt. But deeper, from the core of him, welling up in spite of all he could do to prevent it, he was fighting his fear for Gracie, and his fear for himself because she mattered to him more than he could control or knew how to deal with.

"But 'e knows," she said, watching him. "Remus knows. 'E's so lit up yet could see yer way across London by 'im."

He was still staring at her.

"I saw 'is face in the lamplight in Mitre Square," she repeated. "That's w'ere Jack did Kate Eddowes . . . an' 'e knew that! Remus knew! That's w'y 'e were there."

Suddenly he realized what she was saying. "You followed him there at night?" He was aghast. "By yourself . . . into Mitre Square?" He heard his voice ascend up the scale, trembling and out of control. "Haven't you got the wits you were born with? Think what could have happened to you!" He shut his eyes so tightly it hurt, trying to force away the visions that were inside his head. He could remember the pictures of the bodies four years ago, hideous distortions of the human form, a mockery of the decencies of death.

And Gracie had gone there, at night, following a man who could be anything. "You stupid . . ." he shouted. "Stupid . . ." No word came to him that was adequate for his fear for her.

his rage and relief, and the fury at his own vulnerability—because if anything had happened to her he would never have been happy again.

He was oblivious of people stopping to stare at him, even of an elderly gentleman who hesitated by Gracie, concerned for her safety. Then apparently he decided it was domestic, and hurried on.

Tellman did not want to care so much, about Gracie or anyone else, but particularly about her. She was prickly, wrong-headed about almost everything that mattered; she didn't even like him, let alone love him; and she was determined to stay in service to the Pitts. The very thought of being in service to anyone set his teeth on edge, like the sound of a knife scraping on glass.

"You are stupid!" he shouted at her again, swinging his arm around as if he would smash something on the ground, only he had nothing to throw. "Don't you ever think what you're doing?"

Now she was angry too. She had been frightened before, but he had insulted her, and she was not going to stand for that.

"Well, I found out wot Remus were after, an' that's more'n you did!" she shouted back. "So if I'm stupid, wot does that make you, eh? An' if yer in too much of a rage ter see wot I jus' told yer, an' use it ter 'elp Mr. Pitt, then I'll jus' 'ave ter do it meself! I dunno 'ow, but I'll do it, I'll go an' find Remus again an' tell 'im I know wot 'e's doin', an' if 'e don't tell me—"

"Oh, no you won't!" He caught hold of her wrist as she turned to leave, almost cannoning into a large woman in a striped dress.

"Get off o' me!" Gracie tried to snatch herself away, but Tellman had her tightly, and he was too strong for her. She bent forward and bit him, hard.

He yelled with pain and let go of her. "You little beast!"

The large woman hurried away, muttering to herself.

"Then you keep yer 'ands ter yerself!" Gracie shouted back at Tellman. "An' don't yer try tellin' me wot ter do an' wot not ter do! I don't belong ter nobody, an' I'll do wot I like.

211

Yer can 'elp me an' Mr. Pitt, or yer can stand there an' call me names. It don't make no difference. We'll find out the truth, an' we'll get 'im back—you'll see!" This time she flounced her skirts around and stormed off.

He started to go after her, then stopped. His hand was thoroughly sore. Unconsciously he put it to his lips. He had no idea what to say to Gracie anyway. He felt crushed. He wanted to help, for Pitt's sake, and because it was right, and for Gracie's sake too. She would have to trust him, and he would be more than worthy of it.

But he was terrified for her, and it was a new and dreadful feeling, a fear like no other, cold and knotting him up inside.

She stopped a dozen yards away and swung around to face him again.

"Are you really jus' gonna stand there like a bleedin' lamppost?" she demanded.

He strode over to her. "I'm going to find Remus," he said gravely. "And you're going home to Keppel Street before Mrs. Pitt throws you out for not doing your job. I suppose it hasn't occurred to you that she's worried sick where you are—as if she didn't have enough to be scared about." He projected his own feelings onto Charlotte. "She's probably been awake half the night imagining all sorts of terrible things happening to you. She's lonely, doesn't know what to say or do for the best, and you should be there helping."

She looked at him, weighing her words. "Yer going ter find Remus, then?" she challenged.

"You dear? I just told you I am!"

She sniffed. "Then I reckon as I've told you all I found out, I'll go 'ome an' get summink fer dinner . . . maybe make a cake." She shrugged and started walking away again.

"Gracie!"

"Yeah?"

"You did very well . . . in fact, brilliantly. And if you ever do it again, I'll tan your seat till you have to eat off the mantelpiece for a week. Do you hear me?"

She grinned at him, then kept on walking.

He did not want to smile, but he could not help it. Suddenly there was a joy beside the fear, a fierce, warm ache he never wanted to lose.

Tellman did not even consider remaining by the flower market pursuing the stolen goods. It was still early. If he went straightaway he might find Remus and be able to confront him and discover, either by threat or persuasion, exactly what he knew. For Pitt's sake he must find out what connection it had with Adinett—for everyone's, if Remus really knew the identity of the most fearful murderer ever to strike London, or possibly anywhere. All other names of terror paled beside his.

He walked rapidly away, head down, not looking right or left in case he caught the eye of anyone he knew. Where would Remus be at this hour? It was not yet five past nine. Perhaps he was still at his home? He had been out late enough last night.

He caught a hansom, to save time, giving the driver Remus's address.

If he were not there, then where would he be? Where would he go this morning? What pieces of the puzzle were left to find?

What did he know already? It had something to do with a coach driver called Nickley, who apparently had driven his master's carriage around Whitechapel searching for those five particular women, and then when he had found them, someone had butchered them in the most horrific manner. Why these women and not others? Why had he stopped with five? They had been ordinary enough, prostitutes of one sort or another. There were tens of thousands like them. Yet, according to Gracie, whoever it was had asked after at least one of them by name.

The cab jolted him along the street without interrupting his concentration.

So it was not a maniac simply out to kill. There was purpose. Why had Annie Crook been taken from the tobacconist's shop in Cleveland Street, and apparently ended up at Guy's Hospital? And attended by the Queen's surgeon! Why?

Who paid for it? If she was insane it was hardly a surgical matter.

And who was the young man who had been taken from Cleveland Street at the same time, and also under protest?

He arrived, paid the driver but asked him to wait five minutes while he went and knocked on the door. The landlady told him Remus had gone out ten minutes before, but she had no idea where to.

Tellman thanked her and went back to the cab, directing the driver to the nearest railway station. He would take the underground train to Whitechapel, then walk the quarter mile or so to Cleveland Street.

Through the journey he sat turning the problem over in his mind. If Remus was not there, and he could not find him, he would have to start asking around himself. There did not seem any better place to begin. It all appeared to start with Annie Crook. There were several other pieces that so far had no connection, such as why was it important that Annie Crook had been Catholic?

Presumably the young man was not, and either his family or hers had objected. And her father, William Crook, had ended up dead in the St. Pancras Infirmary.

Who was Alice, that the coach driver had nearly run her down, not once, but twice? Why? What kind of a man wants to murder a seven-year-old child?

There was definitely a great deal more to learn, and if Remus knew any of it, then Tellman must get it from him, one way or another.

And who was the man Remus had met in Regent's Park, who seemed to have been giving him advice and instruction? And who was the man he had quarreled with at the edge of Hyde Park? From Gracie's description, a different man.

He got off at Whitechapel and walked rapidly to Cleveland Street, turning the corner and striding briskly.

This time luck was with him. He saw the figure of Remus less than a hundred yards ahead, standing almost still, as if uncertain which way to go.

Tellman increased his pace and reached him just as he was about to turn left and go towards the tobacconist's shop.

Tellman put out his hand and grasped Remus's arm.

"Before you go, Mr. Remus, I'd like a word with you."

Remus jumped as if he had been frightened half out of his wits.

"Sergeant Tellman! What the devil are—" Then he stopped abruptly.

"Looking for you," Tellman answered the question, even though it had not been completed.

Remus effected innocence. "Why?" He started to say something more, then thought better of it. He knew about protesting too much.

"Oh, a lot of things," Tellman said casually, but without letting go of Remus's arm. He could feel the muscles clenched under his fingers. "We can start with Annie Crook, go on through her abduction to Guy's Hospital and whatever happened to her, and the death of her father, and the man you met in Regent's Park, and the other man you quarreled with in Hyde Park . . ."

Remus was too badly shaken to conceal it. His face was white, fine beads of sweat on his lip and brow, but he said nothing.

"And we could go on to the coach driver who tried to run down the child, Alice Crook, and then threw himself into the river, only he swam out of it again," Tellman went on. "But most of all I want to know about the man inside the coach that drove around Hanbury Street and Buck's Row in the autumn of '88, and cut the throats of five women, ending up disemboweling Catherine Eddowes in Mitre Square, where you were last night . . ." He stopped because he thought Remus was going to faint. He retained his grasp on him now as much to hold him up as to prevent him from running away.

Remus was shuddering violently. He tried to swallow, and nearly choked.

"You know who Jack is." Tellman made it a statement.

Remus's whole body was rigid, every muscle locked.

215

Tellman felt his own breath rasping. "He's still alive . . . isn't he?" he said hoarsely.

Remus jerked his head in a nod, but in spite of his fear there was a light returning to his eyes, almost a brilliance. He was sweating profusely. "It's the story of the century," he said, licking his lips nervously. "It'll change the world . . . I swear!"

Tellman was doubtful, but he could see that Remus believed it. "If it catches Jack that'll be enough for me," he said quietly. "But you had better do some explaining, and now." He could not think of a sufficiently effective threat, so he did not add one.

The challenge returned to Remus's eyes. He snatched his arm loose from Tellman's grip. "You won't prove it without me. You'll be lucky if you ever prove it at all!"

"Maybe it isn't true."

"Oh, it's true!" Remus assured him, his voice ringing with certainty. "I just need a few more pieces. Gull's dead, but there'll be enough left, one way or another. And Stephen's dead too, poor devil . . . and Eddy, but I'll still prove it, in spite of them."

"We," Tellman corrected him grimly. "We'll prove it."

"I don't need you."

"Yes you do, or I'll blow it wide open," Tellman threatened. "I don't care about making a story, you're welcome to that, but I want the truth for other reasons, and I'll get it, whether I make your story or ruin it."

"Then come away from the shop," Remus urged, glancing over his shoulder and back again at Tellman. "We can't afford to wait around here and be noticed." He turned as he spoke and started off towards the Mile End Road again.

The air smelled like thunder, damp and heavy.

Tellman hurried after him. "Explain it to me," he ordered. "And no lies. I know a great deal. I just haven't worked out how it all connects up . . . not yet."

Remus walked a few paces without answering.

"Who is Annie Crook?" Tellman asked, matching him step for step. "And more important, where is she now?"

216

Remus deliberately ignored the first question. "I don't know where she is," he answered without looking at him. Then, before Tellman could become angry, he added, "Bedlam, by now, I should think. She was declared insane and put away. I don't know whether she's still alive. There's no proper record of her at Guy's, but I know she went there and was kept there for months."

"And who was her lover?" Tellman went on. In the distance thunder rumbled over the rooftops and a few heavy spots of rain fell.

Remus stopped dead, so abruptly Tellman was a couple of steps beyond him before he stopped too.

Remus's eyes were wide; he started to laugh, a high, sharp, hysterical sound. Several people turned in the street to look at him.

"Stop it!" Tellman wanted to slap him, but it would have drawn even more attention to them. "Be quiet!"

Remus gulped and controlled himself with an effort. "You don't know a damn thing, do you? You're just guessing. Go away. I don't need you."

"Yes, you do," Tellman contradicted him with certainty. "You haven't got all the answers yet, and you can't get them, or you would have. But you know enough to be frightened. What else do you need? Maybe I can help. I'm police; I can ask questions you can't."

"Police!" Remus gave a guffaw of laughter, full of anger and derision. "Police? Abberline was police—and Warren! As high as you like . . . commissioner, even."

"I know who they are," Tellman retorted sharply.

"Of course you do," Remus agreed, nodding his head, his eyes glittering. The rain was heavier, and warm. "But do you know what they did? Because if you do, the next thing I know I'll be in one of these alleys with my throat cut as well." He took a step back as he said it, almost as if he thought Tellman might make a sudden lunge for him.

"Are you saying Abberline and Warren were involved?" Tellman demanded.

Remus's contempt was withering. "Of course they were! How else do you think it was all covered up?"

It was absurd. "That's ridiculous!" Tellman said aloud, ignoring the rain, which was now soaking them both. "Why would someone like Abberline want to cover up murder? He'd have made a name for himself that would have gone down in history if he'd solved that case. The man who caught the Whitechapel murderer could have called his own price."

"There are some things bigger even than that," Remus said darkly, but the tension and the excitement were back in his face again, and his eyes were bright and wild. The water was running down his face, plastering his hair to his head. Over the rooftops the thunder rumbled again. "This is bigger than fame, Tellman, or money, believe me. If I'm right, and I can prove it, it will change England forever."

"Rubbish!" Tellman denied it savagely. He wanted it to be false.

Remus turned away.

Tellman grabbed his arm again, bringing him up short. "Why would Abberline conceal the worst crimes that have ever happened in London? He is a decent man."

"Loyalty." Remus said the word hoarsely. "There are loyalties deeper than life or death, loyalties deep as hell itself." He put his hand to his throat. "Some things a man . . . some men . . . will sell their own souls for. Abberline is one, Warren's another, and the coachman Netley——"

"What Netley?" Tellman asked. "You mean Nickley?"

"No, his name's Netley. When he said Nickley at the Westminster Hospital, he was lying."

"What's he got to do with them? He drove the coach around Whitechapel. He knew who Jack was, and why he did what he did."

"Of course he did . . . he still does. And I daresay he'll go to the grave telling no one."

"Why did he try to kill the child—twice?"

Remus smiled, his lips drawn wide over his teeth. "As I said before, you know nothing."

Tellman was desperate. The thought of Pitt's being thrown

out of office in Bow Street because he had stuck to the truth infuriated him. Charlotte was left alone, worried and frightened, and Gracie was determined to help, no matter what the danger or the cost. The thought of the whole monstrous injustice of it all was intolerable.

"I know where to find a lot of senior policemen," he said very quietly. "Not just Abberline, or Commissioner Warren, but a fair few more as well, all the way up, if I have to. Those two might be retired, but others aren't."

Remus was ashen white, his eyes wild. "You . . . wouldn't! You'd set them on me, knowing what they did? Knowing what they're hiding?"

"I don't know!" Tellman responded. "Not unless you tell me."

Remus gulped and ran the back of his hand over his mouth. His eyes flickered with fear. "Come with me. Let's get out of the rain. Come to the pub across there." He pointed over the road.

Tellman was glad to agree. His mouth was dry and he had already walked a considerable distance. The rain did not bother him. They were both soaked to the skin.

Lightning flashed in a jagged fork, and thunder cracked overhead.

Ten minutes later they were sitting in a quiet corner with glasses of ale and the smell of sawdust and wet clothes all around them.

"Right," Tellman began. "Who did you meet in Regent's Park? And if I catch you in one lie, you're in trouble."

"I don't know," Remus said instantly, his face pained. "And so help me God, that's the truth. The man who put me onto all this, right from the beginning. I admit I wouldn't tell who he is if I knew, but I don't."

"Not a good start, Mr. Remus," Tellman warned him.

"I don't know!" Remus protested, a kind of desperation in his voice.

"What about the man in Hyde Park that you quarreled with and accused of hiding a conspiracy? Another mysterious informant?"

"No. That was Abberline."

Tellman knew Abberline had been in charge of the Whitechapel murders investigation. Had he concealed evidence, even that he had known the identity of the Ripper, and not revealed it? If so, his crime was monstrous, and Tellman could think of no explanation that justified it.

Remus was watching him.

"Why would Abberline hide it?" he asked again. Then he framed the question that was beating in his mind. "What has Adinett got to do with it? Did he know too?"

"I think so." Remus nodded. "He was certainly onto something. He was at Cleveland Street, asking at the tobacconist's, and at Sickert's place."

Now Tellman was confused. "Who is Sickert?"

"Walter Sickert, the artist. It was at his studio they met. That was in Cleveland Street then," Remus answered.

Tellman guessed. "The lovers? Annie Crook, who was Catholic, and the young man?"

Remus grimaced. "How quaintly you put it. Yes, that's where they met, if you like to phrase it that way."

Tellman assumed from his words that it was more than a mere meeting. But the core of it all still escaped him. What had it to do with an insane murderer and five dead and mutilated women?

"You are not making sense." He leaned a little forward across the table between them. "Whoever Jack was—or is—he wanted particular women. He asked for them by name, at least he did for Annie Chapman. Why? Why did you go asking after the death of William Crook in St. Pancras, and the lunatic Stephen in Northampton? What has Stephen to do with Jack?"

"From what I can tell . . ." Remus's thin hands were clenched on his beer mug. It shook very slightly, rippling the liquid. "Stephen was the Duke of Clarence's tutor, and he was a friend of Walter Sickert. It was he who introduced them."

"The Duke of Clarence and Walter Sickert?" Tellman said slowly.

Remus's voice was half strangled in his throat. "The Duke of Clarence and Annie Crook, you fool!"

The room whirled around Tellman as if he were at sea in a storm. The eventual heir to the throne, and a Catholic girl from the East End. But the Prince of Wales had mistresses all over the place. He was not even particularly discreet about it. If Tellman knew, then probably all the world did.

Remus looked at Tellman's blank face.

"From what I know now, Clarence—Eddy, as he was called—was rather awkward, and his friends suspected he might have leanings towards men as much as women."

"Stephen . . ." Tellman put in.

"That's right. Stephen, his tutor, introduced him to a lot of more acceptable kinds of entertainment with Annie. He was very deaf, poor devil, like his mother, and found social conversation a bit difficult." For the first time there was a note of compassion in Remus's voice, and a sudden sadness filled his face. "But it didn't work out the way they meant. They fell in love . . . really in love. The core of it is . . ." He looked at Tellman with a strange mixture of pity and elation. His hands were shaking even more. "They might have been married . . ."

Tellman jerked his glass so hard that ale slopped over the edges onto the table. "What?"

Remus nodded, shivering. His voice dropped to a whisper. "And that's why Netley, poor Eddy's driver, who used to bring him here to see Annie in Cleveland Street, tried twice to kill the child . . . poor little creature . . ."

"Child?" Now it was plain. "Alice Crook . . ." Tellman gulped in air and nearly choked. "Alice Crook is the daughter of the Duke of Clarence?"

"Probably . . . and maybe in wedlock. And Annie was Catholic." Remus was whispering now. "Remember the Act of Settlement?"

"What?"

"The Act of Settlement," Remus repeated. Tellman had to lean right across the table to hear him. "Made law in 1701, but still in effect. It excludes any person who marries a Roman Catholic from inheriting the crown. The Bill of Rights of 1689 says the same thing."

The true enormity of it began to dawn on Tellman. It was

hideous. It jeopardized the throne, the stability of the government and the whole country.

"So they forced them apart?" It was the only possible conclusion. "They kidnapped Annie and put her in a madhouse . . . and what happened to Eddy? He died? Or did they . . . surely . . . ?" He could not even say it. Suddenly being a prince was a terrible thing, isolated, frightening, one individual lonely human being against a conspiracy that stretched everywhere.

Remus was looking at him with the pity still in his face.

"God knows"—he shook his head—"poor soul couldn't hear half of what was going on, and maybe he was a bit simpler than some. It seems he was devoted to Annie and the child. Maybe he created a fuss about them. He was deaf, alone, confused . . ." He stopped again, his face filled with misery for a man he had never seen but whose pain he could imagine too vividly.

Tellman stared ahead at the scruffy posters and the scribbling on the pub wall, profoundly grateful that he was there and not in some palace, watched over by murderous courtiers, a servant to the throne and not master of anything.

"Why the five women?" he said at last. "There has to have been a reason."

"Oh, there was," Remus assured him. "They were the ones who knew about it. They were Annie's friends. If they'd known what they were up against, they'd have disappeared. But they didn't. Word has it they were greedy, at least one of them was, and led the others. They asked Sickert for money in exchange for silence. He told his masters, and the women got silence all right—the silence of a blood-soaked grave."

Tellman buried his face in his hands and sat motionless, his mind in chaos. Was Lyndon Remus the real lunatic? Could any of this fearful story be true?

He looked up slowly, lowering his hands.

As if reading his thoughts, Remus spoke. "You think I'm mad?"

Tellman nodded. "Yes . . ."

"I can't prove any of it . . . yet. But I will. It's true. Look at the facts."

"I am. They don't prove it. Why did Stephen kill himself? How was he involved?"

"He introduced them. Poor Eddy was quite a good painter. Sight, you see. No hearing needed. Stephen loved him." He shrugged. "In love with him, maybe. Anyway, when he heard he was dead, God knows what he thought, but it finished him. Guilt, maybe, maybe not. Perhaps just grief. It doesn't affect the story."

"So who killed the women?" Tellman asked.

Remus shook his head a little. "I don't know. My guess is Sir William Gull. He was the royal physician."

"And Netley drove the coach going around Whitechapel, looking for them, so Gull could carve them up?" Tellman found himself shaking with an inner cold the warmth of the tavern could do nothing to help. The nightmare was inside him.

Again Remus nodded. "In the coach. That was why there was never that much blood, and why he was never caught in the act."

Tellman pushed away the last of his beer. The thought of eating or drinking made him sick.

"We just need the last pieces," Remus went on, his glass also untouched now. "I need to know more about Gull."

"He's dead," Tellman pointed out.

"I know." Remus leaned forward. The noise around them was increasing, and it was getting harder to hear. "But that doesn't alter the truth. And I need to have every fact possible. All the speculation in the world won't do any good without the facts that can't be argued away." He watched Tellman intently. "And you could get access to things I can't. They know who I am, and they won't tell me any more. I don't have an excuse." He nodded. "But you could. You could say it was to do with a case, and they'd talk to you."

"What are you going to do?" Tellman questioned. "What else do you need? And why? What will you do with it all when you have it, if you ever do? There's no good going to the police. Gull is dead, Abberline and Warren are both retired. Are you after the coachman?"

"I'm after the truth wherever it goes," Remus said grimly. A large man hesitated near them, and Remus waited until he was gone before he continued. "What I really want is the man behind it, the one who sent them out to do these things. He may not have been within five miles of Whitechapel, but he is the heart and mind of the Ripper. The others were just the hands."

Tellman had to ask. The sounds of ordinary life were all around them, talking, laughter, the clink of glasses, the shuffling of feet, the splash of beer. It seemed so sane, so commonplace, that such things as they were speaking of were surely impossible. And yet stop any one of these men in here and mention the horror of four years ago, and a sudden silence would fall, the blood would drain from faces and eyes would go cold and frightened. Even now it would be as if someone had opened an inner door onto a darkness of the soul.

"Do you know who that is?" Tellman's voice was rough. He needed to drink to calm the dryness, but the thought choked him.

"I think so," Remus answered. "But I'm not telling you, so there's no point in asking. That's what I'm going after. You find out about Gull and Netley. Don't go near Sickert." There was sharp warning in his face. "I'll give you two days. Meet me back here then."

Tellman agreed. He had no choice, regardless of what Wetron or anyone else might do. Remus was right; if what he supposed were true, then it was a far bigger issue than any individual crime, bigger even than solving the most terrible murders London had ever seen.

But he could not forget Pitt, and his original reason for asking.

"How much of this did Adinett know?"

Remus shook his head. "I'm not sure. Some of it, that's certain. He knew about them taking Annie Crook from Cleveland Street to Guy's, and taking Eddy away too."

"And Martin Fetters? Where does he fit in? What did he know?"

"Who's Martin Fetters?" Remus looked momentarily confused.

"The man Adinett murdered!" Tellman said sharply.

"Oh!" Remus's face cleared. "I've no idea. If it had been the other way around, and Fetters had killed Adinett, I would say Fetters was one of them."

Tellman stood up. Whatever he was going to do, it must be quickly. If Wetron caught him even once more, he might be dismissed. If he trusted Wetron, or anyone apart from Pitt, he would tell what he knew and be given time, almost certainly help as well. But he had no idea how far the Inner Circle stretched or whose loyalty lay where. He must do this alone.

He left the public house and walked out into the thinning rain.

If Sir William Gull had been the man who had carried out those fearful deeds, then Tellman needed to learn for himself everything about him that he could. His mind was crowded with thoughts and imaginings as he walked towards the main street and the nearest omnibus stop. He was happy to travel slowly. He needed time to absorb the story that Remus had told him and think what to do next.

If the Duke of Clarence had really married Annie Crook, whatever form the ceremony had taken, and there were a child, then no wonder certain people had panicked to keep it secret. Quite apart from the laws of succession to the throne, the anti-Catholic feeling in the country was sufficiently powerful that knowledge of the alliance would be enough to rock the monarchy, fragile as it was at the moment.

But if it was exposed that the most hideous murders of the century had been committed by royal sympathizers, perhaps even with royal knowledge, there would be revolution in the streets and the throne would be swept away on a tide of rage which might destroy the government as well. What would arise afterwards would be strange, unfamiliar, and probably no better.

But whatever it was, Tellman was filled with dismay at the

thought of the violence, the sheer weight of anger that would shatter so much that was good, as well as the relatively little that was not. How many ordinary people who were now going about their daily lives would have everything they knew swept away? Revolution would change those in power, but it would create no more food, houses, clothes, no more worthwhile jobs, nothing lasting to make life richer or safer.

Who would form the new government when the old was gone? Would they necessarily be any wiser or fairer?

He got out of the bus and walked up the slope towards Guy's Hospital. There was no time for subtlety. When Remus had enough evidence in his own mind, he would make it public. The man in Regent's Park who had prompted him would make sure of that.

Who was he? Remus himself had said he did not know. There was no time now to find out, but his motive was clear enough—revolution here in England, the end of safety and peace, even with all its iniquities.

Tellman went up the steps and into the front door of the hospital.

It took him the remainder of that day, talking to half a dozen different people about their recollections of the late Sir William Gull, to gain some impression of the man. What slowly gathered form was a picture of a man dedicated to the knowledge of medicine, most especially the workings of the human body, its structure and mechanics. He seemed impelled more by a desire to learn than by a wish to heal. He was driven by personal ambition and little visible compassion to relieve suffering.

There was one particular tale he heard about Gull's treatment of a man who died. Gull decided to perform a postmortem. The dead man's elderly sister was so profoundly concerned that the body should not be left mutilated that she insisted on remaining in the room during the operation.

Gull had not demurred, but carried out the whole procedure in front of her, removing the heart and putting it in his pocket to take away so that he might keep it. It revealed a streak of cruelty in him to the feelings of patients and their families that Tellman found abhorrent.

But Gull had unquestionably been a good doctor, and served not only the royal family but also Lord Randolph Churchill and his household.

He could find no written record of Annie Crook's stay at Guy's, but three members of the hospital staff recalled her vividly and said that Sir William had performed an operation on her brain, after which she had very little memory left. In their opinion she was certainly suffering from some form of insanity, at least by the time she had been there for the hundred and fifty-six days of her stay.

What had happened to her after that they did not know. One elderly nurse was grieved by it, and still felt a sense of anger over the fate of a young woman she had been unable to help in her confusion and despair.

Tellman left a little before dark. He could wait no longer. Even if he jeopardized Pitt's mission in Spitalfields, which he believed was largely abortive anyway, he must find him and tell him what he knew. It was far more terrible than any anarchist plot to dynamite a building here or there.

He took the train as far as Aldgate Street, then walked briskly along Whitechapel High Street and up Brick Lane to the corner of Heneagle Street. Wetron might very well throw him off the force if he ever found out, but more was at stake than any one man's career, either his or Pitt's.

He knocked on the door of Karansky's house and waited.

It was several moments before the door was opened a few inches by a man he could barely see in the dim light. There was no more than the silhouette of head and shoulders against the background. He had thick hair and was a trifle stooped.

"Mr. Karansky?" Tellman asked quietly.

The voice was suspicious. "Who are you?"

Tellman had already made the decision. "Sergeant Tellman. I need to speak to your lodger."

There was fear in Karansky's voice. "His family? Something is wrong?"

"No!" Tellman said quickly, warmed by a sudden sense of

normality, of life where affection was possible and the darkness outside was a temporary thing, and under control. "No, but I have learned something I must tell him now. I'm sorry to disturb you," he added.

Karansky pulled the door wider. "Come in," he invited. "Come in. His room is at the top of the stairs. Would you like something to eat? We have—" Then he stopped, embarrassed.

Perhaps they had very little.

"No, thank you," Tellman declined. "I ate just before I came." That was a lie, but it did not matter. Dignity should be preserved.

Karansky may not have meant it to, but the relief was in the tone of his voice. "Then you had best go and find Mr. Pitt. He came in half an hour ago. Sometimes we play a little chess, or talk, but tonight he was late." He seemed about to add something further, then changed his mind. There was anxiety in the air, as if something ugly and dangerous were expected, an inward clenching against hurt. Was it always like that here, the waiting for violence to erupt, the uncertainty as to what the next disaster would be, only the certainty that it would come?

Tellman thanked him and went up the narrow stairs and knocked on the door Karansky had indicated.

The answer was immediate but absentminded, as if Pitt knew who it would be and half expected it.

Tellman opened the door.

Pitt was sitting on the bed, shoulders slumped forward, deep in thought. He looked even more untidy than usual, his hair wild and too long over his collar, but his shirt cuffs had been neatly darned, and there was a pile of clean laundry on the chest of drawers, well ironed.

When Tellman closed the door without speaking Pitt realized it was not Karansky, and looked around. His mouth dropped with amazement, then alarm.

"It's all right!" Tellman said quickly. "But I've learned something I have to tell you tonight. It's . . ." He pushed his hand over his hair, slicked back as always. "Actually, it's not all right." He found he was shaking. "It's the most . . . it's the

228

biggest . . . it's the most hideous and terrible thing I've ever heard, if it's true. And it's going to destroy everything!"

As Tellman told him, the last remaining color bleached out of Pitt's face and he sat motionless with horror, until his body began to shiver uncontrollably, as if the cold had gotten inside him.

10

I<small>T WAS NEARLY</small> midnight when Tellman reached Keppel Street, but he would have no chance in the morning to tell Gracie what he had learned, and Charlotte also. They must know. This hideous conspiracy was bigger than any individual's career, or even their safety. Not that keeping it from them would protect them. Nothing he or Pitt said could prevent them from continuing to pursue the truth. In both women, devotion to Pitt, as well as a sense of justice, was far stronger than any idea of obedience they might have possessed.

Therefore they must have the very slight protection that a knowledge of the conspiracy's enormity might give them.

And they might help. He told himself that fiercely as he stood on the doorstep and looked up at the dark windows. He was a police officer, a citizen of a land in very real danger of being plunged into violence from which it might not emerge for years, and even when it did, much of its heritage and identity could be destroyed. The safety of two women, even one he admired and one he loved, could not be placed before that.

He lifted up the brass knocker and let it fall. It thudded loudly in the silence. Nothing stirred right along the street. He knocked again, three times, and again.

A light came on upstairs, and a few moments later Charlotte herself answered the door, her eyes wide with fear, her hair a dark shadow across her shoulder.

"It's all right," Tellman said immediately, knowing what she feared. "But I've got things I have to tell you."

She pulled the door wider and he followed her inside. She called Gracie, and led him through to the kitchen. She riddled the stove and put more coal on. He bent to help her too late, feeling clumsy. She smiled at him and put the kettle on the hob.

When Gracie appeared, tousle-haired from sleep and, to Tellman, looking about fourteen, they sat around the table with tea, and he told them what he had learned from Lyndon Remus and all that it meant.

It was nearly three in the morning before, at last, Tellman went out into the dark streets to return home. Charlotte had offered to allow him to sleep in the front parlor, but he had declined. He did not feel it was proper, and he needed the width and the loneliness of the street to think.

When Charlotte woke it was daylight. At first all she remembered was that Pitt was not there. The space beside her was the kind of emptiness you have when a tooth has been lost, aching, tender, not right.

Then she remembered Tellman's visit and all that he had told them about the Whitechapel murders, Prince Eddy and Annie Crook, and the fearful conspiracy to conceal it all.

She sat up and pushed the covers away. There was no point in lying there any longer. There was no warmth, either physical or of the heart.

She started to wash and dress automatically. Odd how much less pleasure there was in something simple like brushing and curling her hair now that Pitt was not there to see it, even to annoy her by touching it and pulling pieces out of the pins again. She missed the touch of his hands even more than the sound of his voice. It was a physical pain inside her, like the ache of hunger.

She must concentrate on the problem. There was no time for self-indulgence. Had John Adinett killed Fetters because he was part of the conspiracy to conceal the Whitechapel murderer and the royal part in it all? If he had been part of it, then Adinett should have exposed him and made him answer for his crime, to whatever degree he was involved.

But that made no sense. Fetters was a republican. He would

have been the first person to lay it bare himself. The answer had to be the other way around. Fetters had discovered the truth and was going to expose it, and Adinett had killed him to prevent it. That would explain why he could never have told anyone, even to save his own life. He had not been in Cleveland Street asking after the original crime in 1888 but after Fetters's enquiries into it this year. He must have realized that Fetters knew, and would inevitably make it public for his own ends. And apart from his desire to shield the men who had committed the horrific murders, he wanted to keep the secret they had killed to hide in the first place; whether or not he was a royalist, he did not want revolution and all the violence and destruction it would inevitably bring.

She went downstairs slowly, turning the thought over and over in her mind. She walked along the corridor to the kitchen and heard Gracie banging saucepans and the splash of water as she filled the kettle. It was still early. There would be time for a cup of tea before she woke the children.

Gracie swung around when she heard Charlotte's footsteps. She looked tired, her hair was less tidy than usual, but she smiled with quick response as Charlotte came in. There was something brave and very determined in her eyes which gave Charlotte a surge of hope.

Gracie pushed her stray hair behind her ears, then turned and poked the fire vigorously to get the flames high so the kettle would boil. She dug the poker in as if she were disembowelling some mortal enemy.

Charlotte thought aloud while she fetched milk from the larder, watching where she trod because of the cats circling around her as if determined to trip her up. She poured a little into a saucer for them, and then broke off a small crust of new bread and dropped it on the floor. They fought over it, and patted it around with their paws, chasing it and diving on it.

Gracie made the tea and they sat in companionable silence sipping, while it was sharp and pungent, and still too hot. Then Charlotte went upstairs and woke first Jemima, then Daniel.

"When is Papa coming home?" Jemima asked as she

washed her face, being rather generous with the water. "You said soon." There was accusation in her voice.

Charlotte handed her the towel. What should she say? She heard the sharpness, and knew it came from fear. Life had been disrupted and neither child knew why. The unexplained made the world frightening. If one parent could go and not come back, perhaps the other could as well. Which did the least harm: the uncertain, dangerous truth; or a more comfortable lie that would get them over the next few days, but which might catch her in the end?

"Mama?" Jemima was not prepared to wait.

"I hoped it would be soon," Charlotte replied, playing for time. "It's a difficult case, worse than he thought."

"Why did Papa take it, if it's that bad?" Jemima asked, her stare level and uncompromising.

What was the answer to that? He had not known? He had had no choice?

Daniel came into the room, pulling his shirt on, his hair wet around his brow and over his ears.

"What?" He looked at his mother, then at his sister.

"He took it because it was right," Charlotte replied. "It was the right thing to do." She could not tell them he was in danger, that the Inner Circle had destroyed his career in vengeance for his testimony against John Adinett. Nor could she say he had to work at something or they would lose their home, perhaps even be hungry. It was too soon for such realism. Certainly she could not tell them he had discovered an evil so terrible it threatened to destroy all he knew and trusted from day to day. Dragons and ogres were for fairy stories, not reality.

Jemima frowned at her. "Does he want to come back home?"

Charlotte heard the fear in her that perhaps he had gone because he wished to. She had caught the shadow before, the unspoken thought that some piece of disobedience had made him go, that in some way Jemima had not matched up to his expectations of her and he was disappointed.

"Of course he does!" Daniel said angrily, his face flushed,

233

his eyes hot. "That's a stupid thing to say!" His voice was raw with emotion. His sister had challenged everything he loved.

At another time Charlotte would have told him very quickly about his language; now she was too conscious of the tremor in his voice, the uncertainty that prompted the retaliation.

Jemima was stung, but she was terrified that what she feared was true, and that was far more important than dignity.

Charlotte turned to her daughter. "Of course he wants to come home," she said calmly, as if any other idea were not frightening, only silly. "He hates being away, but sometimes doing the right thing is very unpleasant and means you have to give up some of the things that matter most to you for a while, not forever. I expect he misses us even more than we miss him, because at least we are all together. And we are here at home, and comfortable. He has to be where he is needed, and that is not nearly as clean or pleasant as this."

Jemima looked considerably comforted, enough to start arguing.

"Why Papa? Why not someone else?"

"Because it's difficult, and he's the best," Charlotte replied, and this time it was easy. "If you are the best, that means you always have to do your duty, because there is no one else who can do it for you."

Jemima smiled. That was an answer she liked.

"What sort of people is he chasing?" Daniel was not yet willing to let it go. "What have they done?"

This was less easy to explain. "They haven't done it yet. He is trying to make sure that they don't."

"Do what?" he persisted. "What is it they are going to do?"

"Blow up places with dynamite," she answered.

"What's dynamite?"

"Stuff that makes things blow up," Jemima supplied before Charlotte had time to struggle for it. "It kills people. Mary Ann told me."

"Why?" Daniel did not think much of Mary Ann. He was disinclined to think much of girls anyway, especially on such subjects as blowing people up.

" 'Cos they are in pieces, stupid," she retorted, pleased to turn the charge of inferiority back at him. "You couldn't be alive without your arms and legs or your head!"

That seemed to end the conversation for the time being, and they went down to breakfast.

It was well after nine, and Daniel was building a boat out of cardboard and glue, and Jemima was sewing, when Emily arrived to find Charlotte peeling potatoes.

"Where's Gracie?" she said, looking around.

"Out shopping," Charlotte replied, abandoning the sink and turning towards her.

Emily looked at her with concern, her fair eyebrows puckered a little, her eyes anxious. "How is Thomas?" she said quietly. There was no need to ask how Charlotte was; Emily could see the strain in her face, the weariness with which she moved.

"I don't know," Charlotte replied. "Not really. He writes often, but he doesn't say much, and I can't see his face, so I don't know if he's telling me the truth about being all right. It's too hot for tea. Would you like some lemonade?"

"Please." Emily sat down at the table.

Charlotte went to the pantry and returned with the lemonade. She poured two glasses full and passed one across. Then she sat down and told Emily all that had happened—from Gracie's excursion to Mitre Square to Tellman's visit last night. Not once did Emily interrupt her. She sat pale-faced until finally Charlotte stopped speaking.

"That is far more hideous than anything I had imagined," she said at last, and her voice trembled in spite of herself. "Who is behind it?"

"I don't know," Charlotte admitted. "It could be just about anyone."

"Does Mrs. Fetters have any idea?"

"No . . . at least I'm almost certain she doesn't. The last time I was there we found Martin Fetters's papers and it seemed he was a pretty ardent republican. If Adinett were a royalist, and part of this other terrible thing, and Fetters knew it, then that would explain why Adinett killed him."

"Of course it would. But how can you pursue that now?"

Emily leaned forward urgently. "For heaven's sake, Charlotte, be careful! Think what they've done already. Adinett's dead, but there could be any number of others alive, and you don't have any idea who they are."

She was right, and Charlotte had no argument against it. But she could not let go of the thoughts, the knowledge that Pitt was still in Spitalfields, and men who were guilty of monstrous crimes were going unpunished, as if it did not matter.

"We must do something about it," Charlotte said quietly. "If we don't at least try, who will? And I have to know if that's the truth. Juno has the right to know why her husband was murdered. There must be people who care. Aunt Vespasia will know."

Emily considered for a moment. "Have you thought what will happen if it is true, and because of what we do it becomes public?" she said very gravely. "It will bring down the government . . ."

"If they connived at keeping it secret then they need to be brought down, but by a vote of no confidence in the House, not by revolution."

"It isn't only what they deserve." Emily was perfectly serious. "It is what else will happen, who will take their place. Oh, they may be bad, and I wouldn't argue over that, but before you destroy them you have to think whether what you get instead may not be even worse."

Charlotte shook her head.

"What could be worse than a secret society in government that for its own reasons will connive at murdering like that? It means there is no law and no justice. What happens the next time someone gets in their way? Who will it be? Over what? Can they be butchered too, and whoever does it protected?"

"That's extreme—"

"Of course it's extreme!" Charlotte protested. "They are insane. They have lost all sense of reality. Ask anyone who knows anything about the Whitechapel murders—I mean, really knows."

Emily was very pale. The memory of the tales of four years ago was in her eyes. "You're right," she whispered.

Charlotte leaned towards her. "If we cover it up too, then we are part of it. I'm not prepared to be."

"What are you going to do?"

"See Juno Fetters and tell her what I know."

Emily looked frightened. "Are you sure?"

Charlotte hesitated. "I think so. I'm sure she'd rather believe her husband was killed because he knew about this than because he was planning a republican revolution, and that's what she thinks now."

Emily's eyes widened. "A republican revolution? Because of this?" She drew a deep, shivery breath. "It might have succeeded . . . just possibly . . ."

Charlotte remembered Martin Fetters's face in the photograph Juno had shown her, the wide eyes frank, intelligent, daring. It was the face of a man who would follow his passions whatever the cost. She had liked him instinctively, as she had liked the way he had written about the places and people of the '48 revolutions. Through his sight it had been a noble struggle, and she had seen it that way with him. It had seemed the cause any decent person would have espoused, a love of justice, a common humanity. That he had planned violence here in England was startlingly bitter, almost like the betrayal of a friend. She realized it with surprise.

Emily's voice cut across her thoughts.

"And Adinett was against it? Then why not simply expose him?" she said reasonably. "He would have been stopped."

"I know," Charlotte agreed. "That's why it makes far more sense that this was the reason he was killed . . . he knew about the Whitechapel murders, and he would have exposed that when he had the proof."

"And now this man Remus is going to?"

Charlotte shuddered in spite of the warmth of the familiar room. "I suppose so. He surely wouldn't be stupid enough to try blackmailing them?" It was half a question.

Emily spoke very softly. "I'm not sure he isn't stupid even wanting to know."

Charlotte stood up. "I want to know . . . I think we have to."

She took a deep breath. "Will you look after the children while I go to see Juno Fetters?"

"Of course. We'll go to the park," Emily agreed. Then, as Charlotte stood up and moved past her, she reached out and caught her arm. "Be careful!" she said with fear in her voice, her fingers gripping hard.

"I will," Charlotte promised. She meant it. All this she had was frighteningly precious—the children, this familiar home, Emily, and Pitt somewhere in the gray alleys of Spitalfields. "I will. I promise."

Juno was pleased to see Charlotte. Her days were still necessarily tedious. Very few people called and it was not appropriate that she enjoy any form of entertainment in public life. In truth, she did not wish to. But she had more than sufficient means to employ a full complement of servants, so there was nothing left for her to do. The hours dragged by; there was only so much reading or embroidery, so many letters to write, and she had no talent or interest in painting.

She did not immediately ask if Charlotte had news or further thoughts, and it was Charlotte who opened the subject as soon as they were in the garden room.

"I have discovered something that I need to tell you," she said rather guardedly. She saw Juno's face light with eagerness. "I am not at all sure if it is true, but if it is, then it will explain a great deal. It seems preposterous . . . and much more than that, we may never be able to prove it."

"That matters less," Juno assured her quickly. "I want to know for myself. I need to understand."

Charlotte saw the dark shadows around her eyes and the fine lines of strain in her face. She was living with a nightmare. All the past which she treasured, which should have given her strength now, was shadowed with doubt. Had the man she loved ever existed, or was he a creature of her imagination, someone she had built out of fragments and illusions because she needed to love?

"I think Martin discovered the truth about the most terrible crimes ever committed in London—or anywhere else," Charlotte said quietly. Even in this sunlit room looking onto the garden, the darkness still touched her at the thought, as if that fearful figure could haunt even these streets with his bloody knife.

"What?" Juno said urgently. "What crimes?"

"The Whitechapel murders," Charlotte replied, her voice catching.

Juno shook her head. "No . . . How—" She stopped. "I mean . . . if Martin had known, then he . . ."

"He would have told," Charlotte agreed. "That's why Adinett had to kill him, to keep him from ever doing that."

"Why?" Juno stared at her in horror and bewilderment. "I don't understand."

Quietly, in simple words raw with emotion, Charlotte told her all she knew. Juno listened without interruption until she fell silent at the end, waiting.

Juno spoke at last, her face ashen. It was as if she felt the brush of terror herself, almost as if she had seen the black carriage that rumbled through those narrow streets and looked into the eyes, for an instant, of the man who could do such things.

"How could Martin know that?" she said huskily. "Did he tell Adinett because he thought he could trust him? And he found out only in that last second of his life that Adinett was one of them?"

Charlotte nodded. "I think so."

"Then who is behind Remus now?" Juno asked.

"I don't know. Other republicans, perhaps . . ."

"So it was revolution . . ."

"I don't know. Maybe . . . maybe it was simply justice?" She did not believe it, but she would like to have. She should not stop Juno from clinging to that, if she could.

"There are other papers." Juno spoke again, her voice very steady, as if she were making an intense effort. "I have read through Martin's diaries again, and I know he is referring to something else that is not there. I've looked everywhere I can think of, but I haven't found anything." She was watching Charlotte, entreaty in her face, the struggle to conquer the

239

fear inside her. She needed to know the truth because her nightmares would create it anyway, and yet as long as she did not know she could hope.

"Who else might he trust?" Charlotte racked her thoughts. "Who else would keep papers for him?"

"His publisher!" Juno said with a flash of excitement. "Thorold Dismore. He's an ardent republican. He makes so little secret of it most people discount him as being too open to be any danger. But he does mean it, and he's not nearly as bland or eccentric as they think. Martin would trust him because he knew they had the same ideals and Dismore has the courage of his beliefs."

Charlotte was unsure. "Can you go and ask him for Martin's papers, or would they belong to him, as publisher?"

"I don't know," Juno confessed, rising to her feet. "But I'm prepared to try any approach to get them. I'll beg or plead or threaten, or anything else I can think of. Will you come with me? You can call yourself a chaperone, if you like."

Charlotte seized the chance. "Of course."

It was not a simple matter to see Thorold Dismore, and they were obliged to wait for some three quarters of an hour in a smart, uncomfortable anteroom, but they made good use of the time to plan what Juno should say. When they were finally shown into his startlingly Spartan office, she was quite ready.

She looked very handsome in black, far more dramatic than Charlotte, who had not foreseen such a visit and was in a fairly sober soft green.

Dismore came forward with an easy courtesy. Whatever his political or social beliefs, he was by nature a gentleman, and by birth also, although he made little of it.

"Good morning, Mrs. Fetters. Please come in and sit down." He indicated a chair for her, and then turned to Charlotte.

"Mrs. Pitt," Juno introduced her. "She came to accompany me." It did not need further explanation.

"How do you do," Dismore said with a quickening of interest. Charlotte wondered if he remembered her name from the trial or if his interest was personal. She thought it would be the former, although she had certainly seen that sudden flare in men's eyes before.

"How do you do, Mr. Dismore," she replied modestly, and accepted the seat he offered her, a little to the side of Juno's.

When refreshment had been offered, and declined, it was natural to turn to the purpose of their call.

"Mr. Dismore, I have been reading some of my husband's letters and notes again." Juno smiled, her voice warm with memory.

He nodded. It was a very natural thing to do.

"I realize he had several articles planned for you to publish, on subjects very dear to his heart, matters of social reform he longed to see . . ."

A flicker of pain touched Dismore's eyes; it was more than sympathy, certainly more than mere good manners. Charlotte would have sworn it was real. But they were dealing with causes far more passionate and overwhelming than friendships, however long or sweet. As far as these men were concerned it was a form of war, and one sacrificed even comrades for the ultimate victory.

She studied Dismore's face as he listened to Juno describe the notes she had found. He nodded once or twice but he did not interrupt. He seemed intensely interested.

"Have you all these notes, Mrs. Fetters?" he asked when she finished.

"That is why I have come," she answered innocently. "There seem to be certain essential pieces missing, references to other works, especially"—she took a breath, and her eyes wavered as if she would turn to Charlotte, then she resisted the impulse—"references to people and beliefs which I think are essential to the sense of it."

"Yes?" He sat very still, unnaturally so.

"I wondered if he might have left any papers, documents, or earlier, more complete drafts with you?" She smiled uncertainly. "Together they might be sufficient for an article."

Dismore's face was eager. When he spoke his voice was sharp with excitement. "I have very little, but of course you may see it. But if there is more, Mrs. Fetters, then we must search everywhere possible until we find every last page. I am willing to go to any trouble, or expense, to find them . . ."

Charlotte felt a faint prickle of warning. Was that a discreet threat?

"He was a great man," Dismore continued. "He had a passion for justice which shone like a light through every piece he wrote. He could stir people to look again at old prejudices and rethink them." Again his face pinched with sorrow. "He is a loss to mankind, to honor and decency, and the love of good. A man such as can be followed but not replaced."

"Thank you," Juno said very slowly.

Charlotte wondered if the same thoughts were racing through Juno's mind as were in her own. Was this man a dupe, a naive enthusiast, or the most superb actor? The more closely she watched him the less certain she was. There was none of the deliberate menace in him that she had sensed in Gleave, the heaviness, the feeling of power which would be used ruthlessly if tempted. Rather it was an electric, almost manic energy of mind and a wholehearted passion and intelligence.

Juno would not give up so easily.

"Mr. Dismore, I should be so grateful if I might see what you have of Martin's, and take it home with me. I wish above all things to be able to put what he left in order and then offer you a last work as a memorial to him. That is, of course, if you would wish to publish it? Perhaps I am being presumptuous in—"

"Oh no!" he cut across her. "Not in the least. Of course, I will publish whatever there is, in the best form possible." He reached out and rang the bell on his desk, and when it was answered by the clerk, he instructed him to bring all the letters and papers they possessed written by Martin Fetters.

When the clerk had disappeared to obey, Dismore sat back in his chair and regarded Juno warmly.

"I am so glad you came, Mrs. Fetters. And may I say, I hope without impertinence, how much I admire your spirit in wishing to compose a tribute to Martin. He spoke of you with such high regard it is a pleasure to see that it was not just the voice of a loving husband but of a fine judge of character as well."

The color crept up Juno's cheeks and her eyes filled with tears.

Charlotte ached to comfort her, but there was no comfort to give. Either Dismore was innocent or he spoke with the most exquisite cruelty, and the longer she watched him the less sure she became as to which it was. He was sitting a little forward now, enthusiasm lighting his eyes, his face full of animation as he recalled other articles Fetters had written, journeys he had made to the sites of great struggles against tyranny. His own almost fanatic dedication crackled through every word.

Was it conceivable that his ardor for republican reform was the subtlest mask to conceal a royalist who would commit murder to hide the Whitechapel conspiracy? Did his passion for reform of the law actually cover an obsession so ruthless it would expose that same conspiracy in order to foment revolution with all its violence and pain?

She watched him, listened to the cadences of his voice, and still she could not judge.

The papers were brought in a heavy manila envelope, and without hesitation Dismore passed them to Juno. Was that honesty? Or the fact that he had already read through them all?

Juno took them with a smile that was tight with the strain of maintaining her composure. She barely glanced down at them. "Thank you, Mr. Dismore," she said quietly. "Of course, I shall return to you everything that might be worthy of printing."

"Please do," he urged. "In fact, I should very much like to see whatever you have also, and if you discover more. There may be things of value that do not appear to be so."

"If you wish," she agreed, inclining her head.

He drew breath as if to add something further, an additional urgency to his request, then changed his mind. He smiled with sudden charming warmth. "Thank you for coming, Mrs. Fetters. I am sure that together we shall be able to create an article that will stand for the best memorial to your

243

husband, the one he would wish, which will be a forwarding of the great cause of social justice and equality, a real freedom for all men. And it will come. He was a great man, a man of vision and brilliance, and the courage to use them both. I was privileged to know him and be a part of what he accomplished. It is a tragedy that he had to be lost to us so young, and when he is so desperately needed. I grieve with you."

Juno stood motionless, her eyes wide. "Thank you," she said slowly. "Thank you, Mr. Dismore."

When they were outside and safely back in the first passing hansom, she turned to Charlotte, clutching the papers in her hand.

"He's read them, and there's nothing."

"I know," Charlotte agreed. "Whatever it is that is missing from the papers, it's not what he gave us today."

"Do you suppose they are incomplete?" Juno asked, fingering the manila envelope. "And he kept the rest? He's a republican, I'd swear to that."

"I don't know," Charlotte admitted. The core of Dismore eluded her. She felt less certain of him now than she had before they met.

They rode back to Juno's home in silence, then together looked at all that Dismore had given them. It was vivid, beautifully written, full of passion and the hunger for justice. Once again Charlotte was torn by her instinctive liking for Martin Fetters, his enthusiasm, his courage, his zeal to include all mankind in the same privileges he enjoyed, and at the same time a revulsion for the destruction his beliefs would cause to so much that she loved. There was nothing whatever in any of the new material to suggest he knew of the Whitechapel murders, their reason, or any plan to involve Remus to reveal them now, and the rage and violence that could bring.

She left Juno sitting and reading them yet again, emotionally exhausted, and yet unable to put them down.

She walked to the omnibus stop, her own mind in turmoil. She could not speak to Pitt, which was what she wanted above all else. Tellman had very little knowledge of the world in which people like Dismore and Gleave lived, or the others who might be high in the Inner Circle. The only person she could trust was Aunt Vespasia.

Charlotte was fortunate in finding Vespasia at home and without company. She greeted Charlotte warmly, then looked more intently at her face and settled to listen in silence while the story poured out: everything that first Tellman had learned, and then Gracie's realization of the truth as she stood alone in Mitre Square.

Vespasia sat motionless. The light from the windows caught the fine lines on her skin, emphasizing both the strength of her and the years. Time had refined her, tempered her courage, but it had also hurt her and shown her too much of people's weaknesses and failures as well as their victories.

"The Whitechapel murders," she said softly, her voice hoarse with a horror she had not imagined. "And this man Remus is going to find the proof and then sell it to the newspapers?"

"Yes—that is what Tellman says. It will be the biggest story of the century. The government will probably fall, and the throne almost certainly," Charlotte replied.

"Indeed." Vespasia did not move, but stared with almost blind eyes into some distance which lay within her rather than beyond. "There will be violence and bloodshed such as we have not seen in England since the time of Cromwell. Dear God, what evil to match evil! They would sort out one corruption to replace it with another, and all the misery will be for nothing."

Charlotte leaned forward a little. "Isn't there anything we can do?"

"I don't know," Vespasia confessed. "We need to learn who it is that is guiding Remus, and what part Dismore and Gleave play in it. What was Adinett doing in Cleveland Street? Was he seeking to find the information for Remus, or to prevent him from finding it?"

"Prevent him," Charlotte replied. "I think . . ." Then she realized how little she knew. Almost all of it was conjecture, fear. It involved Fetters and Adinett, but she was still not certain beyond doubt how. And there was no room for even the smallest mistake. She told Vespasia about Gleave's visit and his desire to find Martin Fetters's papers. She described her own sense of threat from him, but said here in this clean, golden room it sounded more like imagination than reality.

But Vespasia did not decry the impression. She continued to listen intently.

Charlotte then went on to tell her about Juno's conviction that there were new papers, and their visit to Thorold Dismore, and Juno's belief that he was a true republican and fully intended to use all he could find or create to bring to pass his own purposes.

"Possibly," Vespasia agreed. She smiled very slightly, and with a sadness that lay deep behind her eyes. "It is not an ignoble cause. I do not agree with it, but I can understand much that it strives for, and admire those who pursue it."

There was something in her which prevented Charlotte from arguing. She realized with a sense of loneliness how much older Vespasia was than she, and how much of Vespasia's life there was about which she knew nothing. And yet she loved her with a depth that had nothing to do with time or blood.

"Let me consider it," Vespasia said after a moment or two. "In the meantime, my dear, be extremely careful. Learn what you can without jeopardizing yourself. We are dealing with people who think little of killing individual men or women in order to accomplish their purposes for nations. They believe ends justify means, and think they have the right to do anything they consider will serve what they have convinced themselves is the greater good."

Charlotte felt a darkness in this light room, and a chill as if night had fallen early. She stood up.

"I will. But I must tell Thomas. I—I need to see him."

Vespasia smiled. "Of course you do. I wish I could also, but I realize it's impractical. Please remember me to him."

Impulsively, Charlotte stepped forward and bent to put her arms around Vespasia, and held her, their shoulders close.

246

She kissed her cheek, and then left without either of them speaking again.

Charlotte went home by way of Tellman's lodgings, and to his landlady's consternation, waited over half an hour for him to return from Bow Street. Without prevarication she asked that he take her the following morning to meet with Pitt on his way to work at the silk factory. Tellman protested the danger of it to her, the unpleasantness, and above all, the fact that Pitt would certainly not wish her to go to Spitalfields. She told him not to waste time with protests that meant nothing. She was going, with or without him, and they both knew it, so it would be altogether better if he simply acknowledged it so they could agree upon arrangements and get a good night's sleep.

"Yes, ma'am," he conceded. She saw in his face that he was too aware of the gravity of the situation to make more than a token argument to satisfy conscience. He saw her to the omnibus stop again.

"I'll be at the door in Keppel Street at six in the morning," he said gravely. "We'll take a hansom to the underground railway station, and a train to Whitechapel. Wear your oldest clothes, and boots that are comfortable for walking. And maybe you could borrow a shawl to hide your hair; it would make you less noticeable from the local women."

She agreed, with a sense of foreboding, yet anticipation at the thought of seeing Pitt.

When she got home she ran up the stairs, washed her hair even though she would hide it under a shawl, and brushed it until it shone. She had not intended to tell Gracie, but she could not keep it secret. She went to bed early, and found herself too excited to sleep until long after midnight.

In the morning she woke late and had to hurry. There was barely time for a cup of tea. She drank it too hot and left half of it behind when Tellman knocked at the door.

"Tell Mr. Pitt we miss 'im terrible, ma'am!" Gracie said quickly, blushing a little, her eyes steady.

"I will," Charlotte promised.

Tellman was on the step, the dark shape of a hansom looming behind him. He looked thin-shouldered, gaunt-faced, and she realized for the first time how much Pitt's disgrace had affected him. He might loathe admitting it, but he was deeply loyal, both to Pitt himself and to his own sense of right and wrong. He might resent authority, see its faults and the injustices of differences in class and opportunity, but he expected the men who led him to observe certain rules within the law. Above all, he had not expected them to betray their own. Whatever his origins, Pitt had earned his place as one of them, and in Tellman's world that had meant he should have been safe.

He might deplore the social conscience, or lack of it, among those of the officer class, but he knew their morality, at least he had thought he did, and it was worthy of respect. That was what made their leadership tolerable. Suddenly it was no longer so. When the fixed parts in the order of things began to crumble, there was a new and frightening kind of loneliness, a confusion unlike anything else.

"Thank you," she said quietly as he walked across the damp footpath with her and handed her up into the cab. They rode in silence through the morning streets, the clear, gray light catching the windows of houses and shops. There were already many people about: maids, delivery boys, carters fetching fresh goods in for the markets. The first milk wagons were waiting at the ends of the streets and already queues were forming as they turned in towards the station.

The train as it roared through the black tunnel was far too noisy to allow conversation, and Charlotte's mind was absorbed in anticipation of seeing Pitt. It had been only a matter of a few weeks, but it stretched behind her like a desert of time. She pictured how he would look: his face, his expression, whether he would be tired, well or ill, happy to see her. How much had the injustice wounded him? Was he changed by the anger he had to feel? That thought cut so deeply it caught her like a physical pain.

She sat bolt upright in the train seat. She did not realize, until Tellman moved beside her and stood up, gesturing to the door, how she had been clenching and unclenching her fingers so they ached. She stood up as the train lurched to a stop. They were at Aldgate Street, and they must walk the rest of the way.

It was broader daylight now, but the streets were dirtier, more congested with carts and wagons and groups of men on their way to work, some trudging, heads down, others shouting across to each other. Was there really a tension in the air, or did she imagine it because she knew the history of the place, and because she herself was frightened?

She kept close beside Tellman as they turned north out of the High Street. He had said they were going to Brick Lane, because Pitt would pass that way on his journey to the silk factory where he worked. This was Whitechapel. She thought about what the name meant literally, and how ludicrous a name it was for this grimy, industrial area with its narrow streets; dust; gray, broken windows; dogleg alleys; chimneys belching smoke; smells of drains and middens. Its history of horror lay so close beneath the surface it was sharp and painful in the heart.

Tellman was walking quickly, not to seem out of place among the men hurrying to the sugar factories, warehouses and yards. She had to trot to keep up with him, but perhaps here that was appropriate. Women did not walk beside their men at this time of day, as if they were courting couples.

There was a burst of raucous laughter. Someone smashed a bottle, and the thin tinkle of glass was startlingly unpleasant. She thought not of the loss of something useful, as she would at home, but of the weapon the jagged ends would make.

They were in Brick Lane now.

Tellman stopped. She wondered why. Then, with a lurch of her heart she saw Pitt. He was on the other side of the road, walking steadily, but unlike the other men, he was looking from side to side, listening, seeing. He was dressed shabbily; his coat was torn at the back, sitting crookedly as usual. And instead of his beautiful boots that Emily had given him, he had old ones with the left sole loose and string for laces. His hat was dented at the side of the brim. It was only by the familiarity of his walk that she recognized him before he turned and saw her.

He hesitated. He would not expect to see her here—he probably had not even been thinking of her—but perhaps something about the way she stood attracted him.

She started forward, and Tellman caught her arm. For an instant she resented it and would have torn herself loose, then she realized that running across the street would draw attention to her, and so to Pitt, and she allowed herself to be held back. People around here knew Pitt. They would ask who she was. How could he answer? It would start gossip, questions.

She stood with one foot on the curb, her face hot with embarrassment.

Her brief movement had been enough. Pitt had recognized her. He sauntered across the street, dodging between the carts, behind a dray and in front of a costermonger's barrow. He reached them and after the merest nod to her, he spoke as if to Tellman.

"What are you doing here?" he said softly, his voice jagged with emotion. "What's happened?"

She stared at him, memorizing every line of him. He looked tired. His face was freshly shaved but there was a grayness to his skin, and a hollowness around his eyes. She felt her chest tight with the ache to comfort him, to take him home to his own house, to warmth and a clean kitchen, the smells of linen and scrubbed wood, the quietness of the garden with its scent of damp earth and cut grass, doors that closed out the world for a few hours—above all, to hold him in her arms.

But far more urgent than that was the need to show people that he had been right, to prove it so they would have to acknowledge it, to heal the old wound of his father's shame. She was angry, hurt, helpless, and she did not know what to say or how to explain herself to make him understand, so he would be as pleased to see her as she was just to be close to him, see his face and hear his voice.

250

"A lot's happened," Tellman was saying quietly. He only called Pitt "sir" if he was being insolent, so he had no need to guard his tongue for unintentional betrayal now. "I don't know it all, so it would be better for Mrs. Pitt to tell you. But it's things you have to know."

Pitt caught the edge of fear in Tellman's voice, and his anger evaporated. He looked at Charlotte.

She wanted to ask how he was, if he was all right, what his lodgings were like, if they were kind to him, was his bed clean, had he enough pillows, how was the food, was it enough. Most of all, she wanted him to know she loved him and missing him was more painful, more deeply lonely than she could have imagined, in every way: for laughter, for conversation, for sharing the good and bad of the day, for touching, just for knowing he was there.

Instead she began with what she had been rehearsing in her mind, and probably Tellman could have told him just as well. She was very succinct, very practical.

"I've been visiting Martin Fetters's widow. . . ." She ignored the startled look on Pitt's face and went on quickly before he could interrupt. "I wanted to find out why he was killed. There has to be a reason. . . ." She stopped again as a group of factory women went past them, talking together loudly, looking at Pitt, Tellman and Charlotte with undisguised curiosity.

Tellman shifted his weight uncomfortably.

Pitt moved a step away from Charlotte, leaving her seeming to belong to Tellman.

One of the women laughed and they moved on.

A vegetable cart rumbled down the street.

They could not stand here talking for long, or it would be remembered, and endanger Pitt.

"I read most of his papers," she said briefly. "He was a passionate republican, even prepared to help cause revolution. I believe that was why Adinett killed him, when he discovered what Fetters meant to do. I imagine he didn't dare trust the police. No one might have believed him—or worse, they might have been part of it."

Pitt was stunned. "Fetters was . . ." He took a long, deep breath as the meaning became clear of all she had said. "I see." He stood silently for long moments, staring at her. His eyes moved down her face as if he would recall every detail of it, touch her mind beyond.

Then he recalled himself to the present, the crowded street, the gray footpath and the urgency of the moment.

Charlotte found herself blushing, but it was a sweet warmth that ran through the core of her.

"If that is so, we have two conspiracies," he said at last. "One of the Whitechapel murderer to protect the throne at any cost at all, and another of the republicans to destroy it, also at any cost, perhaps an even more dreadful one. And we are not sure who is on which side."

"I told Aunt Vespasia. She asked to be remembered to you." She thought as she said it how inadequate those words were to convey the power of the emotions she had felt from Vespasia. But as she looked at Pitt's face she saw that he understood, and she relaxed again, smiling at him.

"What did she say?" he asked.

"To be careful," she replied ruefully. "There's nothing I can do anyway, except keep on looking to see if we can find the rest of Martin Fetters's papers. Juno is certain there are more."

"Don't ask anyone else!" Pitt said sharply. He looked at Tellman, then realized the pointlessness of expecting him to prevent her. Tellman was helpless, frustrated, and it was plain in his expression, a mixture of hurt, fear and anger.

"I won't!" she promised. It was said on the spur of feeling, to stop the anxiety she could see consuming him. "I won't speak to anyone else. I'll just visit with her and keep on looking inside the house."

He breathed out slowly.

"I must go."

She stood still, aching to touch him, but the street was full of people. Already they were being stared at. In spite of all sense she took a step forward.

Pitt put out his hand.

A workman on a bicycle whistled and shouted something unintelligible at Tellman, but it was obviously bawdy. He laughed and pedaled on.

Tellman took Charlotte by the arm and pulled her back. His fingers hurt.

Pitt let out a sigh. "Please be careful," he repeated. "And tell Daniel and Jemima I love them."

She nodded. "They know."

He hesitated only a moment, then turned and crossed the street again, away from them, not looking back.

Charlotte watched him go, and again heard laughter from a couple of youths on the farther corner.

"Come on!" Tellman said furiously. This time he took her wrist and yanked her around, almost off balance. She was about to say something very curt indeed when she realized how conspicuous she was making them. She had to behave as people expected or it would look even worse.

"I'm sorry," she said, and followed him dutifully back down towards the Whitechapel High Street. But her steps were lighter and there was a singing warmth inside her. Pitt had not touched her, nor she him, but the look in his eyes had been a caress in itself, a touch that would never fade.

Vespasia was not especially fond of Wagner, but the opera, any opera at all, was a grand occasion and held a certain glamour. Since the invitation was from Mario Corena, she would have accepted it even had it been to walk down the High Street in the rain. She would not have told him so, but she suspected he might already know. Not even the hideous news that Charlotte had brought could keep her from going with him.

He called for her at seven and they rode at a very leisurely pace in the carriage he had taken for the evening. The air was mild and the streets were crowded with people, seeing and being seen on their way to parties, dinners, balls, exhibitions, excursions up and down the river.

Mario was smiling, the last of the sunlight flickering on his face through the windows as they moved. She thought that time had been kind to him. His skin was still smooth, the lines were upward, without bitterness, in spite of all that had been lost. Perhaps he had never given up hope, only changed it as one cause had died and another had been created.

She remembered the long, golden evenings in Rome as the sun went down over the ancient ruins of the city, now lost in centuries of later and lesser dreams. The air there was warmer, with no cold edge to it, heavy with the smell of heat and dust. She remembered how they had walked on the pavements that had once been the center of the world, trodden by the feet of every nation on the earth come to pay tribute.

But that had been the Imperial age. Mario had stood on one of the older, simpler bridges across the Tiber, watching the light on the water, and told her with passion raw in his voice of the old republic that had thrown out the kings, long before the years of the Caesars. That was what he loved, the simplicity and the honor with which they had begun, before ambition overtook them and power corrupted them.

With the thought of power and corruption, a chill touched her that the warmth of the evening could not ease; even the echoes of memory were not strong enough to loose its grip.

She thought of the dark alleys of Whitechapel, of women waiting alone, hearing the rumble of carriage wheels behind them, perhaps even turning to see its denser blackness outlined against the gloom, then the door opening, the sight of a face for a moment, and the pain.

She thought of poor Eddy, a pawn moved one way and then the other, his emotions used and disregarded in a world he only half heard, perhaps half understood. And she thought of his mother, deaf also, pitied and often ignored, and how she must have grieved for him, and been helpless to move even to comfort him, let alone to save him.

They were approaching Covent Garden. There was a small girl standing on the corner and holding out a bunch of wilted flowers.

Mario stopped the coach, to the anger and inconvenience of the traffic around them in both directions. He climbed out and walked over to the girl. He bought the flowers and returned with them, smiling. They were dusty, their stalks bent and petals drooping.

"A little past their best," he said wryly. "And I gave rather too much for them." There was laughter in his eyes, and sadness.

She took them. "How very appropriate," she answered, smiling back, a ridiculous lump in her throat.

The carriage moved on again, amid considerable abuse.

"I'm sorry it's Wagner," he remarked, resettling himself into his seat. "I can never take it all with the right degree of seriousness. The men who cannot laugh at themselves frighten me even more than those who laugh at everything."

She looked at him and knew how profoundly he meant it. There was an edge to his voice like that she remembered in the hot, dreadful days of the siege before the end. They had realized, during those nights alone, when all the work they could do was past and there was nothing else but to wait, that in the end they would not win. The Pope would return and sooner or later all the old corruptions would come back too, bland-faced, pitiless, impersonal.

But they had had a passion inside and a loyalty that gave more than it ever cost, even at the very last. The men who beat them were stronger, richer and sadder.

"They mock because they don't understand," she said, thinking of those who had derided their aspirations so long ago.

He was looking at her as he always had, as if there were no one else.

"Sometimes," he agreed. "It is far worse when they do it because they *do* understand but they hate what they cannot have." He smiled. "I remember my grandfather telling me that if I desired wealth or fame there would always be those who would hate me for it because both are earned at someone else's cost. But if I wished only to be good, no one would begrudge me that. I did not argue with him, partly because he was my grandfather, but mostly because I did not realize then

255

how wrong he was." His mouth tightened and there was a terrible sadness in his eyes. "There is no hatred on earth like that for someone who possesses a virtue you do not have, or want. It is the mirror that shows you what you are, and obliges you to see it."

Without thinking she reached out her hand and laid it on his. His fingers closed over hers immediately, warm and strong.

"Who are you thinking of?" she asked, knowing it was not simply memory speaking, dear as that was.

He turned to her, his eyes grave. They were nearly there and it would be time to alight in a moment, join the throng gathering on the opera house steps, women in laces and silk, jewels winking in the lights, men in shirts so white they gleamed.

"Not a man, my dear, so much as a time." He looked around them. "This cannot last, the extravagance, the inequality and the waste of it. Look at the beauty and remember it, because it is worth a great deal, and too much of it will go." His voice was very soft. "Only a little wiser, a little more moderate, and they could have kept it all. That is the trouble—when anger bursts at last it destroys the good as well as the bad."

Before she could press him further the carriage stopped and he alighted, handing her down before the footman could do so. They went up the steps and in through the crowds, nodding to a friend or acquaintance.

They saw Charles Voisey standing deep in conversation with James Sissons. Sissons was looking flushed, and every time Voisey hesitated he cut in.

"Poor Voisey," Vespasia said wryly. "Do you think we are morally obliged to rescue him?"

Mario was puzzled. "Rescue him?" he asked.

"From the sugar factory man," she said with surprise at having to explain to him. "He is the most crashing bore."

An aching pity filled Mario's face, a regret that filled her with longing for things which could never be, not even all those years ago in Rome, except in dream.

"You know nothing of him, my dear, not of the man beneath the awkward surface. He deserves to be judged for his heart, not his grace . . . or lack of it." He took her arm and with surprising strength led her past Voisey and Sissons and the group beyond them, and up the stairs towards the box.

She saw Voisey take his seat almost opposite them, but she did not see Sissons again.

She wanted to enjoy the music, to let her mind and her heart be fully with Mario in this little space of time, but she could not rid her thoughts of what Charlotte had told her. She turned over every possibility in her mind, and the longer she did so the less could she doubt that what Lyndon Remus had been led to was hideously close to the truth, but that he was being manipulated for purposes far beyond everything he understood.

She trusted Mario's heart. Even after all those years she did not believe he had changed so much. His dreams were woven into the threads of his soul. But she did not trust his head. He was an idealist; he saw too much of the world in broad strokes, as he wished it to be. He had refused to allow experience to dull his hope or teach him reality.

She looked at his face, still so full of passion and hope, and followed his glance across at the royal box, which was empty tonight. The Prince of Wales was probably indulging in something a trifle less serious than the deliberation of the doomed gods of Valhalla.

"Did you choose *Twilight of the Gods* on purpose?" she asked.

Something in her voice caught his attention, a gravity, even a sense of time running out. There was no laughter in his eyes as he answered.

"No . . . but I could have," he said softly. "It is twilight, Vespasia, for very flawed gods who wasted their opportunities, spent too much money that was not theirs to cast away, borrowed money that has not been paid back. Good men will starve because of it, and that makes more than the victims angry. It wakens a rage in the ordinary man, and that is what brings down kings."

257

"I doubt it." She did not enjoy contradicting him. "The Prince of Wales has owed so much money for so long it is only a slow anger left now, not hot enough for what you speak of."

"That depends who he has borrowed from," he said gravely. "From rich men, bankers, speculators or courtiers; to some extent they took their own risks and can be thought to deserve their fate. But not if the lender is ruined and takes others down with him."

The houselights were dimming and a silence fell in the theater. Vespasia was hardly aware of it.

"And is that likely to happen, Mario?"

The orchestra sounded the first ominous notes.

She felt his hand touch hers gently in the darkness. There was still remarkable strength in him. In all the times he had touched her he had never hurt her, only broken her heart.

"Of course it will happen," he replied. "The Prince is as bent on his own destruction as any of Wagner's gods, and he will bring all Valhalla down with him, the good as well as the bad. But we have never known how to prevent that. That is their tragedy, that they will not listen until it is too late. But this time there are men with vision and practical sense. England is the last of the great powers to hear the voice of the common man in his cry for justice, but perhaps because of that it will learn from those of us who failed, and you will succeed."

The curtain went up and showed the elaborate set on the stage. In its light Vespasia looked at Mario, and saw the hope naked in his face, the courage to try again, in spite of all the battles lost, and in him still no generosity to wish victory for others.

She almost wished it could succeed, for his sake. The old corruption was deep, but in so many cases it was part of life, ignorance, not deliberate wickedness, not cruelty, simply blindness. She could understand Charles Voisey's arguments against hereditary privilege, but she knew human nature well enough to believe that the abuse of power is no respecter of persons: it affects king and commoner alike.

"Tyrants are not born, my dear," she said softly. "They are made, by opportunity, whatever title they give themselves."

He smiled at her. "You think too little of man. You must have faith."

She swallowed the tears in her throat, and did not argue.

11

AFTER LEAVING CHARLOTTE, Pitt walked on down
the street towards the sugar factory. The heavy, sickly smell
caught in his nose and throat, but not even the thought of
standing the night watch there could dull the happiness that
welled up inside him at having seen her, even for a short time.
She was so exactly as his memory had re-created her in the
long nights alone: the warmth of her, the line of her cheek,
her lips, above all her eyes as she looked back at him.

He turned in at the factory gates, the huge building towering over him, the men jostling at his sides. All he wished to
know was if they needed him that night. He called by to check
most mornings.

"Yeah," the senior watchman said cheerfully. He looked
tired today, his blue eyes faded and all but hidden by the folds
of his skin.

"Right," Pitt replied regretfully. He would prefer a night's
sleep. "How is your wife?"

The night watchman shook his head. "Poorly," he said with
an attempt at a smile.

"I'm sorry." Pitt meant it. He always asked, and the answer
varied from day to day, but she was failing and they both
knew it. He stayed and talked a few moments longer. Wally
was lonely and he always wanted a listening ear to share his
anxieties.

Afterwards, Pitt hurried back towards Saul's workshop,
now a trifle late. He was late from his first errand too, because

a wagonload of barrels had spilled out onto the street, and he stopped and helped the carter put them back. The little bubble of peace inside him made him impervious to the gray streets, the anger and the fear that set nerves on edge.

He went back to Heneagle Street early. Isaac was not home yet and Leah was busy in the kitchen.

"That you, Thomas?" she called as she heard his footsteps at the bottom of the stairs.

He could smell cooking, sharp, sweet herbs. He was more accustomed to them now and had grown to like them.

"Yes," he answered. "How are you?"

She never responded directly. "Are you hungry? You should eat more . . . and not keep all those late hours at that factory. It's not good for you."

He smiled. "Yes, I am hungry, and I've got to do the early watch tonight."

"Then come and eat!"

He went upstairs first to wash his face and hands, and found the clean laundry she had laid on the chest for him. He picked up the shirt on top, and saw that she had turned the cuffs for him, placing the worn edges to the inside.

A wave of homesickness washed over him so overwhelmingly that for a moment he was almost unaware of the room around him. It was a simple domestic kindness, the sort of thing Charlotte did. He had seen her spend all evening mending, turning collars or cuffs, needle clicking against her thimble, light flashing silver on it as it wove in and out in tiny stitches.

Then he was furious for so many women like Leah Karansky, who were never asked whether they wanted revolution or what price they would pay for someone else's idea of social justice or reform. Perhaps all they wanted was their family safe at home at night, and enough food to put something on the table fit to eat.

He looked at Leah's stitches on his cuff and knew how long it had taken her to do. He must thank her, let her know he was mindful of the kindness, perhaps talk to her about something interesting as he did. Or better, listen to her with all his attention while she talked.

After supper, still smiling at Leah's stories, he walked into the sugar factory yard just as Wally arrived.

"Ah, you again!" Wally said cheerfully. "Wot d'yer do with all yer money, eh? Silk all day and sugar all night. I tell yer, somebody's 'avin' a soft life on yer labor, fer certain."

"Me, one day," Pitt said with a wink.

Wally laughed. " 'Ere, I 'eard a good story about a candle maker an' an old woman." And without waiting he proceeded to tell it with relish.

An hour later Pitt made his first round of his area of patrol, and Wally went in the opposite direction, still chuckling to himself. There was still a skeleton staff working. The boilers never went out, and he checked in each room, climbing the narrow stairs past every floor. The rooms were small, the ceilings low to cram in as many storeys as possible. The windows were tiny; from outside in the daylight the building looked almost blind. Now, of course, it was lit by lamps, carefully guarded because the syrup was highly flammable.

Each room he passed was filled with vats, casks, retorts and huge dish-shaped boilers and pans several feet wide. The few men still working glanced around, and he spoke a few words to them and continued on. The smell of raw, almost rotting sweetness was everywhere. He felt as if he never got it out of his clothes and hair.

Half an hour later he reported back down to Wally. They boiled a kettle on the brazier in the open yard and sat on old hogshead barrels in which the raw sugar came from the West Indies, and sipped the tea until it was cool enough to drink. They swapped stories and jokes; some of them were very long and only mildly funny, but it was the companionship that mattered.

Once or twice there was movement in the shadows. The first time, Wally went to investigate and returned to say he thought it had been a cat. The second time, Pitt went, and found one of the boiler men asleep behind a pile of casks. His slight stirring had upset one of the casks and sent it rolling across the cobbles.

They each completed another round, and another.

Once, Pitt saw a man leaving whom he did not recognize. He seemed older than most of the workers, but then life in Spitalfields aged people. It was the cast of his features which caught Pitt's attention: strong, fine-boned, dark complexioned. He kept his eyes averted, merely raising one hand in a quick salute, and light flashed for an instant on a dark-stoned ring. There was a sense of intelligence in him that remained in the memory even as Pitt returned to the yard and found Wally boiling the kettle again.

"Do many men leave shift at this time?" Pitt asked.

Wally shrugged. "A few. Bit early, but poor devils don't get thanked for it anyway. Sloped off 'ome ter bed, I daresay. Good luck ter 'im. Wouldn't mind me own bed." He took the kettle off the fire.

" 'Ere, did I ever tell yer abaht w'en I went up the canal ter Manchester?" And without waiting for an answer, he carried on with the tale.

Two hours later Pitt was halfway through the next round of the upstairs rooms when he came to the end of the corridor and saw Sissons's office door ajar. He thought it had not been open the last time he was here. Had some worker been in there?

He pushed the door open, holding up his lantern. The room was wider than the others, and from seven storeys up in the very faint light of the false dawn he could see over the rooftops to the south, the silver reflection on the shining surface of the river.

He held his lantern high, turning around the room.

Sissons was sitting at his desk, slumped forward across its polished surface. There was a gun in his right hand, and there was a pool of blood on the wood and leather beneath him. But sharpest, glaring white in the lamplight that caught it, was a sheet of paper untouched by the blood, unstained. The inkwell was on the right of the desk towards the front, set in its own slightly sunken base, the quill resting in its stand, the knife beside it.

Cold, his stomach a little queasy, Pitt took the two steps over to Sissons, careful not to disturb anything, but he could see no footmarks on the bare floor, no drops of blood. He touched Sissons's cheek. It was almost cold. He must have been dead two or three hours.

He moved around the desk and read the note. It was written in a neat, slightly pedantic hand.

I have done all I can, and I have failed. I was warned, and I did not listen. In my foolishness I believed that a prince of the blood, heir to the throne of England, and so of a quarter of the world, would never betray his word. I lent him money, all I could scrape together, on a fixed term and at minimal interest. I believed that by so doing I could relieve a man of his financial embarrassment, and at the same time earn a little interest that I would be able to put back into my business, and benefit my workers.

How blind I was. He has denied the very existence of the loan, and I am finished. I shall lose the factories, and a thousand men will be out of work, and all those who depend upon them will perish likewise. It is my fault, for trusting a man not worthy of honor. I cannot live to see it happen; I cannot bear to watch it, or face the men I have destroyed.

I am taking the only course left to me. May God forgive me.

James Sissons

Beside it lay a note of debt for twenty thousand pounds, signed by the Prince of Wales. Pitt stared at them and they swam before his eyes. The room seemed to sway around him as if he were aboard a ship. He put his hands on the desk to steady himself. Sissons was beyond help. When the first clerk came in, when he was found, and the letter and note of debt with him, it would do more damage than half a dozen sticks of dynamite. An unrepaid loan to the Prince of Wales, for him to race horses, drink wine and give presents to his mistresses, while in Spitalfields fifteen hundred families went into beggary! Shops would close, tradesmen would go out of business, houses would be boarded up and people would live on the streets.

There would be riots that would make Bloody Sunday in Trafalgar Square look like a playground squabble. The whole of the East End of London would erupt.

And when Remus was given the last piece of evidence he needed to expose the Whitechapel murderer as in the service of the throne, no one would care whether the Queen or the Prince of Wales, or anyone else, had known of it or wished it; there would be revolution. The old order would be gone forever, replaced by rage, and then terror, and then unrelenting destruction, the good and the bad torn apart together.

Law would be the first to suffer, the law that oppressed and the law that protected equally, and finally all law, even that which governed conscience and the violence within.

He reached for the letter. If he tore it up, no one else would ever know. Then he noticed beside it a pattern of tiny platters of ink with a large clear space in the center. It was a moment before he realized what it was; then he picked up the inkwell and placed it very carefully over the unmarked patch. It fit exactly. The inkwell normally sat to the left of Sissons! Had it been moved to make him seem right-handed?

Carefully he took the dead man's left hand and turned it over, gently touching the insides of the first and second fingers. He felt the ridge where Sissons normally held a pen. Why?

He had been shot in the right side of his head ... and someone had realized too late that he was left-handed.

A murder made to look like suicide ... but by whom? And who might lie and say Sissons was right-handed, or could use either hand?

He must make certain this was seen as the murder it was. If he got rid of the gun, dropped it in one of the sugar vats, there could be no denying it.

This half of the conspiracy could be stifled. Then even if Remus broke the other story, the rage here in Spitalfields would not erupt. There would be anger, but against Sissons, not against the throne.

Was that what he wanted? His hand stayed in the air,

poised above the paper. If the Prince of Wales had borrowed money for his own extravagance and not repaid, even when it would bring ruin to thousands of people, then he deserved to be overthrown, stripped of his privileges and left as comparatively destitute as those in Spitalfields were now. Even if he became a fugitive, a refugee in another land, it was no worse than what happened to many. He would have to start again as a stranger, just as Isaac and Leah Karansky and tens of thousands like them had done. In the last analysis, all human life was equal.

What justice was there if Pitt concealed this monstrous selfishness, criminal irresponsibility, because the guilty man was the Prince of Wales? It made him party to the sin.

And if he did not, then countless people who had no say in it at all would be consumed by the violence which would follow, and the destruction which would leave poverty and waste behind it, perhaps for a generation.

His mind was in turmoil. Every belief he had lived by forbade he conceal the truth of the debt. Yet even as his thoughts raced, his hand closed over the paper. He crunched it up, then unfolded it and tore it across again and again until it was in tiny pieces. Not yet certain why, he put the note of debt far down inside his shirt, next to his body.

He was shivering, the sweat standing out cold on his skin. He had committed himself. There was no way to turn back.

If this had to be known as murder, then he must make it look like one. He had surely known enough murders to know what the police would look for. Sissons had been dead for at least two or three hours. There was no danger they would suspect him. Better it should be an impersonal robbery than hatred or revenge, which would indicate someone who knew him.

Was there money in the office? He should make it look as if it had been searched, at the very least. And quickly. He must not seem to have stood there debating what to do. An honest man would have raised the alarm immediately. He had already delayed almost too long. There was no time for indecision.

He pulled out the desk drawers and tipped them onto the floor, then the files. There was a little petty cash. He could not bring himself to take it. Instead he put it under one of the drawers and replaced it. It was not very satisfactory, but it would have to do.

He riffled quickly through other pieces of paper to see if there was anything else about the Prince's loan. They seemed to be all concerning the factory and its daily running, orders and receipts, a few letters of intent. Then one caught his eye because he knew the handwriting. Coldness filled him as he read it.

My dear friend,

It is a most noble sacrifice you are making for the cause. I cannot stress how much you are admired among your fellows. Your ruin at the hands of a certain person will set off a fire which will never be extinguished. The light of it will be seen all over Europe, and your name remembered with reverence as a hero of the people.

Long after the violence and the death are forgotten your memorial will be the peace and prosperity of those ordinary men and women who came after.

Yours with the utmost respect.

It was signed with a swirl of the pen which could have been anything. What flared in Pitt's brain like an explosion was the fact that the writer had known about Sissons's ruin, and very possibly even his death. The wording was ambiguous, but it seemed that was what it meant.

He must destroy it also, immediately. Already he could hear footsteps in the passage outside. He had been gone too long. Wally would be looking for him to make sure everything was all right.

He ripped the letter into pieces. There was no time to get rid of it, but at least it would be illegible. He would have to make an opportunity to put the remnants of both letters, and the gun, in one of the vats.

Even as he was moving towards the door he remembered where he had seen the handwriting. He stumbled and banged into the corner of the desk as the full import struck him. It had been during the investigation of Martin Fetters's death—it was John Adinett's hand!

He stood stock-still, dizzy for an instant, his leg throbbing where the desk corner had bruised it, but he was only dimly aware.

Wally's footsteps were almost at the door.

Adinett had known of the plan for Sissons's ruin, and had praised him for it! He was not a royalist, as they had presumed, but as far from it as possible. So why had he killed Martin Fetters?

The door opened and Wally peered around it, the lantern in his hand making his face look ghostly in the upward light.

"You all right, Tom?" he said anxiously.

"Sissons is dead," Pitt replied, startled by how hoarse his voice was, and that his hands were shaking. "Looks as if somebody shot him. I'm going to get the police. You stay here and make sure no one else comes in."

"Shot 'im!" Wally was stunned. "W'y?" He stared across at the figure slumped across the desk. "Gawd! Poor devil. Wot'll 'appen now?" There was fear in his voice and in his face, which was slack with shock and dismay.

Pitt was hideously conscious of the gun in his pocket and the torn-up pieces of the two letters.

"I don't know. But we'd better get the police quickly."

"They'll blame us!" Wally said, panic in his face.

"No, they won't!" Pitt denied, but the same thought was like a sick ache in the bottom of his stomach. "Anyway, we've got no choice." He moved past Wally and out of the door, carrying his own lantern high so he could see the way. He must find an unattended vat and get rid of the gun.

The first room he tried had a night worker in it who looked up without curiosity; so did the second. The third was unoccupied and he lifted the lid of the vat, smelling the thick liquid. The paper would not sink in it. He would have to stir it in, but he dared not be found with the pieces. They could still be placed together, with care. He put them on the surface and used the gun to move them around until they were lost, then he let the gun go and watched it sink slowly.

268

As soon as it was out of sight he went out into the corridor again and ran down the rest of the stairs and out into the yard. He went straight to the gates and down Brick Lane towards the Whitechapel High Street. The false dawn had widened across the sky, but it was still long before daylight. The lamps gleamed like dying moons along the curb edge and shone pale arcs on the wet cobbles.

He found the constable just around the corner.

"Eh, eh! Wot's the matter wi' you, then?" the constable asked, stepping in front of him. Pitt could only see the outline of him because they were between lampposts, but he was tall and seemed very solid in his cape and helmet. It was the first time in his life Pitt had been afraid of a policeman, and it was a cold, sick feeling, alien to all his nature.

"Mr. Sissons has been shot," he said, his breath rasping. "In his office, in the factory up Brick Lane."

"Shot?" the constable said unsteadily. "You sure? Is 'e 'urt bad?"

"He's dead."

The constable was stunned into a moment's silence, then he gathered his wits. "Then we'd better send ter the station an get Inspector 'Arper. 'Oo are you, an' 'ow'd yer come ter find Mr. Sissons? You the night watch, then?"

"Yes. Thomas Pitt. Wally Edwards is there with him now. He's the other night watchman."

"I see. D'yer know where the Whitechapel station is?"

"Yes. Do you want me to tell them?"

"Yes. You go an' tell 'em Constable Jenkins sent yer, an' tell 'em wot yer found at the factory. I'll be there. Understand?"

"Yes."

"Then 'urry."

Pitt obeyed, turning on his heel, then breaking into a run.

It was nearly an hour later when he was back at the sugar factory, not in Sissons's office but in one of the other fairly large rooms on the top floor. Inspector Harper was a very different man from Constable Jenkins, smaller with a blunt face and square chin. Jenkins was standing by the door, and Pitt and Wally were standing in the middle of the floor. It was now early daylight, gray through the dockland smoke, and the sun was silver on the stretches of the river below them in the distance.

"Right now, then . . . what's your name? Pitt!" Harper began. "You just tell me exactly what you saw an' what you did." He frowned. "And what were you doing in Mr. Sissons's office anyway? Not part of your duty to go in there, is it?"

"The door was open," Pitt replied. His hands were clammy, stiff. "It shouldn't be. I thought something might be wrong."

"All right, all right! So tell me what you saw, exactly!"

Pitt had prepared this very carefully, and he had said it all to the duty sergeant at the Whitechapel station already.

"Mr. Sissons was sitting at his desk, slumped over it, and there was a pool of blood, so I knew immediately he wasn't just asleep. Some of the desk drawers were half open. There was no one else in the room and the windows were closed."

"Why d'you say that? What difference does that make?" Harper challenged. "We're seven storeys up, man!"

Pitt felt himself flushing. He must not appear too quick. He was a night watchman, not a superintendent of police.

"None. Just noticed it, that's all."

"Did you touch anything?"

"No."

"Are you sure?" Harper looked at him narrowly.

"Yes, I'm sure."

Harper looked skeptical. "Well, he was shot with a handgun, pistol of sorts, so where is it?"

Pitt realized with a lurch that Harper was suggesting he had taken it. He could feel the guilt hot in his face. Suddenly he knew exactly how others had felt when he had questioned them, men perhaps innocent of the crime but with other desperate secrets to hide.

"I don't know," he said as steadily as he could. "I suppose whoever shot him took it when they went."

"And who could that be?" Harper asked, his eyes wide, pale blue. "Aren't you the night watch? Who came or went, then? Or are you saying it was one of the men who work here?"

"No!" Wally spoke for the first time. "Why'd any one o' us do that?"

"No reason at all, if you've any sense," Harper replied. "More like he shot himself, and Mr. Pitt here thought he'd take a little souvenir. Maybe sell it for a few shillings. Good gun, was it?"

Pitt looked up at him with amazement and met his gaze squarely. It was that instant he realized with horror that crawled over his skin that Harper had known what he was going to find. Harper was Inner Circle, and he intended it to be suicide. Pitt's throat was tight, his mouth dry.

Harper smiled. He was master and he knew it.

Jenkins shifted his feet unhappily. "We got no evidence o' that, sir."

"Got no evidence against it either!" Harper said sharply, without moving his eyes from Pitt's. "We'll have to see what turns up when we look into Mr. Sissons's affairs, won't we?"

Wally shook his head. "Yer got no reason ter say as Tom took the gun, an' that's a fact." His voice shook with fear, but his face was stubborn. "And any'ow, Mr. Sissons never shot 'isself, 'cos I seen the body. 'E were shot in the right side of 'is 'ead, like 'e were right-'anded, which 'e were! 'Ceptin' 'is right fingers was broke an' the wotsits cut, so 'e couldn't curl up 'is fingers . . . so 'e couldn't 'a pulled a gun tight ter shoot it. Doctors wot looks at 'im'll tell yer that."

Harper was confused and angry. He turned to Jenkins and met a blank stare of dumb insolence and immovability.

"Well, then," he said angrily, looking away. "I suppose we'd better find out who sneaked in past our two diligent night watchmen . . . and murdered their employer. Hadn't we?"

"Yes sir!" he responded.

Harper spent the rest of the morning questioning not only Wally and Pitt as to every detail of their watch, but also all the night staff and many of the clerks who came in to start the day.

Pitt did not tell him about the man he had seen leaving. At

first he kept silent more from instinct than thought-out reason. It was not something he could have imagined doing twenty-four hours ago, but now he was in a new world, and he realized with incredulity that for weeks now he had been growing closer to people like Wally Edwards, Saul, Isaac Karansky, and the other ordinary men and women of Spitalfields who were distrustful of the law, which had seldom protected them and which had never caught the Whitechapel murderer. He believed what Tellman had told him about that investigation, about Abberline, even about Commissioner Warren. The tentacles of that conspiracy reached right up to the throne itself.

But it was not the same conspiracy as that which had murdered James Sissons and made it look like suicide, or was feeding Lyndon Remus with information which when complete would expose the greatest scandal in royal history and bring down the government and the crown with it.

And Harper was part of that second conspiracy; Pitt was certain of that. Therefore he could tell him nothing he did not have to.

Second to that, and coming to his realization a moment later, was that the description he could give could fit easily many people he knew: Saul, or Isaac, or a score of other older men. And perhaps Harper would like nothing better than to use that excuse to whip up anti-Semitic feeling. It would suit his purposes very well to blame the Jews for the ruin of the sugar factory. It was not as good as blaming the Prince of Wales, but it was better than nothing.

And so it turned out. By midday, when Pitt was allowed to leave, Harper had suggested, and then paraphrased, answers until he had a definite intruder observed by three different night workers: a thin, dark man of Jewish appearance, carrying something in his hand on which the light gleamed, like the barrel of a gun. He had crept up the stairs, soft-footed, and some little time later crept down again and disappeared into the night.

Pitt left feeling sick and miserable, and more helpless than ever in his life. His concept of the law and all his beliefs were shifted into a new and ugly pattern. He had seen corruption before, but it had been individual, born of greed or weakness exploited, never a cancer that spread silent and unseen throughout the entire body of those who created the law and admonished it, even those who judged it. There was no recourse, no one left to whom the hunted or injured could appeal.

As he walked along Brick Lane up towards Heneagle Street he found himself genuinely and deeply afraid. It was the first time he had felt this way since he was a child and his father had been taken away, and the realization had come that there was no justice to save him, no one who could help. They would never meet again, and he was helpless to make any difference to it.

He had forgotten how terrible that feeling was, the bitterness of disillusion, the loneliness of understanding that this was the end of this particular path. There was nothing beyond except what he himself could create.

But he was a man now, not a child. He could and would effect it! He changed direction and increased his pace towards Lake Street. If Narraway was not in, he would demand that the cobbler send for him. At least he would find out which side Narraway was on, force him to show himself. He had very little to lose, and if Remus succeeded, then nobody would have.

He crossed the street and passed a newsboy shouting the headlines. In the House of Commons, Mr. McCartney had asked whether the conflict between political parties in Ireland would be such as to prevent peaceable citizens from voting. Would protection be provided for them?

In Paris, the anarchist Ravachol had been found guilty and sentenced to death.

In America, Mr. Grover Cleveland had been nominated as the Democratic candidate for the presidency.

As he reached Lake Street he passed another newsboy, this one holding a placard saying that James Sissons had been murdered in a conspiracy to ruin Spitalfields, and the police

273

already had witnesses who had seen a dark-haired man of foreign appearance on the premises, and were now looking to identify him. The word *Jew* had not been used, but it might as well have been.

Pitt reached the cobbler's shop and left a message that he required to speak to Narraway immediately. He was told to return in thirty minutes.

When he did, Narraway was waiting for him. He was not sitting in his usual position, but standing in the tiny room as if he had expected Pitt to the minute and was too restless to make even the smallest concession to the idea that things were as usual.

"Well?" he demanded as soon as the door was closed.

Now that it was the moment, suddenly Pitt was undecided. His hands were clammy, his heart knocking in his chest. Narraway's eyes seemed to be boring into his mind, and he still had no idea whether to trust him or not.

"You wanted something, Pitt! What is it?" Narraway's voice was hard-edged. Was he afraid too? He must have heard of Sissons's murder, and he would understand all its implications. Even if he were Inner Circle, riot was not what he wanted. But there was nowhere else to turn. A phrase came into Pitt's mind: if you would sup with the devil, you must have a long spoon. He thought of the five women in Whitechapel, and the coach that had gone around at night, looking for them to butcher. Was it really better than riot, even revolution?

"For God's sake, man!" Narraway exploded, his eyes dark and brilliant, his face bleached of color with exhaustion. "If you've got something to say, say it! Don't waste my time!"

This time there was no mistaking his fear. It was under the surface, but Pitt could feel it like electricity crawling over the skin.

"Sissons wasn't murdered the way the police suppose," he said, committing himself. There was no going back now. "I was the one who found him, and when I did it looked like suicide. The gun was there in his right hand, along with a letter

274

saying that he had killed himself because he was ruined over a loan he had made and which was now denied."

"I see. And what has happened to this note?" Narraway's voice was soft now, almost expressionless.

Pitt felt his stomach lurch.

"I destroyed it." He swallowed. "I also got rid of the gun." He was not going to mention Adinett's letter or the note of debt.

"Why?" Narraway said softly.

"Because the loan was to the Prince of Wales," Pitt replied.

"Yes . . . I do see." Narraway rubbed his hands over his brow, pushing his hair back into spikes. In that single gesture was a weariness and a depth of understanding that dispelled the outer shell of Pitt's fear. It was peculiarly naked, as if at last it had exposed something of the real man.

Narraway sat down and gestured to the other chair. "So what is this about a Jew being seen leaving the factory?"

Pitt smiled wryly. "Inspector Harper's attempt to find an acceptable scapegoat—not as good as the Prince of Wales."

Narraway looked up sharply. "As good?"

There was no going back, no safety left. "For his purposes," Pitt replied. "Harper is Inner Circle. He was expecting Sissons's death. He was dressed and waiting to be called. He tried to say it was suicide and blame me for stealing the gun. He might have succeeded if Wally Edwards hadn't stood up to him—and Constable Jenkins as well. It was Wally who said Sissons couldn't have shot himself because of an old injury; he didn't have the use of his right fingers."

"I see." Narraway's voice was bitter. "And do I assume from this that you now trust me? Or are you sufficiently desperate that you have no choice?"

Pitt would not add to his lies. And perhaps Narraway deserved better, either way. "I don't think you want the East End in flames any more than I do. And yes, I am desperate."

A black humor showed briefly in Narraway's eyes. "Should I thank you for at least that much?"

Pitt would have liked to tell him about the Whitechapel murders and what Remus knew, but that was taking trust too

275

far, and once said it could not be taken back. He shrugged very slightly and made no reply.

"Can you see the police don't blame some innocent person?" he said instead.

Narraway gave a short bark of laughter, bitter and derisive.

"No . . . I can't! I can't stop this lot from blaming Sissons's death on some poor Jew, if that's what they think will get them out of more trouble." He bit his lip hard, till the pain showed in his face. "But I'll try. Now get out of here and do what you can yourself. And Pitt!"

"Yes?"

"Don't go telling anyone what you did—no matter who they arrest. They won't believe you anyway. You'll only make it worse. This has nothing to do with truth. It's about hunger and fear, and guarding your own when you have too little to share."

"I know," Pitt agreed. It was also about power and political ambition, but he did not add that. If Narraway did not know, this was not the time to tell him; if he did, it was unnecessary. He went out without saying anything more.

12

PITT HAD NEVER felt so profoundly alone. It was the first time in his adult life that he had deliberately placed himself outside the law. He had certainly known fear before, physical and emotional, but never had he experienced the moral division that was within him now, the sense of being an alien in his own place.

He woke up cold, the sheets mangled and knotted, half off his body. The gray morning light filled the room. He could hear Leah moving around downstairs. She was frightened. He had seen it yesterday in her averted eyes, the tension in her hands, which were clumsier than usual. He could picture her in the kitchen, her face tight with anxiety, going about her morning rituals automatically, listening for Isaac's step, perhaps dreading Pitt's coming downstairs because she would have to pretend in front of him. It was difficult having strangers in the house in times of crisis, and yet it had its advantages. It forced one to hide the terror that threatened to swallow one from inside. Panic was delayed.

Sissons had been murdered after all . . . and then it had been made to look like a suicide, and Pitt had altered the evidence—lied, in effect—to make it murder again. He had made the decision to conceal the truth, what he thought was truth, in order to stop riot, perhaps revolution. Was that ridiculous?

No. He knew the violence in the air, the fear, the anger, the smoldering despair that could be ignited by a few words, spoken by the right person at the right time and place. And when Dismore—and then all the other editors—published Lyndon Remus's story about the Duke of Clarence and the Whitechapel murders, the fury would seize all London. It would then take only half a dozen men in positions of power, ready and willing, to overthrow the government and the throne . . . with how much death and waste to follow?

And yet in twisting the truth Pitt had betrayed the man in whose house he now lay and at whose table he would eat his breakfast, as he had eaten last night's supper.

The pain of that knotted in his stomach and forced him to get up and walk across the carefully homemade rug to the dresser and the ewer of water. He poured half of it out into the bowl and plunged his hands in it, then lifted them to his face.

Whom could he turn to for help? He was cut off from Cornwallis, and was certain he was powerless anyhow. Perhaps even Tellman would despise him for this. For all his anger, Tellman was a conservative man, a rigid conformer to his own rules, and he knew precisely what those were. They would not include lies, falsifying evidence, misleading the law—whatever the purpose.

How often had Pitt himself said "The end does not justify the means"?

He had trusted Narraway with at least part of the truth, and that thought rippled a cold fear through him, an uncertainty like nausea. And what about Charlotte? He had so often talked to her about integrity.

He stood shivering a little, sharpening his razor absent-mindedly. Shaving in cold water hurt. But half the world shaved cold!

What would Charlotte say to him about Sissons? It did not matter what she said; what would she think? Would she be so disappointed in him it would kill something of the love he had seen in her eyes only days ago? You could love vulnerability—perhaps more even than the lack of it—but not moral weakness, not deceit. When trust was gone, what was it that was left? Pity . . . the keeping of promises because they had been made . . . duty?

What would she have done had she found Sissons and the letter?

He looked at his face in the small square of glass. It was the same as always, a little more tired, a little more deeply lined, but the eyes were not different, nor the mouth.

Had he always had these possibilities within him? Or was it the world that had changed?

Standing there turning it over and over in his mind would achieve nothing. Events would not wait for him, and his decision was already made in that moment in Sissons's office.

Now he must save from it what he could.

He realized that while he had been scraping at his cheeks, not minding the sting and drag of the blade, it had crystallized in his mind that the only person he trusted and who might have some power to help was Vespasia. He was absolutely certain of her loyalties and her courage, and—perhaps just as important—of her anger. She would feel the same sick, scalding outrage that he did at the thought of what would happen if riot engulfed the East End and spread—or if it were contained and some member of the Jewish population was hanged for a crime he had not committed, because the law was administered by the prejudiced and corrupt.

That too would be a kind of overthrow of government, deeper to the heart. It would appear to affect fewer, but did it not corrupt all eventually? If the law did not distinguish between the innocent and the guilty but was merely expedient for those in power, then it was worse than useless. It was a positive evil, masquerading as good, until finally it deceived no one and became itself a thing of loathing. Then not only the reality of law was gone, but the concept destroyed in the minds of the people.

He had made a bad job of shaving, but it did not matter. He washed in the rest of the cold water and then dressed. He had no heart to face Isaac and Leah at breakfast, and perhaps no time. If it was cowardly, today it was a small sin in the balance.

He said good morning hastily, and without explanation left

the house. He walked hurriedly down Brick Lane to the Whitechapel High Street and Aldgate Station. He must see Vespasia, regardless of the hour.

The newspapers this morning were full of Sissons's murder. There was actually an ink drawing of the supposed killer, made up from the descriptions Harper had drawn from reluctant night staff at the factory and one vagrant ambling along Brick Lane who had seen someone pass. With a little imagination the face in the drawing could have been Saul's, or Isaac's, or that of any of a dozen others Pitt knew. What was even worse was the suggestion in print underneath the drawing that the murder had to do with money lending at extortionate rates and a refusal to repay.

Pitt was furious and miserable, but he knew argument was pointless. Fear of poverty was too high to listen to reason.

When he arrived at Vespasia's house it was still before nine, and she had not yet risen. The maid who answered the door looked startled that anyone, let alone an unusually scruffy-looking Pitt, should call at such an hour.

"It is urgent I speak with Lady Vespasia as soon as she will see me," he said with something less than his usual courtesy. The raw edges of his emotion were audible in his voice.

"Yes sir," she said after a moment's hesitation. "If you would like to come in, I shall inform Her Ladyship that you are here."

"Thank you," he accepted, grateful that he had been here sufficiently often that she knew him, and Vespasia had always been eccentric enough in her affections that his presence was not questioned.

He stood in the golden breakfast room overlooking the garden, where the maid had left him to wait.

Vespasia appeared within fifteen minutes, not dressed for the day, but in a long, ivory silk peignoir, her hair hastily coiled up, a look of concern in her face.

"Has something happened, Thomas?" she asked without preamble. She had no need to add that he looked haggard and no normal occurrence could have brought him here at this time of day and in this state.

"A great deal has happened," he replied, pulling out a chair for her and holding it while she sat down. "And it is uglier and more dangerous than anything I have ever imagined before."

She waved to the chair at the opposite side of the elegant, octagonal table. It had originally been set for one, but a second place had been added by a maid who anticipated her mistress's wishes.

"You had better tell me," Vespasia instructed him. She looked at him critically. "I imagine you could do so over breakfast?" It was not really a question. "Although it might be prudent to suspend your remarks while the servants are in the room."

"Thank you," he accepted. Already he was beginning to feel a little ease from the sense of despair with which he had begun. He realized with surprise how deeply he loved this remarkable woman whose birth, heritage and entire life were so different from his own. He looked at her beautiful face with its perfect bones and fragile skin, the heavy-lidded eyes, the delicate lines of age, and knew the irretrievable sense of loss he would feel when she was no longer here. He could not bring himself to use the word *dead* even in the secrecy of his mind.

"Thomas . . ." she prompted.

"Did you read about the death of Sissons, the sugar manufacturer?" he asked.

"Yes. Apparently he was murdered," she replied. "The newspapers imply it was by Jewish moneylenders. I should be very surprised if that is true. I assume it is not, and you are aware of what is."

"Yes." There was no time to be restrained or careful. "I found him. It was made to look like suicide. There was a note." Briefly he told her what it had said. Then wordlessly he passed over the note of debt.

She looked at it, then walked over to her escritoire and took out a handwritten note. She looked at both pieces of paper, and smiled.

"It is a good likeness," she said. "But not perfect. Do you wish for it back?"

"I think it is safer with you," he replied, surprisingly relieved that it was not, after all, one more piece of self-indulgence.

He told her of the letter from Adinett, and the deduction he had drawn from it. He watched her as he spoke, and saw the sadness in her face, and anger, but not surprise. Her belief was a tiny thread of comfort.

And then it was even harder to tell her what he had done, but there was no way whatever to avoid it. To weigh personal feelings now would be inexcusable.

"I destroyed both letters and took the gun away when I left, and dropped them in one of the sugar vats," he said jerkily, "I made it look like murder."

She nodded very slightly. "I see."

He waited for her to go on, for the surprise, the distancing of herself from the act, but he did not see it. Was she so good at concealing her thoughts? Possibly. Maybe she had seen enough duplicity and betrayal over the decades that nothing shocked her anymore. Or perhaps she had never expected anything different from him. How well did he really know her? Why had he assumed so confidently that she thought of him as honorable, so that anything he did, or failed to do, would mark her more than peripherally?

"No, you don't," he replied, pain and anger sharpening his voice. "I learned from Wally Edwards, the other night watchman, that Sissons had an injured right hand. He couldn't have pulled the trigger himself. I made a murder, disguised as suicide, look like a murder again." He drew in a deep breath. "And I think I saw the man who did it, but I have no idea who he was, except that I have not seen him before."

She waited for him to continue.

"He was older, dark hair graying, dark complexion, fine-boned face. He had a dark-stoned signet ring on his hand. If he was one of the Jews from the area, he's one I don't know."

She sat silent for so long he began to fear she had not heard him, or had not understood. He stared at her. There was an immense sadness in her eyes. Her thoughts were inwards, fixed upon something he could not even guess at.

He hesitated, not knowing whether to interrupt or not.

Questions beat in his mind. Should he not have troubled her with this? Was he expecting far too much of her, thinking her superhuman, investing her with strength she could not have?

"Aunt Vespasia . . ." Then he realized with a wave of embarrassment that he had been too familiar. She was not his aunt. She was his wife's sister's aunt, by marriage. He had presumed intolerably. "I . . ."

"Yes, I heard you, Thomas," she said quietly, no anger or offense in her voice, only confusion. "I was wondering whether it was deliberate or another piece of opportunism. I can see no way in which opportunism is believable. It must have been planned in order to embarrass the crown, or worse, perhaps to cause riots which could then be exploited . . ." She frowned. "But it is very ruthless. I . . ." She lifted one shoulder very slightly. He saw how thin she was under the silk of the peignoir, and again he felt her fragility, and her strength.

"There is more," he said quietly.

"There must be," she agreed. "Alone this does not make sense. It would accomplish nothing permanent."

Suddenly he felt as if they were allies again. He was ashamed of doubting her generosity of spirit. Stumbling to find the right words, he told her what Tellman had said about the Duke of Clarence and Annie Crook, and the whole tragic story.

The clear morning light caught both Vespasia's beauty and her age, the passion of all that she had seen in her lifetime. It was naked in her eyes and her lips, how deeply she had felt it, and understood.

"I see," she said when he finally came to the end. "And where is this man Remus now?"

"I don't know," Pitt admitted. "Looking for the last shred of proof, I imagine. If he had it, Dismore at least would have printed it by now."

Vespasia shook her head fractionally. "I think from what you say that it was intended to break at the same time as Sissons's suicide, and you prevented that. We may have a day or so of grace."

"To do what?" he asked, a sharp note of desperation back in his voice. "I have no idea who to trust. The Inner Circle could be anybody!" He felt the darkness close in on him again, impenetrable, suffocating. He wanted to go on, say something that would describe the enormity of it, but he did not know how to, except by repeating the same desperate, inadequate words over and over again.

"If the Inner Circle is at the heart of this conspiracy," Vespasia said, almost as much to herself as to him, "then their desire is to overthrow the government, and the throne, and replace them with a leadership of their own, presumably a republic of some nature."

"Yes," he agreed. "But knowing that does not help us to find them, let alone prevent it."

She shook her head a little. "That is not my point, Thomas. If the Inner Circle's intent is to create a republic, then they certainly were not the ones who concealed the tragic marriage of the Duke of Clarence or murdered five unhappy women to make sure it was never known." She looked at him steadily, her silver eyes unblinking.

"Two conspiracies . . ." he whispered. "Then who else? Not . . . not the throne itself?"

"Please God, no," she answered. "I cannot swear, but I should guess the Masons. They have the power, and the will to protect the crown and the government."

He tried to imagine it. "But would they . . . ?"

She smiled very slightly. "Men will do anything, if they believe in the cause enough and have sworn oaths they dare not break. Of course, it is also possible it has nothing to do with them at all. We may never know. But someone has broken an oath, or been extraordinarily careless, and someone else has been cleverer than anyone foresaw, because the Inner Circle now has both the power to shatter everything and, it seems, the will to do it." She took a deep breath. "You have delayed them, Thomas, but I doubt they will accept defeat.

"And meanwhile I will have contrived to endanger half the Jews in Spitalfields and almost certainly get one of them hanged for a crime he may not have committed," he added. He hated the self-loathing in his voice the instant he heard it.

She shot him a look of anger that did not yet include pity, but it would be worse when it did. He burned to prove it unjust.

"Is there a way we can find out if the Clarence story is true?" he asked. He was not certain what he was reaching towards, only that inaction was surrender.

"I don't think it matters anymore," she answered him, the anger softening from her eyes. "It could be true, and I doubt anyone could disprove it, which is all the Inner Circle will need. The outrage it would create would not hesitate for an instant to weigh or judge facts. If it is to be stopped, then it must be before it is said aloud by anyone outside the Circle." The ghost of a smile touched her lips. "Like you, I am not certain whom I can trust. No one, I think, for morality. There are times when one stands alone, and perhaps this is one of them. But there are those whose interests I believe I can judge well enough to trust which way they will act when pressed."

"Be careful!" He was terrified for her. He should not have spoken; he was aware even as he said it. It was an impertinence, but he no longer cared.

She did not bother to reply to that. "Perhaps you had better see if you can do something to help your Jewish friends. I think there is little purpose in your pursuing whoever really killed poor Sissons. He seems to have been a dupe all the way along—I think to some degree a willing one. He did not foresee death in the end. He had no idea of the power or the evil of the conspiracies with which he was meddling. There are so many idealists for whom the end will justify any means, men who began nobly . . ." She did not complete the thought. It trailed away, carrying its ghosts of the past.

"What are you going to do?" he pressed her, frightened for her, and guilty that he had come to her.

"I know of only one thing that we can do," she answered, looking not at him but into the distance of her vision. "There are two monstrous alliances. We must turn them upon each

285

other, and pray to God that the outcome is more destructive to them than to us."

"But . . ." he began to protest.

She turned to face him, her eyebrows slightly raised. "You have some better thought, Thomas?"

"No."

"Then, return to Spitalfields and do what you can to see that innocent bystanders do not pay the price for our disasters. It is worth doing."

He rose obediently, thanked her, and did as she had told him. Only when was he out in the morning traffic did he realize that he had still not had breakfast. The servants had been too conscientious to interrupt them with such trivialities as food.

When Pitt had gone, Vespasia rang the bell and the maid came with fresh tea and toast. While she ate it her mind raced over all the possibilities. One thought underlay all of them, and she refused to look at that yet.

First she would address the immediate problem. It hardly mattered that Sissons had not in fact lent money to the Prince of Wales, so long as the Inner Circle had contrived to make it seem as if he had. And she believed they would have taken care of all other appearances necessary to create the fraud. The sugar factories would close. That was the purpose of the murder. The ordinary men of Spitalfields would not riot unless their jobs were lost.

Therefore she must do something to prevent that, at least in the short term. In a longer time some other answer could be found . . . possibly even a grand gesture by the Prince? It would be an opportunity for him to redeem himself, at least in part.

She went upstairs and dressed with great care in a gunmetal-gray costume with sweeping skirt and magnificently embroidered collar and sleeves. She collected a parasol to match, and sent for her carriage.

She arrived at Connaught Place at half past eleven—not a time one called upon anybody, but this was an emergency, and she had said as much on the telephone to Lady Churchill.

Randolph Churchill was waiting for her in his study. He

rose from his desk as she was shown in, his smooth face severe, displeasure only moments away, held in by good manners, and perhaps curiosity.

"Good morning, Lady Vespasia. It is always a pleasure to see you, but I admit your message occasioned some alarm. Please do . . ."

He was about to say "sit down," but she had done so already. She had no intention of allowing anyone, even Randolph Churchill, to set her at a disadvantage.

". . . and tell me what I can do for you," he finished, resuming his own seat again.

"There is no time to waste in pleasantries," she said tersely. "You are probably aware that James Sissons, sugar manufacturer in Spitalfields, was murdered yesterday." She did not wait for him to acknowledge that he was. "Actually, it was intended to look like suicide, complete with a note blaming his ruin upon having lent money to the Prince of Wales, who had refused to repay it. As a consequence, all three of his factories would be ruined and at least fifteen hundred families in Spitalfields sent into beggary." She stopped.

Churchill's face was ashen.

"I see you understand the difficulty," she said dryly. "It could become extremely unpleasant if this closure comes about. Indeed, along with other misfortunes which we may not be able to prevent, it could even bring about the fall of the government and of the throne . . ."

"Oh . . ." he began to protest.

"I am old enough to have known those who witnessed the French Revolution, Randolph," she said with ice in her voice. "They too did not believe it could happen . . . even with the rattle of the tumbrels in the streets, they disbelieved."

He wilted a little, as if the energy in him to protest had been drained away by fear. His eyes were wide, his breathing shallow. His fine, soft hands were stiff on the polished desk surface. He watched her almost unblinkingly. It was the first time in her life she had ever seen him rattled.

"Fortunately," she continued, "we have friends, one of whom happened to be the person who discovered Sissons's

287

body. He had the foresight to remove the gun and the note of debt, and destroy the letter, so the death appeared to be murder. But it is only a temporary solution. We need to see to it that the factories keep working and the men are paid." She met his gaze unflinchingly, a tiny smile on her lips. "I imagine you have friends who would feel as you do, and be willing to contribute something towards that end. It would be a very enlightened thing to do, in our own self-interest, not to mention as a moral gesture. And if done in such a way that the public were to learn of it, I imagine it would meet with a considerable feeling of gratitude. The Prince of Wales, for example, might find himself the hero of the day—as opposed to the villain. That has a certain ironic appeal, don't you think?"

He took a very deep breath and let it out in a long, slow sigh. He was relieved; it glowed in his face in spite of any attempt to mask it. And he was also awed by her, very much against his will, and that was there also. For an instant he considered prevaricating, pretending to consider the idea, then he abandoned it as absurd. They both knew he would do it; he must.

"An excellent solution, Lady Vespasia," he said as stiffly as he was able, but his voice was not quite steady. "I shall see to it that it is implemented immediately . . . before any real damage is done. It—it is fortunate indeed that we had a . . . friend . . . so well placed."

"And with the initiative to act, at considerable risk to himself," Vespasia added. "There are those who will make life exceedingly difficult for him should they learn of it."

He smiled bleakly, pulling his lips into a thin line.

"We shall assume that that will not happen. Now, I must set about this sugar factory business."

She rose to her feet. "Of course. There is no time to be lost." She did not thank him for seeing her. They both knew it was even more in his interest than in hers, and she made no pretenses for him. She did not like him; she had profound suspicions, close to certainty, as to his deep involvement with the Whitechapel murders, although there was no proof. She was using him, and she would not affect to be doing anything else. She inclined her head very slightly as he passed her to open the door and hold it while she walked through.

"Good day," she said with a thin smile. "I wish you success."

"Good day, Lady Vespasia," he replied. He was grateful, but to circumstance, common interest, not to her.

There was one other matter, a darker, far more painful one, but she was not yet ready to face that.

Pitt spent the journey from Vespasia's house back to Spital-fields turning over in his mind what he could do to prevent some innocent man from being made the scapegoat for Sissons's murder. He had heard all the rumors that were on the street as to whom the police suspected. The latest drawings looked more and more like Isaac. It could be only a matter of days at the most, perhaps hours, before his name was mentioned. Harper would see to it. He had to arrest someone to diffuse the mounting anger. Isaac Karansky would do very well. His crime was being a Jew and different, a leader of a clearly identifiable community that looked after its own. Sissons's death was merely the excuse. Usury was a common enemy, an unproven charge, but fixed in the mind over centuries of word of mouth, gossip, and blame for a dozen otherwise inexplicable ills.

Pitt had one advantage: he had been on the scene first and was therefore a witness. He could find a reason to go back to Harper and speak to him.

When he got off the train at the Aldgate Street station he had already made the decision and was only settling in his mind exactly what he would say.

He walked briskly. Someone must have killed Sissons, but as Vespasia had said, it would be a member of the Inner Circle. He would almost certainly never find out who that was. Harper would do all he could to see to that.

By the afternoon the streets were hot and sour-smelling, the gutters nearly dry, refuse piling up. Tempers were short.

There was fear in the air. People seemed unable to concentrate on trivial tasks. Quarrels exploded over nothing: a mistake in change, one man bumping into another, a dropped load, a stubborn horse, a cart badly parked.

Constables on the beat were tense, truncheons swinging by their sides. Both men and women shouted abuse at them. Now and then someone bolder threw a stone or a rotten vegetable. Children whimpered without knowing what they were afraid of.

A pickpocket was caught and beaten bloody. No one intervened, or sent for the police.

Pitt still did not know whether he could trust Narraway, but perhaps he could learn something from him without giving away anything himself.

Narraway might be Inner Circle, or he might be a Mason, and willing to do anything, risk anything, to save the order of things as they were, the vested power, the throne. Or he might be neither, simply what he claimed: a man trying to control the anarchists and prevent riot in London.

Pitt found him in the same back room as always. He looked tired and ill at ease.

"What do you want?" Narraway asked curtly.

Pitt had changed his mind a dozen times as to what he would say, and he was still uncertain. He studied Narraway's face: the level brows, the clever, deep-set eyes and the heavy lines from nose to mouth. It would be unwise to underestimate him.

"Karansky didn't kill James Sissons," he said bluntly. "It's Harper's way of putting the blame somewhere. He's coercing the witnesses, making that description up."

"Oh? Sure of that, are you?" Narraway asked, his voice expressionless.

"Aren't you?" Pitt demanded. "You know Spitalfields, and you put me to lodge with Karansky. Did you think him capable of murder?"

"Most men are capable of murder, Pitt, if the stakes are high enough, even Isaac Karansky. And if you don't know that, you shouldn't be in this kind of work."

290

Pitt accepted the rebuke. He had worded the question too clumsily. His nerves were showing.

"Did you think he was planning insurrection? Or the punishment of borrowers who don't pay usury?" he corrected himself.

Narraway twisted his mouth into a grimace. "No. I never thought he was a moneylender in the first place. He is head of a group of Jews who look after their own. It's a charity, not a business."

Pitt was startled. He had not realized that Narraway knew that. A little of the tension eased inside him.

"Harper thinks he can blame him. Every few hours he's getting closer," he said urgently. "They'll arrest him if they can create one more piece of evidence. And with the high anti-Jewish feeling at the moment, that won't be hard."

Narraway looked tired, and there was a thread of disappointment in his voice. "Why are you telling me that, Pitt? Do you imagine I don't know?"

Pitt drew in his breath sharply, ready to challenge him, to accuse him of indifference, neglect of duty or even of honor. Then he looked more closely at his eyes and saw the disillusion, the inner weariness of a series of defeats, and he let his breath out again without saying what was on his tongue. Should he trust Narraway with the truth? Was Narraway a cynic, an opportunist who would side with whomever he thought would be the ultimate winner? Or a man exhausted by too many losses, petty injustices and despair? Too much knowledge of a sea of poverty—cheek by jowl with affluence. It required a very special depth of courage to continue fighting battles when you knew you could not win the war.

"Don't stand there cluttering up my office, Pitt," Narraway said impatiently. "I know the police are after a scapegoat, and Karansky will do nicely. They are still smarting over the Whitechapel murders four years ago. They won't let this one go unsolved, whether the solution fits or not. They want a resolution that people will praise them for, and Karansky suits. If I could save him, I would. He's a good man. The best advice I can give is for him to get out of London. Take a ship to Rotterdam, or Bremen, or wherever the next one is going to."

Arguments teemed in Pitt's head: about honor, surrender to anarchy and injustice, questions about the very existence of law if this was all it was worth. They faded before he spoke them. Narraway must have said them all to himself. They were new to Pitt. They shook his belief in the principles that had guided him all his life; they undermined the value of everything he had worked for, all his assumptions of the society of which he had thought himself a part. When it came to the final decision, if all the law could say to a man unjustly accused was "Run," then why should any man honor or trust the law? Its ideals were hollow—beautiful, but containing nothing, like a shining bubble, to burst at the first prick of a needle.

He hunched his body, shoving his hands hard into his pockets.

"They knew who the Whitechapel murderer was, and why," he said boldly. "They concealed it to protect the throne." He watched for Narraway's reaction.

Narraway sat very still. "Did they, indeed?" he said softly. "And how do you believe catching him would have affected the throne, Pitt?"

Pitt felt cold. He had made a mistake. In that instant he knew it. Narraway was one of them—not Inner Circle, but Masons, like Abberline, and Commissioner Warren, and God knew who else . . . certainly the Queen's late physician, Sir William Gull. He had a moment's panic, an almost overwhelming physical urge to turn and run out of the door, out of the shop and down the street, and disappear somewhere into those gray alleys and hide. He knew he could not do it quickly enough. He would be found. He did not even know who else worked for Narraway.

And he was angry. It made no sense, but the anger was greater.

"Because the murders were committed to conceal the Duke of Clarence's marriage to a Catholic woman called

Annie Crook, and the fact that they had a child," he said harshly.

Narraway's eyes widened so fractionally Pitt was not certain if he had seen it or imagined it. Surprise? At the fact, or that Pitt knew it?

"You discovered this since you've been in Spitalfields?" Narraway asked. He licked his lips as if his mouth were dry.

"No. I was told it," Pitt replied. "There is a journalist who has all the pieces but one or two. At least he had. He may have them all by now, except the newspapers haven't printed it yet."

"I see. And you didn't think it appropriate to inform me of this?" Narraway's face was unreadable, his eyes glittering beneath lowered lids, his voice very soft, dangerously polite.

Pitt spoke the truth. "The Masons are responsible for it . . . that is what happened. The Inner Circle are feeding it to the journalist piece by piece, to break it at a time of their own choosing. Half the senior police in charge were in on the original crime. Sissons's murder was Inner Circle. You could be either. I have no way of knowing."

Narraway took a deep breath and his body slumped. "Then you took a hell of a risk telling me, didn't you? Or are you going to say you have a gun in your pocket, and if I make the wrong choice you'll shoot me?"

"No, I haven't." Pitt sat down opposite him in the only other chair. "And the risk is worth it. If you're a Mason, you'll stop the Inner Circle, or try to. If you are Circle, you'll expose the Masons and, I daresay, bring down the throne, but you'll have to reinstate Sissons's death as a suicide to do that, and at least that will save Karansky."

Narraway sat up slowly, straightening his back. There was a hard edge to his voice when he spoke. His fine hands lay loosely on the tabletop, but the anger in him was unmistakable, and the warning.

"I suppose I should be grateful you've told me at last." The sarcasm cut, but it was against himself as much as Pitt. For a moment it seemed as if he was going to add something, then he changed his mind.

Pitt wondered if Narraway felt the same anger, the same confusion that the law was not only failing here, but that there was no higher power to address, no greater justice beyond, to which they could turn. It was corrupted at the core.

"Go and do what you can for Karansky," Narraway said flatly. "And, in case you have doubts about it, that is an order."

Pitt almost smiled. It was the one faint light in the gloom. He nodded, then stood up and left. He would go straight to Heneagle Street. It was a bitter thought that he, who had served the law all his adult life, was now helpless to do anything more for justice than warn an innocent man and help him to become a fugitive, because the law offered him no safety and no protection. He would have to leave behind his home, his friends, the community he had served and honored, all the life he had built for himself in the country he had believed would afford him shelter and a new chance.

But Pitt would do it, if he had to pack for them himself and walk with them down to the quay, purchase their tickets in his own name, and bribe or coerce some cargo captain to take them.

Outside, the street was hot and dusty. The stench of effluent hung sour in the air. Chimneys belched smoke, dimming the sunlight.

Pitt walked quickly southwards. He would find Isaac and warn him this afternoon. He passed a newspaper seller and glanced sideways to see the headlines . . . still the same drawing, but now there was a black caption underneath it—WANTED—SUGAR FACTORY MURDERER—just in case anyone had overlooked his offense against the community. The picture seemed to be changing slightly with each reprint, looking more than ever like Isaac.

Pitt increased his pace. He passed peddlers and draymen, carters, beggars, a running patterer making a rhyme about Sisson's murder. He went so far as to say what everyone else was thinking: the killer was a moneylender teaching a bad debtor to pay his dues. It was a clever piece of doggerel. He did not use the word *Jews*, but the suggested rhyme did it for him.

Pitt reached Heneagle Street and went in at the front door and straight through to the kitchen. Leah was standing by the stove. There was a pot simmering, and the smell of herbs was sweet in the air. Isaac was on the far side of the table, and there were two soiled cloth bags on the floor beside him.

He turned sharply as Pitt came in. His face was deeply lined, his eyes dull with exhaustion. There was no need to ask if he had seen the posters or understood what they meant.

"You must go!" Pitt heard his own voice unintentionally sharp, fear and anger in it. This was England. They had done nothing; an innocent man should not have to flee from the law.

"We are going," Isaac answered, putting on his old jacket. "We were only waiting for you."

"Your supper is on the stove," Leah told him. "There's bread in the pantry. Clean shirts are on your dresser—"

There was the sound of heavy knocking on the door.

"Go!" Pitt said desperately, the word choking him.

Isaac took Leah by the arm, half pushing her towards the large back windows.

"There's soap in the cupboard," she said to Pitt. "You'll find—"

There was more thunderous banging at the front of the house.

"We'll get word to you through Saul," Isaac said as he opened the window and Pitt moved towards the corridor.

"God be with you." And he half lifted Leah out.

"And with you," Pitt replied. The pounding on the front door was so loud it threatened to break the hinges. Without waiting to watch them leave, he went along the short corridor and undid the latch just as another blow landed on the panelling which might well have burst the hinge had he not opened it first.

Harper was standing on the other side, with Constable Jenkins beside him, looking profoundly unhappy.

"Well, you again!" Harper said with a smile. "Fancy that, then." He pushed past Pitt and strode down to the kitchen. He found it empty. He looked puzzled, wrinkling his nose at the smell of the unfamiliar herbs. "Where are they, then? Where's Isaac Karansky?"

"I don't know," Pitt said, feigning slight surprise. "Mrs. Karansky just went out to buy something she forgot for the meal." He indicated the pot simmering on the range.

Harper swiveled around on his heel, frustrated but not yet suspicious. He inspected the pot, the half-prepared meal, the domesticity of the kitchen. Isaac's best jacket was hanging on a hook behind the door. Pitt silently thanked God for the knowledge of fear which had driven him to leave it there, in spite of its value. He looked at Harper with a hatred he could not even try to conceal. It burned inside him with a sharp, grinding pain.

Harper pulled out one of the chairs and sat down. "Then we'll wait for them," he announced.

Pitt moved over to the pot and stirred it gently. He had very little idea what he was doing, but there was no point in letting the food burn. Tending it lent an air of normality and allowed him to seem occupied so he did not have to look at Harper. Jenkins stood silently, shifting his weight from one foot to the other.

Minutes ticked by.

Pitt drew the pot over to the edge of the range, off the heat.

"What did she go for?" Harper said suddenly.

"I don't know," Pitt replied. "Some herb, I think."

"Where's Karansky?"

"I don't know," he repeated. "I only just got back myself."

They probably knew that was true.

"You'd better not be lying," Harper warned.

Pitt kept his back to him. "Why should I lie?"

"To protect them. Maybe he paid you?"

"To say Mrs. Karansky's gone to buy herbs?" Pitt said incredulously. "He didn't know you were coming, did he?"

Harper made a sound of deep disgust.

Another ten minutes ticked by.

"You are lying!" Harper exploded, getting to his feet and banging against the table. "You warned them and they've gone. I'll charge you with aiding and abetting a fugitive. And if you're not lucky, maybe with accessory to murder as well!"

Jenkins cleared his throat. "You can't do that, sir; you got no proof."

"I've got all the proof I'll need," Harper snapped, glaring at his junior malevolently. "And I'll thank you not to interfere. Arrest him, like you're told!"

Jenkins remained stubbornly where he was. "We got a warrant for Karansky, sir. We got nothing for Tom."

"You've got my word, Jenkins! Unless you want to end up in a cell beside him, you'll obey my order!"

Shaking his head, his lips pursed, Jenkins told Pitt he was under arrest, then, as Harper glared at him, he put the manacles on Pitt's wrists. He very carefully took the pot off the range and fixed the lid firmly on it, in case Leah should return and find it spoiled.

"Thank you," Pitt acknowledged the action.

Outside they were watched by a crowd of a dozen or so men and women, angry and frightened. They glared at the police with undisguised hatred, but they did not dare intervene. Pitt, Harper and Jenkins left Heneagle Street and walked the three quarters of a mile or so to the police station. None of them spoke. Harper had apparently accepted that at least for the time being Isaac had eluded him, and it infuriated him. They passed sullen men and women in the streets, and more newspapers with pictures that were plainly of Isaac. There were rumors that the sugar factories were closing.

In the police station, Pitt was put into a cell and left.

It was over two hours later that Jenkins came back, smiling broadly. "Sugar factories in't gonna close down arter all," he said, standing just inside the cell door. "Lord Randolph Churchill an' some o' 'is friends 'as put up the money ter keep 'em all goin'. In't that a turn up?"

Pitt felt a surge of amazement and relief. It had to be Vespasia!

"An' you'd better go 'ome, an' all," Jenkins added, his smile turning into a positive grin. "In case the Karanskys come back."

Pitt stood up. "Aren't they wanted anymore?" He could scarcely believe it.

"Oh yeah! But 'oo knows where they is? Could be on the 'igh seas by now."

"And Inspector Harper is prepared to let me go?" Pitt did not yet move forward. He could imagine Harper's fury, and his vengeance against Pitt. It would be the Inner Circle's great satisfaction if Pitt spent a few years in prison for aiding the escape of the sugar factory murderer.

"No, 'e in't prepared," Jenkins oozed pleasure. " 'E in't got no choice, 'cos word came down from the top as yer ter be treated right an' let go. Yer got friends someplace real 'igh. Which is as well fer you."

"Thank you," Pitt said absently, profoundly puzzled as he walked out into freedom and received his few belongings back from the desk sergeant. Vespasia again? Hardly . . . or she would have protected him in the first place. Narraway? No, he had neither the knowledge nor the power.

The Masons . . . the other side of the Whitechapel conspiracies. Suddenly freedom had a dual sweet and bitter taste.

He would go back to Heneagle Street and eat Leah's dinner, then, when he could do it unobserved, go to see Saul, see about raising all the money they could for Isaac and Leah, all the help.

Charlotte was still determined to find the papers both she and Juno were certain Martin Fetters had hidden somewhere. They had exhausted all the places they knew of beyond the house and were back in the library staring around the shelves, searching for further ideas. Charlotte was grimly aware that a few feet away from where she stood, Martin Fetters had been killed by a man he had trusted and believed a friend. Her imagination of that terrible moment hung like a chill in the air. She thought of the instant he saw his own death in Adinett's eyes, and knew what was going to happen, then the swift pain and the oblivion. Surely, Juno must be even more aware of it than she.

Each night Charlotte slept alone in her room, conscious of

the empty space in the bed beside her, worrying about Pitt, frightened for him. Juno slept not only alone but knowing what had happened just a few rooms away from her, and that the worst she could possibly dread was already the truth.

"They must be here," Juno said desperately. "They do exist; Martin didn't know to destroy them, and Adinett didn't have time. He left and he wasn't carrying anything with him, because I saw him go myself. And when he came back again that was when we found Martin . . . I suppose he could have taken something then . . ." She trailed off.

"When did he have time to look?" Charlotte reasoned. "If Martin had them out, then Adinett must have put them away again, and then got them out when he returned. You said he didn't have a case of any sort, just a stick. How did he carry loose papers, or do you suppose it was all written as entries in one book?"

Juno was staring around the walls. "I don't know. I don't really know what we're looking for, or how much, except from what we know—there were lots more plans. They intended to do something positive. They were not just dreamers, meeting to talk over ideas. And if you mean to achieve something, you need to have very precise actions in mind."

"Then surely as a royalist bent on preventing their plans from being acted upon, Adinett would have wanted to destroy them?" Charlotte said thoughtfully. She gazed around at the book-lined shelves. "I wonder where he looked?"

"Nothing seems out of place," Juno replied. "Except the three books that were on the floor, of course. But we always assumed they were there to make it look as if Martin pulled them off when he fell from the ladder."

"I imagine the police would have searched pretty thoroughly anyway." Charlotte felt hope slip away again. "If there'd been anything on the shelves behind the books, it would have been found pretty easily."

"We could always take all the books down," Juno suggested. "We haven't anything better to do. Well, I haven't anyway."

"Neither have I," Charlotte agreed quickly, turning around

one way then the other to gaze at the shelves. "It wouldn't be behind books he took out regularly," she said aloud. "Otherwise it would be seen too easily. Someone would observe it by chance. Do any of the maids take out the books to clean or dust?"

"I don't know." Juno shook her head. "I shouldn't think so, but I suppose they could. You are right. It would be somewhere that no one would pull out. That is if it is behind books at all."

Charlotte felt disappointment fill her again. "I suppose it isn't a very good place. And inside a book would make it fat enough it would be noticed immediately. We're not looking for one or two sheets of paper, I don't think."

"What about . . ." Juno looked up at the top shelves, where there were large reference volumes.

"Yes? What?" Charlotte said quickly.

Juno pushed her hair back off her brow in a gesture of weariness.

"What about really inside a book . . . one hollowed out and replaced? I know it sounds like terrible vandalism, but it might be as safe as it could be. Who else is going to look inside some of those?" Juno gestured up at the top shelf towards the window where there was a row of obscure memoirs of eighteenth-century politicians and half a dozen volumes of statistics on export and shipping.

Charlotte went over to the steps and wheeled them around. Then, holding the pole firmly in one hand, and picking up her skirt in the other, she climbed up. "Careful!" Juno warned, stepping forward, her voice harsh.

Charlotte stopped, balanced precariously. She turned to smile at Juno, who stood pale-faced, drained by the dead black she wore.

"I'm sorry," Juno apologized, moving back again. "I . . ."

"I know," Charlotte said quickly. The steps were quite steady, but she could not help thinking of Martin Fetters, and the way he was first supposed to have died, falling from exactly this position. If she lost her balance from here she would end almost where he had been found, only her head would lie the other way.

She dismissed it quickly. That simple, almost private death was a world away from what they faced now. She reached up and pulled out the first volume, a wide, yellow book on shipping routes, hopelessly out of date. Why on earth would anyone have kept such a thing, except as an oversight, forgetting it was there? It was heavy. She passed it to Juno.

Juno rifled through it.

"Exactly what it says," she said with an effort to mask disappointment. "Martin must have bought it twenty years ago." She put it on the floor and waited for the next one.

Charlotte went through them one by one, and each was examined and then placed on the floor in ever-increasing piles. They kept on because neither of them could think of anything better to try.

It was almost into the third hour and they were both smeared with dust, arms aching, when Juno finally conceded defeat.

"They're all just what they say." The misery in her voice was so sharp Charlotte ached for her. Had nothing more been at stake than the desire to know, she might have encouraged her to abandon the effort. There comes a time when grief must end the struggle to understand, and allow healing to begin.

But she needed to prove to the world that Pitt had been right about John Adinett. She steeled herself to continue.

"Sit down for a while," she suggested. "Perhaps a cup of tea?" She climbed down the steps, and Juno held out a hand to steady her. Her fingers were cool and strong, but her arm shook a little and there was a pallor of strain in her face. She looked away from Charlotte's eyes.

"Perhaps we should stop," Charlotte said impulsively, against all she had intended, but pity hurt inside her too much to listen to sense. "Maybe there's nothing to find after all? It may have been just dreams."

"No," Juno said quietly, still keeping her gaze averted. "Martin wasn't like that. I knew him well." She gave a little jerky laugh. "At least, I knew some parts of him. There are characteristics you can't hide. And Martin always worked to make his dreams come true. He was a romantic, but even if it was something as trivial as getting me roses for my birthday, if he thought of it, he would work until he could accomplish it."

They were walking towards the library door. Juno opened it for them to go downstairs for tea.

Roses for her birthday seemed a very unremarkable gift. Charlotte wondered what made her mention it.

"Did he manage it?"

"Oh, yes. It took him four years."

Charlotte was startled. "Roses grow very easily. I've had them in my garden even at Christmas."

Juno smiled, a sweet smile on the edge of tears. "I was born on Leap Day. It takes a great deal of ingenuity to find roses at the end of February. He insisted I celebrated only on leap years, then he would have a four-day-long party for me and spoil me utterly. He was very generous."

Charlotte found it suddenly hard to swallow for the ache in her throat. "How did he get the roses?" she asked, her voice coming out broken, husky.

Juno swallowed, smiling through tears. "He found a gardener in Spain who managed to force them, and he had them brought by boat when they were in bud. They only lasted two days, but I never forgot them."

"Nor would any woman," Charlotte agreed.

"We've been through all the books." Juno reverted to the search again, closing the library door behind her. "It was a silly idea anyway. I should have known better. Martin loved books. He would never have vandalized one, even to hide things. He would have found another way. He used to mend any books that were broken, you know. He was very good at it. I can see him in my mind's eye, standing with a damaged book in his hands and lecturing me on how uncivilized it was to ill use a book, break the spine, tear it, mark it in any way."

They were going down the stairs and Charlotte saw a maid cross the hall beneath them. Tea was a very good idea indeed.

She had not realized until now how dry her mouth was, as if all the paper and the dust had drained her.

"He would completely rebind them sometimes," Juno went on. "Dora, will you bring tea to the garden room, please."

"Rebind them?" Charlotte said quickly.

"Yes. Why?"

Charlotte stopped on the bottom stair.

"What?" Juno asked.

"We didn't look for books that he bound . . ."

Juno understood immediately. Her eyes widened. She did not hesitate. "Dora! Wait with the tea. I'll tell you when!" She turned to Charlotte. "Come on. We'll go back and find them. It would be the perfect place."

Together they almost ran up the stairs again, skirts in their hands not to trip, and strode along the corridor back to the library.

It took them nearly half an hour, but finally Juno had it: a small book on the Trojan economy, in discreet dark leather with gold lettering, hand-bound.

They stood side by side reading a random page:

The evidence of the loan has, of course, been carefully laid. It will all be in his letter, which will be found on his death. As soon as it is known, the journalist will be given the final piece of proof on the Whitechapel story.

The two together will accomplish all that is necessary.

Juno looked at Charlotte, her eyes questioning.

Charlotte's mind was racing. She understood only part of it, but the reference to Remus was so clear it leaped out from the book, shaking a little in Juno's hand.

"He knew about someone's death in advance," Juno said quietly. "This is part of the plan for the overthrow of the government, isn't it?" Her voice challenged Charlotte to offer some comforting lie.

"It seems so," Charlotte agreed, scrambling in her mind to know whom it referred to. "I know what the journalist

303

is about, and you are right. It is part of the conspiracy for revolution."

Juno said nothing. Her hands shook as she held the book up for Charlotte to read with her, and turned the page.

It was lists of figures of injured and dead in the various revolutions throughout Europe in 1848. From them were projected a new set of figures for probable deaths in London and the other major cities of England when revolution occurred there. The meaning was unmistakable.

Juno was sheet white, her eyes dark in the hollows of their sockets.

They only glanced at the next pages. There were plans and possibilities for redistributing wealth and properties confiscated from those who enjoyed them as hereditary privilege. The document was at least a dozen pages thick.

The last one was a proposed constitution for a new state, led by a president responsible to a senate, not unlike that of republican Rome before the Caesars. It was not set out in a formal way, rather more a matter of suggestions, but there seemed no doubt as to who the first president would be. The writer made reference to several of the great idealists of the past, most especially Mazzini and Mario Corena, the idealist who had so magnificently failed in Rome. But the master himself intended to lead in England.

Charlotte did not need to ask if the handwriting was Martin Fetters's; she knew it was not. There was no resemblance. Fetters's writing was bold, flowing, a little untidy, as if his enthusiasm had run faster than the hand. This was precise, its capital letters only just larger than the rest, little slope to it, no space between one sentence and the next.

She looked up at Juno. She tried to imagine how she would feel if she had found this in Pitt's room. It was passionate, idealistic, arbitrary, violent and utterly wrong. No reform should be brought about by the deception that was proposed here, fomenting riot built on rage and lies, no thought of asking the people what they wanted, or telling everyone honestly what they would lose in order to gain it.

Charlotte turned to Juno and saw horror in her face, and

bewilderment and grief that eclipsed all the pain of the past few days.

"I was wrong," she whispered. "I didn't know him at all. What he planned was monstrous. He—he lost all his true idealism. I know he thought it was for people's good. He loathed any form of tyranny . . . but he never asked if they wanted a republic, or if they were prepared to die for it. He decided for them. That's not freedom; it's just another form of tyranny."

There was no argument that Charlotte could give, nor could she think of any comfort. What Juno had said was true: the plan was the ultimate arrogance, the final despotism, no matter how idealistically intended.

Juno stared into the distance, blinking away tears. "Thank you for not saying something trite," she said at last.

Charlotte made the only decision she was certain of. "Let's have the tea now. I feel as if I've been eating paper."

Juno gave a half smile, and accepted. They went downstairs together and within five minutes Dora brought the tea tray. Neither of them spoke. There seemed nothing sensible to say until they had finished, and finally Juno put down her cup, rose and walked over towards the window. She stared out at the sun on the small patch of grass.

"I was uncomfortable with John Adinett. And I hated him for killing Martin," she said slowly. "God forgive me, I was even glad when they hanged him." Her body was rigid, her shoulders high, muscles locked. "But now I understand why he felt he had to. I . . . hate this . . . but I believe I should tell the truth. . . . It won't bring Adinett back, but it will clear his name."

Charlotte was not so certain what she felt. Overwhelming pity, and admiration definitely. But what about Pitt? Adinett was in some lights justified in killing Fetters, or at least understandable. If people had known at the trial why he had done it they would never have wanted him hanged. They might even blame Pitt for prosecuting him at all.

But then Adinett had refused to give even the slightest explanation. How could anyone know? Even Gleave had said nothing. Presumably he had not known. Then she remembered his face as he had pressed Juno for Martin's papers. He had not threatened them in words, but it had been there in the air, and they had all felt it like a coldness in the bone.

He had known! Only he was on Fetters's side! Poor Adinett . . . there had been no one for him to turn to, no one to trust. Little wonder he had remained silent and gone to his death without attempting to save himself. He had known from the moment of his arrest that he had no chance of winning. He had acted to save his country from revolution, knowing it would cost him his life. He deserved the truth to vindicate him now, at the very least.

"Yes," she agreed. "You are quite right. As Inspector Pitt's wife, I should like to come with you, if I may?"

Juno turned around. "Yes, please. I was going to ask you anyway."

"Who will you tell?"

"I have thought of that. Charles Voisey. He is a judge of appeal and was one of those who sat on the case. He is familiar with it all. I know him a little. I don't know the others. I shall see if I can go this evening. I want to do it straightaway. . . . I—I'd find it very difficult to wait."

"I understand," Charlotte said quickly. "I shall be there."

"I will call by in the carriage at half past seven, unless he is unable to see us. I shall let you know," Juno promised.

Charlotte rose to her feet. "Then I shall be ready."

They arrived at Charles Voisey's house in Cavendish Square a little after eight, and were shown immediately into the splendid withdrawing room. It was decorated in mostly traditional style, of dark, warm colors, reds and soft golds, but with a startling addition of exquisite Arabic brasses, trays, jugs and vases, which caught the light on their engraved surfaces and simple lines.

Voisey received them with courtesy, his curiosity for their call concealed, but he made no pretense at superfluous conversation. When they were seated, and refreshment had been offered and declined, he turned to Juno enquiringly.

"How can I be of service to you, Mrs. Fetters?"

Juno had already faced the worst in acknowledging to herself that Martin was not the man she had loved all the years of their marriage. Telling someone else was going to be difficult, but there were obvious ways in which, if she told the right person, it would be almost a relief.

"As I intimated to you on the telephone," she began, sitting upright and facing him, "I have made a discovery in some of my husband's papers which the police did not find because they were so cleverly concealed."

Voisey stiffened very slightly. "Indeed? I assumed they had made a very thorough search." His eyes flickered towards Charlotte, and then away again. She had the sensation that Pitt's failure pleased him, and she had to make a deliberate effort not to defend him.

Juno did it for her. "They were bound into a book. He did his own binding, you know? He was very good at it. Unless you were to read every volume in the library there would be no way of being certain to find it."

"And you did that?" There was a slight lift of surprise in his voice.

She smiled bleakly. "I have nothing better to do."

"Indeed . . ." He allowed it to hang in the air, unfinished.

"I wished to know why John Adinett, whom I had always believed to be his friend, should kill him," Juno went on levelly. "Now I do know, and I believe it is morally necessary that I should acknowledge it. It seemed to me you were the right person to tell."

He sat quite still. He let out his breath slowly. "I see. And what did these papers say, Mrs. Fetters? I assume there is no doubt they are his?"

"They are not in his hand, but he bound them into a book and concealed them in his library," she replied. "They were letters and memoranda in a cause in which he very obviously believed. I think when John Adinett found out, that was why he killed him."

"That seems . . . very extreme," he said thoughtfully. Now

he completely ignored Charlotte, concentrating his entire attention upon Juno. "If it was something of which Adinett disapproved so passionately, why did he not simply make it
public? I assume it was illegal? Or at the least something
which others could have prevented?"

"To make it public might have caused panic, even have
provoked others of like mind," she answered. "Certainly it
would have caused England's enemies great joy and perhaps
suggested to them ways in which to damage us."

Voisey was staring at her with increasing tension. When he
spoke his voice was harder, anxiety edged in it. "And the
reason you believe he did not report it to an appropriate authority, even discreetly?"

"Because he could not know who else was involved," she
replied. "You see, it is a wide conspiracy . . ."

His eyebrows rose fractionally. His fingers tightened on
each other. "A conspiracy? To do what, Mrs. Fetters?"

"To overthrow the government, Mr. Voisey," she replied,
her voice surprisingly flat for so extreme a statement. "By
violent means—in short, to create a revolution which would
bring down the monarchy and replace it with a republic."

He sat silently for several moments before replying, as if
he was completely stunned by what she had said and barely
able to believe it.

"Are you . . . quite sure, Mrs. Fetters? Could you not have
misunderstood some writings on another country and assumed they were referring to England?" he said at last.

"I wish it were possible, believe me." Her emotion was
clear; he could not have doubted it. He turned to Charlotte.

She met his eyes and was aware of an intense intelligence—
and a coldness of extraordinary, almost uncontrollable dislike. It startled her, and she found herself afraid. She could
think of no reason for it. She had never met him before and
certainly never done him harm.

He was speaking to her, his voice sharp.

"Have you seen these papers, Mrs. Pitt?"

"Yes."

"And do you see in them the plans for revolution?"

"Yes, I am afraid I do."

"How extraordinary that your husband did not find them, don't you think?" Now the contempt in him was unmistakable, and she understood it was Pitt for whom he felt this emotion he could not conceal.

She was stung too. "I don't imagine he was looking for plans to overthrow the monarchy and set up a new constitution," she said coldly. "It would have been a more complete case if he could have found the motive, but it was not necessary. And then Adinett chose to go to the gallows rather than reveal it himself—which indicates how wide he believed the conspiracy to be. He knew of no one he dared trust, even to save his life."

Voisey's face was dark with blood under the skin, his eyes glittering.

Charlotte wondered how much he blamed himself, as a judge who had sat on the appeal, that he had condemned a man he now had to acknowledge as both a victim and a hero. She was sorry she had spoken so bluntly, but she could not bring herself to say so to him.

"And was he mistaken, Mrs. Pitt?" he said softly, his jaw tight. "If he had told the inspector his reason for killing Fetters, would he have met with belief and help?" He left the other half of the question unsaid.

"If you are asking if my husband is a revolutionary, or would have conspired with them—" She stopped, seeing his smile. She knew exactly what he was thinking: that Juno Fetters had believed in her husband's innocence also—and been wrong. "I am certain he would have done what he could to expose the conspiracy," she answered him. "But I take your point that he would not have known any better whom to trust. They would simply have destroyed the evidence, and him also. But he didn't see it, so the question does not arise."

He turned back to Juno, and his expression changed, the pity returned to it. "What have you done with this book, Mrs. Fetters?"

"I have it here," she replied, offering it to him. "I believe that we should . . . that I must . . . see that Mr. Adinett's name is vindicated and does not pass into history as that of a man who murdered his friend for no reason. I . . . I wish I could award that, for my husband's sake, but I cannot."

"Are you certain?" he said gently. "Once you have put the proof into my hands I cannot give it back to you. I must act upon it. Are you sure you would not prefer to destroy it and keep your husband's name as it is: that of a man who fought for the freedom of all men, in his own way?"

Juno hesitated.

"Will it really do good for the public to know that there are such men among them?" he went on. "Men you cannot name, and therefore the rest you cannot exclude, who would over- throw our Houses of Lords and of Commons, our monarchy, and set in their place a president and a senate, however re- formed, whatever justice or equality it offered? Those are strange ideas to the man in the street, who does not under- stand them and who feels safe with what he is accustomed to, even with the ills and iniquities it sustains. John Adinett may well have kept silent because he knew what turmoil knowl- edge of such a conspiracy could cause, as well as not knowing whom he could trust. Have you considered that?"

"No," Juno said in a whisper. "No, I had not thought of it. Perhaps you are right. Maybe . . . if he were afraid to speak then, he would wish it kept silent now. He was a very fine man . . . a great man. I see why it grieves you so much that he is dead. I am sorry, Mr. Voisey . . . and ashamed."

"You have no need to be," he said with a brief smile, full of sadness. "It is not your fault. Yes, he was a great man, and maybe history will yet show him to be, but not yet, I think."

Juno rose to her feet and walked over to the fireplace. De- liberately, she dropped the book into the flames. "I thank you profoundly for your advice, Mr. Voisey." She looked across at Charlotte.

Charlotte stood up too, her head swimming, her thoughts in chaos, but at the brilliant, blazing core of her lay one piece of certainty—Charles Voisey was at the heart of the conspiracy! He knew those papers more intimately than they did. Juno had mentioned a presidency, but she had said nothing of a senate. Nothing of doing away with the Lords and Commons.

"Mrs. Pitt . . ." His voice cut across her thoughts.

"Mr. Voisey," she replied, knowing she sounded awkward, preoccupied in a way for which there was no reason. He was staring at her, his clever eyes studying every expression of her face. Did he guess she knew?

"Perhaps you are right." She forced the words out. Let him think she was disappointed because it would have vindicated Pitt. He hated Pitt. He would believe that. They must get out of here, away from him. Get home safely.

Safely! Martin Fetters had been murdered in his own library. She would have to tell Juno, get her to leave London and go to the country somewhere, completely anonymous. Never be found until they could protect her, or it no longer mattered.

"I believe so," he said with a twisted smile. "It would do more harm than the good of restoring Adinett's good name . . . which he was prepared to forfeit for his country's sake."

"Yes, I see that." She moved towards the door, but she must go slowly, in spite of the almost overwhelming desire to hurry, even to run. He must not guess she knew. He must not sense fear. She actually stopped and allowed him to come closer to her, before going forward to follow Juno into the hall.

It seemed as if they would never reach the front door and the night air.

Juno stopped again to bid him good-bye and thank him for his advice.

Then at last they were outside in the coach and moving away.

"Thank God!" Charlotte breathed.

"Thank God?" Juno asked, her voice tired, disappointed.

"He knew about the senate," Charlotte replied. "You didn't mention it."

Juno reached out and gripped her in the dark, her fingers digging into Charlotte's flesh, locked tight in terror.

311

"You must leave London," Charlotte said grimly. "To-night. He knows you have read the book. Don't tell anyone where you go. Send a message to Lady Vespasia Cumming-Gould—not to me!"

"Yes . . . yes, I will. God, what have we fallen into?" She did not let go of Charlotte's arm as they drove through the night.

13

V ESPASIA STOOD in the morning room staring out of the window at the yellow roses in full bloom at the far side of the lawn. The moment had come when she could no longer avoid facing the question which hurt her the most profoundly. She was afraid of what the answer would be, but she had always believed courage to be the cornerstone of all virtues. Without it integrity perished; even love could not survive, because love was risk, and somewhere, at some time or place, it would always hurt.

She had loved Mario for half a century. It had brought her the deepest, most complete joy and the greatest pain she had known—but never disillusion. She tried to tell herself it would not do so now.

She was still there when the maid came to say that Mrs. Pitt had called to see her.

For once Vespasia would have preferred to not be interrupted. It was an excuse to put the issue from her mind, but she did not wish for one. It changed nothing. But she would not refuse Charlotte.

"Invite her to come in," she replied, turning away from the roses. It must be something urgent to bring Charlotte at such an early hour. It was barely past breakfast.

As soon as she saw Charlotte's face she knew her assumption was correct. The younger woman was pale except for two bright splashes of color on her cheeks, as if she were feverish, and she came into the room in a hurry and closed the door behind her. She rushed straight into speech with barely a gesture to her usual courtesy.

"Good morning. I apologize for calling at such an hour, but yesterday Juno Fetters and I discovered Martin's papers, the ones he hid. He was planning a revolution in England, a violent one to overthrow not only the throne but the whole government as well . . . the Parliament, everything, and set a senate and a president in its place. He expected violence. There are figures quoted for the deaths they foresaw, and the outline of a new constitution, full of reforms."

"Indeed," Vespasia said softly. "It does not surprise me that such papers should exist. I had not realized Martin Fetters would be involved if he knew of the violence. I had believed him a reformer, not a revolutionary. The consent of the people is at the heart and soul of all honest government. I am sorry to hear it." And she was. It was a bitter knowledge, the loss of one more man she had admired.

Charlotte was standing close to her, her eyes dark with hurt.

"So am I," she said with a sad little smile. "I only know him by his writings, but I liked him so much. And it was devastating for Juno. The man she had loved did not really exist." She searched Vespasia's face, her eyes troubled, frightened.

"Sit down." Vespasia indicated one of the chairs and took another herself. "I assume you wish to do something about this."

"I have already done it." Charlotte's voice caught in her throat. "Juno could see straightaway that this information showed why John Adinett killed him and why he could not say so to anyone, even to save himself. After all, whom could he trust?"

Vespasia waited, the idea uneasy in her mind.

"So she decided she must, in honor, make it known," Charlotte concluded.

"To whom?" Vespasia asked, fear opening sharp and bright like a knife inside her.

It was reflected in Charlotte's face also.

"To Charles Voisey," she answered. "We went yesterday

314

evening. She told him most of what was in the papers, but not all."

"I see . . ."

"No!" Charlotte was white now, her eyes wide. "No, you couldn't . . . because just before we left he spoke of it, to persuade Juno to destroy the book rather than cause public alarm by making the conspiracy known, when we cannot name the people involved. And that makes sense," she hurried on. "But in the heat of his argument, he mentioned things we did not tell him! Aunt Vespasia, he is Inner Circle—I think he may even be the head of it. As you know, they wouldn't trust anyone lesser with so much of the information." She shook her head a little. "They don't. They are all in little groups so they cannot be betrayed, each one knowing only what he has to."

"Yes . . ." Vespasia's mind was racing. What Charlotte had said made a terrible sense. Charles Voisey was just the man to emerge as head of state for a new, revolutionary England. He had served as a judge of appeal for many years, been seen to uphold justice, reverse wrong decisions, stand apart from personal or party gains. He had a wide circle of friends and colleagues and yet had stood apart from political controversy so he was not associated in the public mind with any vested interest.

Thinking of all she knew of him, what Charlotte had said was totally believable. Many other things made sense, pieces of conversation she had overheard, things Pitt had told her, even her meeting with Randolph Churchill.

Other things came to mind also, and the tiny, bright sliver of doubt that she had been clinging to vanished at last.

"Aunt Vespasia . . ." Charlotte said quietly, leaning forward in her chair.

"Yes," Vespasia repeated. "Most of what you say is true. But it seems to me that you have one fact mistakenly interpreted, and if you are able to tell Mrs. Fetters, it will comfort her greatly. But her safety is of the utmost importance, and if she has that book then I fear they will not let her be."

"She hasn't," Charlotte said quickly. "She burnt it, right

315

there in Voisey's fire. But what have I got wrong? What have I misunderstood?"

Vespasia sighed, frowning a little. "If Adinett was suddenly made aware of the book, and of Martin Fetters's part in a conspiracy to cause revolution, and this occurred that day in the library, why did he not take the book with him?" she asked.

"He didn't know where it was, and he had no time to search," Charlotte replied. "It was extremely well concealed. Martin bound it to look exactly like . . ." Her eyes widened. "Oh . . . yes, of course. If he saw it then he knew where it was. Why didn't he take it?"

"Whose handwriting was it in the book?"

"I've no idea. Actually, two or three different hands. You mean the book wasn't Martin's?"

"I should imagine we would find at least one of the hands was Adinett's own," Vespasia answered. "And possibly one was Voisey's, and maybe one even Reginald Gleave's. I think the one you would not find there was Fetters's own."

"But he bound it!" Charlotte protested. "You mean as evidence . . . but he was a republican. He never pretended not to be!"

"Many people are republicans," Vespasia said quietly, trying to guard the pain inside her. "But most do not intend to bring about revolution by violence and deceit. They do no more than argue for it, try to persuade with passion or reason—or both. If Martin Fetters was one of those, and he discovered the intention of his fellows was far more radical than his own, then they would have had to silence him immediately . . ."

"Which was what Adinett did," Charlotte concluded. There was fear in her eyes. "No wonder Voisey hated Thomas for persisting with the evidence against Adinett, and for more or less placing him in the position where he himself had to deny Adinett's appeal. After all, if there were three other judges against it already, then his casting his word for it would only tip his hand, as it were, without saving Adinett." A bitter humor flashed in her face for an instant. "The irony would have made it worse." Her mouth softened. "But I'm glad

316

Martin Fetters was not part of the violence. Reading his words I couldn't help liking him. And Juno will be so relieved when I can tell her. Aunt Vespasia, is there anything we can do to keep her safe, or at least help?"

"I shall consider it," Vespasia replied, but important as it was, other things were more pressing, and crowded her mind.

Charlotte was looking at her closely, anxiety clouding her eyes.

Vespasia was not ready to share her thoughts; perhaps she never would be. Some things are part of the fabric of one's being and cannot be framed in words.

She rose to her feet. Charlotte immediately stood also, recognizing that it was time to leave.

"Thomas came to see me yesterday," Vespasia said. "He was well. . . ." She saw the relief flood Charlotte's face. "I think they are looking after him in Spitalfields. His clothes were clean and mended." She smiled very briefly. "Thank you for coming, my dear. I shall consider very carefully what you have told me. At last many things are growing clearer. If Charles Voisey is the leader of the Inner Circle, and John Adinett was his lieutenant, then at least we understand what happened to Martin Fetters, and why. And we know that Thomas was right. I shall see what I can think of to help Mrs. Fetters."

Charlotte kissed her lightly on the cheek and took her leave.

Now Vespasia must act. Enough of the pieces were in place for her to have little doubt left as to what had happened. The Prince of Wales's debt was not real; she knew that from the note of debt Pitt had brought. It was a forgery—an excellent one—but it would not have stood the test in court. Its purpose was to convince the frightened, the hungry and the dispossessed of Spitalfields that their jobs were gone because of royal profligacy. Once the riots had started neither truth nor lies would matter anymore.

On top of that, Lyndon Remus would release his story of the Duke of Clarence and the Whitechapel murders, true or false, and riot would become revolution. The Inner Circle would manipulate it all until it was time for them to step forward and take power.

She remembered Mario Corena at the opera. When she had said what a bore Sissons was, he had told her that she was mistaken in him. Had she known more she would have admired his courage, even self-sacrifice. As if he had known Sissons was going to die.

And she remembered Pitt's description of the man he had seen leaving the sugar factory—older, silver hair in the black, dark complexion, fine bones, average height, a signet ring with a dark stone in it. The police had thought it was a Jew. They were mistaken: it had been a Roman, a passionate republican who had perhaps believed Sissons a willing participant.

It was fifty years since she had known him in Rome. He would not have murdered a man then. But a lifetime had come and gone since that summer, for both of them. People change. Disappointment and disillusion can wear away all but the strongest heart. Hope deferred too long can turn to bitterness.

She dressed in silver-gray, an exquisite watered silk, and selected one of her favorite hats. She had always looked well under a sweeping brim. Then she sent for the carriage to come to the door and gave the coachman the address where Mario Corena was staying.

He received her with surprise and pleasure. Their next engagement had not been until the following day.

"Vespasia!" His eyes took in her face, the soft sweep of her gown. The hat made him smile, but as always, he did not comment on her appearance; his appreciation was in his eyes. Then as he regarded her more closely the joy faded from his expression. "What is it?" he said quietly. "Don't tell me it is nothing; I can see differently."

The time for pretense was long past. Part of her wished to stand in this beautiful room with its view over the quiet square, the rustling summer trees, the glimpses of grass. She could be close to him, allow the sense of fulfillment to possess her that she always felt in his company. But however long

318

or short the time, it would come to an end. The inevitable moment would have to be faced.

She turned and looked into his eyes. For a moment her resolve faltered. He had not changed. Their summer in Rome could have been yesterday. The years had wearied their bodies, marked their faces, but their hearts still carried the same passion, the hope, and the will to fight and to sacrifice, to love, and to endure pain.

She blinked. "Mario, the police are going to arrest Isaac Karansky, or some other Jew, for the murder of James Sissons. I am not going to allow it. Please don't tell me it is for the greater good of the people to sacrifice one that all may benefit. If we allow one innocent man to be hanged and his wife left bereaved and alone, then we have made a mockery of justice. And once we have done that, then what can we offer the new order we want to create? When we use our weapons for ill, we have damaged their power for good. We have joined the enemy. I thought you knew that. . . ."

He looked at her in silence, his eyes shadowed.

She waited for him to answer, the pain inside her building as if to explode.

He took a long, deep breath. "I do know that, my dear. Perhaps I forgot for a while exactly who the enemy was." He looked down. "Sissons was going to take his own life in the cause of a greater liberty. He knew when he lent the money to the Prince of Wales that it would not be returned. He wanted to expose him for the self-indulgent parasite that he is. He knew it would cost many men their jobs, but he was prepared to pay with his own life." He looked up at her again, brilliant, urgent. "Then at the last moment his nerve failed him. He was not the hero he wanted to be, wished to be. And yes . . . I did kill him. It was clean, swift, without pain or fear. Only for an instant did he know what I was going to do, then it was over. But I left the note in his own hand that said it was suicide, and the Prince's note of debt. The police must have concealed them. I cannot understand how that happened. We had our own man in place, on duty, who should have seen to it that suicide was recognized and no innocent person blamed."

319

Confusion shadowed his face, and unhappiness for fear and wrong.

Vespasia could not look at him. "He tried," she acknowledged. "He came too late. Someone else found Sissons first, and knowing what riot it would cause, destroyed the note. Only, you see, it could not have been suicide because James Sissons did not have the use of the first fingers of his right hand, and the night watchman knew it." She met his eyes again now. "And I saw the note of debt. It was not the prince's signature. It was an excellent forgery, designed for just the purpose you tried to use it."

He started to speak, then stopped. Understanding slowly filled his face, and grief, and then anger. He did not need to protest that he had been deceived; she could not have doubted it from his eyes and his mouth, and the ache that filled him.

Her throat hurt with the effort of control. She loved him so fiercely it consumed all of her but a tiny, white core in the heart. If she were to yield now, to say it did not matter, that either of them could walk away from this, she would lose him—and even more, she would lose herself.

She blinked, her eyes smarting.

"I have something to undo," he whispered. "Good-bye, Vespasia . . . I say good-bye, but I shall take you with me in my heart, wherever I go." He lifted her hand to his lips. Then he turned and walked out of the room without looking back, leaving her to find her way when she was ready, when she could master herself and go back to the footman, the carriage and the world.

The whole story of Prince Eddy and Annie Crook remained in Gracie's mind. She imagined the ordinary girl, not so very much better off than many Gracie herself might have passed on the streets of her own childhood—a little cleaner, a little better-spoken perhaps, but at heart expecting only a pedestrian life of work and marriage, and more work.

And then one day a shy, handsome young man had been introduced to her. She must have realized quickly that he was a gentleman, even if not that he was a prince. But he was also different from the others, isolated by his deafness and all that it had done to him over the years. They had found something in each other, perhaps a companionship neither had known elsewhere. They had fallen in love.

And it was impossible. Nothing they could have imagined could ever have touched the horror of what would happen after that.

She still could not entirely rid herself of the memory of standing in Mitre Square, seeing Remus's face in the gaslight, and realizing who it was he was after. Her throat still tightened at the thought of it, even sitting in the warm kitchen in Keppel Street, drinking tea at four o'clock in the afternoon, and trying to think what vegetables to prepare for dinner tonight.

Daniel and Jemima were out with Emily again. She had spent a lot of time with them since Pitt left for Spitalfields. Emily had climbed greatly in Gracie's estimation. Gracie had actually been considering her a trifle spoiled lately. Since she was Charlotte's sister, it was nice to be mistaken.

She was still staring at the rows of blue-and-white plates on the dresser when a knock on the back door startled her into reality again.

It was Tellman. He came in and closed the door behind him. He looked anxious and tired. His shirt collar was as tight and neat as usual, but his hair had fallen forward as if he had not bothered with its customary, careful brushing, and he was about a week overdue for the barber.

She did not bother to ask him if he wanted a cup of tea. She went to the dresser, fetched a cup and poured it.

He sat down at the table opposite her and drank. There was no cake this time, so she did not mention it. She felt no need to break the silence.

"I've been thinking," he said at last, watching her over the top of his cup.

"Yeah?" She knew he was worried; it was in every line of him, the way he sat, the grip of his hands on the cup, the edge to his voice. He would tell her what was bothering him if she did not probe or interrupt.

"You know this factory owner who was killed in Spital-fields, Sissons?"

"I 'eard. They said mebbe all 'is factories would close, then the Prince o' Wales an' Lord Randolph Churchill an' some o' 'is friends put up enough money ter keep 'em goin' a few weeks anyway."

"Yes. They're saying it was a Jew who did it . . . killed him, because he'd borrowed money from a whole collection of them and couldn't pay it back."

She nodded. She knew nothing about that.

"Well, I reckon that was meant to happen about the same time as Remus was supposed to find the last pieces of the Whitechapel murderer story. Only they didn't tell him yet, because the sugar factory thing went wrong." He was still watching her, waiting to see what she thought.

She was confused. She was not sure it made sense.

"I went to see Mr. Pitt again," he went on. "But he wasn't there. They're trying to say it was Isaac Karansky, the man he lodges with, who killed Sissons."

"D'yer reckon it was?" she asked, imagining how Pitt would feel, and hating it for him. She had seen before how it tore at Pitt's emotions when someone he knew turned out to be guilty of something horrible.

"I don't know," he confessed. He looked confused. There was something else in his eyes, dark and troubled. She thought perhaps he was afraid—not with the passing ripple of momentary fear, but deep and abiding and of something he could not fight against.

Again she waited.

"It isn't that." He put the cup down at last, empty. He met her gaze unblinkingly. "It's Remus. I'm scared for him, Gracie. What if he's right, and it really is true? Those people didn't think twice about butchering five women in White-chapel, not to mention whatever they did to Annie Crook and her child."

"An' poor Prince Eddy," she said quietly. "D'yer reckon 'e died natural?"

His eyes widened a fraction. His face went even paler.

"Don't say that, Gracie! Don't even think it to yourself. Do you hear me?"

"Yeah, I hear. But yer scared too, an' don't tell me yer in't." It was not a charge against him. She would think him a fool were he not. She needed the closeness of sharing the fear for herself, and she wanted it for him. "Yer scared fer Remus?" she went on.

"They'd think nothing of killing him," he answered.

"That's if 'e's right," she argued. "What if 'e's wrong? Wot if it weren't nothin' ter do wi' Prince Eddy, an' the Inner Circle is makin' it all up?"

"I'm still scared for him," he replied. "They'd use him and throw him away, too."

"Wot are we gonna do?" she said simply.

"You're going to do nothing," he answered sharply. "You're going to stay here at home and keep the door locked." He swiveled around in his seat. "You should've had that back door locked."

"At 'alf past four in the afternoon?" she said incredulously. "There in't nob'dy arter me. If I kept the scullery locked they'd think I really 'ad got summink goin' on."

He blushed faintly and looked away.

She found herself smiling, trying to hide it, and failing. He was frightened for her and it was making him overprotective. Now he was embarrassed because he had given himself away.

He looked at her and saw the smile. For once he interpreted it correctly, and his color deepened. At first she thought it was anger; then she looked at his eyes and knew it was pleasure. She had equally given herself away too. Oh, well . . . she couldn't play games forever.

"So wot are we gonner do, then?" she repeated. "We gotta warn 'im. If 'e won't be told, then we can't 'elp it. But we gotta try, in't we?"

"He won't listen to me," he said wearily. "He thinks he's onto the newspaper story of the century. He won't give that up, no matter where it leads him. He's a fanatic. I've seen it in his face."

She remembered the wild look in Remus's eyes and the

horror and terrible excitement she'd sensed in him as he had stood in Mitre Square, and she knew Tellman was right.

"We still gotta try," She leaned forward across the table. " 'E's scared as well. Let me come wiv yer. We'll both 'ave a go at 'im."

He looked doubtful. The lines of strain were deep in his face. No one was looking after him. He had no one else to share his fears with, or the sense of guilt he would feel if something happened to Remus and he had not tried to warn him.

She stood up, accidentally scraping her chair legs on the floor. "I'll get yer some tea. 'Ow about bubble an' squeak? We got lots o' cabbage an' taters left over, an' fresh onion. 'Ow'll that be?"

He relaxed. "Are you sure?"

"No!" she said crisply. "I am standin' 'ere 'cos I can't make me mind up. Wot yer think?"

"You'll cut yourself with that tongue," he replied.

"I'm sorry," she apologized. She meant it. She did not know why she had been so quick with him. Perhaps because she wanted to do far more to comfort him, look after him, than he would like or accept.

That realization made her blush suddenly, and she swung around and strode into the larder to get the cold vegetables and start cooking. She brought them back and kept her back to him while she chopped and fried the onions, then added the rest and moved it gently till it was steaming hot on the inside and crisp brown on the outside. She put it all onto a warm plate and set it in front of him. Then she boiled the kettle again and made fresh tea.

At last she sat down on the chair opposite him again.

"So are we goin' ter find Remus and tell 'im just 'ow big this is? In case 'e's so 'ell-bent on getting 'is story 'e in't realized 'oo 'e's up again?"

"Yes," he replied with his mouth full, trying to smile at the same time. "I am. You aren't."

She drew in her breath.

"You aren't?" he said quickly. "Don't argue with me. That's the end of it."

She sighed heavily and said nothing.

He bent his attention to eating the bubble and squeak. It was hot, crisp and fragrant with onions. It did not seem to occur to him that she had given in rather easily.

When he had finished, he thanked her with a touch of real admiration. He remained another ten minutes or so, then left out of the scullery door.

Gracie had followed Remus successfully all the way to Whitechapel and back again. She thought she was really rather good at it. She now took her coat and hat from the peg at the back door and went after Tellman. She did not especially like Lyndon Remus, but she had learned something about him, his likes and dislikes, seen the excitement and the terror in him. She did not want to think of him hurt, not seriously. A little chastening would not harm, but there was nothing moderate about any part of this.

Of course, following Tellman would be much harder because he knew her. On the other hand, he was not expecting her to follow, and she knew where he was going; to Remus's rooms to await his return from whatever story he was working on apart from the Whitechapel murders.

She had only about one shilling and fivepence. There had been no time to look for any more. Unfortunately, there had also not been time to write more than a hasty note for Charlotte explaining where she had gone. Even that had been done in the larder on a brown paper bag, and written with a kitchen pencil. Her spelling was a little uncertain, but since it was Charlotte who had taught her to read and write, she would understand what Gracie meant.

Tellman strode down Keppel Street purposefully towards Tottenham Court Road. He was going for the omnibus. That would make things rather difficult. If she caught the same one, he would be bound to see her. If she waited for the next one, she would be too late by up to a quarter of an hour. But she knew where Remus's rooms were. She had a good chance of arriving there at about the same time if she took the underground train. It was worth the risk.

She turned sharply away in the opposite direction, and then

started to run. If she was lucky, it would work. And she would have enough money, easily.

She paced the platform, and when the train came, sat fidgeting from stop to stop. As soon as it arrived she charged through the door, across the platform and up the stairs.

The street was busy, and it took her a moment or two to realize exactly where she was. She had to ask directions of a muffin girl, then set out at a half run again.

She got there and swung around the last corner and cannoned straight into Tellman, almost overbalancing him.

He swore with feeling and more color than she had known him capable of.

"That's terrible!" she said in amazement.

He blushed scarlet. He was so embarrassed it robbed him temporarily of the ability to stand on his dignity and order her to go home again.

She straightened her hat and stared back at him. "So, 'e in't 'ere yet, then?"

"No . . ." He cleared his throat. "Not yet."

"Then we'd best wait," she pronounced, looking away from him and assuming a position of great patience.

He drew in his breath and started to argue, but after the first word he realized the futility of it and stopped again. She was here. He had no power or ability to send her away. He might as well make an ally of her.

They stood side by side on the corner of the street opposite the entrance of Remus's lodging house. After five minutes of silence and the curious stares of one or two passersby, Gracie decided to give her opinion.

"If yer don't want ter be noticed, we'd do better ter talk ter each other. Like this we look like we're 'ere fer no good. Sayin' nothin' we don't even look like we've quarreled. Nob'dy keeps up a sulk forever."

"I'm not sulking," he said quickly.

"Then talk ter me," she responded.

"I can't just . . . talk."

"Yes, yer can,"

"What about?" he protested.

"Anythink. If yer could go anywhere in the world fer a visit, where'd yer go? If yer could talk ter anybody out of 'istory, oo'd it be? Wot'd yer say ter 'em?"

He stared at her, his eyes wide.

"Well?" she prompted. "An' don' look at me. Watch for Remus. That's wot we're 'ere fer. Oo'd yer meet, then?"

There were faint spots of color in his cheeks again. "Who'd you meet?"

"Florence Nightingale," she said immediately.

"I knew you'd say that," he replied. "But she isn't dead yet."

"Don't matter. She's still 'istory. Oo'd you meet?"

"Admiral Nelson."

"W'y?"

"Because he was a great leader as well as a great fighter. He made his men love him," he replied.

She smiled. She was glad he had said that. It sometimes showed a lot to know who people's heroes were, and why.

He grasped her arm suddenly. "There's Remus!" he said fiercely. "Come on!" He yanked her forward and plunged across the road, dodging in between traffic and reaching the footpath at the far side just as Remus went in through the door.

"Remus!" Tellman called out, stopping just short of actually bumping into him.

Remus turned, startled. As soon as he recognized Tellman his face darkened. "No time to talk to you," he said briskly. "Sorry." He took another step forward, his back to Tellman, and started to close the door.

Tellman put his foot in the doorway, still dragging Gracie with him by the hand, not that she was unwilling.

Remus stopped, his expression changing to one of anger.

"Didn't you hear me? I've nothing else to say, and no time. Now, get out of my way!"

Tellman tensed his body as if to resist a blow, and remained exactly where he was. "If you're still going after the Whitechapel murderer and the story of Annie Crook, you should leave it. It's too dangerous to do alone—"

"It's a damned sight too dangerous to tell anyone about

327

until I've got the proof," Remus retorted. "And you, of all people, should know that!" He turned to Gracie. "And you, whoever you are."

"I know who you can trust," Tellman said urgently. "Let them know. It's the only safeguard you've got."

Remus's eyes were bright, and there was a decided sneer on his lips. "No doubt you'd like me to tell the police. Perhaps starting with you, eh?" He gave an abrupt little laugh, full of contempt. "Now, get your foot out of my door. I know how dangerous it is, and the police are the last people I'd trust."

Tellman struggled to find an argument, and failed.

Gracie could think of nothing either. In Remus's place she would have trusted no one.

"Well, be careful," she said. "Yer know wot they done ter them women."

Remus smiled at her. "Of course I know. I am careful."

"No, you in't!" she challenged, the words spitting out. "I followed yer all the way 'round Whitechapel, even spoke ter yer, an' yer never knowed. Followed yer ter Mitre Square, too, but yer was so full o' wot yer was thinkin' yer 'ad no idea!"

Remus paled. He stared at her. "Who are you? Why would you follow me—if you did?" But there was fear in his voice now. Perhaps the mention of Mitre Square had made him realize she spoke the truth.

"It don't matter 'oo I am," she argued. "If I can follow yer, so can they! Do like 'e says." She gestured to Tellman. "An' be careful."

"All right! I'll be careful. Now go away," Remus replied, stepping farther inside and beginning to push the door closed.

Tellman accepted that they had done all they could, and he retreated, Gracie with him.

Back across the street again he stopped, looking at her questioningly.

" 'E's onter summink," she said decisively. " 'E's scared, but 'e in't givin' up."

"I agree," Tellman said in a low voice. "I'm going to follow him, see if I can protect him at all. You go home . . ."

"I'm comin' wif yer."

"No, you're not!"

"I'm comin'—wif yer or be'ind yer!"

"Gracie . . ."

But at that moment Remus's door opened again and he came out, looked from left to right and back again, and apparently concluding that they had gone, he set out. There was no time to argue. They went after him.

They followed him successfully for nearly two hours, first to Belgravia, where he stayed for about twenty-five minutes, then east and south to the river and along the Embankment just short of the Tower. They finally lost him as he was going east again. It was just growing dark.

Tellman swore in frustration, but this time watching his language far more carefully.

"He did that on purpose," he said furiously. "He knew we were here. We must have shown ourselves, got too close to him. Stupid!"

" 'E mebbe knew we would be," she pointed out. "Or p'rhaps it weren't us 'e were tryin' ter shake? Mebbe 'e were bein' careful, like we told 'im?"

Tellman stood on the footpath, staring along the street in the direction they had last thought they saw Remus, his eyes squinted, his mouth pulled tight.

"We've still lost him. And he's going towards Whitechapel again!"

It was growing dark. The lamplighter was working the farther side of the street and he was hurrying.

"We'll never find him in this," Tellman looked around at the traffic, the rattle and clatter of hooves and wheels over the cobbles, the occasional shouts of drivers. Everyone seemed to be pressing forward as fast as they could. They could barely see fifty yards ahead in any direction in the gloom and the shifting mass of horses and people.

Gracie felt a bitter disappointment. Her feet were tired and she was hungry, but she could not dismiss the fear that Remus had not truly understood the danger he was in; there must be something they could still do to make him realize it.

"Come on, Gracie," Tellman said gently. "We've lost him.

Come and have something to eat. And sit down." He gestured towards a public house on the farther side of the street.

The thought of sitting down was even better than that of food. And there was really nothing else to do.

"Or' right," she agreed, not moving reluctantly so much as utterly wearily.

The food was excellent, and the chance to relax blissful. She enjoyed it with relish, since usually when they ate together it had been in the kitchen in Keppel Street, and she had prepared the food. They talked about all manner of things, about Tellman's early years in the police force. He told her stories of his experiences; some of them were even funny, and she found herself laughing aloud. She had never appreciated before that in his own fashion he had a sharp sense of the absurd.

"Wot's yer name?" she said suddenly as he finished a tale of adventure, and a certain degree of self-revelation.

"What?" He was confused, not certain what she meant.

"Wot's yer name?" she repeated, now self-conscious. She did not want to go on thinking of him as "Tellman." She wanted a name, a name that his family used.

The color deepened in his face, and he looked down at his empty plate.

"Sorry," she said unhappily. "I shouldn't 'a asked."

"Samuel," he replied quickly, almost swallowing the word. She liked it. In fact she liked it very much.

"Hmph. Too good fer yer. That's a real name."

He looked up quickly. "You like it? You don't think it's . . ."

" 'Course it is," she agreed. "I jus' thought I'd like ter know, that's all. It's time I was goin' 'ome." But she made no move to stand up.

"Yes," he said, also not moving.

"Yer know summink," she said thoughtfully. "That Remus thinks 'e's got the answer now. 'E knows the truth, I seen it in 'is face. 'E were tryin' ter 'ide it so we didn't see, but 'e's got it all, an' 'e's gonna tell that story termorrer."

Tellman did not argue. He sat looking at her across the table, his eyes steady, his face pinched and earnest.

330

"I know. But I don't know how to stop him. Telling him all the damage it would do won't help. It's his chance to be famous, and he isn't going to give it up for anyone."

"They'll know that too," she said, feeling the fear well up inside her again, cold and sick. "Yer know, I'll bet 'e's gorn ter Whitechapel again, one more time afore 'e tells 'em ... mebbe afore 'e writes the last bit of 'is piece fer the papers. I'll bet 'e's gorn ter visit them places again—'Anbury Street, Bucks Row an' all."

She saw by the quick widening of his eyes that he believed it the moment she spoke. He pushed his chair back and stood up.

"I'm going there. You catch a hansom and go home. I'll give you the money." He began to fish in his pocket.

"Not on yer life!" She stood up also. "I in't lettin' yer go there by yerself. Don't waste time talkin' abaht it. We'll get the rozzer on the beat ter come wif us from the 'Igh Street, and if there's nothin', we'll look like fools. Yer can tell 'im it were my fault." And without waiting for him she started for the door.

He followed after her, pushing his way past others coming in, calling apologies over his shoulder. Outside on the pavement he waved down the first hansom and directed the driver to the Whitechapel High Street.

He ordered the cab to stop when he saw a constable, a tall, helmeted figure in the gaslight and the mist.

Tellman leaped down and went up to him. Gracie scrambled after and arrived just as he was explaining to the constable that they feared an informant was in danger and needed his assistance immediately.

"That's right." Gracie nodded vigorously.

"Gracie Phipps," Tellman said quickly. "She's with me."

"Where is this informant o' yours?" the constable asked, looking around.

"Mitre Square," Gracie said instantly.

"Hey!" the hansom driver called. "Yer finished wi' me, or not?"

Tellman went back and paid him, then rejoined Gracie and the constable. They set out to walk back along the High Street

331

and into Aldgate Street, then around the corner up Duke Street. They did not speak and their footsteps echoed in the mist. It was far quieter here and it was farther between lamps. The cobbles were slippery. The dampness clung in the throat.

Gracie felt her cheeks wet. She swallowed and could barely breathe. She remembered Remus's face as she had seen it here before, shining with excitement, eyes glittering.

She thought of the huge black carriage that had rumbled down these streets with something unimaginably violent and evil inside, waiting.

She caught hold of Tellman's arm and gripped him tightly as a rat scuttled by, and someone stirred by the wall. He did not pull away; in fact, he gripped her back.

They turned off Duke Street into the alley by St. Botolph's Church, fumbled by the light of the constable's bull's-eye towards the far end, and Mitre Square.

They emerged into emptiness which was faintly lit by the one lamp high on the wall. There was no one there.

Gracie was giddy with relief. Never mind that the constable would think she was a fool—and no doubt be angry. Never mind that Tellman—Samuel—would be angry too.

Then she heard his indrawn breath in a sob, and she saw it, sprawled on the stones in the far corner, arms wide.

The constable moved forward, his breath rasping in his throat, his feet floundering.

"No!" Tellman said, holding Gracie back. But she saw it by the light of the bull's-eye. Lyndon Remus was lying just as Catherine Eddowes had been, his throat cut, his entrails torn out of his body and placed over his shoulder as in some hideous ritual.

Gracie stared at Remus for one terrible moment more, a moment burned into her mind forever, then turned and buried her head in Tellman's shoulder. She felt his arms tighten around her and hold her hard and close to him as if he would never let her go.

Remus had known the truth—and died for it. But what was it? The question beat in her mind. Had the man behind the Whitechapel murders killed him because he knew it was a conspiracy to hide Prince Eddy's indiscretion? Or was it the Inner Circle, because he had discovered it was not true—and Jack the Ripper, Leather-apron, was a lone madman, just as everyone had always supposed?

He had taken his secret to his fearful death, and no one would tell the story he had found—whichever it was.

She loosened herself just enough to put her arms around Tellman's neck, then moved closer again, and felt his cheek and his lips on her hair.

Isaac and Leah's house was silent, almost dead-seeming without them. Pitt heard his own footfalls sounding in the passage. The click of pots and pans was loud as he made supper in the kitchen. Even the noise of his spoon against his bowl seemed a disturbance. He kept the stove going so he could cook and have at least some hot water, but he realized it was Leah's presence that had given the house true warmth.

He ate alone and went to bed early, not knowing what else to do. He was still lying awake in the dark when he heard the sharp, peremptory knocking on the door.

His first thought was that it meant further trouble in the Jewish community, and someone was looking for Isaac to help him. There was nothing Pitt could do, but he would at least answer.

He was half dressed and on the stairs when he realized there was a kind of authority in the knock, as if the person had a right to demand attention, and expected to receive it. And yet it was more discreet and less impatient than the police would have been, especially Harper.

He reached the bottom of the stairs and went the three steps across the hall. He undid the bolt and opened the door.

Victor Narraway walked straight in and closed the door behind him. His face looked haggard in the hall gaslight, and his thick hair was wild and damp from the mist.

Pitt's stomach lurched. "What is it?" Imagination raced hideously through his mind.

"The police have just called me," Narraway answered hoarsely. "Voisey has shot Mario Corena."

333

Pitt was stunned. For a moment the news had little meaning to him. He could not place Corena, and Voisey was only a name. But the look in Narraway's eyes said that it was momentous.

"Mario Corena was one of the greatest heroes of the '48 revolutions across Europe," Narraway said quietly, a terrible weight of sadness in him. "He was one of the bravest and most generous of them all."

"What was he doing in London?" Pitt was still bemused. "And why would Voisey shoot him?" Memories of things Charlotte had said, and Vespasia, came back to him. "Isn't Voisey sympathetic to republican feelings? Anyway, Corena is Italian. Why should Voisey care?"

Narraway's face pinched. "Corena was bigger than any one nation, Pitt. Above all, he was a great man, willing to put all he possessed on the line to fight for a decent chance for all people, for a quality of justice and humanity anywhere."

"Then why would Voisey kill him?"

"He said it was self-defense. Put your clothes on and come with me. We're going to see what it's about. Be quick!"

Pitt obeyed without question, and half an hour later they were in a hansom pulling up outside Charles Voisey's elegant house in Cavendish Square. Narraway climbed out, paid, and strode ahead of Pitt to the front door, which was opened as he reached it by a uniformed constable.

Pitt went up the steps and inside immediately behind Narraway. There were two other men in the hallway. Pitt recognized one as a police surgeon; he did not know the other. It was the second who spoke to Narraway, then gestured towards one of the doors leading off.

Narraway glanced at Pitt, indicating that he should follow, then went over to the door and opened it.

The room was plainly a study, with a large desk and several bookcases and two carved, leather-padded chairs. The gas was turned up and the room flooded with light. On the floor, as if he had been walking from the door towards the desk, lay a slender man with a dark complexion and dark hair liberally threaded with white. On his fine-boned hand was a signet ring with a dark stone in it. His face was handsome, almost beautiful in the passion of its form and the peace of its expression. The lips were curled in the faintest smile. Death had come to him with no horror and no fear, even as a long-awaited friend.

Narraway stood motionless, fighting to control emotion.

Pitt knew the man. He knelt and touched him. He was still warm, but apart from the bullet hole in his chest and the scarlet blood on the floor, there was no mistaking death.

Pitt straightened up again and turned to Narraway.

Narraway swallowed, looking away. "Let's go and speak to Voisey. See how he can . . . explain this!" His voice was choked but the rage poured through it.

They went out, and Narraway closed the door softly, as though the room were now a kind of sanctuary. He walked across the hall to where the second man stood waiting. They exchanged only a glance of understanding, then the man opened the door and Narraway went in, Pitt on his heels.

This was the withdrawing room. Charles Voisey sat on the edge of the large sofa, his head in his hands. He looked up as Narraway stood in front of him. His face was drained of all color except for the livid marks where his fingers had pressed into the flesh of his cheeks.

"He came at me!" he said, his voice rising high and cracking. "He was like a madman. He had a gun. I tried to reason with him, but he wouldn't listen. He—he didn't seem to be hearing anything I said. He was . . . a fanatic!"

"Why would he want to kill you?" Narraway asked coldly.

Voisey gulped. "He—he was a friend of John Adinett, and he knew I had been also. He thought I somehow . . . betrayed him . . . by not being able to save him. He didn't understand." He glanced at Pitt, then back to Narraway. "There are loyalties higher than friendship, no matter how you . . . regard someone. And there was a great deal that was fine in Adinett . . . God knows . . ."

"He was a great republican," Narraway said with an edge to his voice, a mixture of passion and sarcasm that Pitt could not read.

"Yes . . ." Voisey hesitated. "Yes, he was. But . . ." Again he stopped, uncertainty in his eyes. He looked at Pitt, and for a moment the hatred in his face was naked. Then as quickly he masked it again, lowering his gaze. "He believed in many reforms, and fought for them with all his courage and intelligence. But I could not deny the law. Corena could not understand that. There was something of the . . . savage . . . in him. I had no choice. He came at me like a lunatic, swearing to kill me. I struggled with him, but I could not take the gun from him." The flicker of a smile touched his lips, more in amazement than any kind of humor. "He had extraordinary strength for an old man. The gun went off." He did not add any more; it would have been unnecessary.

Pitt looked at him and saw the blood on his own shirtfront, at the right height to have matched Corena's wound. It could have been true.

"I see," Narraway said grimly. "So you are saying it was self-defense?"

Voisey's eyebrows shot up. "Of course I am! Good God—do you think I would have shot the man on purpose?" The amazement and incredulity were so intense in his whole being that in spite of his own feelings, Pitt could not help but believe him.

Narraway turned on his heel and strode out, leaving the door swinging on its hinges.

Pitt looked at Voisey once more, then followed after Narraway.

In the hall, Narraway stopped. As soon as Pitt caught up with him he spoke very quietly.

"You know Lady Vespasia Cumming-Gould, don't you?" It was barely a question. He did not even wait for an answer. "Perhaps you didn't know that Corena was the greatest love of her life. Don't ask me how I know; I do, that is enough. You should be the one to tell her this. Don't let her read it in the newspapers or hear it from someone who doesn't know what it means to her."

Pitt felt as if he had been hit so hard the breath had been forced out of him, and he could not fill his lungs again. Instead there was an ache inside him almost enough to make him cry out.

Vespasia!

"Please do it," Narraway said urgently. "It shouldn't be a stranger." He did not beg, but it was there in his eyes.

There was only one possible answer. Pitt nodded, not trusting himself to speak, and went back to the front door and out to the quiet street.

He took the first hansom and gave Vespasia's address. He rode through the darkness without thinking. There was no point in rehearsing how he would say such a thing. There was no way.

The cab pulled up and he alighted. He rang the doorbell and to his surprise it was answered within moments.

"Good evening, sir," the butler said quietly. "Her Ladyship is still up. Would you care to come in, and I shall tell her you are here."

"Thank you . . ." Pitt was confused, walking in a nightmare. He followed the butler into the yellow room and stood waiting.

He had no idea whether it was two or three minutes, or ten, before the door opened and Vespasia came in. She was wearing a long silk robe of almost white, her hair still coiled loosely on her head. She looked fragile, old, and almost ethereally beautiful. It was impossible not to think of her as a passionate woman who had loved unforgettably one Roman summer half a century ago.

Pitt found the tears choking his throat and stinging his eyes.

"It's all right, Thomas," she said so quietly he barely heard her. "I know he's dead. He wrote to me, telling me what he would do. It was he who killed James Sissons, believing it was what Sissons himself had intended, but at the last moment lost his nerve to be a hero after all." She stopped for a moment, struggling to keep her composure. "You are free to use this, to see that Isaac Karansky is not blamed for a crime he did not commit—and perhaps that Charles Voisey is, although I am not certain how you can accomplish that."

Pitt loathed telling her, but it was not a lie that could live.

337

"Voisey says he shot him in self-defense. I don't know that we can prove otherwise."

Vespasia almost smiled. "I'm sure he did," she agreed. "Charles Voisey is the leader of the Inner Circle. If they had succeeded in their conspiracy to cause revolution, he would have become the first president of Britain."

For an instant, the beat of a heart, Pitt was astonished. Then the beat passed, and it all made perfect sense: Martin Fetters's discovery of the plot, his facing Adinett—who was probably Voisey's friend and lieutenant—and being killed because he wanted reform but not revolution. And then for all his power and his loyalty, Voisey could not save Adinett. No wonder he hated Pitt and had used all his influence to destroy him.

And Mario Corena, a man driven by a simpler, purer fire, had been used and deceived to destroy Sissons. Now, realizing it at last, he had tried to turn it back on Voisey.

"You don't understand, do you?" Vespasia said softly. "Voisey meant to be the ultimate hero of all reform, to be the leader into a new age . . . perhaps originally his aims were good. He certainly had some good men with him. Only his arrogance led him to believe he had the right to decide for the rest of us what was in our best good and then force it upon us, with or without our consent."

"Yes . . . I know . . ." Pitt began.

She shook her head, the tears glistening in her eyes. "But he can never do that now. He has killed the greatest republican hero of the century . . . above any one country's individuality or nationalism."

He thought he began to see just a glimmer, like a distant star. "But it was self-defense," he said slowly.

She smiled, and the tears slid down her cheeks. "Because he discovered the conspiracy to overturn the throne, to invent this spurious debt of the Prince of Wales, and murder Sissons and create riot—and when Mario realized he knew, he attacked him, so of course Voisey had to shoot. He is a very brave man! Almost single-handedly he has uncovered a terrible conspiracy and named the men in it—who will certainly be at the least disgraced, maybe arrested. Perhaps the Queen will even

338

knight him ... don't you think? I must speak to Somerset Carlisle and see if it can be arranged." Then she turned away and walked out of the room without speaking again. She could no longer keep within her the grief and the longing that consumed her.

Pitt stood still until her footsteps died away, then he turned and walked back into the hall. It was empty except for the butler, who showed him out into the lamp-lit street.

Almost exactly a month later, Pitt, superintendent of Bow Street again, stood beside Charlotte in the throne room in Buckingham Palace. He was acutely uncomfortable in a new suit, an immaculate shirt, collar high and straight, boots perfect. Even his hair was well cut and tidy. Charlotte had a new gown, and he had never seen her look lovelier.

But it was Vespasia, a few feet away, who held his attention. She was gowned in dove gray with pearls at her throat and ears. Her hair gleamed silver, her chin was high, her face exquisite, delicate, very pale. She refused to lean on Somerset Carlisle's arm, even though he stood ready and watchful to help.

A little in front of them, Charles Voisey knelt on one knee as another old woman, short, dumpy, sharp-eyed, moved a trifle clumsily to touch the sword to his shoulder and command him to arise.

"We are sensible of the great service you have given us, for the throne and the continued safety and prosperity of your country, Sir Charles," she said distinctly. "It is our pleasure to acknowledge before the world the acts of selfless courage and loyalty which you have performed in private."

The Prince of Wales, standing a few yards away, beamed his approval and even more heartfelt gratitude. "The throne has no more loyal servant ... or friend," he said appreciatively.

There was a rustle of enthusiastic applause from the audience of courtiers.

Voisey tried to speak, and choked, as he would be choked from now on, should he ever again raise his voice for a republic.

Victoria was accustomed to men being overcome in her presence. She ignored it, as good manners required.

Voisey bowed and turned to leave. As he did so he looked at Pitt with a hatred so violent, so intense, his body shook with it, and there were beads of sweat in his face.

Charlotte grasped Pitt's arm until her fingers dug into his flesh even through the fabric of his coat.

Voisey looked at Vespasia. She met his gaze unblinkingly, her head high, and she smiled with that same passionate calm with which Mario Corena had died.

Then she turned and walked away so he should not see her tears.

Read on for a preview
of Anne Perry's next thrilling novel

SOUTHAMPTON ROW,

featuring Thomas and Charlotte Pitt

Coming in hardcover in spring 2002.
Published by The Ballantine Publishing Group.

─────── 1 ───────

"*I'M SORRY*," Assistant Commissioner Cornwallis
said quietly, his face a mask of guilt and unhappiness. "I did
everything I could, made every argument, moral and legal.
But I can't fight the Inner Circle."

Pitt was stunned. He stood in the middle of the office with
the sunlight splashing across the floor and the noise of
horses' hooves, wheels on the cobbles and the shouts of
drivers barely muffled beyond the window. Pleasure boats
plied up and down the Thames on the hot June day. After the
Whitechapel conspiracy he had been reinstated as superintendent of the Bow Street police station. Queen Victoria herself had thanked him for his courage and loyalty. Now,

Cornwallis was dismissing him again! "They can't," Pitt protested. "Her Majesty herself . . ."

Cornwallis's eyes did not waver, but they were filled with misery. "They can. They have more power than you or I will ever know. The Queen will hear what they want her to. If we take it to her, believe me, you will have nothing left, not even Special Branch. Narraway will be glad to have you back." The words seemed forced from him, harsh in his throat. "Take it, Pitt. For your own sake, and your family's. It is the best you'll get. And you're good at it. No one could measure what you did for your country in beating Voisey at Whitechapel."

"Beating him!" Pitt said bitterly. "He's knighted by the Queen, and the Inner Circle is still powerful enough to say who shall be superintendent of Bow Street and who shan't!"

Cornwallis winced, the skin drawn tight across the bones of his face. "I know. But if you hadn't beaten him, England would now be a republic in turmoil, perhaps even civil war, and Voisey would be the first president. That's what he wanted. You beat him, Pitt, never doubt it . . . and never forget it, either. He won't."

Pitt's shoulders slumped. He felt bruised and weary. How would he tell Charlotte? She would be furious for him, outraged at the unfairness of it. She would want to fight, but there was nothing to do. He knew that, he was only arguing with Cornwallis because the shock had not passed, the rage at the injustice of it. He had really believed his position at least was safe, after the Queen's acknowledgment of his worth.

"You're due a holiday," Cornwallis said. "Take it. I'm . . . I'm sorry I had to tell you before."

Pitt could think of nothing to say. He had not the heart to be gracious.

"Go somewhere nice, right out of London," Cornwallis went on. "The country, or the sea."

"Yes . . . I suppose so." It would be easier for Charlotte, for the children. She would still be hurt but at least they would have time together. It was years since they had taken more than a few days and just walked through woods or over fields, eaten picnic sandwiches and watched the sky.

Charlotte was horrified, but after the first outburst she hid it, perhaps largely for the children's sake. Ten-and-a-half-year-old Jemima was instant to pick up any emotion, and Daniel, two years younger, was quick behind. Instead she made much of the chance for a holiday and began to plan when they should go and to think about how much they could afford to spend.

Within days it was arranged. They would take her sister Emily's son with them as well; he was the same age and was keen to escape the formality of the schoolroom and the responsibilities he was already learning as his father's heir. Emily's first husband had been Lord Ashworth, and his death had left the title and bulk of the inheritance to their only son, Edward.

They would stay in a cottage in the small village of Harford, on the edge of Dartmoor, for two and a half weeks. By the time they returned the general election would be over and Pitt would report again to Narraway at Special Branch, the infant service set up largely to battle the Fenian bombers and the whole bedeviled Irish question of Home Rule, which Gladstone was fighting all over again, and with as little hope of success as ever.

"I don't know how much to take for the children," Charlotte said as if it were a question. "How dirty will they get, I wonder . . ."

They were in the bedroom doing the last of the packing before going for the midday train south and west.

"Very, I hope," Pitt replied with a grin. "It isn't healthy for a child to be clean . . . not a boy, anyway."

"Then you can do some of the laundry!" she replied instantly. "I'll show you how to use a flatiron. It's very easy— just heavy—and tedious."

He was about to retaliate when their maid, Gracie, spoke from the doorway. "There's a cabbie 'ere with a message for yer, Mr. Pitt," she said. " 'E give me this." She offered him a piece of paper folded over.

He took it and opened it up.

Pitt, I need to see you immediately. Come with the bearer of this message. Narraway.

"What is it?" Charlotte asked, a sharp edge to her voice as she watched his expression change. "What's happened?"

"I don't know," he replied. "Narraway wants to see me, but it can't be much. I'm not starting back with Special Branch for another three weeks."

Naturally she knew who Narraway was, although she had never met him. Ever since her first encounter with Pitt eleven years ago, in 1881, she had played a lively part in every one of his cases that aroused her curiosity or her outrage, or in which someone she cared about was involved. In fact, it was she who had befriended the widow of John Adinett's victim in the Whitechapel conspiracy and finally discovered the reason for his death. She had a better idea than anyone else outside Special Branch of who Narraway was.

"Well, you'd better tell him not to keep you long," she said angrily. "You are on holiday, and have a train to catch at noon. I wish he'd called tomorrow, when we'd have been gone!"

"I don't suppose it's much," he said lightly. He smiled, but the smile was a trifle downturned at the corners. "There've been no bombings lately, and with an election coming at any time there probably won't be for a while."

"Then why can it not wait until you come back?" she asked.

"It probably can." He shrugged ruefully. "But I can't afford to disobey him." It was a hard reminder of his new situation.

He reported directly to Narraway and he had no recourse beyond him, no public knowledge, no open court to appeal to, as he had had when a policeman. If Narraway refused him there was nowhere else to turn.